A CLOCKWORK VAMPIRE

A CLOCKWORK VAMPIRE

A Clockwork Vampire #1

K.H. KOEHLER

The Monster Factory

A Clockwork Vampire

A Clockwork Vampire #1

K.H. Koehler

A Clockwork Vampire (A Clockwork Vampire #1) Copyright © 2011 K.H. Koehler

All rights reserved.

The characters and events portrayed in this book are fictitious. Any similarity to real persons, living, dead, or undead is coincidental and not intended by the author.

No part of this book may be reproduced, or stored in a retrieval system, or transmitted in any form or by any means, electronic, mechanical, photocopying, recording, or otherwise, without express written permission of the publisher.

No part of this book was created with Artificial Intelligence.

Paperback ISBN: 979-8-8692-1572-7
Ebook ISBN: 979-8-8692-1573-4

Cover design by: KH Koehler Design
https://khkoehler.net

CONTENTS

I	1
II	20
III	35
IV	44
V	61
VI	79
VII	86
VIII	101
IX	112

X	138
XI	151
XII	174
XIII	185
XIV	198
XV	219
XVI	238
XVII	259
XVIII	288
XIX	308

About the Author 315

"Oh bliss, bliss and heaven...Oh, it was gorgeousness and gorgeousity made flesh...And then, a bird of rarest-spun heaven metal, or like silvery wine flowing in a spaceship, gravity all nonsense now...I knew such lovely pictures."
—Anthony Burgess, A Clockwork Orange

| i |

Miss Eliza Book took the gold, scarab-shaped key on the chain from the bedside table, inserted it into the vampire's dead heart, and gave it six good turns. Five was never enough, and seven left him overwound. And an overwound vampire is never a pleasant thing first thing in the morning.

She stood by his bed and listened while the escapement mechanism of the vampire's clockwork heart made its first full rotation of the day. She knew it would be several minutes before her employer was legally alive again, so she went about the task of digging through his wardrobe and picking out his clothes for the day.

He enjoyed an awful lot of outdated tweeds, but it was summertime, and she didn't want him going about his day talked about, so she chose the black frock and green cotton plaid trousers he seemed to favor. By the time she was done laying everything out, Edwin Oliver McGillicuddy—O. E. Wodehouse to his legion of readers—was awake and sitting up, though he looked somewhat disheveled. He had been up all night wrestling with writer's block on his latest project.

Mr. McGillicuddy was a man of impressive height and build. A combination of childhood malnutrition in his early mortal years and a rough upbringing in the East End of London had intersected in just such a way as to produce a lank, mean, fighter's build. He had wiry auburn hair, devilish eyebrows, and the pale, startling hazel eyes of a wolf. That, combined with his impressive, claret-colored wings, lent him a positively devilish visage.

There were only two things that kept Mr. McGillicuddy from being absolutely perfect. The first was his fashion sense, of which he had none. The second was his mouth. He had a long history of attracting loose women—at least until he opened his mouth, at which point they went scrambling for a Cockney rhyming dictionary. Eliza bore it all with the dignity of a lifelong soldier. As his secretary and all-around His Girl Friday, it was her job, after all.

"Good morning, Miss Book," Mr. McGillicuddy said, staring at her with enormous appreciation. "I take it you slept well? I didn't keep you up?"

Mr. McGillicuddy made a habit of banging around his office at all manner of ungodly hours—but most often at night. Eliza had long learned to appreciate noise-canceling headphones as she slept in the room down the hall. "Very well, thank you, sir," she said as she finished brushing his slacks down, which she had left at the foot of his bed. "Breakfast is waiting in the kitchen."

She lost her smile some ten minutes later when he stepped into the kitchen and she saw what getup he had on today. He had once more ignored the carefully coordinated clothes she had set out. The awful outdated tweed trousers…the T-shirt with the happy vampire smiley face…the red suspenders he'd long ago made a staple of his wardrobe, such as it was…it was all she could do to keep from screaming.

Instead, being a professional, she turned to the stove to make tea, though she did shake her head tiresomely. Edwin McGillicuddy was the most unvampire-like vampire she had ever met.

The kitchen of the townhome they shared was really more of a kitchenette, made smaller still by the roving devices that Eliza had invented to help her carry out her daily tasks. There was a sink that washed dishes, a stove that cooked food unaided, and the "secretary," a sphere that happily followed anyone around and reminded them of their most important engagements of the day. The free-roaming teapot had just poured her the first cup of the day when she sensed a presence closing in behind her.

She jumped, then relaxed when she saw it was only Mr. McGillicuddy reaching for the newspaper she had left folded on the kitchen countertop.

Mr. McGillicuddy smiled an apology. "Sorry, love, don't mean any offense."

She relaxed but still edged slowly away from him, making up excuses about needing to clean up the terrible mess he'd made in his office the night before. Living with a vampire was precarious at best, and something Eliza was still getting used to.

* * *

Five months earlier, when Edwin first met Eliza Book, she had been as wary as a wounded animal and as thin as an Indian fakir. For her interview, she wore what looked like a borrowed day dress that was too large on her underfed frame and a hat and well-mended gloves. When she'd had to demonstrate her typing skills, she removed her gloves. Her nails were pitifully chewed and jagged, and there were holes gnawed into the corners of her thumbs, but he did not comment on such things. She was a lovely typist, quiet and accurate. He'd always been a creature of instincts, and so he hired her on the spot.

He'd thought they had made terrific progress, but when he saw her flinch, he realized his mistake. After downing the mug of blood substitute she had warmed for him, he offered her his best "forgive me" look and went back to the bedroom to change into the clothes she had chosen for him. Over the past two centuries of his existence, he had made kings and queens crumble with his boyish smile.

Miss Book, however, was inured to vampire charms. When he arrived at his office, she had his daily planner in hand and a pen tucked behind her ear. In her grey tweed skirt and vest, her wild tangles of black hair piled atop her head in a mangled bun, she was a fetching sight for his old eyes.

"You have a busy day ahead, sir. Tea at noon with your agent Mr. Dumphrey, a Zoom interview at two, and you must have at least fifty pages of the latest book ready for your editor by tomorrow, no later." She wagged a finger as she spoke. "Mr. Dumphrey was quite insistent you speak."

Edwin groaned and turned to peruse the morning correspondence the mechanical mail snail had thoughtfully brought in. He'd penned no less than a half dozen serious detective novels before finding publication with Doctor Blood, Vampire Detective under his pseudonym of O. E. Wodehouse. Funny thing was, he'd written the damned thing on a dare, with no thought put into it whatsoever. It was nothing but blood, sex, and guns, but it was what his editor and his agent Dumphrey kept asking for, and what the reading public kept thirstily drinking up, no pun intended.

"Tell me again why I write these bloody stupid books?" he asked, glancing at the fan mail, catalogs, and, of course, never-ending flow of bills. There was even a folded flyer that read, "Do you know who just moved in next door?" and had a picture of a shady character peeking at his neighbor through an upstairs window. Anti-vampire propaganda. Hate crimes had been on the rise all over the country. With the new vampire rights amendment bill presently going through Congress, he knew it would only get worse before it got better.

Meanwhile, Miss Book had whipped out her reading glasses and the notepad she carried with her at all times. "I made a short list of editing suggestions for the new book. Please consider them this time."

Edwin let the flyer droop. "Why do you call them a short list when they're always so bloody long?"

Miss Book looked up, and the same shadow he'd spotted earlier passed behind her eyes as she tried to ascertain if he was criticizing her or just being a tease. It was always the latter, but she still hadn't gotten used to that, it seemed. "You do realize you like making up your own words?"

"Abso-freakin'-lutely not," he insisted and smiled to show he was kidding.

"Inordinary? What is an inordinary day? You could just as well have used extraordinary." She bent over the desk and started penning in more notes, which had the inadvertent effect of causing her cascade of hair to fall away enough to expose the side of her light brown neck.

He ogled her from behind the flyer, trying not to be too obvious about it. "But extraordinary doesn't convey the exact feeling. It was not an extraordinary day, merely an inordinary one. Slightly more than ordinary, not quite standoutish."

"There you go again," Miss Book insisted. She stood up and pointed her pen at him. Her deadly serious, almost dangerous, demeanor made him shift uncomfortably, but not for the reason she probably thought. Truly, she was a gorgeous black-haired tigress when she was angry.

"Don't make up your own words, sir!" she said. "Hasn't the English language suffered enough abuse?"

Haven't I? he wondered, trying not to give into a teeny tiny fantasy. Too late.

Growling, he pressed her back against the desk and kissed her. Belatedly, Miss Book realized he'd done nothing to deforest his morning wood. But the moment she felt what effect she'd had on him, she kissed him back, winding her arms around his neck, and offering up her throat to him for a little vampire kiss.

He brushed everything off his desk in a grand gesture and laid her down upon it. She writhed beneath him as he kissed her...everywhere. "Oh, sir, yes," she said, "like that...oh!"

Edwin had been made a vampire young, at the tender age of nineteen—maybe a year older than Miss Book. It was a time when most young men had beauty on their side as well as raging hormones. It was a lethal combination.

"Shift just a little, Miss Book. Like that, yes. Oh, Miss Book, how delicious you are, love...!"

"Yes, sir. Of course, sir..."

"Sir?" she said, interrupting him.

He refocused on the present. "What was that, Miss Book?"

"Have you been paying any attention, sir?"

"Aye, of course," he said, having no idea what she'd been banging on about over the past few minutes or so.

Miss Book huffed. "Really, sir. What do I do with you?"

You could throw me to the floor and have your wicked way with me, love.

"My apologies, Miss Book," Edwin insisted, straightening up, though he kept the mail down low, covering the lower half of his body. With his free hand, he indicated the typewriter. "Shall we begin?"

Miss Book sat down to take his dictation while he narrated the continued adventures of Doctor Blood, Vampire Detective. Luckily, they were coming upon the chapter where Doctor Blood inevitably seduced the black widow he had been hired to protect. It was almost a relief. At least he could channel some of his sexual frustration into the character.

* * *

Beyond the old walls of the townhome, New York City was in full motion.

The streets were full of early morning traffic. Airflow and Slipstream sedans roared up and down Flatbush Avenue, vendors stood at curbs, hawking their wares, and pedestrians moved in undulating waves. And backlighting it all was the opulent art deco styles of cinema theatres, storefront churches, X-rated peepshows, and fifty-foot television screens advertising the newest tech. Hanging in the sky like ever-watchful eyes were half a dozen airships cruising steadily by. The city, protected as it was by a subtle layer of bluish UV from orbiting satellites—a subtle method of staving off the killing rays of the sun so the things that abhorred sunlight could move about it undisturbed during the day—carried on.

Standing across the street from the townhome was a man in a charcoal grey trench coat. His head was tilted up as he watched a recap of last evening's news on the side of a passing airship. An anti-vampire religious group had marched up to the White House only the night before, demanding that the new civil rights amendment—which, if passed, would grant vampires full citizenship—be pigeonholed indefinitely. They had even dragged a number of so-called abuse victims with them to prove their point. The screen panned across the gaggles of screaming, outraged faces, many toting GOD HATES VAMPIRES signs. He shook his head of dark, evenly trimmed hair, sighed at such a gauche display of bigotry and ignorance, and turned his attention back on the humble downtown Brooklyn brownstone.

The place was cozy but not opulent in appearance. Invisible. The owner could have certainly afforded a much grander home if he wanted, the man—whose name was Mr. Stephen—reflected.

Mr. Stephen had worked in the employ of vampires all of his life and knew a fair bit about them. The vampire he was about to approach was not the humble kind, so this situation was unusual, to say the last.

Following World War II, the first major war where vampires and shapeshifters served extensively alongside human soldiers, nonhumans were finally recognized as important members of the U.S. population. And, not long after, vampires began immigrating to the United States from Europe and abroad. The first government-approved blood substitutes were marketed at that time, the country's sensible response to the demands of its growing vampire population. At the same time, new laws were drafted to protect human rights, and it became a felony punishable by death for a vampire to feed on a human being without their consent.

But synthetic blood was merely food; it did nothing to address the other basic needs of America's newest minority group. Primarily, the need for intimacy and companionship. The solution came in the form of Poppets, synthetic humans created in labs from cloned embryos in vitro and genetically engineered to fit the specific needs and aesthetics of vampirekind.

A perfect solution, it was. After years of debate, the UN and even the Vatican eventually came to the same conclusion. Since the clones had never known the inside of a human womb, they could not technically be categorized as human beings with human rights. Of course, there were laws in place to prevent the mishandling of Poppets, but vampires were seldom guilty of such heinous crimes. The price attached to making, nurturing, and training a Poppet at a Scholomance—the frightfully high-end academies that trained Poppets to serve properly—was simply too great. That was akin to abusing a monstrously valuable racehorse. Unfortunately, most pro-human radical groups didn't see it that way. As far as they were concerned, vampires were monsters in need of eradication, and all Poppets everywhere were their hapless victims.

It was Mr. Stephen's opinion that the exploitation of Poppets by the government in the function of underpaid laborer was a far greater sin than any crime being committed by the many Vampire Courts. Poppettown, the underground city where Worker Poppets ran the machines that kept the city running, was an appalling slum. Working conditions were perilous, living conditions mean and spare, and crime rampant. But no one was interested in Mr. Stephen's opinion, because Mr. Stephen was a Poppet and had no rights outside of his Court.

As a light, shivery morning rain began falling over the city, making orangey smears of the sodium streetlights that marched in an even line up the avenue, Mr. Stephen unsheathed his umbrella and crossed the street, his heart thudding in his throat. His master had entrusted him with a responsibility that no Poppet had ever known before. It was a matter of life and death—literally. His life and death, as well as his master's. It was an enormously humbling task, and it made him hesitate a moment before pushing the button on the talk box of the innocuous little townhome in downtown Brooklyn.

* * *

The visitor said his name was Mr. Stephen and he wished to speak to Lord Edwin McGillicuddy. Eliza frowned before speaking into the kitchen talk box. She asked Mr. Stephen to wait while she came to fetch him. She set Edwin's lunch tray down and made her way out to the foyer.

She did not know until that moment that Edwin was a Vampire Lord, a vampire who had come fully into his power. He seemed far too young. But, then, he could be as old as the sands of time, for all Eliza knew. Edwin was very private about that part of his life.

A bad feeling started somewhere down near her toes and began inching its way up her legs and then her spine. Something wasn't right. She stopped in the hallway and checked herself in the mirror on the wall. She searched for any flaws, anything that might give her away for what she was, but everything seemed to be in order. Lastly, she checked to make certain the beautiful, gold-plated Derringer she kept in a hidden pocket of her skirt was loaded.

A man in a smoky grey raincoat and bowler hat was waiting to be let in. He was tall and broad-shouldered, handsome, with a perfectly symmetrical face, hair cut on even, mathematical angles, and eyes so blue they looked fabricated and sewn on. He was definitely a Poppet, a caricature of male beauty. More importantly, a Courtier Poppet, a kept man—one owned by a wealthy vampire, if the cut of the razor-tailored Savile Row of London suit he wore under his open raincoat was any indication.

The man turned to her and smiled courteously. His perfectly even set of teeth were two shades whiter than Mr. McGillicuddy's best set of china. "Hello there, miss." He removed his hat and bowed low to her. His speech was formal and his bow was executed flawlessly as only a Courtier can do. "My name is Mr. Stephen. I've come on a mission of great importance."

"You're a Courtier," Eliza blurted out. She couldn't help herself; she glanced down at his left hand.

The Poppet noted her look. Unashamedly, he lifted his left hand and ungloved it to reveal a well-manicured hand and the blooding bracelet he wore around his wrist. It gleamed in the moody lighting of the foyer's hanging lamp—ornate, priceless, a pretty manacle. From it, a vampire could drink anytime he or she wished to from a sterile and eternally open wound.

"Indeed," the man agreed. He spoke in a soft, friendly voice as if afraid of spooking her. "And you are...miss?"

She almost forgot herself. "E-Eliza. Eliza Book. Mr. McGillicuddy's secretary."

"You are very young," he observed, looking her over carefully. "You must be a very smart young woman to be working for a Vampire Lord."

She smiled at that even though she disliked his condescending tone, the way he made it sound like something scandalous. Eliza was eighteen, but she was not young.

"Would the man of the house be available? Lord Edwin McGillicuddy?" Mr. Stephen pulled his sleeve down to hide the bracelet.

Eliza crossed her arms behind her back and rubbed at her own wrist, at the scar there. She stared long and hard at Mr. Stephen while her hidden right hand slid soundlessly into the invisible slit in her skirt. She fingered the Derringer.

* * *

Normally, Edwin allowed Eliza to handle all of their visitors, but not today. The man in the doorway sounded too formal, like a trained Courtier. And where Courtiers went, vampires were soon to follow. The idea didn't sit well with Edwin; he liked his retirement too well.

He stood up slowly from his desk where he was doing the edits that Miss Book had meticulously marked on his newest manuscript. He knew a thing or two about Vampire Courts, having worked as an Enforcer for one of the more powerful ones. Clutching his teacup, he silently wended his way down the spiral staircase from his office on the third floor to the foyer below.

Miss Book stood with her back to him, facing their visitor, her hand in her skirt pocket as she fingered a small gold Derringer he had seen her carry with her in the past. Miss Eliza Book was a practical young woman with more than a few of her own dark secrets, but he could respect that. He knew a thing or two about secrets as well.

Beyond her, a Courtier who looked rather familiar stood smiling in a perfectly charming way that made the hackles on the back of his neck stand on end.

* * *

As soon as the vampire stepped into the foyer, Mr. Stephen went on full alert. Lord Edwin McGillicuddy was tall and rangy, with a dangerous scrapper's build. Beyond that, he didn't seem like much—a kid playing truant from school. Until one saw him in action, that is. He certainly did not look like what he was—a Vampire Lord two hundred years steeped in his power.

Mr. Stephen smiled. Lord Edwin's wardrobe was much better these days. Normally, he dressed rough, like a man better suited to bare-knuckles fisticuffs in the worst part of London than a Vampire Lord. But, beyond that, little had changed with the very unconventional Lord Edwin McGillicuddy.

Without missing a beat, Mr. Stephen went down on one knee and bowed his head properly. "Greetings, my Prince. I've come seeking your very urgent help on a matter of great importance."

Lord Edwin glowered but indicated he should follow him into the drawing room.

"Thank you, Miss Book. Quite excellent of you," Mr. Stephen said a few minutes later, accepting a cup of tea from the free-roaming tea set floating past them. He considered himself well-traveled—he was not one of his lord's more cloistered Poppets, good for only warming his lord's bed—but he still managed to be mildly surprised by the wide variety of inventions scattered around the room. Miss Book was certainly an interesting young woman.

The tea set zoomed away. Miss Book followed it to the kitchen, though he sensed her lurking just out of sight.

"She's not your Poppet? How very progressive," Mr. Stephen said when they were alone, sipping his tea. "Shall I take it you sympathize with those radical groups that would free the Poppet population from...slavery, as it were?"

Edwin McGillicuddy, refusing to be baited into a debate, stayed on his feet in the drawing room and leaned against the wet bar. "What are you doing here, Stephen?"

Mr. Stephen lifted the embroidered napkin to his lips, his face professionally blanked of emotion. "I see. Direct as always, my Lord."

"Out with it."

"I bear a message—a request, one might say—from a mutual friend." He withdrew a boarding pass from his jacket pocket and extended it to Lord Edwin.

Edwin, on the other hand, remained absolutely still, revealing nothing. Mr. Stephen knew how he felt about Vampire Courts. Though one of the most powerful young Lords to come out of his master's Court, something had happened in his past, some upset or unspoken tragedy, which had caused him to avoid all things vampire like the plague.

"Foxley," Lord Edwin said, recognizing the corporate seal on the boarding pass, a fox wrapped around the world. "You're on a mission from Lord Foxley's Court?"

"That's correct. I was told..."

"Mr. Stephen, are you a Favorite?" Edwin asked suddenly. His hand was rock-hard, the cords of his forearm standing out like tensile wires as he clutched his teacup. His eyes looked darker and moodier, and when he spoke, his teeth looked sharper in his mouth. Most vampires considered it a fashion faux pas not to have their teeth rigorously capped and molded to look acceptably human, but Lord Edwin, because of his past as an Enforcer, had not cut his teeth.

Stephen, still dressed in his raincoat, inclined his head. "I am my Lord's most trusted valet. His Favorite, yes."

Edwin smiled humorlessly. "You sleep with him."

Stephen shifted uncomfortably in his seat. "I fulfill all of the roles expected of me. Friend, confidante, lover."

"And gopher," Edwin said, and his smile grew. "His most valued servant, and yet he sends you to accomplish the potentially dangerous task of approaching another Vampire Lord to deliver an invitation—a task that could be accomplished with a phone call or an email, or even a courier." Slowly, Edwin crouched down until he was sitting on the divan across from Mr. Stephen's chair. But he stayed tense and on high alert, an especially vampire-like poise.

It made Mr. Stephen sweat. He wondered if Edwin would spring at him. If Edwin would rip his throat out just for the fun of it. He knew the Prince's reputation.

"You seemed concerned, little Poppet on a string," Edwin taunted him with a sly, knowing smile.

* * *

Eliza hovered just inside the kitchenette, listening to the conversation. She knew a great deal more about Court life than she let on, even to Mr. McGillicuddy. Like Mr. Stephen, Eliza had been born in vitro, a Poppet, a future Courtesan, genetically engineered for the satisfaction of the Vampire Lord who'd commissioned her design.

She'd spent fifteen wonderful years at the Scholomance wallowing in obscene luxury like a spoiled heiress. She'd had toys and pets of every kind, tutors who'd schooled her in dance and Court etiquette, and she'd had a glorious bedroom in shades of pink and soft dove fit for a Disney Princess. She'd had gifts of cake and ponies and pink birthday roses which, over time, slowly evolved into gowns, diamonds only of the first water, and red, red roses, all sent to her by way of the Vampire Lord who owned her—a lord she had yet to meet.

Later, in her early teens, her life consisted of debutante parties, wild shopping sprees, and all-night reveries, all in preparation for her first meeting with her future master, the man she would spend the rest of her life with.

She was fifteen when her Lord finally came calling on her. He was tall, aristocratically beautiful, and fascinating. All the girls at the Scholomance giggled and mock-swooned when he passed by. He took her to the opera, dinner, and a horse and carriage ride through Central Park, and then it was back to his white-glove penthouse apartment on Fifth Avenue. There he spent the rest of the night raping her repeatedly until her throat tore and she could cry no more. All of which gave way to the realization that she was not a girl at all. Like Mr. Stephen, she was a toy to be groomed, dressed, and played with according to the ever-evolving whims of her vampire master.

For the first fifteen years of her life, Eliza had lived a content, picturesque life as a wonderfully ignorant doll with pretty hair and pretty dresses and not a single dark thought in her head. The year at her master's Court that followed was an education in hell.

"What exactly is a Favorite?" she asked, stepping boldly into the room. She was afraid Mr. Stephen might suspect her and she wanted to appear as innocent and wide-eyed as possible. She was good at looking innocent when she needed to, and vampires were very popular and fashionable at the moment. She wanted to look interested.

Mr. Stephen raised his eyebrows at that. Ignoring Mr. McGillicuddy, he turned his full attention to her. "Clearly, your master has not explained many things about Court life to you."

"Certain celebrities are considered Favorites, aren't they? The ones in the paper always photographed on the arm of some Vampire Lord while on their way to the Academy Awards?"

Mr. Stephen rolled his eyes, which was exactly the reaction she was looking for. She was just another befuddled human female who gained all her vampire gossip via rag mags and reality television programs. She knew nothing at all about real Vampire Courts.

"A Favorite is understood to be a Courtesan or Courtier who is next in line to receive an Inheritance from his or her Lord."

"That's a euphemism for being turned into a vampire, isn't it?" she said, knowing it to be true.

"That's correct, miss."

She fluttered her hand like a silly girl. "How exciting for you. So you will be a vampire someday, Mr. Stephen?"

"If my Lord deems it."

"They never do it," Mr. McGillicuddy suddenly spoke up. "But we remain hopeful, don't we, Mr. Stephen?"

Mr. Stephen's face darkened and a wave of almost palatable anger poured off him. "We are all hopeful our dear Lord Foxley will favor us as he has favored you, Lord Edwin."

Eliza stiffened at this new information. She'd had no idea that Mr. McGillicuddy's master was the elusive, never seen, or photographed Lord Foxley, reputed to be the oldest and most powerful vampire in the world.

Edwin shrugged it off as he stood up. Slowly, he relaxed. "That's neither here nor there. What does Foxley want with me, Mr. Stephen?" He smiled nicely.

Mr. Stephen's jaw stiffened as he worked on containing his anger. "Lord Foxley has requested an audience with you tomorrow aboard his gyro, the *Gypsy Queen*." He paused to let the implications of that statement sink in. "We shall remain in orbit over the city of

New York for the next two weeks. You may even consider it a form of holiday, if you will."

"The *Gypsy Queen*? That's the largest gyro in the world," Eliza suddenly said.

She couldn't help it; she was fascinated by the giant spherical ships hanging in the stratosphere over the Earth like great fat moons. Vampires invented them in an attempt to counteract the effects of daylight in a time before UV protection, but now they were invariably linked to the greatest Vampire Courts in the world. The great ships were large enough to orbit against the rising of the sun, perfect for creatures who shunned daylight. Living on board a gyro was like living in a state of perpetual night, with all the glamour and dangers associated with it.

Gyros had gyroscopic centers, hence the name. Gyroscopes, she knew, helped the ships stay in orbit above the Earth by generating their own gravity fields. Eliza had long dreamed of visiting a gyro and studying how it operated, the engineering marvel that it was, but she wasn't willing to jeopardize her freedom for such a fancy.

"Lord Foxley owns the *Gypsy Queen*?" Eliza glanced at the passport in Mr. Stephen's lap.

"He built it, in fact," Mr. Stephen explained. He appeared to be enjoying this opportunity to educate a mere human. "And his hospitality naturally extends to visiting his estate aboard the ship. New Versailles is the grandest Vampire Court in the world. None can compare."

He went on to explain that the *Gypsy Queen* was over twenty square miles in size, making it fall just a hair short of the island of Manhattan. It regularly boasted over half a million visitors, had a hundred major casinos, hotels, and resorts, twelve hundred restaurants and nightclubs, and a permanent staff of over a hundred thousand people. The Academy Awards, the Miss Universe Pageant, and five different reality shows were regularly filmed on board the *Gypsy Queen*, a veritable paradise of leisure and debauchery. Mr. Stephen explained all this with a great flourish like a travel agent trying to sell a package deal.

Eliza knew better. If Edwin's master was summoning him home, something very terrible was likely going on.

Mr. Stephen sat up, eying her carefully. "Lord Edwin, why not bring your charming companion with you? I think she would very much like to see the ship." He turned to eye the vampire querulously. "May I tell my Lord that he can expect to see you tomorrow? It is considered a supreme honor to be called into the audience of Lord Foxley."

Mr. McGillicuddy snorted. He knew, as she did, that only royalty, major celebrities, and politicians ever visited New Versailles, the estate of the "King of the World," as the media called Lord Foxley. And, even then, they were usually disappointed to find themselves dining with agents and representatives, never with the Lord himself. Foxley never made any public appearances or allowed anyone to photograph him. He preferred to remain secreted away in his gauche palace with his hordes of Poppet servants.

But, she wagered that things would be different if she and Mr. McGillicuddy boarded the *Gypsy Queen*. For that…yes. She suspected that Lord Foxley would put in a personal appearance.

Mr. Stephen added, "Your accommodations are to be at the Palace of New Versailles, in apartments directly adjacent to Lord Foxley's private quarters. All expenses paid."

Mr. McGillicuddy, arms crossed, never lost his smile when he said, "Get out."

"Excuse me?" Mr. Stephen looked confused.

"Just so," Edwin stated simply, dropping his arms and taking a menacing step toward the Courtier. "I have a book to write and no desire to see New Versailles."

Mr. Stephen looked vaguely sick. "Of course, you do not have to stay at New Versailles. Lord Foxley can arrange other accommodations. A casino, perhaps? Or one of the five-star golfing resorts...?"

"No." Mr. McGillicuddy said, his anger crackling in the air between them as he took another step toward Mr. Stephen. His entire demeanor had suddenly changed. Eliza actually jumped at the sound, for he rarely spoke above a loud whisper.

Mr. Stephen jerked mechanically to his feet, clutching his umbrella so hard that his powerful Poppet fingers managed to snap the stem.

Mr. McGillicuddy narrowed his eyes and Mr. Stephen visibly shirked as if the vampire had struck him a glancing blow.

"Mr. Stephen, I suggest you remember who I am." Mr. McGillicuddy took another step toward the Poppet, who backed up automatically toward the door. Eliza had never seen her employer so incensed. It was as though he were a totally different person. "You may tell your lord from me that he can take his fancy, gilded invite, roll it up, and stick it up his arse! Now, I must insist you leave my premises immediately!"

Mr. Stephen scrambled for the door, so flustered that he managed to drop his poor, abused umbrella in his haste to escape the Prince's wrath.

Eliza clutched her elbows at the display.

Well, now!

| ii |

Mr. McGillicuddy's publisher had wisely decided to hold the release party for the newest Doctor Blood book at the Theatre des Vampires, one of the city's hottest nightspots. Formerly the Astor Opera House in lower Manhattan, the old washed stone building had been converted into a rave palace about ten years ago. It was the place to see and be seen—just with vampires. And, tonight, the party had attracted a surprisingly elite audience.

Eliza, whose job was to get Mr. McGillicuddy there on time and to stay there for the duration of the party, glanced around the vast dance floor, recognizing a fair number of celebrities, social media influencers, and, of course, loyal fans.

Everyone was dressed to the nines, with many dressing up as characters from Mr. McGillicuddy's books, or just any of the literary vampires they envied. She saw dozens of Doctor Bloods, the blood-drinking, crime-solving coroner that had made Mr. McGillicuddy famous, as well as Draculas, Lestats, Carmillas, Lady Bathories, and many others. They seemed to glide rather than walk across the mirror-polished floors.

She watched young people flutter together into brief, glittery, black-clothed cliques and then break apart, some heading to the open bar while others migrated to the floor to writhe to the goth and trance music the DJ was spinning. Vampires were very fashionable these days, she reflected. Though, of course, few humans truly understood what they were emulating.

She knew Mr. McGillicuddy was hiding somewhere amidst the melee, probably dancing the night away with a pretty young thing or two. Edwin loved raves and nightclubs—it was the only vampire-like thing he seemed to enjoy—and because he looked so young, he could easily pass as a teenager if he wanted to. But she hoped he behaved himself tonight and didn't wind up in a closet somewhere, making out with one of his fans or drunkenly fighting the barkeep in the alley behind the club. It was such a bother. She knew if she didn't keep a close eye on him, he would wind up on the front page of the gossip newspapers in the morning.

Perhaps, though, she had little to fear. Normally, he reveled in release parties, but he'd seemed uncharacteristically subdued when they arrived. She had a feeling he was still thinking about that very disconcerting visit by Mr. Stephen a few weeks ago.

Her suspicion was confirmed when the crowd parted and she spotted her employer in the VIP lounge on the catwalk. He was surrounded by his fans, as usual, but he seemed to be ignoring most of them. She did notice he was quietly romancing a young man dressed like David, the punk vampire from The Lost Boys. They were having drinks that looked like blood (but were not) and Mr. McGillicuddy was whispering something into the David's ear that was making the boy positively blush.

She tried not to let it bother her, but of course, it always did. Not that she had any claim on her employer, of course. They worked together and she would never cross that professional line. But she hated watching him pick up floozies and one-night stands. They were all bouncy, squealing, empty-headed fans. He was a vampire. One would think he'd worry more about his reputation.

She wiped nonexistent lint from her dress. She had carefully selected it for the evening, a conservative wine-red evening dress and black pearls. It was only kind of/sort of vampire-like, and it helped her to fit in with this crowd without standing out too much.

Surprisingly, Mr. McGillicuddy had worn the evening suit she had chosen for him without complaint. His suit was pinstriped charcoal with lovely if slightly outdated swallowtails, and his shoulder-length auburn hair was cinched back in a queue. It made him look particularly roguish, like a highwayman or swashbuckler. It drove the girls—and many of the guys—absolutely crazy.

He looked up, spotted her, and immediately signaled that she should join him on the catwalk. As always, she shook her head at his invitation. It was their thing. He always tried to include her; she always turned him down.

"Behave yourself, Mr. McGillicuddy," Eliza whispered, clutching her trusty clipboard against her bodice like a bit of armor. With a tired sigh, she made her way to the bar to order a Shirley Temple. She didn't drink very often, not liking the loss of control that alcohol could cause.

While she waited for the barkeep to fetch her drink, voices buzzed like a giant swarm of wasps caught under the roof of the Theatre. Almost everyone was discussing the sudden appearance of Lord Foxley's gyro. Sometime last night, while the city slept, the *Gypsy Queen* had suddenly appeared in orbit over the west end of the island of Manhattan like a gigantic gunmetal moon.

The coincidence was not lost on her. Eliza kept craning her neck and searching for the telltale sign of a large crowd that would indicate that a Vampire Lord was moving in their midst, surrounded by servants, security, and the press. So far, nothing untoward had happened tonight.

She had to keep reminding herself that vampires had no civil rights. Lord Foxley might be the most powerful vampire in the world, but he was still only a vampire. He could do no more than politely request someone's audience. If they refused his invitation, he couldn't force them. If he did anything improper, he could find himself endangering the Vampire Bill going through Congress, and then vampires would never win civil rights. She didn't think he would do that. At least, she hoped he wouldn't.

It made logical sense when she thought about it, yet she felt an odd static charge in the air even as she spotted Robert and Juliana heading toward her across the dance floor. Her spirits were immediately lifted on seeing some familiar faces.

Eliza had met Juliana over a year ago at a dinner party thrown by Edwin's publisher. She'd been there to support her boyfriend's first book release, and she and Eliza had clicked almost from the start.

Juliana, an artist, musician, and full-time riot grrrl, was everything Eliza was not. Loud and brash, she often organized civil disobedient sit-ins and Gandhi-like peace rallies to raise awareness and money for nonhuman civil rights organizations. Her hair was always a dozen different colors and her outfits outrageous. Once, she wore no clothes at all and just painted them onto her body to attend one of these affairs. Eliza had no idea what the girl was doing being friends with someone as mousy and soft-spoken as herself.

After greetings and hugs, Robbie said, "Rum and Coke, darling?"

"Only if the ingredients are naturally sourced. Will you ask, darling?"

"Don't I always?" With a wry grin, Robbie turned to order them drinks.

Alone finally, Juliana clenched Eliza and squealed. Juliana thankfully wore clothes tonight, a shimmery bustled dress in a shocking shade of azure with a long skirt that seemed to be made of broken hardware. Eliza was pretty sure she'd had the dress designed as a satiric commentary on consumerism. All the jangling metal brought out her wide, girlish blue eyes and complimented her sparkling ringlets of red, red hair.

"Dear heart, I absolutely love that dress!" she cried even though she had seen it half a dozen times before. It was Eliza's only formal dress. "And those earrings are so darn cute! Tell me you made them!"

"I did," Eliza admitted with a grin. She turned to let Juliana see her earrings, which she had fashioned from junk she had found in the trash. They were little cogs with a watch face in them. Juliana squealed again when she saw that they actually told the time.

"How are you so smart to have made those?"

"I just read a lot."

"No, you are amazing. And they are darling. I must commission a pair."

"Do you think it's too much on me?" Eliza asked worriedly. She didn't want to stand out. She never wanted to stand out.

"I don't think it's enough! Oh, I do wish I could invent! Leeza, I could improve on so many things. Do you know that down in Poppettown they use industrial fibers in the uniforms of the Poppets who work the steam shops? They don't breathe! I said to Robert that things must change. Things will change. But let's not talk about me tonight."

Juliana grinned, wrinkling up her snub little freckled nose, and linked an arm through Eliza's, walking her to the stairs that led to the upper catwalk where it was easier to talk without having to shout at each other above the pounding music. "What do you think of the Vampire Bill? Is your Mr. McGillicuddy excited?"

"I'm not sure if he is even aware of it. He seems rather...apolitical. And he isn't mine!" she laughed.

Juliana laughed, too. "Of course he is yours, dear heart. Your very own vampire all wrapped around your little pinky finger!"

"He certainly is not!"

"He's wearing a suit, Leeza."

Eliza rolled her eyes. "As opposed to pajamas, which is probably what he'd wear if I wasn't after him all the time."

"He does it to please you!"

"He does not!"

Juliana wagged her finger as if unconvinced. "Robbie is the same way. One moment I worry he's not paying attention, and the next he's giving me jewelry for no reason at all. It's that or he's guilty of something." She laughed. "Do you know he wants to take me to Egypt?"

If Juliana had one flaw, it was a touch of ADHD. But living with a high-strung, Gaelic vampire had given Eliza a unique skillset. She knew exactly what conversations to pick up and which to let go of.

"Egypt. How exciting." She tried to sound upbeat about the news, but it left her sad all the same. She knew she would never meet anyone who would ever take her to Egypt. Or anywhere. It made her feel lonely even amidst her friends.

Thankfully, Juliana didn't notice her lapse. She was too busy talking about LGBT+ rights in Egypt.

Robbie drifted back to them with drinks in hand. He was big in the gaming world and wrote a popular series of LitRPG books. He often threatened to poach her and her talents from Mr. McGillicuddy. He raised his glass to her now as if to thank her for taking Juliana off his hands for a little while.

Robbie, like Mr. McGillicuddy, was a member of a most unique subset of the human race—the nonhumans. Robert was a head taller than even Edwin's impressive six-foot-four-inch height, was gifted with a mouthful of teeth to die for, and sported eyes like beautifully polished aquamarines. He liked to call himself a minority of one, seeing how he was not only African-American but also a were-leopard. But, for all his charm and his talents, she knew even he needed a break from Juliana from time to time.

"...I mean, we've talked about it...but I can do so much more good for nonhumans as I am," Juliana was saying as she hung all over Robbie. She was getting soused on rum and Coke and her voice was getting louder. Juliana raised her eyebrows with interest. "Do you think I should?"

Eliza had to backtrack to figure out what she was saying. "Convert?" She looked up at Robbie, who was just grinning and going along with what his girlfriend was saying. "I mean...I don't think it's my place to comment, but..." She let her voice trail off.

"You wouldn't? Has your vampire ever tried to nibble on you?"

Eliza stiffened, suddenly uncomfortable with the turn of their conversation. "We don't have that kind of relationship. And I told you, he's not m—"

"So you never would?" Juliana interrupted.

"Never would what?"

"Feed him."

"No!" Eliza said a bit too loudly. She immediately lowered her voice and frowned. "That would be...inappropriate."

Juliana grinned as if she had not heard her. "I hear it's an amazing experience. Positively orgasmic. And you know Mr. Vampire would if you asked him to..."

Eliza drank down her drink so she wouldn't need to answer but choked when Juliana said orgasmic, then started looking around as if she had lost something. She didn't want to talk about this.

"The suit, Leeza!" Juliana reminded her.

"What about the suit?" Robbie inquired. He suddenly looked interested, and Juliana laughed and smacked him on the shoulder.

"Leeza got Edwin into an evening suit!"

"Ooooh," Robbie said, observing. "Eliza has magic powers!"

"She has him under her spell!"

Despite their good-natured ribbing, Eliza felt her mood sullen considerably. She wasn't an idiot. She knew Mr. McGillicuddy probably liked her in a way that went beyond her simply being a good secretary or picking out nice clothes for him. She'd seen the way he looked at her, and she'd read his stories, which had become increasingly sexier and more explicit during the time she'd worked for him. But she couldn't pursue such a path. It wasn't safe.

She couldn't afford to let him any closer than he already was.

If they kissed...if he tasted her...he would know what she was. Then things would spiral out of control. He might fire her and send her away for lying about what she was. Or—the worst-case scenario as well as her worst nightmare—he might turn her over to the authorities as lost property. Then she would need to go home to him. And that was never going to happen. Not while there was breath left in her body.

No, better they keep things professional at all times.

A glint of eyes in the crowd below made her start. She leaned over the safety rail, looking out across the preening crowds of people.

"Is everything okay?" There was an edge of concern to Juliana's voice.

"I don't know. I hope so," Eliza said.

"Is your Mr. McGillicuddy in some kind of trouble?" Juliana asked, suddenly very sober. She, like Eliza, had finally noticed a slender female figure sitting in almost total shadows beside Mr. McGillicuddy. Only her eyes were visible when they caught the gleam of the stage lights. The cute wannabe David was gone and this stranger had taken his place. But she was no ordinary raver or teenage fan, Eliza realized.

Why was Mr. McGillicuddy meeting with another vampire?

* * *

"Claire, it's been forever," Edwin remarked and smiled bitterly at his "old friend" after she chased away the adorable fan who'd wanted to get to know him better.

The white shadow sitting beside him looked over, her face professionally blank, but her pale blue eyes smoldering. Claire was the product of a Double Inheritance, a young half-breed Japanese prostitute that he and Lord Foxley had picked up in the dangerous Shinjuku region of Tokyo during the turn of the last century. Foxley had loved her coloring and had encouraged Edwin to drink her while he watched, though it wasn't long before Foxley joined them. Together, they drained her almost to the point of death and then enjoyed filling her up with their own version of life.

Their new creation immediately began a kind of sibling rivalry with Edwin for Foxley's full affection. She had still been fighting for her place in the hierarchy of their collective relationship when Edwin left Foxley's Court almost fifty years ago.

Claire was a young chit by vampire standards, the undead equivalent of a bratty preteen, and not just because she looked the part. She was the result of Foxley's fetish for very young blood. She looked it, too—tiny, white, mealy, and dressed in a bustled white ragdoll dress that showed off decidedly underdeveloped breasts, a sunken ribcage, boyish hips, and her great milky white wings. Her face was tiny and thin-lipped, and her upslanted eyes predatory. Her hair was done up in enormous dreads that fell like a holocaust of white about her narrow shoulders, making her head seem much too large for her body. She wore a pair of welding goggles atop her head—a popular trend among the youth that she was trying to emulate—and enormous moonwalker boots with five-inch platforms.

Claire offered him a bitter smile. "It's Lady Claire now."

"Lady," Edwin exclaimed. He stuck an unlit cigarette in the corner of her mouth. "You've become your own Lord?"

"Not just a Lord. An Enforcer. Foxley's Enforcer. You're surprised?"

"Not really." After he'd left Foxley's employment, Foxley would naturally have chosen the best he had as a replacement, and as loathed as Edwin was to admit it, Claire was the best. He knew because he had trained her.

Claire narrowed her eyes, her power crackling against his skin almost like the fluttery touch of her razor-sharp wings.

"Foxley's pups always do come to power fast."

She offered him a humorless smile. "You would know."

Like her, Edwin had been a "child of the street." He'd been born in a whorehouse in Mile End in the East End of London in the early part of the Nineteenth Century. Back then, it had been the Yiddish slums full of panhandlers, music hall girls, and theater troupes—thieves and cutthroats, more than anything. Edwin never discovered who his mum was, or what had become of her, but he'd counted himself a lucky lad nonetheless. Instead of one mum, he'd had dozens, as all of the working girls had taken turns raising him. He learned to pickpocket almost before he could walk, and by the time he was nine years old, he could drink gin, smoke pipes, and swear and fight as well as any man who lived south of the Bow-bells. He lost his virginity at age twelve, and his innocence at nineteen.

A house client, an evil old git like Fagin in the book, had been beating one of his many mums with a martinet. Edwin, who loved all women everywhere and who had stayed on at the whorehouse to work as security, heard about what was happening and used a pair of harness reins to subdue the bloke. It took four police officers to drag Edwin—tall, lanky, and wiry-strong—off the lifeless, strangled remains of the man.

Edwin was certain he would hang, his life over before he ever reached twenty. He even welcomed it. He reckoned it was one way out of Mile End, and he was certain that whatever hell looked like, it couldn't be any worse than the hell pit he lived in now. But on the night of his hanging, Lord Foxley showed up, impressed by Edwin's strength, savagery, and cockiness. His pride, more than anything.

Foxley said he was a beautiful devil, a mongrel with a life of pickpocketing and prostitution that stretched out forever before him—if he managed to survive the next few days and the hangman's noose. He said Edwin had enormous potential if nurtured correctly...assuming he was willing to join Foxley's Court. It was a binding contract, Foxley explained. He would intervene on Edwin's behalf and save his neck from the noose. In exchange, Edwin would work for two hundred years as his Enforcer.

The idea of being Foxley's Enforcer—and a vampire—had been overwhelmingly nauseating to Edwin. Despite what he had done, he still believed in God and in the sermons he'd heard preached in church. The churchmen believed that to be a vampire was to be irrevocably damned, set apart from God forever. Rejected. But as zero hour loomed and Edwin watched the other condemned prisoners being led to the gallows by the head executioner, his fear kicked in. He decided that he would rather live and be damned than die and still be damned.

He might be a mongrel, a nothing, but he was nobody's fool.

Even now.

Edwin pinned Foxley's new Enforcer with his best predatory look, pushed his power inside of her, and watched Claire stiffen and tremble. Regardless of her feelings for him, or her jealousy, he was still her master, her maker. If she forgot that, he was more than willing to remind her.

"What's the bloke got to say for himself? Did he share any fond memories?"

Claire clenched her fists and scrunched up her face nastily. "Just that I was to speak to you tonight. To deliver his message. Our Lord wants you to come home."

Edwin laughed at that. He couldn't believe Foxley's audacity! "You're dotty in the head, you are, chit." He waved away his power. The absurdity of the situation had killed his appetite for any power play. "And so is he. I fulfilled my contract with Lord Foxley years ago. I'm my own Lord now. He has no right to command me."

"Lord Foxley is attempting to be civil."

"Lord Foxley has no idea how to be civil. I've already conveyed my response to the esteemed Mr. Stephen. The answer remains the same: No."

Claire opened her mouth to speak, then closed it to reconsider. "Very well. If that's your answer—and Lord Foxley said it would be—then I must offer you a new contract on behalf of our Lord."

"Really, now?" This was turning out to be more entertaining than the rave!

Lady Claire smiled, showing off catty incisors. "Two hundred years of service as Lord Foxley's Enforcer...in exchange for the life of your little plaything up there." She nodded upward, toward where Miss Book stood watching him.

* * *

Run!

The need was urgent and instinctual.

Eliza raced past her friends to the tune of their confusion. She reached the bottom of the steps before she became aware of a presence. She turned and recognized Mr. Stephen standing beside her.

Smiling benignly, he took her solicitously by the arm as if he meant to waltz with her. Another man came up beside her. For one spare moment, she thought it was Edwin. He was tall like Edwin, with Edwin's pale, redheaded coloring, but with a thicker, weightlifter-type upper-body build. Like Mr. Stephen, he looked like a gorgeous valet or some kind of supermodel for a man's fashion magazine.

Another Poppet.

"Mr. Laurel," Mr. Stephen greeted the man with a nod.

Mr. Laurel nodded in response and took Eliza by the other arm, his fingers squeezing her painfully. Eliza, suddenly panicked, jerked away from them both, but both Poppets were stronger than they looked, and their grip on her arms felt like vices.

She thought about screaming, but the DJ was spinning some thundering techno, and she knew no one would hear her. Besides, did it matter? The Scholomance had rigorously trained her in different forms of martial arts as a young Poppet in an attempt to induce poise and balance. She'd been a very apt pupil.

Eliza did a kind of improvised pirouette and locked her heel behind Mr. Laurel's, sweeping his feet out from under him. Mr. Laurel lost his grip on her wrists and went down hard on the stairs on his face, cursing her.

At the same time, Eliza danced back, jerking her arm loose from Mr. Stephen's grip. Mr. Stephen grunted and looked at her with new eyes.

"You're not human," he said.

She grunted in response to that. Before she could shift into a more defensive position and reach for the Derringer in her garter, Mr. Stephen was upon her, stepping on her hem and winding a long black garrote about her neck. She fought the garrote, kicked at him, dislodging the Derringer but accomplishing nothing with it. He too was strong.

"Little Poppet, that will be quite enough," Mr. Stephen said, softly, benevolently, in her ear. "Lord Foxley wishes to speak to you and your master, and we should not keep a Vampire Lord waiting."

He tightened the garrote and Eliza's world went black.

* * *

Swearing, Edwin made it to the stairwell in record time, a useless endeavor since he already knew that Miss Book was gone. He did find her Derringer lying abandoned on the floor and her friend Juliana babbling about two men who had abducted her best friend in plain sight of everyone.

His surge of anger was such that his wings ripped free of the confines of his suit jacket, ruining it forever as he fully extended them. At the same time, a white blur rushed past him, encircling him.

Lady Claire. He launched himself at her, cursing under his breath, but Claire had something ridiculous like inline skates on the bottoms of those moon boots of her. As he closed his hands around her throat, she turned suddenly with the fluid, surreal grace that only vampires could display and kicked him squarely in the chest with the force of a jackhammer.

The blow knocked the wind from his body and sent him flying backward into one of the ten-foot-tall mirrors that decorated the wall behind the bar. It exploded in an apocalypse of glittering glass shards, those razor-sharp fragments ripping through his clothes and flesh and sticking out of him at odd angles like quills. He sagged to the floor on his hands and knees in his torn suit, feeling like a human porcupine.

"Bloody hell, I'll kill you," he warned Lady Claire through clenched teeth as she danced about him like some kind of demented ballerina.

"Poor Lord Edwin," she singsonged, dark eyes glinting like pieces of black flint. "You're losing your touch, Prince." She withdrew a large Oriental fan painted with flocking cranes. He noticed it was made of stainless steel.

Undeterred, Edwin lumbered out from behind the bar, ready to fight the vampiress—barehanded, if need be.

The club was suddenly dead quiet as guests tried to understand what was happening. Someone nearby screamed at the sight of him, probably Juliana. Edwin swiped at Claire's legs as she danced merrily by, but the glass in his body restricted his movements.

Lady Claire grinned, her cutting fan flicking out and catching him somewhere under the chin. The world suddenly went grey in the corners of his vision as the little bit of blood in his body began leaking down the front of his suit. The suit he wore just to impress Miss Book...

She was the last thing he thought about as he collapsed.

"Sleep well, sweet Prince," Lady Claire said as Edwin's world faded to black. "We'll see each other very soon."

| iii |

Eliza woke to a deep, serene humming. She lay with her eyes half-closed, not dreaming, but not quite awake, either. Then she remembered how she had gotten here—Mr. Stephen speaking to her, the horrible pressure of the garrote about her throat!—and she jerked upward and opened her eyes, clutching reflexively at her throat with a black, lace-gloved hand.

She was lying on an enormous bed of red crushed velvet in an unfamiliar red and gold bedchamber. The room was brilliantly posh, like something that belonged in Buckingham Palace. The thought did not make her feel at all safe. It was obvious she was a long way from her safe, sensible bedroom in New York. The walls were burnished gold and heavily carved with scrollwork and floral motifs, the floor was a furry, scarlet plush carpeting so deep it looked like an ocean of blood, and the cathedral ceiling above, past the blinding crystals of the chandelier, displayed one of the most obscene ceiling murals she had ever seen.

The Renaissance-inspired art depicted a great host of beautiful angels and black-winged devils having sex. She'd seen similar murals during her time as a Courtesan. They were a popular artistic expression among the more gauche Vampire Lords and were often painted on removable panels so the pictures could be changed out if the Lord grew tired of it.

She had a terrible thought, then. Maybe she'd woken up at Court, and the last three years of her life as a free woman had been a dream.

Panting suddenly, almost on the verge of a panic attack, she got slowly to her feet. Her dress was shorn, her hairnet gone, and her loose hair crackled about her shoulders like a black halo as she moved toward the only door in the room, praying it was unlocked. She wished she still had the Derringer, as small and pathetic as it was. Any type of weapon would make her feel better at the moment. Unfortunately, it was gone.

"Hello there, lady," came a soft voice as she reached the door.

She started and turned to find a child sitting on a divan in the shadows near the door. He was playing with a hand-held game and fit into the shadows so well that she'd missed him initially.

He looked about twelve years old, pitifully thin and pale. He wore a pair of hip-hugging denim trousers and a white shirt open to reveal the slightly sunken chest and shadowy ribs of a painfully underfed youth. His skin was pale gold like a boy with a forever fading tan, and his hair nearly colorless, the white, white blond of the very young before age has a chance to darken the strands. It made his pale skin seem positively radiant. His eyes, half-hidden by the waves of thick hair, were the color of sun-worn slate and looked huge in his thin, malnourished face.

Eliza approached him carefully, studying the delicate, almost girlish beauty of what could only be a young Poppet as he concentrated on the game, his thumbs flying knowledgeably over the buttons.

Nausea rose up in her throat. It was positively perverse how young the Poppets were becoming that the great Vampire Lords kept these days. But, in this place, with such a mural leering down upon their heads, it didn't surprise her at all.

"Damn!" The boy sat up on the divan, pushed his long pale hair out of his eyes, and stared up at Eliza. "Final boss got me again. Do you know how to play this game?"

Eliza stood rooted to the floor, afraid to move. Afraid to even speak.

The boy watched her suspiciously. "You're new, aren't you?"

She ignored his question. "What's your name?"

"Henry." The boy had a sweet, lilting voice and big innocent eyes.

"Where are we, Henry?" She glanced around the ridiculously excessive bedchamber. "Is this a...Vampire Court?"

"It's the Palace of New Versailles." Henry watched her with interest and confusion. "We're at Lord Foxley's Court. Aboard his gyro."

Eliza felt her stomach lurch upward. She reached out and closed her hand over the boy's delicate shoulder, feeling an instant kinship with him. "He hasn't hurt you, has he?"

The boy shook his head, his pale hair shushing around his painfully young face. "Nah. He's really nice, actually. Really generous. He gave me this game!" He held it up to show her.

She made a decision then: Somehow, she would escape Lord Foxley's Court just as she had escaped her own Lord's Court so many years ago, but she wouldn't be leaving without Henry. She crouched low so she could better meet his eyes. She clutched both his shoulders in an effort to build a better connection with him.

"Would you like to leave here with me?" She had no idea if she should make any such promise, but she had to try. This couldn't go on. "Would you like to come back to Earth with me, Henry?"

He didn't answer.

"We could help each other," she persisted. "We could...we could be free. If that's what you want?"

"You're really pretty."

"Thank you, Henry."

Henry laughed suddenly. "Very desirable," he responded in a very different tone of voice, "and what I want, Poppet, is to throw you to the floor and have my way with you."

* * *

Voices floated to him out of the dark.

"He's a bloody mess." It sounded like Lady Claire.

"You threw him into a mirror, Claire. What did you expect?"

Claire made a harrumphing noise. "I thought he was more…durable than this. The old Prince is getting soft, I think. That's what you get when you play around with the humans too long."

"You're just lucky you didn't harm him more. Do you want to upset Lord Foxley?"

"No." The voice this time was cut with worry. "Of course not."

Edwin groaned as he came around and opened his eyes. He was lying face down on a bed so plush it felt like he could fall through it. Surrounding him were ornate, gold-plated walls bordering on hideous. Only one person loved such gauche décor, and that person was Lord Foxley. He immediately knew where he was without even needing to ask: New Versailles, on board the *Gypsy Queen*.

Two people sat on the bed with him, a man and a woman. In another life, he might have found that proposition interesting and full of possibilities, but one of the people was Lady Claire, and that killed his mood almost at once. Mr. Stephen was the other, his big latex-gloved hands moving with practiced ease over Edwin's back and buttocks under his shredded clothes, but there was nothing particularly erotic in Mr. Stephen's touch; he was merely looking for glass shards he had missed. When he encountered one, he took a large pair of tweezers and plucked it loose, the sensation queasy.

Edwin marveled at how things always felt so much worse coming out than they did going in—knives, bullets, stakes, and now, glass shards. It never got any easier, and in his time as an Enforcer, he'd experienced all those and more.

"He's awake," Claire said when he flicked his wings with annoyance

"Help me turn him over."

Together, the two of them rolled Edwin over so he was lying on his back on the obscenely soft bed, staring up at the tackiest ceiling mural he'd ever seen, cherubs dancing around a giant naked man with two hard-ons. He would have shuddered, but his body felt like a sack of concrete, and there was absolutely no strength in his limbs.

"Blimey, that's an ugly ceiling."

Mr. Stephen turned to Lady Claire. "I think he's going to live."

"Unfortunately, I think you're right."

Edwin moved his eyes analytically across the lot of them. "Which one of you blokes emptied me out?"

Claire skated backward. "Why?"

"Because after I fill up, I'm getting off this bed and kicking your arse."

Mr. Stephen and Lady Claire exchanged worried glances.

"Should we do it?" Claire asked.

"It was a direct order from Lord Foxley," Mr. Stephen reminded her.

"What was a direct order?" Edwin asked.

"You're at New Versailles," Lady Claire informed him. "You're attending Lord Foxley's Court—"

Edwin cut her off. "I'm aware of all that. Get on."

Lady Claire let out an exasperated sigh. "Lord Foxley extends his hospitality to you. He has also ordered that all Courtesans and

Courtiers in his Court be available to feed you anytime you require it. It's a hospitality he only extends to his most—"

"Bloody hell! I'm aware of Court etiquette, Claire. I attended Foxley's Court for two hundred years!" he snapped. "Are either of you going to feed me or just stand there and leave me mostly dead all day?"

Mr. Stephen shrugged and sat down beside Edwin on the bed, looping his long, muscular arm around Edwin's shoulders. He rolled up his sleeve to produce the blooding bracelet and then slid a panel back on the mechanism.

The scent of Mr. Stephen's blood was as strong as vinegar to Edwin, only sweeter. Edwin didn't have to do a thing; his body did it all for him, forcing him to lunge forward and press his tongue against the open, seeping wound. He didn't even taste it, he was so starved.

Mr. Stephen grunted, and Lady Claire took a concerned step toward him before he motioned to her to stay put. Edwin knew why. The last thing he wanted was someone coming between himself and a starving vampire physically attached to his arm. Edwin, with his uncut feeding teeth, could have ripped Mr. Stephen's hand off at the wrist.

Already, the initial frenzy was beginning to wear off. Edwin was now cradling his arm, pressing his teeth and lips to the wound, but his mouth was working more fastidiously as he exerted more control over his bloodlust. It wouldn't be an issue, and Mr. Stephen knew that.

Mr. Stephen was just beginning to relax when the Poppet suddenly lurched and grunted under a sudden and unexpected wave of pleasure that ripped up his back, practically bowing it. Claire gasped in surprise but didn't try to intervene this time. Mr. Stephen bit his lip to keep from crying out. He'd never fed Edwin before, so, naturally, he didn't know about the side effects.

Edwin rode his hunger hard. It flowed and ebbed, rushing into his gut and then just as quickly receding as he drank and drank. Mr. Stephen's blood was the blood of a Poppet, incredibly nourishing. He didn't know that, having lived in a time when they didn't exist. Poppets were as different from normal human beings as water was from wine.

Mr. Stephen writhed and made small whimpering noises, as far gone as anyone could get. Blimey, Edwin thought as he drank, he'd forgotten about that.

In years past, his lovers had often said that Edwin's bite was like shooting up on some crazy aphrodisiac. He'd known lovers to complain about being horny for days after being with him. It would have been a terrific superpower if it didn't create so many creepy stalkers. It even happened to other vampires, which should have been impossible, seeing how vampires were supposed to have a natural immunity to that kind of stimulation. It was one of the reasons Foxley had valued him so much. He was the street drug. An elite, high-end vice that could corrupt even Foxley's most stalwart enemies and make them putty in his hands.

After a few moments, Edwin forced himself to close his greedy mouth to the wound and, finally able to move, extradited himself from the bed. Mr. Stephen lay clutching the bedclothes, convulsing, with his eyes rolled into the back of his head like a man experiencing a seizure. Edwin hadn't seen someone this high in years.

He leaned down and slapped Mr. Stephen's cheek. His eyes rolled down and the spasms wracking his body slowed. "As high as a bloody kite. Your girlfriends are going to have a hell of a party tonight."

Mr. Stephen tried to sit up, then immediately clenched his eyes shut and lay back down. "Dear God. What did you do to me?"

"You'd think you'd be grateful." Edwin brushed invisible dust from his clothes, which were a bloody mess and ruined beyond repair. Miss Book was going to kill him. "I gave you a hit, mate. Might as well enjoy it while it lasts."

Edwin stopped to sniff the air. He was sure he'd caught Miss Book's scent, and not very far off. He turned to the door, but Claire immediately took a step toward him.

"You can't leave! Lord Foxley's ord—"

"Claire, love," Edwin said, charging for the door, "bugger off."

* * *

Henry pushed Eliza to the floor, wrested her arms down, and bared his shocking, saber-sharp incisors. Eliza was just about to scream when Edwin's voice echoed through the doorway of the bedchamber, halting the boy.

"How bloody sad." Edwin sounded rough and deep, not like himself at all. "Even after all these years, you still enjoy threatening women like some common rapist, Foxley."

"Foxley?" Eliza croaked.

Henry chuckled, his voice rich and old and wicked, not like a child's at all. "Edwin, my boy."

He released Eliza and sat up, addressing the doorway. "The prodigal son returns."

Mr. McGillicuddy stepped fully into the room, face darkened with anger, demonically red wings fully extended to make himself look bigger. He looked like hell. He also looked like he'd recently been through hell. His swallowtail suit hung in bloodstained tatters and his wiry auburn hair was unkempt and half-fallen into his eyes, which blazed with an amber rage. There was blood, candy-apple-red, on his hands and suit, but also on his face and mouth.

"Let her go," Mr. McGillicuddy warned. There was little humanity in his face, eyes, or voice. "She has nothing to do with any of this. Or with us."

Eliza thought, This then is the Prince. She tried to move, but some irresistible force held her down so she felt she was somehow magnetized to the floor. She started to struggle, whimpering deep in her throat.

Foxley observed her struggles. "I like her, Edwin. She's pretty, real, not like the usual sluts you prefer." His voice was deep, confident, and without accent. He ran a finger over the curve of Eliza's cheek, leaving a thin red line. "I can see why you've chosen her to be your Courtesan."

Mr. McGillicuddy practically leaped forward. "She is not my Courtesan, Foxley. She's my employee. Now unhand her!"

Foxley stood up, brushing his hair out of his eyes and showing off heartlessly beautiful teeth. Suddenly, he didn't look so young. Not young at all.

"M...Mister...mmm..." Eliza didn't want to sound like some panicked damsel in distress, but this was the first time she had ever experienced any kind of paralysis like this. "I...I can't move!"

Edwin glared at Foxley—not a friendly look. "That's because he's controlling your blood."

"I don't understand!"

"Foxley is a powerful bloodkinetic. He can control and maneuver the blood inside living beings."

"I've never heard of such a thing."

"There are only three vampires in the world who can do it," Foxley explained with an impish smile. "And two of them are standing in this room right now."

His eyes grew facetiously large as he turned to soak in the sight of Eliza's distressed face. "Pretty girl," he said, this evil, eternal child, "hasn't Edwin told you anything about himself?"

| iv |

Foxley had a retinue of Security Poppets escort his guests to his personal office, if one could call it that. It was so elaborate it looked like something one would expect to find in a Turkish palace, circa 1897—if the Marquis de Sade were visiting.

Eliza looked with vague distress upon the gold-plated furnishings, the fountains, the BDSM-inspired instruments of torture spread throughout the room. Her eyes lingered on a human-sized, gold-gilded birdcage with furry handcuffs hanging from the ceiling.

Once inside the chamber, the Security Poppets drifted back into recesses in the walls, less like people and more like pieces of bulky furniture. They made no move to restrain her or Mr. McGillicuddy, but they both knew it was useless to try to escape. They were on board a gyro, orbiting a thousand feet over the City of New York. All Foxley had to do was inform the shuttle base that taxied people on and off the *Gypsy Queen* that all the exits must be shut down for security reasons. There was no other way off the gyro unless they learned to fly in a hurry, and that was something that maybe Mr. McGillicuddy could do, but she was trapped.

Mr. McGillicuddy shifted closer to her and reached out to examine the scratches on her face. She didn't know how she felt about his presence.

"Are you all right, Miss Book?"

"I...guess?" Eliza stared at the holes in her employer's clothes, at all the bloodstains. The disheveled hair and dried blood on his lips. He was more frightening than even Foxley at the moment, but she decided to stick close to him anyway. He was her only ally in an unfamiliar Court. Maybe he could negotiate her a way back home?

"What does Foxley want with me?" she asked suddenly. She had to suck back the tears that threatened to spill from her eyes. "I'm nobody. I'm nothing..."

"Not you. Me. And I have no bloody clue. But we'll get through this. I promise." He smiled encouragingly and tweaked her nose so she smiled. He then moved to explore the view through the big Plexiglas picture window. She joined him, rubbed the wetness from her eyes with her sleeve, and found it looked down upon a city in miniature.

The Palace of New Versailles rested on a high manmade plateau surrounded by exotic arboretums and Japanese-style gardens. Below them crouched an urban sprawl of pointlessly baroque casinos and resorts built to look like a Disneyland version of the Las Vegas Strip. Everywhere she looked, she spotted rich, fat tourists milling about like busy insects, burning off their disposable incomes. The horizon was outlined against a sky colored a ridiculously upbeat and unchanging blue, complete with fluffy clouds—a holographic display to disguise the gunmetal grey underside of the gyro walls that made this place absolutely safe for vampires to mingle all day and night among the unsuspecting human population.

A door shushed open behind them. Together, they turned and watched Lord Foxley, the master of this manufactured, off-world paradise, step into the room, accompanied by his Enforcer, Lady Claire, who stood on his right, and his two favorite Poppets, Mr. Stephen and Mr. Laurel, who stood on his left.

Mr. Laurel glared hostilely at Eliza, a hand hovering to touch his bandaged, broken nose. She glared back, a polite smile quirking one corner of her mouth.

If Lord Foxley had been a child before, now he was a god. He still wore the dress shirt and faded Levis that were such a popular trend with businessmen these days, but he'd added a waistcoat in a brilliant red tapestry pattern and a jet black jacket so rich and plush it looked like leopard fur—and probably was. He wore twelve rings on his small, white, glove-like hands and black, knee-high equestrian boots with modest heels. Lord Foxley didn't need the extra height—he was painfully thin but possessed of an almost archaic height as if he descended from a clan of people whose children grew tall and lean before they were fully fleshed out.

He'd scraped his shoulder-length white-blond hair back into a sleek queue. It made him look older, crueler, drawing in deep relief his narrow, pearl-white face, razor-sharp cheekbones, determined mouth, and grey eyes so pale they looked ghostly. As he moved, artificial sunlight poured over him from the floor-to-ceiling windows, turning his hair the nearly blue-white of milk and washing out his eyes so all that remained were the tiny black pinpoints of his pupils. It made him look more alien than vampiric. Eliza decided that vampires did not look good expressed in full lighting.

Well, now she knew why the infamous Lord Foxley never left his gyro, why he refused pictures, why he never made public appearances and sent agents to run all his errands for him.

"How...?" she began, and then stopped herself. Did she really want to know the archaic secrets of his existence? She wondered what it felt like to be a child with a man's—and a vampire's—hunger forever.

Lord Foxley smiled cunningly at her as if he knew damned well what she was thinking. Though he resembled a child, his sly, ancient eyes were anything but childish. He said in a booming, unnatural basso, so at odds with his young, barely developed body, "My master was an incredibly cruel man."

Slowly, he turned to face Edwin, smiling. "It's been too long, my boy." He moved to where his desk squatted in one corner of the suite, swept aside all his papers and electronic devices as if they meant nothing to him, and hopped up onto the edge, crossing his long, slender legs. His wings flickered and settled around him, a pale angelic gold that fooled Eliza not at all.

Foxley's retainers moved to stand behind the desk while he patted the empty place beside him. "Come here, my boy. Let's have a look at you after all these years."

Edwin stiffened. Slowly, he shook his head.

Lord Foxley lifted one thin hand and put it absently to his lips, a decidedly old-fashioned gesture, something Eliza expected to see on a swooning debutante in a Jane Austen novel. "Edwin, my boy. I've missed you. Come to me."

Edwin ignored him. "I'd like to change my clothes, if you wouldn't mind."

Foxley smirked and looked him up and down. "But I like seeing you covered in blood. It recalls the good old days."

"'The good old days.'" Edwin's voice was flat and dead. "Funny. I don't recall them being all that good."

Foxley ignored the brush-off. "I take it you've fed? Yes, I think you have. Your color is quite good."

Edwin held Foxley's even gaze even as he blushed at the words, then immediately cut to the chase. "Your reason for bringing us here?"

Behind Foxley, Mr. Stephen's face was professionally blank, but he kept periodically shifting his weight from foot to foot and pulling at the front of his trousers. Eliza wondered what that was about.

Foxley knew, of course. "How was he? He's one of my best. The sweetest I've ever owned. And he tells me you're rather good yourself, Edwin, the best he's ever had. But then, I knew that." He glanced over at Eliza and made a light, dismissive gesture with his hand. "Forgive me, pretty Poppet. I don't mean to talk around you as if you don't exist. Your master turned a trick on Mr. Stephen. It was, as the Americans say, 'good for them both.'"

Eliza felt a dull shock pass through her body. She'd suspected as much, but having her suspicions confirmed hurt like a physical ache inside her, one she did not want to examine. And worse than that...far, far worse...was the fact that he knew what she was. Lord Foxley knew.

And now, so did Mr. McGillicuddy.

When her employer glanced over at her, she immediately looked away, a terrible dread sitting like a cold stone in her stomach. She felt small. A small, wretched, ashamed thing. A Poppet. She wasn't even human. What must he think?

She expected him to say something. Instead, he turned his attention back on Foxley. "You have an awful lot of gall dragging us up here, Foxley. Do you have any idea what could happen if you're found to have kidnapped another vampire's Poppet?" Again, he glanced aside at Eliza but then quickly switched his attention back to Foxley. "You could start a war with another Court."

Foxley shrugged as if he were completely unperturbed by the fact that he'd just openly committed a crime that could start a war that lasted centuries—or however long the vampires involved lived. "Edwin, I want you to come here. Now."

"Said the spider to the fly. I like standing here."

"Edwin..."

"Piss off, you bloody annoying little midget!"

"Edwin, Edwin...you are much too stubborn a boy for your own good." Foxley's voice had changed again, but not like before. Foxley rolled his words, and there was a faint Germanic inflection in his voice.

Raising his hand, Foxley made a sudden, violent pushing gesture.

Mr. McGillicuddy grunted as the tremendous pressure of Foxley's bloodkinetic power lifted him off his feet and forced him back, pinioning him to the far wall, his arms crucified to either side. It all happened in seconds, too quickly for Eliza to even react. Edwin just hung several inches off the floor like a puppet on invisible wires.

Eliza thought about rushing forward to help him, but she had no idea what she could do under the circumstances. "Mr. McGillicuddy!" She gaped at the display. "How...?"

Foxley laughed boyishly, his hand frozen in mid-gesture. "This is bloodkinetics, my pretty Poppet. He cannot move until I will it." He quirked a wicked, now familiar smile. "I've spent many nights holding your Edwin against walls. He didn't often complain about it back then."

Eliza felt a surge of rage. It came from a dark hole deep within herself, a place she rarely visited these days. But she was acutely aware of its existence. It had opened up the night her master forced himself on her. And, even now, it was a gaping wound on her soul.

Vampires. She was appalled and disgusted by them. Their deathless, pointless cruelty...

"Bastard..." she breathed. She reached down, picked up Foxley's laptop where it lay broken on the floor, and heaved it at the vampire's head.

After that, things pretty much went to hell.

* * *

"I gave you two hundred years of service, Foxley. What more do you want from me?" Edwin asked after the Security Poppets had properly restrained both him and Miss Book. He leaned against the back of the Eton bench he was currently chained to, his arms securely cuffed together behind his back with unbreakable iron manacles lined in soft fur. He was trying not to look in the direction of Miss Book. He chose instead to watch Mr. Stephen carry in a heavy portfolio.

Foxley's valet set it down on a small, Queen Anne-style writing desk situated before him, making Edwin wonder if they were about to descend into one of Foxley's disturbing little schoolhouse fantasies. He'd always hated those.

"One hundred and ninety-eight years, seven months, and fourteen days," Foxley corrected him. "You did not fulfill your contract with me."

Edwin gaped at his creator's sheer pettiness. "You have got to be farking kidding me."

Miss Book watched everything from her place across the room, locked in the human-sized birdcage—put there by the Security Poppets after she pulled that stunt. She looked frightened half to death, and he desperately wished he could give her reassurances. In fact, he was trying to with his eyes without making it too obvious to everyone in the room, but he knew anything he said was merely a platitude. She was fully aware of the danger she was in. What danger they were both in.

He was a fugitive of Foxley's Court, and her situation was nearly the same. The only difference was she belonged to some other Vampire Lord. The thought made him irrationally angry. He wished she had told him she was a runaway Poppet at some point in their relationship. He might have been better able to protect her from the Courts.

Foxley smiled. "The Poppet is fine. Unharmed." He marched across the room with a flogger tucked under his arm. "And it's not as if the creatures feel pain anyway."

"Bugger off, Foxley," he spat, showing his teeth.

Foxley laughed at that. "You care about the Poppet? Does the little pet warm your bed? Or do you use her as your wineskin when you grow tired of that wretched blood substitute you live on?"

"I told you. We don't have that kind of relationship."

But he saw Miss Book look away as if mortified.

"Ah," said Foxley, quickly catching on. "Another heart to join the ranks of the Marquise de Peze, Maria Antoinette, Amelia Earhart, Belle Starr, Charlotte Bronte, and that Russian prince you fancied so...what was his name?"

Foxley turned to face Miss Book. "Edwin's conquests are many and varied, in case you didn't know." He smiled again as he circled her cage. Edwin knew he enjoyed the shadow of pain lurking just behind the fear in her eyes. It was the air he breathed.

Edwin clenched his eyes shut. Bugger. He never wanted Miss Book to know about his past. He'd been a different person back then.

Returning to Edwin, Foxley extended his arm, the flogger resting on Edwin's shoulder. He grinned, enjoying all the damage he was wrecking. "We will return to this soon. For now, I want you to take a look at these." With the flogger, he flipped the portfolio open.

Edwin looked down as Foxley turned the pages. Anything was better than looking into Miss Book's pain-wracked eyes.

The first thing he saw in the portfolio was a death certificate, followed by an official police report written in Upyrese, the flowing, squiggly script of the high Vampire Courts. After that came witness reports, forensic reports, and pictures of different angles of one of the worst mutilations he had ever seen—and he'd seen his fair share, that was for sure.

What he saw looked like a body—if that body had been processed through a meat grinder. The photos were grainy black and white photostats, but, somehow, that made it even worse. Edwin's overactive imagination automatically kicked in, filling in all the gruesome little details, the red, meaty smell of death on the air, the chunks of warm, still-steaming meat, the tremendous gore splashed across the white furnishings of the posh penthouse suite where this terrible act had taken place.

Foxley pushed the photographs around and Edwin noted that other bodies littered the premises in similar states of...deconstruction. He didn't know how else to think of it.

"That is—was—Lord Wyndham," Foxley explained.

Edwin felt a tick in his throat. Lord Wyndham was—had been—a tall, bony English vampire with an appetite for expensive brandy, racy cars, and ten-year-old girls. Not a nice bloke by any stretch of the imagination, but he dated back to a time when the Brits were still calling themselves Britons and the Roman Empire was still hanging in there. He certainly was no pup. He was surprised to see someone had ended the bastard so completely.

Foxley turned more pages, and Edwin saw the other pictures and autopsy reports. Lady Espirito, a Spanish noblewoman over seven hundred years old. The location of the slaughter was her keep, Castillo de Penafiel, the "unconquerable" castle that had housed the Lady and her entourage of servants for centuries. Another old one. Not as old as Wyndham, perhaps, and a mite more pleasant to know, but still powerful. Lady Espirito was one of the first vampires to observe that Edwin's bite caused delirium in both humans and vampires. She used to call him El Mal de Amor, the "Lovesickness."

The remains were less horrible this time, but only because the castle was more remote, surrounded by mountainous regions and wilderness, and scavengers had been at the Lady's and her servants' remnants before they were discovered by some backpacking American tourists, according to the report. Lady Espirito and every member of her Court had been slaughtered, no witnesses. And no suspects.

"There are others," Foxley informed him. "All old ones. All slaughtered along with their Courts."

Edwin swallowed hard. "How many?"

"Five, so far."

The news surprised him. It wasn't inconceivable that such an old one might be slain, particularly by a skilled assassin or vampire hunter. But he had to admit it was bloody unlikely to have happened five times. What's more, according to the forensic reports, the Poppets themselves had done the slaying in each of the cases. They had killed their own masters in a fit of rage, then turned on each other. Pleasure Poppets, Security Poppets—everyone murdered in what seemed to be a giant murder-suicide pact.

Edwin frowned, finally intrigued. "Are they all like this?"

"Yes. As my Enforcer and the former head of my security, what is your take?"

Edwin ogled the bodies carved up like so much bloody steak.

"Don't think. Just react," Foxley prompted.

"It's the Poppets who did this in every instance?"

"Yes."

"Rage. Bloodlust. Murder. And no one knows why they did it?"

"No one."

Edwin leaned forward and used his chin to drag a forensic report closer. "Were the remains tested for drugs or other substances?"

"Nothing of importance came back from the lab—some light recreational drugs, but nothing known to induce this kind of violence."

"Did the Poppets in all of these cases know each other?"

"No. Different ages, different cultures, separated by oceans or thousands of miles. Most did not even speak the same language. None of the Courts knew each other. It is a mystery."

"What do the investigators think?"

"A berserker rage. A flaw in the genetics."

"Do you believe that?"

Foxley looked grim. "No."

Edwin slowly shook his head. "This is organized, not some random genetic quirk. And even if it was, there's no bloody way it would happen again and again like this." He'd done enough research for his books to know there were organized and disorganized serial killers. Hell, he knew that from experience while working for Foxley. Despite the obvious chaotic feel of the crimes, this looked tight, organized, high IQ. Whoever had done this knew exactly when, how, and where to hit a great many isolated individuals.

"This looks like urban combat or a terrorist organization of some kind," he observed.

"You grasp the situation. What else do those pictures tell you?"

Edwin stared long and hard at the photostats in all of their gory black-and-white splendor. "It's a message of some kind. A warning."

"That was my initial analysis, as well."

"What do the High Courts say?"

"The High Courts convened a few weeks ago to discuss the matter, and we agree the crimes are likely being committed by some kind of extremist group, perhaps one in opposition to the Vampire Bill, except..."

"This can't be the work of humans," Edwin finished for him. "Not alone. Humans couldn't control all of these Poppets like this." He thought about that for a second. "But a vampire in possession of bloodkinetics could do it." He eyed Foxley suspiciously.

"I had considered that, yes."

"That makes you a suspect." Edwin offered Foxley a small, wry smile. "You and Lord Rathbone."

Rathbone was the only other known bloodkinetic in the world capable of controlling so many people at once. He was old, dating back to Pharaonic Canaan in North Africa. The problem with his theory was that Rathbone had disappeared over ten years ago, presumed dead.

Foxley leaned against the desk and indicated the torrent of files. "An investigation is still ongoing into Rathbone's past. We all agree the crimes are following some sort of pattern, and that they will continue to do so until they are stopped."

"Terrific. So you lot spent the better part of several weeks sitting around agreeing that what's happening really is happening." Edwin rolled his eyes—their vampire taxpaying dollars at work. "Is anyone investigating Rathbone's present whereabouts?"

Foxley grimaced. "He cannot be found."

Edwin would have thrown his hands up had they not been chained behind his back. The Courts were predictably useless, as usual. It was the same with vampire sex offenders. If a vampire was found abusing the Poppets under his care, the High Courts just moved the vampire around until everyone forgot about it.

"Have any of you thought to contact MI6...the FBI...Interpol? Anything?"

Foxley looked insulted. "Human police? All the victims were vampires or Poppets owned by vampires. Why would the humans take any interest in our problem?"

Foxley was unfortunately right.

"What are the Courts doing now?"

Lord Foxley made a dismissive gesture. "They do not know. They have no leads." He placed a hand across his middle. It was a genteel gesture, one seldom seen anymore because gentlemen used to do that when they felt the need to go for a blade on their belt. Foxley was afraid. Edwin had never seen his master so afraid before.

"I suggested bringing in human detectives or hiring private investigators, but the other Courts ruled against it. I was overruled."

Edwin leaned back uncomfortably in his seat and stared long and hard at Foxley. The iron chains crisscrossing his chest were itching something awful as they smoldered. "I'm not a detective, you know, I just write about them. And, by the way, by now the leads are so bloody cold I'm not sure Sherlock Holmes shagging Miss Marple could investigate this." He indicated the top file. "It's called a cold case, Foxley. I'm way out of my league here."

Foxley gave him a serene smile. "You are the Prince, and the Prince is never 'out of his league.'"

Edwin laughed. "Is that why I'm here? You want me to hold your hand, protect you from the big bad vampire slayers killing off all of your mates?"

Foxley looked sullen. "Have you forgotten how to be the Prince?"

"No," Edwin answered automatically, smiling humorlessly. "I just don't like you, Foxley, and I don't want to work for you. I gave you two hundred years—give or take a couple of them."

Foxley laughed, the sound high and clear and polished. "Edwin. My boy. You are my Heir, my magnum opus. I have poured more of my power into you than in any other." He placed the flogger under Edwin's chin and tilted his head up. "A thousand years away from my Court could not erase that."

"Bugger off, old boy."

Never losing his smile, Foxley moved the flogger down to the key around Edwin's neck, pulling it deftly from his shirt with the flogger. "I enjoy your rebellious nature, it's true," he said, extraditing it from around Edwin's neck. "But you remember how things went the last time you disobeyed a command of mine."

"You sent a lunatic assassin after me." Edwin held his master's eyes. "And the answer is still no."

Foxley's pale, hooded eyes slowly shifted to Miss Book in her cage.

"You leave her out of this. She has nothing to do with us!" Edwin insisted, baring his teeth.

"Don't be naive, Edwin. Everything—and everyone in your life—has to do with us."

Lord Foxley bit back a smile and stepped back, then strolled to the cage, his eyes sparkling like a hungry cat eyeing a plump little canary just out of reach.

Miss Book, her face piqued with terror, took a step back, then another, backing up as far as the cage would allow her.

Foxley paced back and forth in front of her, narrowing his eyes as he picked up on all sorts of signals. He had that ability, too. Not vampire magic; merely experience. "Oh, poor pretty Poppet. You like him, don't you? You are in love with the Prince!"

"No..." Miss Book insisted, but her voice quavered with shame. Wearing a miserable expression, her back hit the back of the cage with a clank.

Foxley raised the flogger, showing her the gold scarab key. The key, literally, to Edwin McGillicuddy's heart, one could say.

It winked in the forced lighting. "You must be truly special to him that he should allow you to wind him up—so to speak. But do you truly know him, Poppet?"

Miss Book remained silent, though a small noise escaped her throat.

Foxley inclined his head, eyes glittering. "When Edwin worked for me, he drew the blood of my enemies—he bathed in it. The Prince took enormous pride in his work." He let that sink in before continuing. "My enemies cringed and crawled on their bellies before him, but he never once allowed mercy to taint his work. When it came to pain, Edwin was a true artist. One of his favorite methods was a slow, careful degloving of his victim's face to extract information. And if the results were unsatisfactory...well, there was always the victim's family, their friends...their loved ones. Edwin was quite ingenious in how he meted out pain. He knew exactly how to get under a victim's skin, so to speak."

Edwin cringed in his seat and closed his eyes. He couldn't bear to see Miss Book's face. If Foxley wanted his loyalty, if he wanted another two hundred years, he could have it, just so long as he let Miss Book go. Just so long as he didn't have to see her expression.

His master really was a bastard. It would be easy to just turn Miss Book into the authorities and let fate take its natural course. Her master, whoever he was, would then come to take her away, and Edwin would probably never see her again. But Foxley didn't do easy even when he was punishing members of his Court. And it was obvious Edwin's relationship with Miss Book disturbed Foxley very much or he wouldn't be putting so much effort into spoiling Edwin in Miss Book's eyes.

After a few awkward seconds of silence, Miss Book spoke up. She sounded surprisingly angry. "I don't believe you! Edwin has always been kind to me. He wouldn't do such horrible things!"

"Do you believe that, pretty Poppet?" Foxley asked, his voice dripping with niceties. "Do you really believe he is some beautiful, romantic figure, no blood on his hands? Poppet, he is a vampire, a monster, one of the most dangerous I have ever made." He hooked one arm inside the cage like a cat playing with a bird.

Miss Book jumped in response though there was nowhere left in the cage to go.

"Edwin has no respect for anything except for the taste of blood. He is not capable of love, whatever you may think."

Miss Book shuddered and closed her eyes. Slowly, she sank to the floor, her back to the bars of the cage. Her hands drifted to her face as if she wanted to cover it, but she forced them down and wrapped them around her upturned knees instead.

Foxley giggled, and Edwin decided in that moment that he would find a way to get his master back for this. He would destroy his maker—somehow and in some way.

"Now, then, Lord Edwin. You are well aware of Court etiquette, and you have always been a strong supporter of it." Foxley smirked, turning to him. "You possess another Lord's property. You really ought to give it back—"

"I'll do it," Edwin said suddenly, hurriedly. "Stay here. Protect you. Whatever you need to make up for the two years I owe you. Or two hundred, if that's what you want. But only if Miss Book remains safe and unchanged." He knew he had to specify. Foxley had a talent for manipulating contracts the same way he manipulated people. "And, of course, only if she is returned to Earth unharmed."

Foxley slipped up into a nearby window well as he considered the offer, his eyes burning black in his narrow, vulpine face. After a few moments, he again brought his fingers to his lips in that archaic gesture. Edwin could tell he was pleased. "Two thousand years of service. The penalty for breaking your contract with me."

Edwin shuddered. He thought at first he hadn't heard right. But then he realized how ridiculous that was. For a creature as old as Foxley, two thousand years was a mere drop in an eternal bucket.

He sucked in a quick breath. "Done. But...I have conditions."

"Speak them."

"I want a moment alone with Miss Book. I want to say my goodbyes."

Foxley thought about it. Then he indicated with a dismissive hand wave that the Security Poppets should leave the room. Once they were gone, he slid to the floor and approached Edwin.

As Foxley leaned into him, Edwin edged back as best he could in his current position.

Reaching behind Edwin, Foxley easily broke the chains binding his wrists, then the ones across his chest. He stepped back, the chains smoldering in his hands. He dropped them to the floor, but despite the red marks they left on his hand, Foxley hardly seemed to notice the pain.

Edwin stood up, rubbing at his sore wrists. He knew better than to try to attack Foxley. His maker, despite his small stature, could break Edwin in half like kindling with barely any effort. Besides, with Foxley, it was always honey, not vinegar, that got you what you wanted. He knew that all too well from hard-won experience.

"Thank you," Edwin said and held out his hand for the gold key. He forced himself to be civil. He knew Foxley would respond to that. "Now, I want to speak to Miss Book. Alone."

Foxley returned the key but made no move to leave the room.

Ignoring Foxley for the moment, Edwin went up to the cage.

Miss Book sat hunched on the floor, her head tipped forward, her face hidden by the spiraling reams of her wildly and beautifully abundant hair. She barely moved when he spoke.

"Miss Book...Eliza..." Edwin's voice was little more than a whisper.

After a minute or so, Eliza stirred and lifted her head. But after seeing him, she scrunched herself against the bars as if she didn't recognize him. Didn't trust him. He couldn't say he blamed her. The things that Foxley said...the way he had ripped open all of her private thoughts and laid her heart open and bare for anyone to pick apart...he couldn't imagine what she felt, though he recognized the mortification in her red cheeks and fever-bright eyes. That and the fear.

Edwin closed his eyes and sucked the rage and horror back down inside of himself, wallowing in the tragedy of it all. They might have had a chance to have a real relationship one day, but Foxley had destroyed that for his own petty reasons.

He put his hand upon a bar of the cage. "Listen, love, I know you don't trust me, but I'm asking you to try. Foxley won't harm you so long as I do what he asks." He nodded solemnly. "I will make absolutely certain you are returned unharmed to New York. I promise on my soul as a vampire and as a man, you will be free."

Slowly, too slowly, Miss Book got to her feet and approached the bars, her eyes wet but determined.

| V |

Eliza stood there, staring at the man she thought she knew with quiet horror, trying not to let it show on her face—though, of course, it did. The man before her looked like her employer, Mr. McGillicuddy. He still looked like the man she had been tasked to take care of for the past six months of her life. But she was seeing him in a new light.

He was an Enforcer. A master vampire's Enforcer. Christ. He had spent centuries hurting others—vampires, humans, anyone—at the whim of his master and to forward his master's agenda.

Mobster. Monster.

The cage, Foxley's threats...these things were horrible, yes, but they were nothing compared to what she felt in this moment. The pain of having her world ripped apart like this. She felt like a great knife was probing her heart, cutting it out by the root.

Ultimately, though, it was her own damned fault, wasn't it?

How could she have liked him? How could she have liked a vampire after what her master had done to her? She was such a fool. Such a sad and pathetic fool.

Sad little Poppet, she thought.

She felt the awful onslaught of tears. But she wouldn't cry, she promised herself, not in front of him.

"He's lying," she said after swallowing hard. "Foxley's lying. He will never let me go."

She knew it was true. Foxley was never going to keep his word, and she would eventually become another slave of his Court. One of his many Poppet playthings. And if Mr. McGillicuddy didn't understand that, then he was as much a fool as she was and didn't know his master at all.

Mr. McGillicuddy looked surprised at her insight. He seemed to be at a loss for words.

"What was it like?" she demanded suddenly, growing angrier by the moment. She glared at him through the veil of her tears. "When you hurt those families, did you make the women cry? Did you hurt the children? Did they beg while you hurt them? Or did you hypnotize them so they just sat there and let you do it to them?"

He hesitated. "It wasn't like that."

"What was it like?" she challenged him. "Tell me. I want to know."

"Don't, love...please," he begged.

"Don't call me that. I'm not your love."

She watched him. His face was twisted into a mask of utter despair—disgust. He looked horrified at himself. Good.

The silence between them stretched on. During that time, Mr. McGillicuddy played with the key to his clockwork heart. He held it against his chest, rubbing at the gold. Finally, he said, "I have my regrets and my nightmares."

"Good."

"I'm not that person now."

"I don't believe you."

He ignored that. "I will return for you. And, when I do, I will take you back to New York. I promise on my soul as a vampire and as a man, you will be free."

He swallowed so hard that she heard the click in his throat. He glanced over at Foxley, who was enjoying their little drama from his place in the window well. He was lying on his stomach, his chin on his fist as if he were watching a particularly engrossing drama on television.

Mr. McGillicuddy looked back at her. "You have my word you will be safe."

She couldn't help herself. She leaned forward and spat on him, though he never flinched at the assault. From the corner of her eye, she saw Foxley smile at that, which only made her angrier.

"You're a vampire," she finally said, surprised by how steady her voice was. "Your word means nothing."

Mr. McGillicuddy opened his mouth, closed it. He dropped his attention to the floor.

Eliza suddenly clenched the bars and rattled them. She wanted to die. To cease to exist for all time. All of her life had been a nightmare. Why should this be any different? He had made a fool of her.

Please, whatever higher power exists, let me die...

But, of course, she did not. She was denied even that.

Finally, Mr. McGillicuddy looked up. "Miss Book...Eliza..."

"Don't." She held up a hand for silence. "Just crawl back to Foxley where you belong, vampire."

He watched her a long, hard moment, then wiped the spit off his cheek. Slowly, he reached between the bars of the cage and set the gold key down on the floor a few feet from her. "I don't know what to say. I don't know how to fix this." He stared hard at the key. "But now you have this. You have this power over me. I have to return to you. I have to make sure you are safe. I hope it's enough."

She thought about that, about his gesture. She pressed her lips together bitterly. "Go to hell, Mr. McGillicuddy. Just go to fucking hell."

There was nothing left to say, so Edwin turned and left the room.

***

A few hours later, Lord Foxley summoned Edwin to his private sleeping quarters. It was a chamber as gauche as the little Lord of New Versailles himself. Murals of gods and monsters decorated the walls and ceiling, the carpeting was as plush as the white fur of an arctic fox, and every piece of furniture in the room was plated in 24-carat gold, from the tiny sitting tables and Queen Anne desks to the king-sized, four-poster bed draped in blood-red valances and veils.

The bed was the only thing of consequence in the room; everything else had been scaled down a size or two, closer to child-size. Foxley's conceit knew no bounds, nor his insecurities. If he could not present himself to the world in adult-size, he would reduce the size of his private world.

There were no lights on when Edwin entered the room, not that he needed them. Instead, votive candles flickered here and there, their light slanting across golden statues of angels with devil wings stretching toward the heavens. The candles threw the gold-plated room into sharp relief and made it look more like the flickering burial chamber of an ancient Pharaoh than an actual bedroom.

At the center of the room was a tiny table only a little larger than a dinner platter overlaid in several brocade tablecloths. The table had been set for a formal vampire supper—embroidered cloth napkins, narrow-stemmed glasses spiraling upward like unicorn horns, and, between the two glasses, a dark, thin, long-necked bottle that Edwin assumed contained the real thing since Lord Foxley would rather die a thousand deaths than drink synthetic blood.

Foxley stepped out of the shadows to greet him, and he was dressed in a parochial schoolboy uniform like a vampiric version of Angus Young. He loved to dress in costume. Stunning an unwilling audience gave him a perverse pleasure. Foxley's hair fell like a white curtain around his coy, rain-pale eyes.

He indicated a seat with a flourish, his rings crackling in the firelight. Speaking in Upyrese, he said, "I'm glad you've decided to join me tonight, Edwin." As if Edwin even had a choice in the matter. "Please sit."

Edwin knew without looking that Poppets were installed in various parts of the bedchamber. He could smell them, see their faintly glinting eyes. They stood in deep shadows or perched on cushions and chairs. One thin young Poppet barely of age sat on the edge of the king-sized bed, twined in veils, so beautiful she looked like a fabricated doll. Like the palace and its furnishings and the surrounding gardens, Foxley's Poppets were only of the first water, the most beautiful manufactured human beings in the world. Edwin noted their greedy cat eyes flickering over him as he made his way to the table.

"Spotty outfit," he said in English, looking Foxley over.

Foxley waved a hand. "You used to adore me like this, my boy."

"And then I grew up."

Foxley hesitated. "I want to celebrate your return. And I thought you might be hungry. You are hungry?"

Edwin considered lying, but it was true.

"You always were so hungry, both as a human and as a vampire." Foxley's smile grew. "I remember." He drew a chair out like a maitre d'. "Sit, Edwin. Allow me to serve you tonight."

Edwin sat. The table was much too small. When Foxley seated himself, he felt Foxley's legs glide gently against his own, which was probably the idea. He put his napkin properly in his lap.

"I'm pleased you remember your manners."

"I don't want to talk about the past," Edwin snapped.

Foxley hesitated, searching for some neutral ground. "The suit looks lovely on you," he said as Mr. Stephen slipped out of the dark and reached for the bottle on the table between them to pour them their dinner. "I'm pleased you decided to take advantage of the wardrobe I have provided."

"It's outdated," Edwin complained. "How long have you kept it, expecting I would return?"

Foxley pouted. His romantic dinner was not going according to plan. "We were good together, you and I. We had fun. They were not all bad times, Edwin. Do you remember Venice, 1878, the carnival, and those delicious twins?"

Edwin gave his master a hooded look.

Mr. Stephen finished filling the two long-stemmed glasses and then glided back into the shadows. The rich, unique bouquet of a fine Sicilian vintage from a family a hundred years dead filled the room. Edwin picked up the glass and swirled it. "Wine?"

"I cannot abide blood substitute."

"It's useful enough." Edwin sipped the wine. "What's the point of the wine?"

Foxley smiled. "The wine is merely an appetizer. This is supper." With a flick of his hand, the Poppets emerged from their pockets of shadows. Some stalked toward Edwin with paralyzing grace, swinging their hips like models on a catwalk. Some crawled along the furry white carpet on hands and knees, their huge, feline eyes beseeching him. The Poppets were perfect and beautiful, and they converged on him like ravenous animals. They surpassed male, female, human. A perfumed wall of soft, lush bodies pressed against him, touching him, begging him to touch them in return.

Once, these little pretties would have driven him crazy. Now, he just felt sad, remote. Disconnected. It meant nothing. It was all empty desire. Useless hunger. Miss Book hated and distrusted him. Nothing else mattered anymore.

"Oh, my pretties. Such a treat for you." Foxley petted the dark-skinned female where she heeled at Edwin's feet. "Tonight you taste El Mal de Amor, the Prince. What lucky little pretties you are!"

And still, Edwin sat there like a stone in his chair, drinking his wine and hardly tasting it.

A Poppet had gotten his dress shirt open and was licking across his exposed skin. Edwin drank and drank.

Foxley smiled with approval. "You're so thin, my boy. You haven't been eating properly. Tonight you'll make up for that."

The harem of Poppets were mewling like cats, imploring him.

When the Poppet licking him hit a certain spot on his chest, Edwin choked, the wine spilling over his lips. Another Poppet leaned down and kissed away all the wine. Soon, they swarmed him as if they were starving animals and he was the main course, instead of the other way around.

He should have been pushing them away. He knew that. But he needed Foxley distracted. He needed to give Miss Book time.

"We're not done," he growled at Foxley through the great veils of long, perfumed Poppet hair that obscured his vision. "We're far from finished, Foxley."

Foxley smiled and got up to leave. "Edwin, I dare say you're about to finish any minute now."

A Poppet lowered her head and expertly tongued up all the wine dribbling down his chest. Edwin arched his back and cried out as over a dozen expert Poppet mouths descended upon him all at once.

* * *

Eliza sat on the floor of the cage, getting sadder and angrier even as the shadows grew longer in the room. Artificial night coming down over New Versailles.

She had stopped crying a few hours ago. Now she was just angry as hell. "Goddamn it!" she yelled at the ceiling, clutching the key she'd thought was to Mr. McGillicuddy's clockwork heart. The one he had offered her in plain sight of everyone in the room.

It wasn't.

Somehow, amid all the chaos and drama, Mr. McGillicuddy had liberated the key to the gilded cage from Foxley's pocket, had switched it out for the one around his neck, and passed it to her in clear sight of Foxley...and he'd never even noticed. It was the ultimate sleight of hand.

He had delivered her a means of escape.

She held up the key to the cage, watching false night winking off it. After their row and all she had learned about him, she'd wanted to hate her employer forever and ever. It had felt so good to do so, but Mr. McGillicuddy was making that increasingly difficult to do!

***

Edwin woke sometime after midnight with a massive headache, a soft, heavy Poppet lying slantwise across his legs, and blood all over his mouth and chin. Not one of his shining moments, he decided as he squirmed out from under the Poppets.

He stood up—too fast, because he had to hold his head as the room seemed to expand and contract around him. Blimey, he was hung over.

Bodies lay tangled with bodies, some on the bed and some on the floor. Others were sort of half on and half off. Poppets lay everywhere like victims of mass slaughter, except that they breathed and every single one sported incredibly satisfied smiles. At least it was good for them, he thought miserably.

"Lord McGillicuddy, sir?" came a soft, imploring voice.

Edwin squinted through his headache at the Poppet on the floor at his feet, a beautiful palomino male.

"Sir, are you well?" the Poppet asked with concern, staring up like a lovesick puppy.

"No, I'm not bloody well. Where the hell's the loo in this joint?"

The Poppet directed him to a washroom bigger than his entire apartment at home. Edwin knelt before the toilet and threw up blood all over the seat. "Blimey," he groaned. Throwing up too much food while alive had been bad enough; throwing up blood was just as horrible as it sounded. He crossed himself. "Hail Mary, full of grace, the Lord is with thee; blessed art thou among women..."

The Poppet waited patiently for him to finish his liturgies.

Eventually, Edwin ran the taps and splashed the coldest water he could get onto his face. He checked his pocket watch, noting that he had less than an hour before his pacemaker stopped for the night.

He hated winding himself up, but he had no choice under the circumstances. The last thing he needed was to run down while asleep in one of Lord Foxley's bedchambers. God knows what would become of his body.

Taking the key from his pocket, he pressed it into his chest just above the pacemaker, the spike biting through his skin and locking into the keyway. He jerked at the sensation. Half a century and he still wasn't used to this. Normally, Miss Book did this for him in the early morning hours before he was even conscious.

He missed Miss Book. Missed her so much. Too much.

He breathed in quick, shallow spurts. Once he had the nauseating pain under control, he wound himself up six times. This time, the escapement mechanism ground with resistance as he forced it to turn over for another day without a proper rest period. He knew he couldn't do this indefinitely. If he wound himself up more than three days in a row, he'd become so overwound that the pacemaker would lock up and forcibly shut down his heart—maybe forever.

A sobering thought. That meant he had only two days to live. And he couldn't trust Foxley with the key. Anyway, what was the point? That would give Foxley yet more power over him. Better he die than go back to this life. Foxley's world was nothing but a giant gilded birdcage like the one he'd locked Miss Book in.

As for him and Miss Eliza Book, he had no idea how to fix something so broken.

Two days. How odd, he thought as he slid the chain of the key around his neck and fingered it. Despite a life filled with death, he'd never actually thought about dying himself, not in practical terms. Death had been but an abstract concept until now.

He turned to face the palomino Poppet, a plan forming in his head, something that could aid Miss Book in getting home faster, even if he never did. He reached out and traced the male's lips with his thumb. The contact was enough. The Poppet practically jumped his bones, molding himself to Edwin's body.

"What's your name, mate?" He tried to make his voice sleek and seductive but succeeded at neither. He always came off sounding like some low-class cocker idiot.

"Jeremy, sir."

"Jeremy," Edwin mused. He brushed blond hair out of the Poppet's huge, eager eyes. "Jeremy, old boy, I need you to do me a favor."

"Whatever you require, sir," he said dreamily. "Whatever you want."

"There's a good lad."

* * *

Eliza found herself lost amid the maze of sterile white corridors that made up the Palace of New Versailles. One corridor looked the same as another. All of them had vaguely glowing white honeycomb walls broken up only by equally white steel doors. She felt like she was lost in a vast alien spaceship—a deliberate design "flaw" on Foxley's part, she figured. Even if one was able to escape his cage and the room it was in, it would be virtually impossible to find an exit from this liminal space, and the maddening sameness of the layout would get you all turned around, allowing security to scoop you up with no trouble at all. She couldn't even tell which direction she was going in any longer.

Just ahead, she heard a quick step as someone headed toward her around a blind corner. Working to keep herself from panicking, she quickly tried several doors, all of which had some kind of electronic scanning protocol that required a keycard or maybe a handprint or retinal scan. She got red lights on the first two she tried, but the third one turned green and opened on what seemed to be an empty, generic office of some kind, maybe the kind a traveling accountant would use.

Breathing a sigh of relief, she slid inside, and the honeycombed-patterned door closed silently behind her. The room was dim and quiet, and even the windows were shuttered. Quickly arming herself with a paperweight from off the tidy and virtually empty desk, she moved to stand beside the door, sliding it open just a crack so she could see who was marching down the corridor.

The man was dressed as a Security Poppet but looked rather lost as he moved restlessly back and forth. "Miss Book!" he whispered. And then louder: "Miss Book!"

She wouldn't allow him to put her back into that cage! But she also didn't want him alerting others.

Taking a deep breath for courage, she pushed the door fully open and stepped out into the corridor, ready to smash in his head with the paperweight, but the Poppet spun around and smiled down at her.

"Miss Book!" He was young, tan, and well made, but there was a simple quality to his face that didn't belong on a Security Poppet.

She just barely stopped herself from bashing in his face. "Y-yes?"

The Poppet looked at the paperweight hovering inches from his head but never lost his happy smile. He put a finger to his lips. "I'm Jeremy."

His odd response gave her heart a small, hopeful lurch. Maybe he wasn't here to drag her back to that awful cage?

"Lord McGillicuddy sent me," Jeremy further explained. "He said you would want to leave now, and that you might want this." He reached inside his tough plastic security armor and pulled out a spitter handgun, popular with security firms because it used forced air instead of live ammunition and could knock suspects out cold without killing them.

She looked at him, then at the gun he was giving her. It was larger than the type of gun she was used to, and because it didn't fire real bullets, there was an almost toy-like quality about it, but she would make do. She took it.

"Lord McGillicuddy said I'm to accompany you wherever you want to go and not to leave you alone," Jeremy insisted.

"Did he now?"

"Those were his instructions."

"So, now he's bullying the Security Poppets around."

"No, no." The boy's expression remained pleasant as he touched his chest. "Pleasure Poppet. But Lord McGillicuddy said I should make myself look like Security." He touched the uniform he wore up. "And that I should help you escape New Versailles."

Eliza hated this. How was she to continue to hate Mr. McGillicuddy when he insisted on aiding in her escape this way?

"Lord McGillicuddy said."

She pursed her lips when she saw the bite mark under his uniform collar. "Lord McGillicuddy has turned a trick on you."

The Poppet shook his head. "No trick. Lord McGillicuddy is nice."

Oh dear god, the Pleasure Poppet was in love with him!

Eliza nodded all the same. She didn't care how she got out just as long as she did. "Jeremy, lead the way."

* * *

Clutching the gun tight to her hip, Eliza let Jeremy guide her through the labyrinth of hallways. Although he got turned around a couple of times, Jeremy was still more familiar with the palace than she would ever be.

Eventually, they found a sign that pointed to the shuttle pad on the roof of the palace. Jeremy was simple, like most Pleasure Poppets, but when she gave him a moment to think, he seemed to know his way around the complex.

They passed several Security Poppets, but no vampires, thank god. When they encountered someone, Eliza had Jeremy guide her by the upper arm. She was a prisoner being moved, nothing to see here, folks. Security Poppets glanced their way—but with little interest. Foxley gave them their marching orders, but it was obvious they knew very little about the importance of the duties they performed. The only thing they cared about was following orders so they didn't get in trouble.

It still made her uneasy. "How far is it?" she asked when they had navigated what felt like miles of twisting hallways.

"We're here." Jeremy steered her down yet another corridor and turned sharply left where a blue steel door lay in a deep recess.

She tested it, finding it unlocked. "This will lead to the shuttle pad?"

"Yes, Miss Book."

Beyond the door lay a narrow industrial stairwell that led up into darkness. She started climbing with Jeremy bringing up her rear like a loyal dog. "You don't need to come along, Jeremy."

"Yes, I do," he insisted. "Lord McGillicuddy said."

She paused when she heard footsteps echoing from below. Someone was in the hallway below, calling up to Jeremy. Someone must have spotted him wandering around and gotten suspicious.

Eliza, suddenly worried they would be found out, gathered her skirts and started hurrying up the stairs, her heeled shoes clanking alarmingly loud on the steel steps. She grimaced, wishing she had thought to take them off.

The voice called up again, sounding angry.

She stopped, waving Jeremy away. "You should go back," she whispered. The last thing she needed was an entourage of Security Poppets attracted to the ruckus.

"No," Jeremy said, louder than she was comfortable with. "I must stay with you. Lord McGillicuddy said."

Instead of wasting more time arguing with Jeremy, Eliza started up the stairs again, hurrying despite the terrible racket she was making. At the top, she found another blue metal security door, this one firmly locked, with another of those security keypads, this one locked. She pressed on it but it kept giving her a red light. Swearing under her breath, she dropped to one knee to examine the keypad.

"Jeremy, what are you doing up there?" called up a grumpy, familiar voice.

"Dammit." Eliza froze in place, her heartbeat escalating in her ears.

Mr. Laurel, her least favorite of the Brides of Dracula, was pounding up the stairs after them. And she still didn't understand how the keypad worked, the electronics unfamiliar to her. If she'd had some tools and time, she might have been able to bypass whatever security measures were in effect. But she hadn't counted on needing her toolbox the night she was abducted at the club. She thought about using the gun on the mechanism, but she was afraid that, unlike the action movies she had seen, the blast would destroy the lock and leave the door permanently closed. Plus, she would alert all of New Versailles.

"Dammit!" she said again, hammering the keypad with the side of her fist.

She felt a spark as if the device carried some kind of electrical charge. She jumped and looked at her hand in alarm.

"Jeremy, there you are!" The moment Mr. Laurel spotted them, Eliza in particular, his eyes narrowed, he touched his broken nose, and his hand moved to the comm in his ear, which was attached via a wire to a device he wore in a pocket of his shirt.

"Yes, Miss Book." Jeremy fairly flew at Mr. Laurel as he was clicking the comm.

The two clashed and grappled at the top of the stairs. Mr. Laurel accidentally yanked the comm out of his ear and the radio pinged around the stairwell a few times before starting its long descent to the floor below.

"You bitch!" Mr. Laurel roared, trying to climb past Jeremy, who was clinging to him like a barnacle. "How did you get out of your cage?"

He made a grab for Eliza, but she danced back a step and kicked him briskly in the shin. Mr. Laurel howled.

Even though it was childish, she stuck her tongue out at him. "Don't you remember what happened last time, Mr. Laurel? Stairs are not your friend." She returned to the security door and spread her fingers over the keypad. Again, she felt that peculiar charge. This time, she forced her hand to stay put. Given the current emergency, she had no better ideas.

The keypad grew hot under her hand. She clenched her eyes shut when her mind was suddenly struck with the intricate picture of a complex grid system that she immediately recognized as a circuit board, though she had no idea why she should suddenly be thinking about that. But as Mr. Laurel snarled at her, telling her what all he planned on doing to her, she was willing to accept just about any explanation just to get off this funhouse of the damned.

She saw the circuit board clearly in her mind and all the little ways it worked. All she needed to do was to send an impulse to the proper release mechanism...

The whole keypad lit up green and the lock disengaged. Eliza sobbed with relief.

"Bitch, I'm going to drag you back to your cage by your garters!" Mr. Laurel said as he pushed past Jeremy and reached for her.

"How uncouth!" Eliza cried as the door slid open and grey light washed inward, along with a strange, almost metallic scent—the artificial air inside the dome of the gyro, she realized. She fell backward away from him.

Still clutching the spitter gun and hoping to use it for leverage to get Mr. Laurel to back down, she scurried out onto a wide, black-paved shuttle pad with Mr. Laurel hot on her heels. Once she was halfway across it, she swung around, looking for Jeremy, but Mr. Laurel had knocked him down and was now practically on her heels.

"I'll show you uncouth, Miss Book!" Mr. Laurel snarled. He leaped at her, both arms extended.

Eliza swung the gun around, which made him stop momentarily. She squeezed the trigger but only got a dry click as the gun hit on some safety mechanism she didn't know she had to undo. By then, he was on her, grabbing her, so she decided to knock him in the head with the gun, something he didn't expect.

The blow drove him to the pavement. She brought the gun down hard over his head again, just for good measure. Mr. Laurel grunted and lay still. "There is no excuse for uncouth behavior, Mr. Laurel!"

Sweating, disheveled, terrified out of her skull, Eliza turned back to the shuttle pad. She was standing on the roof of the palace, the rambling Greco-style structure stretching out beneath her in every direction. Beyond it lay all of New Versailles, with gardens so lush with fruits and flowering trees that they didn't seem real and more like an artist's rendition. Far below, she saw Poppets frolicking like water nymphs among the white Grecian fountains or tossing balls and running games amidst the unrealistically perfect gardens.

So beautiful.

So hideous.

It made her shiver with revulsion. She turned away, the wind plucking at her hair and rustling long skirts, and searched for some means of escape.

There were ten slot-like bays set up on the launch pad, most occupied by small, compact shuttles used to transport people on and off the gyro. They were called Hummingbirds in the tech magazines she read, aerodynamically avian, with fins and wings folded tightly to the body. They were built for speed and high maneuverability on and off gyros. She'd never flown a Hummingbird before, but how hard could it be?

Eliza pulled at the latch on the nearest one and scrambled into a tight cockpit, wriggling around until she had her legs positioned correctly in the footwells, then slammed the door shut. She let out her breath, unaware that she'd been holding it all this time. She was hot, tired, shaking, and so very frightened. She stared at the cockpit's control deck and felt even more frightened by the dozens of buttons, levers, dials, and blinking lights. She was no pilot. Sweet Christ, she was going to crash!

"Stop it, Leeza, get control of yourself, girl." She breathed slowly in and out. She set her hand on the control panel, wondering if she could do to the Hummingbird what she had done to the lock mechanism on the door...

...and just at that moment, she was hit once more with a bombardment of images.

A great, complex schematic opened up behind her eyes. It included circuit diagrams, engineering mechanics, electronic design automation, digital circuits, and even the way the machine's parts worked together to lift and propel the shuttle. It was almost as if the craft were showing her in real time what it was capable of doing, performing for her approval. A dull, throbbing headache bloomed behind her eyes, along with the certainty that she had some strange rapport with the machine, as insane as that sounded.

Keeping her hands firmly attached to the cockpit controls, she willed the craft to understand her wishes and act accordingly. A dull humming started under her and she felt the Hummingbird rise several inches off the pad. There were two joysticks in front of her —steering controls, she supposed. She chanced taking her sweating hands off the cockpit controls to set them on the joystick, clenching it so tightly her fingers hurt. She felt like her thudding heart had been relocated to her throat. She could hardly swallow past it.

Eliza asked the machine what steps she needed to take to get off the gyro. The machine responded by flashing a systematic how-to guide in her head, complete with images and a map of the *Gypsy Queen*. Finally, it deployed its fins and wings, eager to please.

Okay, girl, she thought, trying to calm her mind. We can do this.

She was going to fly or die.

| vi |

As long as Eliza kept her attention focused on the task ahead and not on the idea that she was rocketing hundreds of feet through the air and that crashing would hurt very much, she was all right. She wasn't panicky at all. Well, almost.

It was even a little bit fun, watching the milky grey light of dawn rushing toward her as it grew into the brighter fabricated blue of pseudo-day aboard the gyro. She marveled at its manmade and manually controlled sky. Down below glittered little colored checkerboards representing decorative villages, exotic resorts, and the nearly painful green of parks and reserves. It wasn't long before other Hummingbirds pressed in around her as they all prepared to exit the gyro as she was. Ahead, she saw a giant floating spherical building. She thought it might be the departure gate.

The front of the control deck flashed Lord Foxley's corporate seal, and, beside it, glowing red text that read: WELCOME TO EXIT GATE 14. PLEASE STAY INSIDE YOUR VEHICLE AND PREPARE FOR DEPARTURE SCAN. WE HOPE YOU ENJOYED YOUR VISIT ABOARD THE *GYPSY QUEEN*. PLEASE COME AGAIN!

Staying inside the shuttle seemed like a good idea, but she wasn't keen on the whole "departure scan" thing. Whatever strange power she had developed in the last few hours would likely not help her in avoiding detection, especially if Foxley had a dragnet out looking for her. She chewed her bottom lip nervously as she navigated along the thoroughfare, following another shuttle into one of the many huge, honeycomb-like tunnels.

Another message flashed: YOUR VEHICLE WILL BE CHECKED MOMENTARILY. PLEASE TURN OFF YOUR ENGINE. YOUR PATIENCE IS APPRECIATED.

She sent a mental command to the shuttle, and the whole craft settled down, the humming ceased, and she was left in the almost pitch-blackness of the tunnel. She glanced around, noting that the other vehicles were sandwiching her in on all sides. There was no escape now. What was worse, a hundred feet down the tunnel, she spotted the day-glo uniforms of Security Poppets manually checking each vehicle with flashlights as they went down the line.

She swore softly under her breath, grabbed the latch on the door, and let herself out of the Hummingbird. The coolness of the tunnel felt good on her face after the hot, sweaty cockpit. She clicked the shuttle door shut, patted it goodbye like a loyal pet, and crossed the medium into the next lane. She approached the passenger side of a random vehicle and tapped on the glass.

A short, neckless, middle-aged man in a bad leisure suit turned his head to look at her. She gave him her cheekiest smile as he fumbled to unlock his vehicle.

When it was unlocked, she pulled the door up and scooted inside. "Hello, 'ere, luv," she said from the passenger seat, doing her best to imitate Mr. McGillicuddy's Cockney accent—rather badly, she feared.

He looked confused. Then his eyes slid over her and lingered longer than was appropriate on her generous cleavage. "Can I help you?"

When she went to the club or attended other formal affairs, she often had to retreat to the catwalk or any upper level that had fewer people on it just to be left alone. She knew that despite her timidity and quiet nature, her Poppet charms were strong. She had been created to seduce, after all.

Eliza crossed her legs and smiled prettily while her eyes quickly took in the interior of the shuttle—the pile of suitcases, the gift bags from one of Foxley's exclusive casinos, the fuzzy dice memoir on the dashboard. "Help me, luv?" she asked as seductively as possible, batting her lashes. "Doubtful, but I can certainly help you."

"I don't understand."

"You won the automatic drawing at the casino. Don't you remember?"

"I did?"

Eliza tittered—badly, she thought. "Naughty man, you didn't claim your prize." She reached out to pinch his nose.

"My prize?"

"You won one free day with a Pleasure Poppet."

The man's jaw dropped like a nutcracker. He put a hand over his heart and fluttered it as if he was experiencing a coronary embolism. Eliza scooted over on the seat until she was pressed tight against him and she could smell his aftershave, hair tonic, and the light sweat he was working up rather quickly under his clothes.

Forcing herself to be bold—she was never going to get out of this hellhole otherwise—she put her hand on his knee.

The man reached into his pocket, withdrew an amber pill bottle, and flicked two pills into his mouth. Then he smiled. His teeth were nicotine-stained.

"What's your name?" she asked.

He trembled. "Um...Maurice?"

"You don't know?"

Maurice laughed nervously. His face went blotchy red and he seemed to be developing hives in the little triangle of bare skin above his open dress shirt. "Um...are you...coming with me, then?"

"I thought we might go somewhere more private," she cooed.

Someone knocked on the shuttle's door. The sound of it slid down Eliza's spine like an ice cube. She leaned over, grabbed Maurice by the ears, and kissed him full on the mouth. Maurice tasted like coffee and spearmint chewing gum. She kept her back to whoever was standing outside the shuttle while Maurice's hands wandered up her back. A searchlight circled through the window, then disappeared when the Security Poppet didn't find anything particularly interesting.

When she was sure they were alone again, she fell back in her seat, sighing with relief. Maurice sat there, disheveled and glasses crooked, grinning. "Do you want to drive or shall I?"

"You drive," she demurred, her attention set straight ahead of her. "I can tell you're the type of man who likes to take control."

* * *

They parked the Hummingbird in a car park in lower Brooklyn and picked up Maurice's sedan from the valet parking. Maurice drove down Old Fulton Street with one hand on the wheel and one hand planted on her knee, giggling insanely about some plumber fetish he had.

Eliza had to keep reminding herself to smile and snuggle against him and not lean to the other side of the car. After a few miles of Maurice pawing her pantaloons, she pointed out an Italian eatery under the Brooklyn Bridge and complained about being hungry. They parked and he escorted her inside, keeping his hand planted firmly near her ass.

While Maurice ordered from the menu, Eliza excused herself to visit the ladies' room to "powder her nose." Once inside, she slid open the old-fashioned hinge window and wriggled out onto the weedy back lot beside a giant blue dumpster. She got stuck only once, cursing the big breasts her genetic designers had foisted upon her.

Downtown Brooklyn was laid out before her in broken parsecs of abandoned rail yards, tall, sad-looking redbrick projects, weathered bistros, and little failing mom-and-pop shops. It looked poor, struggling, and unkempt...and it was one of the most beautiful sights she had ever seen. It was home.

A home, she realized rather miserably after ten minutes of walking down the avenue, that she could never return to. They would have staked out the townhouse. They probably had a Silver Alert out for her. They would be waiting for her, prepared to pounce on her the moment she stepped into the light. They would hurt her. They might hurt Juliana or any of her friends. She stopped amidst the mad bustle of foot traffic, staring blankly at the storefront windows of dozens of familiar local shops as a giant invisible fist squeezed her heart to pieces. They could be watching her even now.

She wondered bleakly what had gone wrong with her life, how she could have gone to the club as a professional woman doing her job and returned alone, bereft. A fugitive. It didn't seem possible. It didn't make any sense. It certainly wasn't fair.

She had worked so damned hard to build her life here. She had kept her head down. She had kept to the shadows.

Her entire body started to tremble, and she had to make a concentrated effort not to burst into tears like a little girl. She rubbed at her tired eyes with her sleeve and eyed the people out walking, mostly couples going to dinner or to the theatre. She felt hunted. Alone. She had to find safety, somewhere where she could just sit and think things through properly.

Ahead of her loomed the darker, dingier recesses of downtown, otherwise known as The Gate, the slums that led to Poppettown. With nowhere else to go and no one to turn to, Eliza started walking purposely in that direction. She only stopped many blocks later when the business district started giving way to generic projects, derelict-looking pool halls, and rundown grocers and steam shops, where anyone who had the money could buy an implant as easily as a tattoo. Broken bags of trash littered the streets, and the sidewalks were pocked with puddles of stagnant rainwater from the broken drainpipes overhead. Narrow little alleys full of impenetrable shadows snaked between the tall buildings. No cars passed her. Most people had more sense than to go driving through The Gate this late at night.

Heavy footfalls echoed down one of the alleys behind her. Eliza turned and looked, dreading what she might see. Shadows flitted under the eaves. Was it just some derelict staggering her way, someone taking a shortcut home, or something more sinister than that? A mugger? A gang? Them?

She couldn't take any chances. Her life and freedom depended on her making good choices in the next few minutes. She fled as fast as her heels would carry her. Behind her came the slap of shoes on wet pavement as her pursuer took up the chase. She turned a bend, raced down a backstreet, then turned another bend, finding herself in a blind delivery alley bordered on one side by a derelict machine shop and on the other by a tavern advertising BAD FOOD, WARM BEER in bright pink, neon letters.

Cut into one side of the machine shop was a bright red door. Eliza felt a swell of hope at the sight of it. When she was a much younger Poppet at Court, she'd learned about the Society of the Red Doors from the other Poppets. They were an underground organization that aided Poppets in escaping abusive Vampire Lords. If a building in the city had a brightly painted red door, chances were good that it was a Poppet safe house. You just had to knock a special code onto the door.

She started hurrying toward the machine shop, desperately hoping there was someone to answer her distress call. The footsteps behind her kept up a steady pace. She tried not to panic; she had to remember the code. But when she finally reached the securely locked door, she found her mind was drawing a blank. She pounded on the door, trying to hear if there was anyone on the opposite side. Her hackles felt positively electric.

"Is anyone there?" she begged, pressing an ear against the door. "Anyone! Please! Open the door! I require sanctuary!"

Behind her, the footsteps began closing in. She heard a muttered curse as her stalker reached her. Eliza turned abruptly as a nondescript man in a raincoat that positively screamed secret agent lunged for her. She kicked him soundly in the stomach, driving him down like a pile of rags at her feet. The man, obviously a human not used to the unusual strength a Poppet was capable of, rolled around a little in the wet gutter before recovering and scrambling for a gun in a pancake holster under his arm. His eyes rolled in his head like an animal full of rage.

No one was answering the door. She was alone. On her own.

Eliza gritted her teeth and pulled the spitter handgun from the pocket in her dress. She aimed it squarely at the man getting to his feet, muttering curses. She'd been through too much to give up now. If she was going to die tonight, she would die fighting!

| vii |

Lord Henry Foxley disliked people in general and humans in particular. It wasn't a superiority complex; it was simple good taste. Human beings were crude and insipid. He'd met those who were not, of course. But when he did, he usually preserved them as vampires, so they didn't really count. In a way, he liked to think of himself as a connoisseur of human beings, an earthbound god saving those he deemed fit and disposing of those who were damaged goods.

He'd survived over twelve thousand years of life. He was richer than all of the billionaires in Earth's history combined. He was stronger, smarter, and faster than any vampire or shapeshifter in the world. Mentally, he was unmatched in every field of human endeavor, be it science, mathematics, or art. He had invented several common languages, a number of different art forms, and he had capitalized on the interactions of ancient peoples in order to create the science of politics. Like the fox he was named for, he was a survivor, a realist, a pragmatist, and a dreamer all at once. He could live under the worst possible conditions.

If he had any one flaw, it was a touch of loneliness. It was very lonely at the top.

He had come a very long way. His people had been a clan of savages clothed in animal furs who lived in crude mud huts in what would one day be Scandinavia, centuries before the Viking expansion took place. His people hadn't known how to build houses or ships, though they could construct antler-tipped spears with which they stabbed and wrestled large, wooly animals to the earth, tearing the body apart so they could feed upon the raw, steaming insides. At night, they huddled in circles for warmth, fire being unknown to them, and told stories to stave off the fear of the prehistoric hunting animals that called to each other in the dark. When one of their own died, they divided the body up using crude knives made from fish bones and ate the pieces in an effort to absorb the strength and knowledge of their fallen kin.

His father had been Clan King of the Fox Tribe, not because he had earned the role in a fair fight but because he'd been clever. One night, his father snuck into the Old King's hut and cut his throat using a fish scaler. Foxley had been seven summers old at the time. His name then had been Ilya, which in his people's tongue meant "Little Yellow Sun."

The New King summoned Ilya and the rest of the clan to bear witness. As the prince of his people, Ilya was expected to drink the blood of the dead Old King. In this way, Ilya would prove himself his father's heir and the future King of the Fox Clan.

Ilya drank the blood of the Old King and threw up. The new King was enraged by Ilya's lack of fortitude. He declared his son unfit to be the future leader of their clan and sent Ilya, naked and without food or tools, into exile, expecting the elements to dispose of him. Ilya did not fight his father's judgment, nor did he protest; this was just their way.

Ilya wandered, starved, cold, and near death, for days before he came upon the group of shipbuilders by the sea, dark-haired, bronze-skinned travelers from a distant land, though their leader, Chrysanthos, was a man of smooth, shining white skin who clothed himself in black wolf fur. Chrysanthos said he came from the land called Hellas, which meant nothing to Ilya; Ilya did not even know the name of the land he wandered in.

Ilya was fascinated. He had never met such a beautiful man before. Chrysanthos took Ilya into his tent and revealed himself to the boy. Under the wolf fur, Chrysanthos was golden all over, and so perfect that Ilya couldn't stop touching him. He thought that this must be the god Dellingr—the "day spring," sometimes known as the "shining one"—fallen to Earth from Valhalla, even though Chrysanthos turned his face away from the dawn.

Chrysanthos took Ilya. He drank Ilya's blood and declared it bitter. Afterward, Chrysanthos told Ilya he loved his white Nordic skin, pale eyes, and white, dawn-touched hair. Chrysanthos even loved his name, calling him his "Little Sun." He promised to teach Ilya shipbuilding.

The seasons passed. But as Ilya grew, some part of him was still his father, still the noble savage. When he was twelve summers old, he'd learned all he could from his master, including how to please him in every way—even those ways that he knew his father the Clan King would have disapproved of. Ilya was torn. Even though he sometimes still dreamed about his father, he had learned to love his master's touch, his master's blood kiss.

By then, Ilya had grown taller and was very strong for his age; he could easily build ships with the other grown men. He had never feared hard work, and he had learned to harness pain as an ally.

Chrysanthos sensed Ilya's indecision. He said he did not wish for his little sun to go out, so, one night, he remade Ilya in his own image so that Ilya too could bestow the blood kiss on others.

At first, this seemed a blessing. He would never sicken, and he would never grow old or tremble like the old men of his tribe. But as the years passed and the shipbuilders around him grew crooked and white-headed, their eyes full of cataracts, Ilya realized something else: He would also never be a man. No wife would have him, and he would never bear children in the conventional sense. What's more, the new, young shipbuilders that Chrysanthos took on treated him like a child even though he was old enough to be their grandfather.

One day, drunken on blood and enraged by this realization, Ilya went in unto Chrysanthos with a fishbone knife and cut his master's throat while he slept. Ilya drank every last drop of Chrysanthos's blood. He then cut his master apart and ate some of the flesh as well, taking into himself all of Chrysanthos's years and power.

He did not throw up. After that, he became the leader of the shipbuilders. Like Chrysanthos and his father, he was fair-handed but stern, rewarding those who obeyed him and slaying those who were a disappointment. From there, he sailed to other lands and conquered other people.

The world is trivial. That's what Ilya learned from his master and his many travels. The world is trivial, and men petty and cruel. Survival was all. The fox that his clan worshiped could survive anything—drought, famine, extremes of heat and cold. And so would he. When he ceased to think of humans as anything but prey animals to be used, he could do anything he wanted to them and suffer no guilt in the consequences. His father had hunted huge beasts that could gut a man and stamp him into the snow. Ilya could do better. He would hunt men. And he did.

Ilya became powerful, untouchable. He became Lord Henry Foxley, the King of the World. But since none could match him, and none could stand against him, he was alone. He was always alone.

But then had come Edwin, and Foxley's lonely world of endless power and money changed. His world expanded.

When Foxley stepped into his private library, he found exactly what he expected. Edwin sat in his favorite wing chair, a badly stacked collection of books on the table beside him with not a few on the floor—How Edwin loved his books!—and one of Foxley's favorite pretties straddling his lap.

Edwin's arms were wrapped tightly about her delicate waist and his teeth buried to the root in the tough muscle between her neck and shoulder. A single drop of blood raced down her bare back, obscenely red in the glow of the candlelight. The Poppet was whimpering and writhing against him, though hardly in pain. Edwin was very meticulous about pain. Edwin ran his pale, long-fingered hands gently down the Poppet's spine, smearing the drop of blood across the canvas of her back.

Despite what he had told Edwin's lovesick little Poppet, Foxley had often found it difficult to encourage his Heir to mete out enough pain unless his victim was quite deserving. Edwin was stubborn and high-handed. He did not understand that he, too, was an animal. In fact, he was so much like a wolf that there were those in the Vampire Courts who would sometimes mistake him for a shapeshifter. Edwin worried about justification, though the gods knew he had reason enough to be angry with the world. Edwin's early mortal life had been filled with nothing but hideous poverty, hunger, and despair.

It was one of the reasons why Foxley had chosen him. They were far more alike than even Edwin would admit to. They both had their pain. And both of them had ultimately survived it, learned to harness it. As vampires, they now fed on the pain of others.

Foxley moved seamlessly to the side of the wing chair and perched on the armrest. He was happy to see Edwin wearing one of the fine black suits he'd had tailored just for him. It made him seem huge, his skin as pale as glass, his eyes golden. Foxley gazed upon the face he knew so well. How many nights had he touched that face, drunk in the scent of that white cream skin? It was never enough.

Gathered around Edwin's chair were ten or twelve of his best Pleasure Poppets, stroking his legs or lying across his feet like loyal pets, all waiting for their turn with the Prince. They did not usually gather around like this unless they were truly taken with a Vampire Lord. They trusted Edwin, loved him, were in love with him. Foxley could always tell the measure of a vampire by how his Poppets reacted. This went beyond desire, beyond the mere raw ecstasy of Edwin's bite. This was greater than El Mal de Amor.

Love.

The thought was a source of thrilling fear for Foxley. Strange, disturbing. Enthralling. From the moment Foxley laid eyes on Edwin in that sad little cell in the East End of London, he'd known he must be his. He'd made many vampires over the long centuries of his existence, but as far as he was concerned, Edwin was his magnum opus. He never made another after Edwin left him, not because he did not want to, but because he knew in his heart that no other vampire could compare.

Edwin released the female. She slid down his long legs and lay contentedly against the base of his chair, her eyes closed and her breathing so deep and regular she seemed to be sleeping. Edwin leaned back in his seat, the candlelight carving out the smooth, golden plains of his face, and touched the blood painting his lips, his throat working, savoring the taste with closed eyes.

Foxley loved to watch Edwin feed. It was like gazing into a painting by Michelangelo. No matter how much one studied it, one could still discover something new and beautiful.

In life, Edwin McGillicuddy had been beautiful, instilled with that particular male grace that was both carven and smooth, dark and light, day and night. In undeath, he was divine. He looked like the prince at the end of the fairy story, the one who makes all things right again with a kiss and a spell.

"My lovely boy," Foxley sighed in contentment.

"Blimey, you're a wanker."

Foxley jerked. "Excuse me?"

Edwin licked the tips of his fingers, an act Foxley would have been more than willing to do for him. One of the male Poppets clutched his legs and laid his head down in Edwin's lap, his long, rustling blond hair draped over Edwin's legs like a shawl. He did nothing more than that—just lay there in Edwin's lap and closed his eyes like some mythological creature offering itself up to the pure of heart. Though, of course, Foxley knew better. Edwin had not been pure of heart in a very long time.

Edwin absently touched the Poppet's hair. "Uber-wanker."

"I beg your pardon."

"You're such a perv, old boy." Edwin was beautiful until he opened his mouth. Then it all went to hell. He turned his head, glaring at Foxley with bright, keen eyes that reflected the candlelight like tiny hearts of fire.

"You'd think after twelve thousand years you'd learn to knock. Didn't yer father ever teach you manners? Oh, that's right; he was a barbarian."

Foxley leaned back against the chair uncomfortably. His eyes were cold. "I enjoy watching you feed." He shrugged. "It pleases me."

"It would." He shifted uncomfortably and wiped his mouth on his sleeve.

"You are ashamed to feed in front of me? After all we have been through?"

Edwin looked away. "You're like some dirty old man, the Hugh Hefner of the vampire world. Well, except that you're stuck in that body." He brushed the Poppet in his lap away, rose from his seat, negotiated the sea of Poppets surrounding his chair, and moved with an effortless grace to the bookshelves. He gave Foxley his back as he picked out a new book.

Foxley considered getting up, getting angry, but the view, such as it was, was very good and compensated for Edwin's lack of manners, especially when Edwin stretched upward to reach a book on a higher shelf and the frightfully expensive broadcloth of his tailored trousers was stretched taut across his ass.

"Like Hefner, you just hide in your little bubble up here, getting fat and lazy with your wenches, your head stuck in the sand. You're such a pathetic, wanky vampire."

Foxley narrowed his eyes. He was willing to take a lot from Edwin, but he had his limits. Edwin had a cute ass, but it wasn't that cute.

"I'm not fat," Foxley insisted, sliding a hand over his middle to test the pliancy of his eternal body. He was as thin as the day he had died, and he kept his weight strictly controlled through meticulous exercise and a regiment of purging up at least half of the blood he drank on a daily basis.

"Regardless," he continued, dropping his hand and working to control his temper, "if you had stayed with me, I would not have had to hide up here in my...little bubble, as you put it. I would be down there on Earth with you."

"You're up here because you're afraid, Foxley. People scare the piss out of you. You feel inadequate, a freak. Body Dysmorphia, much?"

"I beg your pardon."

Edwin laughed. "Stop chasing the ghost of your dead father, Foxley. He's been gone twelve thousand years. Let the old bloke rest already."

Foxley stiffened. "What's that supposed to mean?"

Edwin chose a book at random and started paging through it. "If I have to explain it to you, it kind of misses the point."

"Edwin, why must you defy me?"

Edwin rolled his eyes. "Piss off." He placed the book back on the shelf and chose another. "I've always defied you, Foxley. You know that. How distressingly redundant—you'd think by now you'd be used to it."

He turned and showed Foxley the current book in his hand. A Doctor Blood book, well worn, with the spine broken where all the really good sex scenes were. He held it up as if to say, Really?

"When you left me, Edwin, you didn't just break my heart. You also hurt my pride."

"Your transgressions. Let us count the ways."

"I don't understand."

"You never did. I agreed to be your Heir, Foxley, not your toy, your lapdog. But you took all my choices away from me. You always have. You don't treat me like an Heir. You treat me like one of the collectibles in this room, something you own. And you expect me to be happy?"

Edwin indicated the whole room. "Now, you've turned into such a shut-in, you can't even recognize good Court etiquette anymore." He slapped the book against his chest. "I am my own Lord now, worthy of having my own Court. That should mean something to you. Yet you keep me trapped up here like some young Heir who's still wet behind the ears."

Foxley was silent a good long time. He was old. He had gotten that way because he knew how to play hardball, especially when it was his neck on the block.

Finally, he sighed. "Until this thing with Rathbone is settled, I cannot afford to let you go, Edwin. Afterward...well, perhaps we can have some kind of truce between us."

Edwin looked unconvinced.

Foxley made a grand sweeping gesture, indicating the whole of New Versailles. "Really, Edwin, is this the worst you've ever had it? I may not have always been kind, but never have I neglected you or your needs. I have always given you everything you wanted." The room was filled to brimming with the books that Edwin loved, as well as an endless parade of Poppets willing to keep him well fed and satisfied. What more could any vampire need?

But as Foxley glanced at the Poppets he had assigned to Edwin, he noted that despite the marks on their necks, none looked particularly disheveled. None smelled like him. That wasn't Edwin's way. How curious.

"You haven't been sexing my pretties. How peculiar of you."

"Don't change the subject."

The Poppets were coming awake as if aware they were the topic of discussion. Sex-starved, they swarmed over Foxley like pretty zombies, covering him in kisses and caresses. He closed his eyes as they tugged at his clothes, letting his imagination run a little wilder than usual. "You are biting and then love-starving my pretties? Edwin, really. Is this because of her? That Poppet?"

"Leave Eliza out of this," Edwin said with disgust as he watched a Poppet squeeze her way into his lap. It took some doing, Foxley being a mite smaller than she was.

"How valiant. I think I shall be ill." Foxley playfully laid one arm across his forehead. Then, turning the gesture around, he hooked his arm around the neck of the Poppet in his lap and brought her throat within easy biting distance of his mouth.

Edwin leaned against the bookshelves and waited for Foxley to finish. "Speaking of being ill…is there some reason you're buggering me with this crap?"

Foxley, having exhausted his hungers for the moment, pushed the Poppet off his lap. She dropped to the floor at his feet, blood leaking from the small marks at the base of her throat. He smeared the Poppet's blood over his lips. "It seems your little plaything has gone missing."

"I know."

"Really?"

Edwin shrugged. "Your Poppets like to talk. You should be more careful about that."

Foxley sat back in his seat and wiped his mouth with a handkerchief. "Aren't you the least bit concerned about that? No desire to rush in and save her, the knight-errant?"

"Miss Book is resourceful. She doesn't need some bloke rescuing her."

"And yet, I get the feeling you wouldn't mind," Foxley mused. His eyes moved across the room full of Poppets. "Who told you about her escape?"

"Mr. Laurel. The unhappy wanker you had made to look like me. The one who looks in need of a good shit."

"You are crass and offensive, Prince," Foxley said, wiping at the blood on his disheveled clothes.

Edwin smiled. "Those are my best parts."

Foxley narrowed his eyes. "I remember some other parts being much better." He reached for Edwin through the air and through his own blood.

Edwin immediately lurched back against the bookshelves as if he'd been sucker-punched by an invisible fist. He gritted his teeth as Foxley's power dragged him up the bookcase and toward the ornately painted vaulted ceiling high above.

Foxley looked up, noting with pleasure that today's mural was of a giant spider's web full of naked Adonises trapped in the webbing and awaiting the grotesque, human-faced spider crouched in one corner. Edwin, always the rebel, kicked and clawed at the books, ripped at the wood, and flitted his wings even though he knew it was useless. Foxley's power was irresistible. Absolute.

In the back of his mind, Foxley plied the trick against his own blood. He spread his wings and rose up until he was hanging in mid-air, eye to eye with Edwin, light as a feather. See, not fat at all. He reached out and touched Edwin's face.

Edwin jerked and his face scrunched up in disgust, but despite his reputation, he was young by vampire standards and powerless to resist. Exactly what Foxley wanted.

Unable to pull away, Edwin closed his eyes. Meanwhile, Foxley drew a wistful finger down his cheek. "What are your plans regarding Miss Book?"

Foxley thought about that. "To discover her whereabouts, of course. To bring her back to my Court. It's only a matter of time."

"You won't find her," Edwin said, keeping his eyes tightly shut. "If Eliza chooses not to be found, you'll never see her again."

"I shouldn't worry about that. I have Chimera hunting her even as we speak. I can't just have a lost Poppet out there on the streets, wandering about."

Edwin stiffened, and Foxley sensed the outrage and violence in his body. It was because of Chimera that Edwin now had his unique...condition. "Chimera is a bloody lunatic! You'll be lucky if he doesn't bring her back in ten pieces."

Chimera was a part-time bounty hunter and full-time sociopath, one of the vampires that the Courts kept moving around because no one knew what to do with him. Years ago, Edwin, burned out on vampire politics, requested a sabbatical from Foxley's Court. Foxley had been outwardly congenial about the whole affair, letting him take the personal time without argument, but he knew better. He knew Edwin, knew his Heir would do a runner, and he wasn't disappointed.

Less than a week later, Foxley hired Chimera to hunt his Heir down and bring him back alive. Unfortunately, Chimera didn't seem to understand that Foxley had meant alive and not mostly dead. By then, Chimera put a bullet in Edwin's heart. And still, somehow, Edwin managed to get away, though not for long.

Grievously wounded and near death, his Heir had had no choice but to return to Foxley's Court, and it was there that Foxley's best scientists built him the mechanical pacemaker that now kept him alive—after a sense. He never did tell Edwin the details of that little snafu, of course, but Foxley couldn't help but wondered if he suspected something.

Perhaps he did because Edwin reached up and clutched the back of Foxley's neck, fingering the slender, boyish bones. The desire to snap Lord Foxley's neck and end his twelve thousand years of life must have been powerful in Edwin. Foxley felt it like the bottomless hunger within him—a hunger that demanded immediate fulfillment.

"Go ahead," Foxley said in a soft, seductive little-boy voice. The voice he had used on Chrysanthos even up until the end. "Try."

Edwin did. He tried to close his fingers but something was wrong with the mechanics between his brain and his hand because his fingers trembled with strength but wouldn't close at all.

"A vampire cannot harm his master. It is nearly physically impossible."

"Nearly," Edwin reminded him. "Yet you killed your master."

"Yes," Foxley agreed, smiling. "And perhaps one day you will kill me. But not today, Edwin. You don't have that power. Yet."

They hung in the air like that, creature and creator.

Foxley stroked Edwin's cheek and watched the shadows and sadness fill his eyes. "I'm glad all of this has come to pass and that we are together again. I do believe that awful Poppet has defanged the Prince."

Edwin looked sad.

Foxley knew that look. He recognized it in his own face when he looked in a mirror. Edwin was in love with a Poppet! A manufactured sex toy! That in itself was both a comedy and a tragedy.

Foxley clutched his Heir fiercely as they hung together in midair. He felt a pang. Once, he'd wanted to see the whole world through Edwin's young, crystal clear eyes. He would have given

Edwin that world, wrapped it up in a big red bow, if only Edwin had asked for it. Edwin could have been powerful. He could have been strong—not thin and starved, subsisting on synthetic blood and living between humans and Poppets. But Edwin was stubborn, and trying to deter him from his path, Foxley knew, was like trying to move mountains.

How awful, he thought. The bloodlust had died in Edwin's eyes. He couldn't find it anywhere. He wanted to weep.

"She's a Poppet," Foxley exclaimed. He moved very close to Edwin's face to whisper. "Just that. Why, Edwin?"

"You wouldn't understand, Foxley, even if you lived another twelve thousand years."

"Then make her like you. Like us."

"I love her, Foxley. I don't want to change her."

Frustrated with their game, Foxley clutched the sides of Edwin's head and shoved—physically, mentally, and psychically—so Edwin was pressed flush to the ceiling above, stuck to the center of the painted spider's web. Edwin gasped, eyes glittering with panic, fingers clawing at the ceiling mural even though Foxley had no intentions of letting him fall.

Foxley would never let Edwin fall.

"I don't want your explanations…your books. They're nothing but pale substitutes." He sprang at Edwin, landing atop him with catlike agility. He smiled savagely as they both hung upside down from the ceiling. "What I want is you. All of you."

He put his hand over Edwin's mechanical heart, clutched it, and kissed him with lips and sharp little teeth, rouging Edwin's mouth in his own blood even as he struggled. Edwin didn't understand. The world was trivial, and, when everything was stripped away, all that remained was flesh, hunger, and gears. The world was a vampire.

Edwin grunted when Foxley broke the kiss, blood pouring from the torn flesh of his mouth. It made him look just beautiful, like an angel. An angel of hell.

Just like the good old days.

Foxley, in a frenzy of hunger and passion, reached up and ripped at his own shirt until the buttons popped and he'd bared his throat and shoulder on the left side. It had been too long since he'd sampled El Mal de Amor, the Lovesickness.

He slid his hands up Edwin's smooth lapels, smiling with desperate hunger. "Edwin, my boy, show me Valhalla."

| viii |

The door opened behind her and Eliza fell inward, the gun still extended in her hands. Foxley's agent fell on top of her and she jerked the trigger reflexively. The gun was not designed to be shot at such close quarters, and the percussion blew a good-sized hole right through his chest, splattering Eliza with blood and unnamable stuff.

She experienced a moment of quiet, panicky horror, followed by a longer moment of strangely calm determination. She was not going back to Foxley's Court. She would not be some Vampire Lord's plaything. She'd sooner die—or kill—before allowing someone to touch her without her permission. It was as simple as that.

As she looked down at the remains, she felt a moment of extreme satisfaction at what she had done. The Poppet who had opened the door for her helped get the dead body off her so she could stand up. It took several moments for her to stop shaking. Then she turned to the young, pale Poppet who had helped her.

They stood in a rusted steel construction elevator that almost seemed to hang suspended in the dark. An unhealthy, rose-red steam surrounded them, and some dull glinting lights pierced the unfathomable depths of the clanking, steaming darkness that lurked far below the city. It looked like an industrial version of Dante's hell, but she knew it was simply the guts of the city.

She looked at the sentinel, hoping he understood, that he would not bar her way down after what she had done. "Please," she said, scanning his face for understanding, "I need to get below."

He looked at her wordlessly—with pride? Horror?—then he nodded.

Eliza felt her heart leap inside her like a stabbed fish. Relief. Anger. Trembling fatigue. She didn't want to go down into that darkness. She'd hoped she would never again have to return to Poppettown. But now she had no choice. The city beneath the city was the only place Foxley's agents would never venture to look for her

She watched the sentinel as he activated a series of pulleys. And then the old metal car began its shuddering descent into the seething darkness far below.

* * *

Poppettown.

It was the rotten, rusty heart of New York City. Twenty square miles of underground slums stretching from the Bronx down to Staten Island, and populated by the simple-minded Poppets that ran the great steam machines that kept the city running in good order. Originally called Steamtown, it was built and then populated by the poor and by immigrants who had nothing to offer the city but their backs and their sweat. But, as tends to happen to a people overworked, overcrowded, and underpaid, the miniature underground metropolis eventually turned into a ghetto full of slipshod projects, sleazy taverns, gambling halls, and implant parlors. The immigrants were long since gone, replaced by synthetic humans to run the synthetic city. Not that the Poppets were apt to complain. Most did not care if they lived in poverty. Most were not even bright enough to know what the word meant.

When she was sixteen years old and living as her master's Courtesan, Eliza learned about the Red Doors, who frequently helped higher-functioning Poppets escape their Courts. She researched and then coordinated an escape. All but two of them were recaptured and returned to her master's Court. She and her friend Derek made it out. But to what end? she often thought during that first year of freedom.

The Red Doors had gotten her below, but she soon found herself in a deplorable little coldwater flat, sharing the space with two other Poppets. No skills. No education past what she'd been taught as a Poppet. No real hope. But she'd persevered, educating herself through books and television. She was a very good typist, and she remembered everything she read with absolute clarity. She was ecstatic the day the temp agency said they could place her.

Dory, one of the Poppets she'd been living with at the time, told her she was crazy even to consider returning to the above, that it wasn't safe. She might be found out and returned to her Vampire Lord. But Dory turned tricks every night in the red light district and came home with bruises all over her face and body, so Eliza wondered just how much "safer" they really were down here.

As she set foot in Poppettown again, Eliza thought about Dory, and also about her old life. It seemed so long ago, yet all the old memories came flooding back at once. The streets were lined with old-fashioned iron streetlamps that splashed their sallow light onto the wet black cobblestones—wet, not from rain, of which there was none here underground, but from the heavy, clammy steam that hung over the city, generated by the machines that operated hundreds of feet above, just under the surface of the street. Through the dimness that could never be cut by any amount of light, she saw Poppets lumbering up and down the avenue. Not slender, androgynous Pleasure Poppets like at New Versailles, but big, blocky ones like broken refrigerators—Worker Poppets built for a life of hard, endless labor. They moved purposefully in and out of shops or climbed on or off steam trolleys, the only available means of public transportation here.

One of the vast, bullet-shaped slipstream trolleys rocketed by her, tolling its bell and spattering her with muddy rain and debris, its wake ripping at her skirts. It was carrying a heavy load of Worker Poppets on their way to the steam factories, all of them clutching lunch pails and standing about-face like one creature duplicated many times over. Eliza stepped back from the curb and looked around foolishly.

She picked a direction at random and started walking even though she had no idea where she was going or what she would do when she got there. Gradually, Poppets closed in around her, their silent, empty zombie eyes making her skin crawl. She lowered her head, pulled at her skirts, and tried to figure out what to do.

The first thing she needed was shelter. Most taverns and boardinghouses had no trouble putting a new Poppet up so long as she didn't mind working in deplorable conditions for peanuts. Before she'd gone above, Eliza had been a laundress, a waitress, and a seamstress. Later, she'd made a small fortune removing blooding bracelets for newly freed Pleasure Poppets. She glanced around, wondering about her prospects. She could probably carve out a niche for herself if she played her cards right. She certainly was confident enough in her skills.

She had options, she reminded herself. The dark depression of the Poppettown slums didn't have to consume her. She didn't have to sink to the level of empty desolation that she saw reflected in the dirty faces and blank gazes of the people surrounding her. She was free; she was still in charge of her own destiny. She was alive, dammit.

She lifted her head proudly as she reached the bustling business district. There she detached herself from the hoard of zombie

Worker Poppets and chose a side street lined on both sides with the neon-lit picture windows of taverns advertising topless girls and no-tell motels that sold rooms by the hour. Lights dappled the cobblestone streets, making them glitter as if Poppettown were paved with dirty black diamonds. Rats scampered through the garbage pouring out of overturned trashcans. Poppets hung back in sunken doorways—young, skinny females hunting johns, worn old women selling cheap trinkets out of handmade baskets, watery-eyed males so drunk all they did was sit befuddled in doorways and rock to their own internal miseries.

She glanced at the various help wanted signs. Most of the establishments were looking for barmaids or exotic dancers. She felt her hopes wither. She didn't know if she could endure being groped every night. She felt closer to the old beggar women trying to scrounge out a living in the gutters. And, everywhere she looked, she saw predatory eyes like carrion birds trying to decide if she was worth their time to pick her bones.

At least she still had the gun.

She got halfway down the street before she decided to rest.

She found a somewhat clean stoop in a deep, dark recess of a project. She wiped the soot away with one dirty gloved hand, sat down with the gun in her lap, covered her face, and wept.

* * *

"She's pretty enough. Dead, I think."

Eliza was startled awake. Someone was tugging on her and, for one moment, she had no idea where she was. Her world was dim, alien, made of dark, sharp-edged concrete pierced through with bright, filthy lights. She was slumped in a doorway, her cheek cooling against the doorjamb. There was a terrible ache down her back from her neck to her tailbone. She felt cold and hungry and bleak and empty all at once.

Three figures in coarse clothes and cloth hats and scarves stood over her like nightmare versions of the Three Bears. Two were big and looked like aging Courtier Poppets, but the one in the middle was as thin as a snake, with broken teeth and an ugly grin. He looked human, probably one of the many confidence men who made their homes underground, where it was easy to fleece Poppets with subpar intelligence. He was the one pulling on her skirts, trying to get the gun out of her lap.

Eliza panicked. The spitter gun was the only protection she had. Now, these brutes were trying to steal it—the only thing of value she owned. Eliza felt a great wellspring of despair open up inside of her. She yanked the gun out of the con's grasp.

"Well, hello there, Poppet," said the Baby Bear. He grinned at her, impressed with her strength and determination. "Not so dead, after all, are we?" He loomed over her, blocking the light. His breath could have derailed a locomotive. "Not yet, anyway." He reached for her.

"Get away from me!" she screamed, wrapping both hands around the gun and raising the weapon even though she noticed it was out of charge. Useless.

"Gimme the gun, Poppet."

She tried to cold-cock them as she had Mr. Laurel, but her first blind swing missed. She was cold and tired and uncoordinated. The men easily grabbed her hand.

Eliza dropped the gun and leaped to her feet. Thankfully, the con men were more interested in the weapon than they were in her. She was barely able to sprint down the alley, her skirts tangling her all up as she headed toward what looked like streetlights up ahead. She could hear the Three Bears calling to her to come back, that they had something real nice for her. She ignored all of her aches and pains and raced for the end of the alley, hoping someone would notice and stop them. But the souls lurking in the dark recesses of the alley looked on with dull interest; her drama was no concern of theirs.

Panting heavily, Eliza lunged into bright lights—and a chain-link fence that cut across the alley. A dead end! She let out a little exhausted cry, took a deep breath, and leaped for the fence, hoping to scramble overtop it. She hooked her fingers in the chain links and started kicking at the fence, trying to find purchase, but the Bears were suddenly upon her, their fingers digging into her back, yanking on her hair, pulling her down to the filthy concrete littered with garbage, dirty glass, and syringes.

Eliza whimpered and whipped around, ready to fight them off. She would not be a victim...!

The Three Bears' leader pop-punched her in the eye and her head snapped back hard against the concrete. Darkness leaked into the corners of her eyes. She felt him pulling on her clothes, tearing at them with his dirty fingernails as he told her what an undeserving whore she was.

Oh, god, please, let me die! she begged. She couldn't endure this. She just couldn't...

She thought she was hallucinating when a shadow swooped down from somewhere on high. There was a wet crunching noise as a pair of great white hands twisted the little Bear's head at a funny angle. His chin dropped down onto his chest, blood spattering from his nostrils, and the body suddenly crumpled to one side. Eliza scrambled back, trying to make herself small against the fence, wondering what new indignation was about to be heaped upon her.

A tall, slender figure stood before her, dressed in a long black coat and a man's wide, flat-brimmed hat. A red scarf was tied around the mouth and chin The Shadow-style so all she could make out was a bone-white face and pale green eyes that shimmered faintly in the dull light that filtered into the alley. Two great white wings flashed outward threateningly, making the figure look like a fair angel of destruction.

Eliza bit back a cry of surprise. The vampire looked at her hungrily with its bright, night-seeing eyes.

The two big Bears moved to surround the new figure, to grapple with it. The vampire casually reached out and caught both men at the back of the head like a referee about to explain a play to two opposing teammates...then smashed their heads together so abruptly that they dropped like bags of bloody flour to the ground at its feet.

"You should be more careful," the vampire said in a deep, throaty voice. "This part of the city is dangerous at night."

Eliza gripped the links of the fence and used them to haul herself to her feet. The vampire edged back a step, moving with a dancer's balanced grace. It stared at her so intently that Eliza felt goosebumps race along her arms. She was certain she was next, that the creature would set upon her, but the vampire turned its back on her and shushed its wings closed.

"Wait," Eliza said, clinging to the fence. "Wait, please. Don't go."

She had no idea why she wanted the vampire to stay, except that it had helped her when no one else had, and that meant something. That meant she might have an ally.

The vampire hesitated, turned, then gave her nervous eyes. It glanced past her, past the chain-link fence, where some kind of demonstration was going on. About two dozen Poppets stood huddled together in a vacant lot while one of their own stood, literally, on a soapbox, preaching about taking actions against the Vampire Overlords, whatever that meant.

"It's not safe here for me," whispered the vampire. It tried to slip backward, but Eliza boldly stepped forward to stop it, a hand on its cold wrist.

"Are you like a vampire superhero?" she said. As far as she knew, there weren't many vampires down in Poppettown, despite the perpetual night that might have appealed to them. Vampires had a bad habit of disappearing here or of winding up dead in ways they couldn't recover from.

The vampire laughed at that. Its eyes flickered over her as if it didn't know what to make of her.

On a whim, Eliza reached up and pulled away the hat and scarf. The rain-pale hair beneath was cut short around the ears, which were a little too big. The face was long and lean but distinctively female. The eyes were huge and beautiful, jeweled like a cat's, though the face was really rather plain.

"Do you belong to Lord Edwin?" the vampiress asked suddenly. Her voice was deep and hoarse, startling. It made Eliza want to clear her throat. "Are you his Poppet?"

"I..." She decided it would take too long to explain everything. She didn't even know where to begin. And, anyway, the vampire might leave her if she said no. So she said, "Yes. Do you know him?"

"The Prince? Of course." The vampiress smiled fondly, a look that lit her whole face up and made her seem, at last, beautiful. Eliza's words seemed to galvanize her.

She grabbed Eliza so quickly that she didn't have a chance to react, to even cry out, and pressed her back against a nearby brownstone. The body under the coat was hard and soft, a queer combination. The vampiress turned her head and nuzzled Eliza's ear, inhaling her scent. "You smell of Lord Edwin."

"Is that good or bad?" she asked, trembling with fright. She pressed her hands against the vampiress's rather negligent bosom in an attempt to separate them, but it was like trying to move a brick wall.

"I've missed Lord Edwin," the vampiress mused. Her rough, catlike tongue scraped along the line of Eliza's neck, raising goosebumps.

Then she let Eliza go and withdrew to the shadows under the eaves of the brownstone. "You must be careful. Others may notice you are his. Others may desire to harm him through you."

Eliza watched the vampire carefully.

"Avoid the riots." The vampiress's pretty, glittering eyes moved analytically to the demonstration in the vacant lot. "The riots are dangerous. There is something wrong with the Poppets here. They've become...unnatural."

That said, she extended her great white wings again.

Unnatural Poppets? Eliza stepped toward the vampiress. "Wait, please...I don't understand!"

But Eliza found she clutched at shadows. The vampiress had flown away.

* * *

Eliza resolved to be more careful. Her time above had obviously softened her reflexes and instincts. She crossed the street and walked several blocks south, being sure to stay well away from the darker, dingier alleyways. She wouldn't make the same mistake twice.

She passed a great many Poppets assembled into loose militia groups in the streets. She stopped and gazed up at a man standing atop an overturned barrel.

He had the build of an ex-Pleasure Poppet and he was handing out printed posters. "My little brothers and sisters, time has brought us to the edge of the abyss," he said, scattering posters. "My children, heed the words of the Great Mother, for she has called you forth out of the dark. Heed me, for I walk with her and I feel her pain..."

He turned and offered Eliza a poster and a longsuffering smile. "My little sister." His face was dour, mad, and holy as only the truly devout can be. "Heed the words of the Great Mother. Open your heart to her, for she is our salvation."

Eliza took a poster from the man and tried to look vapid like a Pleasure Poppet without a thought in her head. She didn't need any more suspicion falling upon her. Avoid the riots, the vampiress had said.

The Poppet tenderly touched her face like a prophet. Then he smiled at her benevolently before turning back to his task—distributing as many posters as possible to passersby.

Eliza moved on, glancing at the poster. It was covered with a tiny, cramped script all run together with no punctuation. It had the mark of a Poppet who had never had a formal education. It seemed to be a call to arms, a rally to overthrow the Vampire Overlords and support the Queen and the Hive, whatever that was. It didn't make a lot of sense. Then again, much of her life was that way now.

As she walked, she turned the sheet of paper over, discovering the other side was a flier advertising FREE GAMES! and BEAUTIFUL GIRLS! from the nearby Starlight Casino. The zealot Poppet was using the backs of posters ripped from walls to print his propaganda. She clutched the poster in her gloved fingers, rocking slightly on her feet. The Starlight Hotel & Casino was where she'd worked as a waitress when she first arrived below. She, Dory, and Derek had all worked there together,

Derek, she thought, feeling a deep pang that made breathing difficult.

Maybe he would remember her. Maybe he would make a place for her. He was all she had now.

| ix |

Derek Wall was a tall, garish caricature of a Poppet. The Lord who had commissioned his design had been partial to movies featuring Errol Flynn and Clark Gable. As a result, Derek was well formed and square-jawed, with a stubborn, mischievous slant to his full, expressive lips. His midnight-black hair curled in silken waves behind his ears, and his eyes were the blue of a Caribbean sky after a violent storm. He wore his suits exactly two sizes too small so they hugged his broad shoulders and slim hips, and he regularly sported leather buccaneer boots, even in bed. The ladies loved them.

Derek liked the attention he received. It was the air he breathed. It was also his bread and butter. In the Starlight Casino, he was known as a "Snake Eyes"— a double zero. His job was twofold as a gambler and a hustler. He attached himself to vulnerable female high rollers, wined and dined them, gambled away their retirement funds, gave them a good roll in the sheets, and then got them out the door at the end of the weekend. In the end, they had only two things to show for it: broken hearts and empty pockets. Double zeroes.

Derek was very good at what he did. As a result, he had a certain arrangement with the Starlight Casino. He would do any woman he was assigned to, even several at once if the money was right, but he would not do men. And never, under any circumstance, would he do a nonhuman. It was his only conceit. At Starlight, such conditions were normally unheard of, but Derek was always in demand, so the casino capitulated to his demands.

Derek was running his game on the casino's main floor, flushing away the pensions of two middle-aged divorcees from Orange County, when he spotted the Poppet across the crowded casino hall. She had just stepped into the room and was staring in wide-eyed wonder at all of the tables jam-packed with rich, drunken marks.

He knew she was a Poppet right off. Tall, short, thick, or thin, all Poppets had a certain common body type that didn't change no matter how they aged—cartoonishly large breasts, petite hands and feet, big eyes, and perfectly symmetrical faces that made them look surreal. The woman was definitely a Poppet.

He also knew her. Intimately.

Derek swore, his lips hovering at the edge of his whiskey tumbler. Alisa! A few years older, and perhaps not as whip-thin as she once was, but it was definitely Alisa. He recognized her as much by her proud, proper walk as by her features, which were prettier than a human but somewhat understated by Poppet standards. Dark skin and deep blue eyes, with an angelic halo of wild black hair. It was her style and strength that made her what she was, that made her Alisa.

Suddenly, he was awash in nostalgia. His memories of Alisa were of clinging to her hand as a child at the Scholomance where they both grew up, Alisa doctoring his bruises, wiping away his tears. Alisa there, her arms embracing him like an angel—the closest thing to family that something like Derek could ever hope to have.

He dropped his cards and stood up, almost toppling the table. The two Orange County ex-wives were complaining about something, but he hardly heard them.

Across the room, Alisa lifted her chin and stared straight at him. He too had aged, he knew. It had been, what, three years? But he knew that she recognized him nonetheless. The flare of remembrance in her eyes told him so.

Leaving the table, the women, everything, Derek cut a shark-like path across the floor.

Alisa too rushed toward him, her steps so light and fast that when they finally met in the middle of the casino floor, Alisa was holding up her skirts and running full tilt into his arms.

They clenched. Derek swung her up and around, up and around, like a child he was amusing. Alisa laughed—a tired, sad, joyous, sensual laugh that he would have recognized anywhere.

"Derek!" she cried, wrapping her arms around his neck. "Oh, Derek!"

"Alisa." He swung her down, went to one knee, and wrapped his arms tightly around her waist, resting his head on her heart as if they were still children huddling together in the frightening, uncertain darkness of the Scholomance.

* * *

Eliza let Derek escort her into a dimly lit lounge done up in a quasi-Asian motif. There were shoji screens to partition the booths for privacy and red paper lanterns to shed a romantic light. Derek led her to one of the more secluded booths near the back.

A pretty, young Asian waitress appeared, dressed in a glittering red and gold cheongsam. "Derek, what can I get you tonight?" She looked over at Eliza, then blanked her face professionally. Derek often brought his marks here, and the staff had long since grown inured to it.

"Whatever Alisa wants," he said with a flourish of his hand. "Are you hungry?"

"Oh, god, you have no idea!" Eliza glanced at the menu, her hands positively jittery. "Give me whatever's fastest, and plenty of it!"

"We'll have two of that," Derek laughed.

"The special it is, then." The waitress diligently disappeared.

"I remember you being a much pickier eater," he joked.

"I don't care tonight! I'd go out back and slaughter the cow myself if I had to."

Derek smiled nervously.

Eliza looked Derek over, noting his infallibly good tastes in clothing. His well-muscled, six-foot-even frame was sculpted into a Western suit coat, formal shirt, and leather jeans. He wore a belt with a big, brass, snakelike buckle, giving him a kind of Old West hustler look that very few human men could have pulled off effectively. Derek did it admirably. His dark hair was perfectly coiffured, emphasizing his shocking blue-green eyes, his sharp-as-stones cheekbones, and his wry, smirking lips.

Eliza touched her hair and her terrible black eye. She felt like a squat, ugly, unkempt elephant by comparison. "I really should clean up."

"You look beautiful," Derek insisted as he rolled some ice cubes from his water glass into a cloth napkin and handed it to her. "You always do."

Next, he reached for the flask of sake that sat in a wire basket between them and poured her a drink. "It's good to see you, Alisa. But I know you wouldn't be here if you weren't in trouble. What's happened?"

She held the ice to her black eye and struggled to maintain his gaze. They had grown up together at the Scholomance. There was little she could conceal from him. Back then, Derek had been a positively exquisite child. When he was five, he'd wound up in a pushing match with another Poppet who'd called him a girl. Eliza, then Alisa, fought off his bully, biting and kicking at him until the other Poppet started crying. Derek had immediately attached himself to her, and after that, they were inseparable.

Derek had been good at whatever he did, be it sports, ballroom dancing, or etiquette. It should have given him certain advantages, as Poppets well loved by their vampire masters had the power to move up quickly in rank. But, unlike Eliza, Derek didn't know when to swallow his pride and do as he was told. Derek rebelled.

By the time he was eleven years old, the master who had commissioned him had forbidden anyone from striking Derek, as the constant beatings he received by the headmaster were beginning to leave scars on his property. Eliza hoped that things would change after that. But, of course, they didn't. When the headmaster could no longer handle Derek's temper tantrums, his future Court stepped in and took him away for days at a time. He always returned. But when he did, he seemed to be worse.

She later learned that when Derek was taken away, it was to be pre-conditioned, as they called it. She never learned what that entailed, and Derek never told her, but she could well imagine it. She sometimes woke in the middle of the night to the sound of Derek's screams echoing through the dormitory. Sometimes, she had to crawl under his bed just to coax him out.

After they graduated from the Scholomance, they were both sent to the same Court, a lucky happenstance since it meant Eliza could continue to watch over Derek. By then, she had been comforting him for so long that it seemed the most natural thing in the world that they should become lovers. But Derek wore her down. She had more than enough to deal with just trying to navigate Court etiquette, find a niche in her Lord's Court that was comfortable and safe, and stay out of trouble. Troublesome Pleasure Poppets seldom came to good ends. Often, they were shipped off to a workhouse for a chemical lobotomy, then auctioned into Poppettown as Worker Poppets, a fate literally worse than death.

She tried to impress this on Derek, but he insisted they didn't have to live cowed and obedient. She didn't have to live like the pretty, mute little Poppet that she was. She knew in her heart that he was right, but life was difficult enough without locking horns with your own vampire master, which Derek did for years.

One day, restless and bored, she went looking for Derek, only to find him in their Lord's quarters, folded into a corner like a frightened animal, nursing a broken arm. Without really thinking about it, Eliza guided Derek back to her private quarters, had him lie down on her bed, and started to devise an escape route with several other Poppets she knew were interested.

"What are you doing?" Derek asked her, worried.

"We're leaving." They were the most difficult words she had ever spoken. "I've heard the other girls talk. They say there's sanctuary underground, that the Lords won't go down there because vampires aren't welcomed. It won't be pleasant, but we can be free."

She sat down beside him on the bed and gently took his hand. She would take an electronic door pass from one of the cleaners, make a copy—something she knew she could do—then return it without anyone the wiser. After that, they would run. They would take nothing and make no indication that anything was up. That way, no one would notice they were missing for a few hours, which would give them an advantage.

"They'll hunt us down," the other frightened Poppets told her.

"I don't think so." Eliza was all but invisible compared to the other almost supernaturally beautiful Poppets their Lord kept. She was what they often referred to as a "token," a Poppet created off-pattern from their Lord's preferences to fulfill a diversity quota. As a result, their lord seldom summoned her to his bedchamber, and with her dark looks, the other Poppets considered her too plain and bookish to join in their reindeer games. She didn't have many friends, and the ones she did were mostly tokens themselves.

"But you might have to wait a day or two before I can make a pass. Can you hang on that long?"

Derek, holding his arm, looked at her with tear-struck eyes. "You can do that?"

She stroked his hair. "I can do anything!"

"But you're happy here."

"I won't be happy if you aren't happy, Derek."

A couple of days later, they made it to The Gate, and without incident. After wandering around the slums for a while, she recognized one of the red doors. Down below, it was as awful as she had imagined, crowded and stinking and as dangerous as a jungle full of wild animals. She felt like they stood on the outer edge of hell itself. But because Derek was happy to be away from their Lord, she was happy too. She would endure for his sake.

The first thing she did was find Derek proper medical care in the form of an old, gelatinously fat, filthy implant specialist who was able to set his broken arm. He demanded payment for his services, of course, and Eliza had nothing to offer him but her body, which he happily, and greedily, accepted.

She never told Derek. Derek had enough to deal with. After he'd healed, they found work in one of the casinos.

Derek was a hit. He was tall and handsome and made the women giggle like schoolgirls. Eliza chose to work in the hotel's Laundromat. Sometimes she mended the staff's clothes or waited table when the restaurant was short-staffed. After the incident with the implant specialist, she couldn't bring herself to sell her body to anyone. She felt tainted. She could scarcely stand to let Derek touch her.

Eventually, she and Derek met another Poppet named Dory who worked the streets around the hotel. She let them stay in her vile little basement hovel. They split the rent three ways, and it was there that they began to make real plans for the future.

Eliza didn't make the money that the people who worked the casinos did, of course, but it wasn't long before she found she had a special rapport with mechanical devices. She could fix almost anything. She could also remove blooding bracelets without amputating a Poppet's hand below the wrist, and that gave her a magnificent advantage. Suddenly, she found herself commanding outrageous fees for her removal services, and it wasn't long before she had enough to return above.

Derek wasn't pleased with her plans to get a job in the city. He accused her of betraying her own people, of destroying what they had together, which wasn't very much, really. They were more like brother and sister than lovers. She'd stopped sleeping with him a long time ago. There was a great deal of drama, crying, and manipulation.

She came to realize that she could no longer live with Derek; he was dragging her down and down. Soon, she would be just like him, another soulless inhabitant of Poppettown. Resolved, she left for the world above with hope in her heart and what felt like a huge weight pressing down against her shoulders. She wasn't happy, exactly, but she was determined. Resolute. She had to do what was right for herself for a change.

Now, she was back, looking to Derek for comfort, for sanctuary. It was so ironic that it made her sick, and she damned Edwin McGillicuddy for putting her in this position, for making her eat her pride with a side order of crow. She remembered the girls who worked at the casino telling her that Poppettown was a backfilling trap. Once you were in, you never got out.

Derek leaned forward, touching her hand. He seemed much more self-assured than she remembered. "Tell me about yourself. Have you been well?"

"Well enough." She forced a smile. "I work as a secretary now. I have a lot of responsibilities."

"My brilliant Alisa." He stroked her hand. "Who do you work for?"

Eliza licked her lips nervously. They were descending into dangerous territory. Derek had no love for vampires. "No one you know," she answered simply.

"I see." He released her hand as the waitress appeared with two steaming platters of the house special.

Eliza had no idea what it was. She simply ate it all, not tasting the food at all and sopping up all of the gravy with her bread. Her stomach nearly rebelled; it felt like days since she'd had a decent meal. The spices warmed her, and the food helped her think. She drank more sake and tried not to meet Derek's gaze until the end.

Derek sat there, watching her. "Alisa, how deep are you in?"

"I'm alive. Hopefully, that counts for something."

"Is it...him?" He sounded righteously angry.

She knew what he meant. She swallowed and watched his eyes, feeling her heart trip in her chest when she realized how indignant Derek was about someone harming her.

"No," she explained. She looked down at her demolished plate, wondering how much of her story she could trust to him. He didn't just hate vampires; he was frightened to death of them. If she told him about Foxley, about Mr. McGillicuddy, he might toss her out into the street, and she had nowhere else to go. She didn't want to use him, but she was completely out of options.

"I just need somewhere to lie low. I thought of you. I didn't know who else to turn to." She pulled nervously at her hair, which had all kinds of knots. "I'm sorry." It sounded pathetic even to her.

"You've helped me so many times, Alisa. You know I'm at your disposal. Anything you need, I'll help you with...even though I know you're only telling me the partial truth."

She looked up.

He smiled knowingly. "You always play with your hair when you lie."

She let go of her hair and sat back in her seat. Suddenly, it was too much, too overwhelming, and she realized she couldn't stop the tears. She was so damned tired. "I've made a mistake coming here…" She started to get up.

Derek took her hand, halting her. "The only mistake you've made is thinking you need to justify yourself to me. Whatever you need, Alisa, it's yours. Whatever you want, I'll give you."

He brought her hand to his lips and kissed it. "I'd prefer you didn't lie to me. But if that's the way it has to be…" He shrugged.

She stared at Derek long and hard, amazed by the changes in him. Once, he had turned to her for comfort in the dark. Now, she felt perfectly at ease leaning on him.

* * *

They were crossing the casino's parking lot, heading toward Derek's restored classic silver roadster, when the trouble started. She'd forgotten bout Derek and his cars. He loved beautiful cars, the more gauche the better. "What now?" she asked.

"Back to my place." He aimed his key ring at the car and deactivated the car alarm. "I have the penthouse apartment on Broad Street now. You'll be safe there."

She was impressed. Broad Street was a long way from the slums where they'd lived. Derek was doing all right for himself. "Do you know what became of Dory?" she asked suddenly.

A shadow passed behind Derek's eyes. "Dory's gone, Alisa."

She felt numb. "You mean dead."

"She got involved in an urban terrorist group. They did a suicide bombing of a building on Walk Street where some vampires were holed up. There were no survivors."

"Oh, god." She covered her mouth with her hand. That wasn't at all like sweet, cowed Dory, so afraid of the vampires who had once enslaved her that she wouldn't even work the districts where they were rumored to troll the streets. Eliza was about to ask Derek how Dory—Dory, of all people—could have become involved in a terrorist group when she suddenly froze a few feet away from the roadster. She felt like someone was running a razor blade up her spine.

Her hesitation, her sixth sense, whatever you wanted to call it, saved her life. A moment later, a shot chipped the asphalt in front of her foot. If she hadn't stopped, she would have intercepted the shot perfectly.

Someone was shooting at her.

The world slowed to microseconds. Eliza didn't think, just did. She dived behind the cover of the roadster, Derek still attached to her arm, even as another shot rang out. This time, she heard the report, but only because now she was listening, and now she could hear the petite hiss of the sniper rifle beneath the roar of activity on the avenue.

Derek grunted in surprise as the bullet whizzed harmlessly past the car.

Staying in a low crouch, she searched the dim, steamy street, the buildings rising almost crookedly like black mountains before her, the windows winking like eyes, but the shooter could be anywhere, on any of a dozen different rooftops. Then something that felt like a punch to her shoulder knocked her flat to the ground, making her gasp for breath. She thought it might be a genetic-seeking round, the kind of programmable bullet that could go around corners to find its target.

Derek was on his feet in seconds, his arm fully extended, and a silver, ivory-handed old-fashioned colt that looked much too beautiful to be anything deadly in his hand. He stood very still as he sighted down his target like a professional gunfighter.

She saw a brief flash, possibly the reflection of streetlights on the rifle's scope, and then she realized that Derek was tracking the shooter. He squeezed the trigger and the gun made a surprisingly powerful cough. A window chattered apart high above. Derek squeezed off two more rounds. One went wild; the other tagged someone atop the building directly across the street from them, knocking the black-clad shooter off the ledge he was perched on.

"Aces!" Derek cheered, watching the man fall. He wore a look of satisfaction on his face. The man crashed down atop a car parked on the curb, setting off its siren-like car alarm. Derek, never missing a beat, let out his breath and yanked open the driver's side door of the roadster.

"Get in!" he said.

Eliza gripped the bloody hole in her shoulder with one hand and tried to pull herself up with the other. The initial flare of almost electrical pain was finally lessening, leaving a sickeningly numb sensation in its wake that told her that the bullet was probably still lodged in her shoulder somewhere.

"Alisa!" Derek pushed her into the car ahead of him.

Seconds later, they tore out of the parking lot with a rubbery burn and swung onto the street, missing a slipstream trolley by seconds. Derek, spinning the wheel, swore and said, "Who the hell did you piss off?"

The lurching sensation made Eliza want to throw up. "Very bad people," she managed through gritted teeth as she bled all over Derek's beautiful white leather interior.

He swerved to avoid a drunken Poppet staggering in the curb and pulled alongside the smashed car with the shooter bleeding all over the roof. Before Eliza could say anything, Derek leaped out and ripped the black ski mask off the man, examining him briefly before returning to the idling car.

"It's a Poppet, a local." He slid back into the driver's seat and put the roadster into gear. It leaped into the street like a cat. Derek turned to pin her with a look. "You didn't answer my question. Who's after you?"

Eliza groaned in response.

"We need to get you to a doctor."

"No doctors," Eliza insisted. She felt like her arm was being wrenched from the socket with every breath she took. She could hardly think through the pain, never mind construct a decent lie.

"I don't care! You need—"

"Derek," she interrupted. "I've got trouble that runs very deep, and enemies that go very far up. You don't want to take me to a doctor, trust me. It would be like handing me over to him."

"Who? Our master?"

She swallowed hard against the nausea. "Foxley."

Derek drove with one hand on the wheel and one on the gearshift, his foot as heavy as lead on the gas. He looked at her with pale-faced shock, as if she had admitted to cold-blooded murder. As they swerved down one dark, slick street after another, Eliza thought about begging him to slow down before they crashed, but she wasn't sure he would listen.

"Lord Foxley?" he shouted.

Eliza nodded, biting her lip. She did not want to have this conversation right now.

"How in the hell did you get mixed up with Lord Foxley?"

Smeary lights flickered across the windshield. "It's a very long story, Derek."

"This is turning out to be a very long night."

Within minutes, they were pulling into the underground parking garage of Derek's building, a tall, white-glove apartment complex complete with a doorman and valet parking. It looked more like a posh hotel than an apartment building. Eliza leaned against

Derek as they made their way inside, his coat covering her shoulder wound. The doorman held the door for them, and some security guards in the lobby leered as Derek walked her like a drunken floozy toward a bank of elevators.

Derek's penthouse apartment was sterile and generic. It was obvious he didn't entertain very often and was more at home in the casino where he worked than in his own flat. Once inside, she nearly collapsed. Derek carried her like a bride into the master bedroom and set her down on a bed that looked seldom used.

"Derek, I'll bleed all over your bed," she insisted, trying to sit up.

"Don't worry about that." He piled pillows behind her neck. "Just lie back."

She grimaced. The constant, burning pain in her shoulder felt like a hot butter knife was being thrust in and out of her flesh. She could feel her own heartbeat under her hand where she clutched the seeping wound.

Derek hovered undecidedly. Without his jacket, Eliza noticed how taut his shirt was over his model-like build, the white linen so thin that a dark matting of hair was visible as a shadow around his nipples and in a thin line that edged downward toward his belt buckle. The pain of the gunshot was enough to make her want to grind her teeth down to stumps, but at least the view was nice.

Derek leaned down and undid the front of her ragged dress, which had seen far too much violence in the last few days. He examined the wound, careful not to touch it. "Well, Alisa, you have a very impressive hole in your shoulder and a bullet that needs to come out. Any suggestions?"

This close, she could smell Derek's cologne, dark and spicy. "You'll have to dig it out."

"I don't know if that's such a good idea."

A doctor was out of the question, and she was done with illegal implant specialists. "I know enough about human anatomy to guide you," she insisted, hoping it was true. She struggled to talk through the waves of almost dizzying pain. "But...first...you'll have to get a few things for me."

She glanced around, saw a legal pad for phone messages on the nightstand beside the bed, and nodded at it. "I'll dictate a list. Get the items and then get back here as soon as possible."

She must have passed out, because sometime later, she heard Derek whispering her name. She opened her eyes and saw he was sitting at her bedside with a shopping bag in hand. She shook her head to clear the tears of pain from her eyes. "Get me undressed."

Together, they pared her down to her chemise and knickers. She had Derek cut the blood-soaked chemise off with a pair of scissors so she was naked to the waist, the chill of the room cooling the feverish sweat on her upper body and making her shiver. She had him spread out the items she had requested on a clean towel.

He offered her a hit of strong whiskey, but there was no way she was going to be able to operate if she was floating somewhere outside of her own skull. First, she had him soak a pair of forceps in alcohol, then she had him disinfect the wound, added cold compresses around the entry point, and then had him go to work digging out the bullet before she completely lost her nerve.

She passed out three times. The third time was even a relief.

She had a strange fever dream. She dreamed she was home, lying in her own bed, but Mr. McGillicuddy was there with her, making love to her—urgent, ravenous, all consuming. He was kissing her, running his sharp little teeth over her lips and chin and throat. It was a pleasurable sensation until he dropped his head and began biting at her shoulder. She screamed. She told him to stop, but he didn't. She woke with a start, choking, sweating, her body lit from within with misery and pain.

She was alone, her bandaged shoulder burning coolly. The pain was different now, the bullet gone. The room was dim, and her body was full of equal parts of pain and painkillers so she felt like she was floating in the dark, her back not quite touching the mattress.

She was crying, her face damp with sweat and tears. She didn't want to think about vampires. And she especially didn't want to think about how Mr. McGillicuddy had upset her life. Yet, each time she closed her eyes, she found herself thinking about him, wondering where he was, if he was thinking about her, or maybe just laughing about her with all of his vampire friends. And then she felt like her heart was being pulled out of her chest all over again.

She was so tired. So very tired. She turned to her other side so she wouldn't aggravate her wounded shoulder. She saw her dirty, bloodstained dress lying on the floor at the side of the bed. She looked at it as she slowly began to drift back into darkness.

RIP, dress, she thought. And my life.

It was such a nice life, too.

***

"Tell me about your job," Derek said the following morning as he carried in a tray of food and set it on the bed beside Eliza. "What do you do all day?"

She sat up in bed, eyeing him warily. She felt groggy and vaguely nauseous from all of the pain meds, and she had a dull headache that seemed to extend from her skull all the way down her spine to her tailbone. At least her shoulder hurt less today. "There isn't much to tell, really. I take dictation and arrange engagements for my employer. Pretty mundane stuff."

"What kind of mundane stuff?"

"Release parties, book signings. I also edit his books for him."

"Working for a famous writer." Derek sounded impressed. He was dressed in a casual blue day suit that was nothing like the hustler clothes he'd worn down in the casino the night before. The blue of his suit brought out his eyes.

"You're not working today?" she asked, trying to detract him from the subject of her day job.

"I asked for today off so I could baby you." He started undoing the dressing to check her wound. "What's his name? Your writer?"

Eliza faltered. She looked at the food on the plate, hardboiled eggs and toast, but couldn't find her "That's rather uncommon."

"He's British."

"A British novelist. Fancy."

She didn't want to talk about this

Derek had gotten the sling and bandages off her shoulder and was examining her wound with great interest. She knew without asking that the quality of the gunshot was good. As a Poppet, she was genetically enhanced to heal quickly and to be able to take a great deal of abuse.

"Why does Foxley want to kill you?" Derek sounded so indignant, as if he meant to ride out and slay the big bad vampire for her. "Why, Alisa? You're nobody. He doesn't even know or care about our ex-Lord."

It sounded cruel when he put it that way, but she knew what he meant. He had questions, and he'd been so good to her. He deserved at least partial answers. "To...to manipulate Edwin."

"Your employer the famous British writer."

"Yes."

"Is Edwin a Courtier?" he asked, sounding hopeful. "A runaway like us?"

She bit her lip. "No."

Derek sat back slowly, blinking. "Well, what is he then?"

She felt numb in her extremities. "He was Foxley's Enforcer."

She waited. She felt her heart ticking in her chest like a time bomb ready to go off.

"Edwin McGillicuddy?" Derek suddenly said, his voice rising in notches. "Lord Edwin McGillicuddy?" He dashed the breakfast tray to the floor.

Eliza shuddered, holding very still, not wanting to look at him, certain that Derek would strike her. But after a moment or two of deadly, cancerous silence, he got up and stalked out of the bedroom, slamming the door soundly behind him. In another room, something heavy hit the wall and smashed, making her jerk in response. The rest was silence.

At first, she was afraid. Then she got angry. Derek could smash every piece of furniture in his posh apartment if he liked, but that did not give him the right to treat her like a child who had disappointed him. Maybe she had made some questionable choices in her life—she was even willing to admit that Edwin McGillicuddy was one of the bigger ones—but Derek had no business judging her.

Furious, she got out of bed. Her dress was a weary, un-wearable rag, so she explored Derek's closet, picking through his clothes for something that fit. The huge assortment of garments for both men and women confused her. She finally grabbed one of Derek's old shirts and hastily buttoned it up. It fell to mid-thigh on her like a chemise. She jerked the bedroom door open and went in search of him.

She found him on the wide parapet just beyond a pair of open French doors that led off the living room. Derek had set up a target practice range on his rooftop. He stood a hundred feet from the target, sighting it down with his colt. She joined him where he was standing in front of the target.

Derek squeezed off five rapid-fire shots in one long procession. Three hit dead center. He was a pinhole shot, she remembered. That was the reason he'd been able to shoot the sniper in such dim lighting. As a boy, he'd dreamed about being a cowboy.

"Do you have any idea who that McGillicuddy bastard is?" he asked very calmly as he reloaded the colt from the box of ammo in his pocket.

Eliza stood her ground. "Yes. I lived with him. I know him, Derek."

"Do you? They call him the Prince, Alisa. The Angel of Hell." He glanced at her. "He's a gangster. A devil. The devil. Before he disappeared, he was Foxley's heavy, his right-hand man. Drugs, racketeering, prostitution. That's who McGillicuddy is."

Eliza shuddered. Her memories of him were very different. She didn't know who he was when the temp agency sent her to him, but he was kind and funny. He listened to her and treated her like she mattered. Like she was an equal. When Foxley captured her, he had gotten her out of the cage and even convinced a Poppet to help her escape the *Gypsy Queen*. Could a truly evil man be capable of all of that?

"Foxley made him that way, Derek."

"Why are you defending him?"

She jerked reflexively at the loud sound of his voice. She supposed it was pride. She hated being caught doing something foolish. And working for Edwin McGillicuddy had been an extremely foolish thing to do.

"He hit you." Derek slid new bullets into the colt's chamber. "He tried to kill you."

Now he was crossing the line. "No, he didn't," she insisted. "Mr. McGillicuddy has never hit me. He has never so much as raised his voice to me. And he wouldn't try to kill me. I know that."

"And yet, Foxley's agents tried to kill you. A vampire McGillicuddy worked for. He may as well have done it himself." Rage was simmering in Derek's fiery blue eyes. He aimed the gun at the target.

She watched him shoot five more bullets into the target. She said nothing. Lying sleepless in bed last night, she'd had plenty of time to work a lot of this out in her head. She no longer believed the shooter on the rooftop was working for Foxley the way the agent who'd been stalking her had. In fact, the more she thought about it, the more she was sure.

"It wasn't Foxley who shot me. He's evil, not stupid. He wouldn't try to kill me. He needs me alive so he has at least some leverage over Edwin or he might leave him again." She took a deep breath. "The shooter was someone else."

Derek gave her a suspicious look as if he suspected there was more between her and Mr. McGillicuddy than she was letting on. "Who?"

She sighed tiredly and glanced out across the dark expanse of Poppettown, at the horizon of smog-enshrouded, crooked buildings. "I'm not sure. I do know Foxley is terrified of a rogue vampire named Rathbone. He has a talent for killing old vampires and wiping out entire Courts. But no one knows why he's doing it, or how. They don't even know where he is." She went on briefly about what happened aboard the *Gypsy Queen*, concluding with, "Maybe Rathbone knew I escaped from Foxley's Court and sent his man after me. Maybe he thinks I know something about the violence down here. The Poppets going rogue."

"You think this Rathbone is behind the terrorist activity down here?"

She reached up and touched her lips. For some reason, she wanted to think about her fever dream, which was ridiculous. "Maybe."

She decided she needed a lead on Rathbone very badly. If she could find him, pinpoint his exact location, she could talk to him, prove she was on his side and not Foxley's. Weaponize him. Yes.

She wanted Rathbone to wipe out Foxley's whole Court. Or, maybe she could convince the two vampires to destroy each other. She was fine with either scenario, though she wondered if there was a way to save Mr. McGillicuddy from becoming a casualty of whatever insane inter-vampire war was going on.

She had no other options. She certainly couldn't go to the police. They would only scan her chip and send her back to her master.

"Does anyone in Poppettown know anything about Rathbone or his Court?" she asked.

"Nobody here would go anywhere near a Vampire Court if they could help it, Alisa. Most of us started out there, remember?"

"Are there any Poppets here who used to work in Rathbone's Court?"

"None that I know of—unless they're not saying."

Watching Derek slowly reload his gun, it suddenly hit her. She knew exactly how to track Rathbone. The sniper had shot the clue right into her shoulder.

* * *

"Highly compressed titanium," Eliza stated, standing at Derek's kitchen counter and examining the crumpled bullet that had been in her shoulder only a few hours ago. It sat smoldering at the bottom of a large glass Pyrex. She had set it in a corrosive solution she had made from a collection of common household chemicals.

Derek stood leaning against the cooking island, watching her carefully.

"It was probably made in a vacuum space. Pressure changes the molecular structure, making it stronger but still giving it reasonable density," she explained. "It's almost completely non-corrosive."

"What does that mean? Why would anyone make bullets out of titanium? "

"So the ammo won't jam in the humid atmosphere of Poppettown." Using a pair of long forceps, she fished the bullet out of the homemade hydrochloric acid and held it up to the light. There was no serial number—that meant it was definitely contraband. Homemade. She knew of only one person in all of Poppettown with access to titanium, a material virtually impossible to find in any mass quantity.

"Is Dr. Grott still alive?" she asked.

Derek frowned. "I haven't seen Grott in years, but I assume so. He used to work on Wet Street, right on the edge of the factories, right?"

"Right." When she worked as a flesh mechanic, removing blooding bracelets for Poppets, she and Dr. Josef Grott would often recommend patients to each other's practices. He was a very sweet old eccentric with many fantastic and impractical ideas in his head, including the belief that he could one day replace Worker Poppets at the great steam machines with manmade "machine-men." She'd spent many hours discussing it with him over tea and biscuits. He'd meant to make his machine-men out of compressed titanium so they would never rust in the endlessly wet conditions of the underground.

If the bullet came from Dr. Grott's lab, then that was as good a place to start as any.

* * *

For the trip downtown, they decided to take public transportation to avoid anyone recognizing Derek's car, and she decided to pose as a young man—Derek's lover. Derek was less than enthused about the idea. He had always been a little homophobic.

"You could pose as my brother," he suggested from the doorway of the bathroom, watching as she stood before his vanity mirror, clipping off long strands of her blue-black hair.

She shook her head and looked down at the pile of long, coiled black hair she was accumulating in his sink. "We don't look enough alike, Derek. And, this way, if we do act suspicious, it will only make people think you're uncomfortable with being seen with your lover."

"I am. This could hurt my career," he said somewhat grumpily, staring at her as if she'd asked him to put his hand in a box full of live vipers.

She ignored him and looked at herself in the mirror. Her forehead loomed and her ears looked too big with all of her long hair gone, but she was certain she could pull this off. She was plain-faced enough, she thought. Anyway, losing her hair was preferable to a bullet in her back, as far as she was concerned.

Still angry but out of arguments, Derek returned to his bedroom to change, leaving Eliza alone with her thoughts and her fears.

Am I doing the right thing?

She had no idea, and she had no one to ask. She'd been alone all of her life.

Later, as they crossed the lobby, Eliza wearing a baggy dark suit and coat, a cloth cap pulled down over her brow and a scarf wound around her neck to hide her lack of an Adam's apple, she considered the wisdom of her idea for maybe the thousandth time. This was the big test.

The doorman held the door for them and smiled nicely, but even though he raised his eyebrows at Derek, he paid her no mind. Eliza considered herself a success.

Derek's jaw ticked. He didn't say as much, but Eliza knew that with the clothes and lack of makeup, she made a very convincing boy. Everything was working together to make her look like one of the many young rentboys who hung out around the more expensive districts, hoping for a rich John to come along.

She linked her arm through his and leaned against his arm in a familiar way as they turned down the avenue, the noise of the city closing in around them.

Vendors and hawkers hemmed them in on all sides, along with a number of the soap boxers she'd observed the day before. She and Derek stayed close to the buildings and as far away from the groups of protesters as they could without being too obvious about it. The vampiress who saved her had warned her to avoid the riots.

"Is Edwin McGillicuddy gay?" Derek suddenly asked.

"What kind of question is that?" she said, not answering it.

On the avenue, they jumped onto a slipstream trolley. Derek paid and they took their places at the back. The trolley was less than half-full. It was mid-morning and the Worker Poppets had already gone off to their factories all over the city. With only a few people down in the front, they were able to whisper without being overheard.

"He's done men, you know," Derek said, holding her hand.

Eliza sighed and closed her eyes. "I don't care what he is or who he's slept with. Why did you come, if you feel so uncomfortable?"

"I'm not uncomfortable."

"But you are."

"This is all just very strange." He turned his face away, looking sullenly out the window. Derek had a perfect movie-star profile: the straight nose and soft lips, the black hair curling artistically around his ears. Their Vampire Lord had been quite a fan of Rhett Butler's character, as she recalled. "What kind of a relationship do you have with him?"

Suddenly, she understood. Derek was jealous. Of Mr. McGillicuddy!

Eliza sighed. This was how he'd looked the night she left him for the city above. Stone silent and wounded, unwilling to speak to her or even meet her eyes, even though it might be the last time for them both. She'd wanted to explain herself, explain her dreams of being something, being a gentlewoman who could make her own way in the world, but he looked so angry, so hurt. She knew what he was thinking but was too passive-aggressive to say—that she was betraying him, betraying her own kind by abandoning him for the world above. She'd wanted to do this for them both, but he was much too afraid of leaving Poppettown, afraid their former master would discover them.

The next day, she packed a lone suitcase, took the small fortune she had built up in the underground, and left alone for the overworld. And, alone, she had begun to build her dreams.

Edwin McGillicuddy once told her he believed strongly in Anam Cara, the idea of the soul mate. He said that it was deeply rooted in the history of the Gaels, his ancient people. Your Anam Cara was the one who challenged you. The one who completed you. The one who was difficult to live with. Surely, Derek was her Anam Cara, the one she was meant for, the one she loved and could not live with or without.

"I had to leave, Derek," she explained as they rumbled up and down the streets, past faceless brownstone buildings and bridges, all made up of the same grey, sunless, despondent stone. "This place is just too dark and sad for me."

"And Edwin?"

She waited for another volley, another attack on his character, but Derek merely sat there waiting. "Edwin was beautiful and fascinating. I was young and desperate. What do you want me to say?" She pinned him with a dire look. "I can't undo my mistakes. I can only live through them."

Derek seemed to sense her pain and her insult. He moved his arms to embrace her on the seat. His body was firm and near perfect as only a Courtier Poppet can be. She thought about the gorgeous gunslinger figure that he cut, standing in the street as he took aim at the shooter, and she felt her body respond to that. He had changed so much, hardened and matured since last she'd seen him.

She looked into his electric blue eyes, so like the sea under a bad storm.

"I'm sorry." He sounded genuinely remorseful. "I am so sorry, Alisa."

"I'm sorry, too," she said.

He put his hand on her cheek and rubbed his thumb across her lips. His eyes were still fierce, but also full of years. And desire. "I don't say or do rational things around you, Alisa. You know that."

He felt like Derek as he touched her. She touched his hand on her face.

He leaned down, his mouth seeking hers. He kissed her gently, shyly. It was a very different kind of kiss from her dream of the night before. There had been a subtle violence to her fantasy kiss with Edwin, as if he could scarcely keep himself from devouring her whole. Derek was all soft yearning, and his mouth tasted like tears and rain.

Their mouths were still clinging in a kiss when the trolley rolled to its first stop at midtown, their signal to disembark. They were only a few blocks from Wet Street, a brisk five-minute walk. But as they climbed down to the street hand in hand, Eliza found herself wishing it was much farther.

| X |

Edwin was running out of time. Running out of life. Literally.
    He had to get to Earth and warn Eliza about Chimera. He had to protect her, despite what she thought of him. He told himself it was a matter of pride. A part of who he was. He had always protected his women. He'd protect Eliza, too, no matter the cost, no matter that she probably hated and feared him.

Edwin, accompanied by Lord Foxley's head of security, walked the gaudy, red-carpeted floor of one of his more lavish casinos under the guise of a routine security check. He was trying to formulate a decent plan of action.

The Clocks looked a great deal like the White Sands casino, only tackier, and filled with an even greedier clientele of high rollers. Politicians and movie stars turned to check him out as he passed, probably wondering if they had a shot with him. Fifty years ago, he would have been flattered. Now, it just made him angry. He was nothing but a piece of ass to these people.

He was dressed in one of Foxley's tailored all-black suits but had added a white, ankle-length leather coat to it. He wasn't sure if that made him look angelic or demonic—perhaps a little bit of both. From the looks he was getting, he was turning into an unwilling showstopper.

Celebrities loved vampires. They loved getting it on with them. But they saw vamps at their best, wearing the seductive, diplomatic public faces they put on for show. They didn't understand a damned thing about vampire politics or what kind of creatures they were playing around with. If they did, they wouldn't go anywhere near his kind. Hell, he didn't want to be anywhere near his own kind.

Edwin half-listened to the eager young officer chattering on. The Clocks was by far one of the largest casinos on the *Gypsy Queen*, sporting ten gambling halls, fifty "private lounges" where one could engage in every type of debauchery imaginable, and over five hundred posh hotel rooms, all of which were booked solid every single night. Edwin squinted under the fierce lights of the massive glass chandeliers hanging overhead, cringed inwardly at the unholy amounts of money being fed into the one-armed bandits and blackjack tables, and tried to focus on what the young officer was saying.

The kid was yammering on about what he thought could be done to upgrade security and how the pickpockets had run wild on the floor. Edwin grunted noncommittally while in the back of his mind he mulled over bigger issues.

As Lord Foxley's Enforcer, he had nearly as much power as Foxley himself. He could steal a Hummingbird and leave anytime he wanted, and no one would be any the wiser. They certainly wouldn't question him. The only problem was that he couldn't pilot, and he couldn't even bite a pilot, infect him with the Lovesickness, and force him to fly the aircraft. There was a reason they warned people not to operate vehicles while under the influence. He wasn't big on the idea of sitting in an aircraft several hundred feet in the air beside a pilot tripping balls. The whole fiery crash thing worried him a tad.

So here he was, walking the halls of the casino, trying to decide on a more reasonable course of action. Several young Security

Poppets on the floor turned to glance his way as he passed, whispering low to one another. He was the Prince, after all. As such, it was his job to search for security breaches or to keep an eye out for suspicious behavior, especially in light of what had been happening in the other Courts. He had the highest security clearance in the entire casino. He was the second most powerful man on board the *Gypsy Queen*.

But the officers watched, he knew. And, certainly, more than a few were expected to report back to Lord Foxley.

The officer who walked with him was a night supervisor, a young, blond human in his early twenties with a stern, ambitious face. He'd seen this one before. A good soldier, the young man kept his eyes focused ahead of him at all times as he marched Gestapo-like down the halls of the casino, trying to impress on Edwin his value as a team player, his face revealing no emotion.

Yet, when they'd first met, Edwin noticed something very telling. Even though his face showed no reaction to meeting the Prince in the flesh, the man's scent had changed dramatically, becoming more pungent with a sudden light sweat. He was either terrified of Edwin or…something else. If it was fear, Edwin could do little about that. But, if Edwin's suspicions were correct, he might just have found a way off the *Gypsy Queen*.

The young officer was going on about how he had stopped several young drug pushers the night before when Edwin finally interrupted him.

"Do you like your work here?"

The supervisor immediately blanched with surprise. "Sir?" His posture went rigid as if he had some serious military training in his background.

"At ease, soldier." Edwin smirked.

The supervisor met his eyes but then dropped them shyly. Ah.

He was likely in possession of a clearance card that allowed him to enter and exit the air space around the gyro without throwing Foxley's security systems into the defense mode. Edwin looked him over, being rather obvious about it. He was slender, but with nice muscles, a generous natural tan that hinted at something spicy and vaguely Hispanic in his genetic background, and pretty, cornflower-blue eyes. Movie star material.

Edwin glanced at the nametag affixed to the breast pocket of his braided gold and red uniform. "Officer Cesar. How did a young bloke like yourself come to be head of security of The Clocks?"

Cesar looked momentarily confused by the question. His lips formed the words before he managed to say them. "I...uh, put in for it after I left the military."

"Army?"

"Air Force."

Edwin smiled. "Excellent. I may have a new job for you, flyboy."

Cesar looked terrified by the idea, his eyes never leaving Edwin's face. "Sir?"

They were coming upon one of the private lounges. Edwin tested the doors until he found one that was unlocked. He pushed it open and waved Officer Cesar ahead of him.

Once inside the room, the door closed and securely locked, Edwin turned to scan the space. It was filled with racks of BDSM-inspired equipment, some he didn't even know the names of. Blimey, he was turning into an old fogey, he thought.

"Help yourself," he said, indicating the conservative wet bar in one corner.

"I'm sorry, sir. I'm on duty." Cesar sounded disappointed by that. He was a few inches shorter than Edwin, but it was obvious he worked out. His uniform fit him exactly, creases so sharp they could have drawn blood. His white-gold hair was cut short and neat around his ears, nothing left to chance. A meticulous man, obsessed with details. He had probably climbed the ranks fast.

Edwin leaned against the wall beside Cesar. "Go ahead, flyboy. I won't tell."

Cesar gaped at him, evidently deciding it was a test of some kind. "I'm very sorry, sir, but I can't."

"Are you always so stuffy? Were you born with that stick up your arse, soldier?"

Cesar swallowed nervously.

Edwin laughed. "I've been asked to go on a special assignment for Lord Foxley, extremely classified. Only Foxley knows. I need a reliable pilot to take me to Earth. Can you pilot a Hummingbird?"

Cesar stood up straighter, brightening at the news. "Yes, sir." He started reaching for the radio on his hip. "I'll have to clear it with Lord Foxley first, of course."

Edwin put his hand on Cesar's where it rested on his hip. "Lord Foxley doesn't want you using the radios. We believe there may have been a security compromise."

"Yes, sir. I see." Cesar swayed slightly as if he was trying to unstick himself from the floor. "I'll have to speak to Lord Foxley in person, then."

Edwin, one hand set on the wall above Cesar's head and the other still on his hand, turned his body slightly, boxing Cesar in. "Don't you trust me, lad? I am Foxley's Enforcer, you know—his most trusted Heir."

"Yes, sir. Of course." Cesar held his eyes like a mouse mesmerized by the cat that means to consume it. He swallowed again, this time with more difficulty, his Adam's apple bobbing.

Edwin smiled, showing just a hint of teeth, the smile that had made kings and queens toss their fortunes at his feet just to spend a night with him. "Do I make you nervous, Cesar?"

"Yes, sir," Cesar answered, unable to look away, to even blink. "You're the Prince."

Edwin leaned close and tapped Cesar on the nose. "Nervousness will keep you alive, lad. I like that. I can tell you'll go far."

"As you say, sir." Cesar sounded breathless, on the verge of swooning.

Enough games; time to move in.

Edwin shifted closer until Cesar was backed against the wall—no room for escape, not that Cesar looked particularly interested in escape. "Ever dream about making it with a Vampire Lord?" he asked in an intimate little whisper, playing with a button on Cesar's uniform. It was polished to a mirror shine.

It took Cesar a moment to answer. "No, sir...I mean...I...don't know, sir."

Edwin smiled at the almost boyish indecision on Cesar's face, bent his head, and laid a light, nearly chaste kiss on the corner of Cesar's mouth. His face was so smooth it was like kissing a woman. Cesar must shave at least twice a day, he thought.

He waited to see if Cesar would bolt. If he did, it would be unfortunate for Cesar, because that would necessitate Edwin killing him to keep him from alerting Foxley.

But Edwin had chosen well, it turned out. Cesar didn't disappoint. He closed his eyes and held perfectly still while Edwin kissed him a great deal less chastely. Edwin moved a hand to cup Cesar's chin, holding him in place while he deepened the kiss, biting gently at Cesar's lips and sliding his tongue deep into the boy's mouth. Cesar groaned in appreciation.

Cesar's hands moved slyly down his back to embrace his ass. Cesar, he decided, had just a little more experience with this type of thing than he was letting on. Edwin turned his head, running the sharp edge of his teeth along Cesar's neck, but without breaking the skin. He needed a compliant accomplice, not a dead drunk one.

Cesar whimpered, his fingers digging deep into Edwin's flesh. His cheeks burned red at his own reaction.

Edwin didn't mind. He was used to it.

As they kissed, Cesar's hands drifted around to the front of Edwin's trousers, his dexterous fingers quickly undoing his belt and buttons as only another man can. Edwin braced his hands against the wall of the lounge as he had done in hundreds of other drawing rooms throughout the long years of his existence. Cesar sank slowly to his knees, his lips following a predetermined path. Thankfully, Cesar was both adroit and fast, since Edwin was in a bit of a hurry.

* * *

"Sir, we're nearly there."

Edwin tried to pry his eyes open, but it was as if his eyelids were permanently superglued shut. His back remained ramrod straight in his seat, and his fingernails had dug permanent grooves into the smooth fiberglass armrests of the co-pilot side of the cockpit. He couldn't understand it at all. He'd been perfectly fine all through takeoff. He'd even found the Hummingbird's speed and altitude somewhat exhilarating. Then, while they were roughly a thousand feet above the patchwork landscape of the *Gypsy Queen*, he made the mistake of looking down and nearly vomited all over himself and the cockpit. Cesar quickly deployed an airsick bag, which saved his clothing, if not his pride. He'd used it four times since.

"Sir?"

Edwin groaned when the Hummingbird dipped into a stomach-lurching descent as it came in for a landing at the shuttle depot adjacent to JFK Airport. "Just kill me now," he whimpered, hunching his shoulders and hanging his head as his stomach begged to be emptied for the umpteenth time. "I want to die. Again."

He wondered how Miss Book had done this. Of course, Miss Book was a crazy inventor type, sort of like Doc Brown, just with an amazing rack. She read techie manuals, and she had likely taught herself how to pilot a Hummingbird through sheer hands-on experience. He groaned as the craft taxied to a stop, the familiar New York landscape rushing by in a nauseating blur of early evening activity.

Cesar had to drag him out of the Hummingbird almost by his collar, and even then, the earth felt like it was still lurching under his feet when he finally touched down on it. He walked in circles for a while, wondering if he was going to fall down. He finally decided on sitting on the cool tarmac as he tried to get his bearings.

"Lord Edwin?" Cesar asked with concern as he stooped over him.

"Aye." Edwin climbed slowly to his feet and tested his footing. He did not fall down. Good.

Cesar glanced at the bulge of Edwin's wings under his suit coat. "Don't you fly?"

Edwin gave the boy a murderous look. "No, I don't bloody fly. That's insane!" Pulling himself together, he started lurching toward the airport runway where a fleet of taxicabs was waiting to pick up fairs. Cesar was clearly not right in the head. If vampires were meant to fly, they would have been given wings…well, wings and no bloody fear of heights.

Cesar jogged alongside him. He looked concerned, a deep frown marking the space between his brilliant blue eyes. "I need your instructions."

"What?"

Cesar looked annoyed. "Your instructions regarding the mission. What are they?"

"The mission," Edwin said, thinking about that. "There's a lounge called The Cockpit on West Twenty-Second Street that requires your immediate attention, soldier."

Cesar shook his head. "I don't understand."

Edwin gave the boy a poignant look. "Here's a hint: It's not an aviation lounge."

It took a moment for Cesar to catch on, but when he did, the look of confusion on his handsome face was quickly replaced by a snarly look of rage. "You tricked me!" Cesar cried, startling Edwin. "You lied about the mission! Foxley gave you no such instructions."

"You're astute. I told you you'd go far."

Edwin could feel waves of anger radiating off the boy. It was most impressive. He tried to ignore it, but Cesar was boring a hole right through the back of his head with his baby blues.

"What?" Edwin asked, signaling a cab headed their way.

"You realize I can't go back!" he shouted. "If I go back, Lord Foxley will punish me. Probably kill me."

"Sucks to be you."

Cesar grabbed his arm just as the cab coasted to a stop beside them and the driver rolled down his window. Cesar's eyes were cold and savage. Edwin was impressed. Cesar certainly had some guts to put his hands upon a Vampire Lord. "You really are a bastard, aren't you, Prince?"

Edwin hedged on a response. The words cut deeper than he expected they would. A hundred years ago, he would have laughed this naïve little boy under the table and called him a fool. A hundred years ago, he would have broken Cesar's arm for daring to touch him. But times change, he supposed. Instead of being annoyed, he felt only sad, alone, and vaguely ashamed.

Miss Book would have taken him to task for the way he had treated the boy. As far as he knew, vampires became more stoic and austere with age, not more wishy-washy. Obviously, there was something very wrong with him.

Edwin smiled to cover up his discomfort. "You're just buggered about the buggering."

Cesar narrowed his eyes. "I'm not some mentally deficient Pleasure Poppet, you know. You used me."

Edwin arched an eyebrow at that. "Lad, I don't remember forcing you to go down on me like some starving Whitechapel whore. Do you know how badly it chafed when you did that tongue thing?"

He remembered the Pakistani cabbie who was sitting in the car, the engine running, and listening with rapt attention to their row. He turned and smiled nicely, saying, "Sorry. A misunderstanding."

The cabbie made a little salute off his forehead as if to say Go on with ya.

Cesar's grip on Edwin's arm increased dramatically. His hand shook. He had quite a grip, that Cesar. "There is no misunderstanding, Prince. You screwed me."

"That's not how I remember it."

Cesar shook his arm violently. "You ruined my career! My life! You owe me! You're taking me with you."

With a pinched expression firmly affixed to his young, scorned face, he yanked open the backseat of the cab and slid down onto the vinyl seat, leaving the door ajar. Edwin thought about slamming the door and summoning the next cab in line. It really would be in his best interests to get rid of the indignant Officer Cesar as soon as possible. But, well, the lad had a point. He couldn't go back to his job. He couldn't go back to the Gypsy Queen. Ever. He owed the kid something for using him. Didn't he?

Bloody hell, he really was turning into an old fogey!

With a snort of frustration, Edwin ducked into the backseat beside Cesar.

Cesar glared at his profile, looking for all the world like a sulky teenager who wasn't getting his way.

Edwin gave the cabbie the address of a pool hall on Canal Street that had quick access to Poppettown. Then he shot Cesar a look. "I'll take you below, but no farther. Once we're down, you're on your own, lad."

Cesar's mouth quirked up on one side. "We'll see about that, Prince. I'm yours now, part of your Court. You have to take care of me." He crossed his arms, looking smug.

"Don't push it, kid." Edwin dug a cigarette out of his jacket pocket and stuck it unlit between his teeth. "You weren't that good."

* * *

Edwin and Cesar were down in Poppettown less than two hours, hoofing it through teeming streets full of hot steam, pollution, and zombie-like Poppets when they came upon the demonstration in the ruins of a burned-out building. Edwin stopped and hooked his fingers in the links of the chain-link fence that surrounded the demolition zone from the street and stared in pale-faced horror at the unlikely sight before him.

In the center of the lot was a mixed group of Poppets, some Pleasure, some Workers. All were standing at rapt attention, listening to a bagman in a ratty pea coat preaching from atop an overturned milk crate. Besides the crate was a large pile of wooden refuse taken from the surrounding buildings. In the center, a tall pole had been erected and what looked like a young vampiress bound to it. It was difficult to tell, since the vampire was on fire and screeching bloody murder, bits of her flesh and hair flaking off like fiery flotsam to land amidst the crowd.

"Bloody hell," Edwin said in horror.

Cesar stopped at the fence and all the color drained from his face.

"Behold the Vampire Masters! Look upon the devils that enslave us!" the ragged bagman was screaming overtop the vampire's cries, presenting the burning girl to the audience. She was little better than a ragged black stick figure with skeletal wings at this point. He started going into a diatribe about God hating vampires and some other nonsense about the Hive and the Great Mother, but Edwin hardly heard.

He didn't have a lot of camaraderie with his fellow vampires, but he wasn't one to let something this barbaric go on. Emitting a growl of rage, he ripped a hole through the chain link with his fingers and ducked through it, charging the demonstration. He was tired, frustrated, and hungry, and he missed Miss Book more than he ever believed was possible. He was also angry as hell, and his anger required attention. He needed a target.

He leaped to the top of the milk crate so he was practically nose to nose with the zealot.

The man didn't recognize him at first, not until Edwin dropped his coat in a puddle at his feet and slowly unfurled his wings for all to see. Large and blunt, they were armored in thick red, dragon-like scales as sharp as shards of broken glass. He could have easily cleaved the head off a man with one twist of his shoulders. He'd seen it done.

The zealot's face flushed when he saw those wings glinting over him like scythes. "You!" he screamed, grabbing Edwin by the front of the suit jacket and shaking him. "Devil-spawn! The Hive will eat your soul, devil! You...will...burn!"

"I'm already burning—with rage!" he shouted back. "You have no idea how much!"

His wings flapped in supreme annoyance, blowing trash all over the lot. He grabbed the zealot by the back of the neck, thought about tearing the scream from his throat with his teeth, then thought better of it. There was only one monster here tonight, and it wasn't him. Instead, he flung the man down among his followers.

"The Vampire Masters!" a woman shouted, pointing her long, thin finger at him.

"Kill the devil!" someone else cried in response, shaking his fists. "Kill the winged ones!"

Edwin grinned wickedly, showing off his great white teeth. He spread his arms and unfurled his great red wings, hoping he looked as demonic as he felt in that moment. "Come and get me, you vile dogs!"

The crowd rushed him as one.

| xi |

Dr. Grott's house, like so many buildings built on the edge of the factories, was nearly obscured by a thick, eye-watering shroud of steam and pollution. Eliza stepped off the trolley, moved to the tall, familiar, iron-barbed gate, and stopped, a handkerchief over her nose. A dull thumping carried like a giant's heartbeat through the ground, the vibration of the great steam machines that worked far above in unseen towers. The air was wet and almost touchable this close to the steam machines, hence the name: Wet Street.

"That's it, isn't it?" Derek asked, coming up beside her.

She nodded. The red-bricked warehouse sat solemnly on a dirt lot so desolate even the trash in the street seemed to shun it. No one lived on Wet Street. No one normal, anyway. The constant underground thumping was enough to drive even the sanest man over the edge. Not that Dr. Grott minded; he'd taken the bend long before he'd ever found himself down in Poppettown.

Eliza remembered him as a big, stoop-shouldered, grandfatherly man with crazy zealot eyes, a crushing depression, and a stuttering speech impairment. He'd been a great professor once, in another life. As a young man, he'd lectured all over the country on biochemistry and flesh mechanics. Then, one day, his wife and daughter died in a particularly gruesome airship disaster. He never recovered from it, or from the years of isolation and alcoholism that followed.

Eventually, the universities threw him out and he found himself down among the Poppets, the only people who would have him. He'd adopted their cause and had pushed to replace Worker Poppets with automatons, but his experiments were seldom successful, and his theories impractical and unworkable.

Eliza tested the gate. It swung inward, creaking like something out of an old horror movie. She started down a footpath worn down to rock but with no discernable markers and cautiously approached the building.

Little had changed. The warehouse loomed, though it seemed to lean a bit more than in the past, the bricks darkened by pollution and covered in arcane graffiti. The door was still a crooked wooden affair with a ring in it, like something that belonged on a medieval barn. It was slightly ajar. She hesitated and put her hand in her pocket where Derek had lent her a small handgun, afraid she might be interrupting a break-in. She listened but heard nothing. She realized she could stand here all day and probably hear nothing.

Taking a deep breath, she pushed the door slowly open.

The warehouse stretched out ahead of her, as dark and ominous as a steel-lined throat, with an iron catwalk running the full circumference of the place two stories above their heads. Her memories of the lab were of Dr. Grott crowding every inch of the dank, sad space with long trestles full of lab equipment.

She glanced around in surprise and wonder, fingering the gun. Most of those tables were overturned. Lab equipment like microscopes, skinner boxes, bio-safety cabinets, lab glass, and computers lay in broken heaps across the concrete floor. Someone had come in with a blunt instrument and wrecked the place so thoroughly that it was almost unrecognizable.

Derek whistled. "Someone didn't like your Dr. Grott."

Eliza moved between all the glittering debris, looking around in wonder and confusion. "I don't understand this." She opened a random medical cabinet only to find more broken bottles and dented canisters lying on their sides. "Dr. Grott was harmless, a crazy old inventor," she said with a mounting sense of panic. "This doesn't make any sense!"

"Maybe some kids were looking for drugs. It happens here all the time."

A glass beaker fell and shattered at her feet. "Dr. Grott didn't have any drugs! Everyone knew that."

"Look at this." Derek moved toward a darkened corner and ran his hand over the smooth surface of a long, white tube-like appliance made of heavy gauge steel. It had survived through sheer resilience. "It looks like some kind of torpedo."

"No," said Eliza, moving toward it. "That's a hyperbaric chamber. It's used to compress metals, to test them or to make them stronger."

"Like the titanium."

"Yes." She examined it closely. "Exactly." A few feet away, half-buried by debris, she spotted a heap of scrap metal lying on the floor. It looked dusty, years old...and vaguely humanoid. "Oh, my god."

"What the hell is that?"

She knelt to uncover it. "I think this is one of Dr. Grott's machine-men. He actually did it!"

She started explaining about Dr. Grott's theory about automatons—"machine-men," as he liked to call them—eventually coming to replace the Worker Poppets at the steam machines, all the while examining the metal corpse. The humanoid figure was darkened with age but not rusted. No corrosion.

"It's so resilient! His titanium must be worth a fortune down here as contraband." Lying overturned beside the machine-man was a box full of munitions. She took one of the bullets out of the box to compare it to the one in her pocket. As she had suspected, they were made of the same substance.

Derek crouched beside her. "So Dr. Grott has been making these bullets?"

"Yes, but I don't understand why. He's a humanitarian."

"Maybe he was bought off."

She glared at him. "If you knew him, you wouldn't say that."

"Maybe if we can find him, we can ask."

A door slammed on a downstairs level, making them both jump in response. Obviously, the warehouse wasn't as empty as she first assumed.

Without saying a word, Derek pressed a finger to his lips, drew his Colt, and moved toward a door on the far side of the room, the one that led to the basement. He tested it, finding it unlocked. He moved his hand away from the doorknob, keeping his gun at the ready.

Eliza moved to the opposite side and drew her borrowed gun. She wasn't familiar with it, but after a few seconds of playing with the weapon, she had it loaded and ready. Derek raised his eyebrows in appreciation. He always said she was a quick study.

She nodded at the door as light footsteps made their way up the stairs.

The moment the door creaked open, Derek reached out, snagged the arm of a thin, ragged teenage girl, and folded her slight weight against his body, pushing the gun against her cheek.

Eliza immediately lowered her weapon. "Wait, Derek. Stop!" she said, and Derek's hold on her eased, though not by much.

The girl had pale, almost colorless hair that fell in knotted tangles around her face and huge, dark, quag-like eyes. She looked like she'd come from a battlefield, her pinafore dress dirtied and torn at the shoulder, her apron spattered with blood. She barely reacted at all to the gun that was kissing her cheek.

Derek slowly let her go, though he didn't immediately return the gun to his holster.

The girl swayed in the middle of the destroyed lab, looking like a corpse exhumed from her own grave, her face papery white and bruised. There was blood not just on her clothes, Eliza saw, but in her hair as well, and blood masking half of her face when she turned her head to stare at them both.

The girl watched them, her breath hitching in her throat. Then, unexpectedly, she dropped to her knees as if her body had no bones in it at all, wrapped her arms about her own thin shoulders, and began to scream hysterically.

***

The girl's name was Maria Hand and she was sixteen years old, an ex-Pleasure Poppet like Eliza and Derek. She was only two years younger than Eliza.

It was the usual sad story. When life had become unbearable at her Court, she had run away, taking sanctuary in the underground like so many before her. A pimp had immediately seized upon her—she was young and fresh, and like most Pleasure Poppets, she knew how to please a man. Those were not good years, she said, talking as if she was a hundred years old. But then she discovered she had other skills, like fixing mechanical devices. That led to her taking work as Dr. Grott's assistant. She owed Dr. Grott a great deal for helping her to get off the streets, she said—more than she could ever thank him for, especially now.

Eliza went to one knee before Maria's chair and laid a cold cloth against the girl's jaw. It was bruised almost black as if someone had punched her repeatedly. Maria never even flinched. She was young but tall, with the typical oversized breasts and exaggerated small hands and feet of a Pleasure Poppet. Her face had been pretty, once. Now, her lip was so broken it was nearly bisected, one of her eyes was mashed shut, and one whole half of her face was a mass of spongy purplish bruises.

Eliza, her heart squeezing inside of her at the sight of the girl, moved the cloth to the bruised side of Maria's face, trying to combat the extreme swelling. Again, the girl never flinched, as if the pain meant almost nothing to her. As if she had become inured to it through sheer force of constant exposure.

"Where's Dr. Grott now?" Eliza carefully asked.

Maria whimpered, her one good eye going wide as she started down the road to a panic attack once more. Eliza took the girl in her arms, shushing her and resting Maria's head on her shoulder. That seemed to quell her. Maria was all loose bird-like bones, a typical undernourished Poppet, practically starved from the day of her birth to maintain an unrealistically slender figure for her vampire masters.

The thought made Eliza sick to recall. "Easy, sweetie. We won't hurt you." She cradled Maria's head of dirty, unwashed hair. "We'll protect you. We came here to see Dr. Grott."

The girl shook her head slowly back and forth.

"Dr. Grott is gone?"

"Dead, I think."

Eliza felt a shock. "Where...where is he?"

Maria sucked back on the tears in her throat. "Downstairs."

She looked up at Derek, who nodded and started down the stairs to the basement, his gun drawn. Eliza turned her attention back on the girl, cupping her swollen face carefully in her hands. "Can you tell me what happened?"

Maria nodded but didn't immediately speak. Her dress was soaked with blood. There were gaping tears in the bodice, and the skirt was shorn to bits. Bruises crawled up Maria's legs. Eliza was terrified to discover what kind of damage lurked beneath the fabric.

"Who did this to you?" she asked, her voice raw with horror.

Maria swallowed. "The clockwork man."

"A clockwork man did this to you?"

Maria began to tremble.

"Did this same clockwork man hurt Dr. Grott?"

A nod.

"Do you know why?"

Maria gave her a glassy look. "Dr. Grott wouldn't tell him about his work."

Derek came back up the stairs and gave Eliza a funny look. He looked paler than usual. "You should probably see this."

* * *

Downstairs, they found an unfinished concrete basement that Dr. Grott had been using for storage. It was filled with the debris of his work and many of his half-finished devices, but adjacent to that was a small, dank root cellar lined with jars of foodstuffs and other supplies. Spattered across hundreds of broken bell jars was the blood of the old man, and at the center of the room, Dr. Grott himself.

He was tied to a chair, quite dead. His face was a mask of bloody black bruises, his toes smashed, most of his fingers sliced off, and his teeth scattered like dice across the dirty floor. Eliza smelled the blood long before she ducked into the low-ceilinged room. The dirt floor had absorbed much of the spillage, but the thick, meaty stench of vicious open wounds lay heavy on the air, making the place stink like an abattoir.

Eliza felt her pulse ticking in her throat as she came around to examine Dr. Grott's remains. Her stomach did a somersault at the sight, and she covered her mouth with both hands and jerked away, racing for the room next door. Dr. Grott was unrecognizable, which was a good thing, she supposed. She threw up in the corner only once. If he'd looked more like the Dr. Grott she remembered, she would have wound up crawling out of that room.

The last two days of her life had officially become nightmare fodder. She would never sleep again without a light on. And, she knew, she would never be able to erase the image of Dr. Grott's death from her memory, the pathetic visage of a dead old man, his face so raw and full of broken bones and teeth that his own family wouldn't have been able to identify him, had they still lived.

She huddled against the basement wall to get her bearings. Derek approached her with wary concern like she was a rabid animal that might snap at any moment.

"It just happened. Maybe a couple of hours ago." She was very proud of herself. At least she hadn't passed out.

"Should we take the doctor's body up?" he asked softly.

"We shouldn't disturb the evidence. The police will want to investigate this."

"You must be kidding me."

She looked up at him.

Derek indicated the basement area, the gun still in his hand. "You've been in the overworld too long, Alisa. Do you really think the police will care about any of this? This is Poppettown. Unless someone very rich or very famous dies, the police don't do shit. Some crazy old man who was trying to make robots isn't even going to make their radar."

"What about the girl?" she insisted, her blood boiling now. "She needs to file an assault charge."

Derek sighed. "The girl is a Poppet, Alisa. She's no more important than you or I am. They won't investigate, trust me."

He was probably right. She wanted to cry...it infuriated her so. It made her want to scream and pound her fists against the wall until they bled. There had to be something they could do, someone out there who would hold the person who did this responsible. And if not...well, she'd find this creature herself. This clockwork man. She'd find out where he lived and what places he frequented. She'd hunt him down, make his life a living hell. She'd make him pay for what he'd done to Dr. Grott. And to Maria.

Eliza leaned against the wall, shaking with rage. She had to work to make her voice even and unhurried. "The one who did this...Maria called him the 'clockwork man.' What does that mean?"

"Sounds like Talos to me," Derek said. He glanced behind as if afraid the very mention of the name might conjure something deadly out of the dark. Satisfied they were safe and alone, he put his gun back into his armpit holster. "If he has a real name, but no one knows it. They just call him Talos."

"Is he a vampire?"

"No, a Poppet...well, he was." He sounded bitter. "A Red Collar...an assassin for hire. He takes work from anyone. He has some very expensive habits."

"Drugs?"

"Implants. His body is mostly made up of prosthetics. That's why he's in high demand. But he burns all the money he makes on more implants, so he's always looking for work."

Eliza rubbed her forehead where a tremendous headache was stomping through her skull with combat boots on. "The kind of mercenary that a Vampire Lord like Rathbone might use," she mused as much to herself as to Derek. "Do you know where this Talos hangs out? Where he gets his assignments from?"

Derek shook his head. "You don't want to go anywhere near Talos, believe me. He's nastier than any vampire."

Eliza narrowed her eyes and glared up at him. "I don't want to go anywhere near Rathbone, either, but I may need to. If he's the vamp who sent the shooter after me, then he got his bullets from Dr. Grott. Dr. Grott is dead now, and that's an awfully big coincidence, don't you think?"

Derek gave her a knowing look. "You think there's a connection?"

"If I can find Talos, maybe I can get an audience with Rathbone."

"Alisa...don't you think all of these people are a little out of your league?"

She couldn't believe this! She threw up her arms in despair. "I am so far out of my league that it isn't even funny anymore! But that won't stop the Vampire Courts from coming after me. And that means I could be trapped down here for the rest of my life."

She pointed savagely at the root cellar. "And if I stay here, it won't be long before I wind up like that. Now, unless you have a better idea of where to go from here, where can we find this Talos?"

Derek hunched his shoulders as if he was sustaining blows. "Alisa, please. You just want to find Talos so you can hurt him for hurting Maria." He shook his head. "I know you. You think you're some kind of urban avenger. You need your brain checked."

"My brain is fine!" she yelled, pushing herself back to her feet through sheer force of rage. "And if you won't help me, then get the hell out of my way!" She pushed past him and headed for the stairs.

Someone had shot her, threatened her, hurt an innocent little girl, and tortured and murdered an old, dear friend of hers. If some petty mercenary addicted to plastic surgery was the key to finding Rathbone, then they absolutely had to talk. And if it ended with Talos's grey matter splattered across the floor at her feet, so be it!

Derek took her by the arm, halting her mid-step. "Alisa," he warned, shaking his head, "if you kick this wasps' nest, something bad is going to come out. What do you think you're doing?"

"Doing? I'm being proactive." Eliza set her jaw and narrowed her eyes. She thought about the agent she had shot. It hadn't been so hard to do. "First, I find out if Talos was hired by Rathbone. Then I kill the bastard."

"And if he wasn't?"

"I kill the bastard."

"You're serious, aren't you?"

"Never more so."

Derek nearly laughed at her bravado.

"What?" she demanded.

"I was just remembering," Derek explained. "As a child, you were always the smallest and scrawniest of us all. And yet, you were always the toughest and the bravest among us. All the other kids at the Scholomance turned to you, you know. They knew you would protect them."

She hadn't known that and hedged on a response.

Derek gathered her into his arms. "This isn't the world above, Alisa," he whispered in her ear. "We're not in New York, and there are no rules. You know that, right?"

It took her a moment to unclench her jaw and answer. "I know. It's more like hell. But I'm not afraid."

"You're not, are you?"

She shook her head vehemently.

He pulled her tight against his body, holding her the way she had held him in the dark that had frightened him so badly all those years ago. "You realize you don't have anything to prove, right? You could just come home with me, stay with me, and forget all of this. I can protect you."

He touched her face, her hair. He was close enough to kiss her again. "Do you believe me, Alisa?"

She nodded.

"Then why do this?"

"Because I'm tired of crying! I'm tired of being afraid! I'm tired of running!" She stared at him, numb and yet full of rage and fire. "Why should I let them win? Why should I let them drive me underground and make me afraid? It isn't fair!"

He smiled. "You do know that life isn't fair, right?"

"I know!" she cried. "I just refuse to accept it!"

***

Upstairs again, Eliza took a few moments to get her temper under control. There was no point in frightening Maria with another outburst. Afterward, she put her suit coat around Maria's narrow, shivering shoulders and gave her a cup of water.

"Do you have any idea why the clockwork man would do this to you or to Dr. Grott?" she asked.

Maria frowned. "Don't know. Dr. Grott was very upset these past few days. But that wasn't unusual for Dr. Grott."

"Why do you say that?"

Maria licked her lips nervously, her voice velvet soft. "He was always worried about his work being stolen. He even memorized all his notes and then destroyed them and deleted all his files. He said he wouldn't be working for them anymore."

Maria paused but didn't immediately elaborate on who they were. "So, when the clockwork man came, he couldn't find anything. He tried to make Dr. Grott tell, but he wouldn't do it, not even when he was hurting me." She squinted out of her swollen face at them both. "The clockwork man said he would kill me too, and I guess he tried, but I didn't die."

He'd gotten close, though, Eliza realized. Had Maria not been a Poppet, her bones reinforced and her flesh tougher and harder to hurt than a human's, there was a good chance she'd have wound up dead just like poor Dr. Grott downstairs. "Who is them?"

"The people Dr. Grott was working for."

"Do you know their names, sweetie?"

Maria shook her head. "He never told me."

"When you say his work, do you mean the machine-men he was making?"

Again, Maria shook her head. She glanced over to where the machine-man lay face down on the floor. "No. the machines were no good. They were too expensive to make. He stopped doing that a long time ago and started making the guns instead."

Eliza raised her eyebrows at that. With the hem of her shirt, she wiped at a particularly nasty raw scrape at the corner of Maria's mouth. Maria never flinched. "What kind of guns?"

Maria shrugged. "Don't know. I just helped Dr. Grott with little stuff. I ran errands for him mostly or repaired things when they broke."

Leaving Maria with Derek, Eliza started rummaging through the debris of the lab, tossing over shelves and moving tables, but there were no notes, notebooks, computer disks, nothing. But then, Talos probably took all of that, she reflected. She glanced around the workshop, finally settling on the CPU that lay overturned and fire-blackened on the floor. She picked it up and righted it on a nearby workbench. The monitor and keyboard were broken, useless. She threw them away.

"What are you doing?" Derek asked. He glanced up from where he was checking his munitions.

"You know, if Talos was just here, he might come back anytime and throw the place one more time just to see if he missed anything. We should get out of here."

"I know," she answered. "I think that's a great idea, Derek. You should do that. And take Maria with you."

But Derek didn't move.

She wiped debris off a chair and stationed it in front of the CPU. If it was true and she had some queer talent for communicating with machines, she saw no reason why she couldn't read the information from the computer's hard drive. Anyway, it was a theory. And since there was no permanent way to wipe a hard drive, she figured it was worth a try. Worst-case scenario, she'd look like a fool in front of Derek, who probably already suspected she was crazy.

She sat in the chair, put her hands on the burned-out CPU, and closed her eyes. For a while, nothing happened. She listened to Derek moving around restlessly and started feeling very foolish indeed. In time, her mind started to wander and she had to refocus her attention.

It took a long time, but then, she felt a sudden and familiar spark. Her fingers felt welded to the still-warm metal of the device, and a nauseating collage of images struck her head like a series of hammer blows. There was too much! There was at least a teragig's worth of files on the hard drive—the equivalent of an ocean full of data. She had to find a way to narrow it down.

Guns, she thought. Show me guns. Schematics. Statistics. Documents. Guns.

She felt a jolt as the CPU responded. At her command, she watched a series of complex schematics open up. Thousands of documents, hundreds of illustrations. She saw everything related to guns on the hard drive. There was still too much—weapon engineering had been consuming Dr. Grott's life for the past three years. She narrowed it down further to only the more recent files.

"Alisa?" Derek's voice sounded very far off, like a cosmic signal off a distant planet. "Your eyes are glowing."

"That's...interesting," she responded. After searching through a few thousand file folders in a matter of microseconds, she finally found something interesting. She read three or four hundred pages worth of documents almost at once, analyzed them, and then stored them away in her brain for later analysis.

Enough, she thought, growing panicky now. Her head felt like it was full of wasps, and her skull felt like it was developing a crack down the center. She felt the tickle of a nosebleed starting. That's enough!

The images fluttered by, then switched off like a TV screen going black. Eliza lunged back in her seat, a drop of blood flowing from her left nostril.

The CPU before her sat smoldering. She had sucked out a dizzying amount of data, overloaded it, and burned it out…again.

"Alisa, are you all right?" Derek asked, hovering at her side. He looked terrified by what he had just witnessed.

Eliza wiped at the blood in her nose with her handkerchief. "Couldn't be better, Derek. Couldn't be better."

* * *

The three of them jumped a trolley back to midtown.

Eliza and Derek sat in the back again, this time with Maria wedged between them. Eliza had blanketed the girl's bruised body with her coat to forestall any questions from concerned passengers. Then she realized how silly her fears were. The trolleys were automated, so there were no drivers, no conductors. As a result, their car was empty, not that the Poppets, assuming there were any on board, would be self-aware enough to notice Maria's injuries.

Derek took her by the elbow and looked her in the eye. "What did you do back there?"

She dabbed at her nose with a tissue. It came away red. Everything felt so surreal. "I read the computer, Derek."

"You read Dr. Grott's computer?" he said in blatant surprise.

"Yes." She wasn't about to lie about it.

Derek shook his head in confusion. He looked ready to ask about that, then seemed to change his mind. "What did you…read about?"

"Guns," she answered. "The guns he was making."

Maria perked up beside her but didn't interrupt.

Eliza's eyes filled with unwelcomed tears. "Dr. Grott was a great man, Derek. A true humanitarian. He cared about Poppets even though he himself was human."

"He couldn't have been that great a person if he was inventing guns."

She bit her lip, the loss of her friend cutting down into her soul like the sharp edge of a knife. "He had so many great dreams, and the machine-men really did work. But no one took him seriously. No one helped him. He was all alone. All his research...his whole life...all of it was wasted."

She closed her eyes, briefly but quickly shuffling through the gigs of information in her head. "According to one of Dr. Grott's journals, a client visited him and offered to finance his dreams of building the machine-men if Dr. Grott was willing to manufacture arms and munitions."

"The titanium bullets."

"Yes."

"So, someone did buy him off."

Eliza shuddered. Did Derek have to be so blunt?

"Dr. Grott didn't want to make firearms for the client, but he was desperate. He was becoming increasingly worried about the Poppets. There has been so much unrest here these past few years..."

She bowed her head and stared at her feet as the trolley coasted up and down the hills. "The client returned several times, demanding even bigger and more elaborate weapons. Dr. Grott didn't want to work with the client anymore, but by then, he was desperate for money; he'd accrued too many debts down in the bars and casinos. Eventually, Dr. Grott invented a gun called a sonic boomer, hoping it would satisfy the client and make him go away. It works by generating high-frequency sound waves so powerful that they can disrupt molecules. Even a small handgun can collapse an entire skyscraper with a single shot."

"Is that why Talos killed him? Because of the boomer gun?"

"I don't know why Talos killed him. There's nothing in Dr. Grott's notes about Talos, and the client was never mentioned by name. Dr. Grott's notes are mostly his idealistic fantasies about the machine-men. That and the design for the gun. But the gun is bad, Derek. A weapon of mass destruction."

"Did Dr. Grott finish the gun?"

"I don't know. I don't think so. There were no field tests."

Derek turned to Maria and put his hand on her shoulder. She flinched noticeably. "Do you know if he finished the boomer gun? Was there a prototype made?"

Maria stared up at him with one eye swollen shut and one round with terror.

Derek shook her. "What was Grott doing when Talos visited you?"

Eliza sniffed back the sticky blood in her nose. "Stop it, Derek. She's been through enough, and it's obvious she doesn't know much. There were no tests conducted; hopefully, that means there are no actual working guns. We'll find out when we talk to Talos."

Derek glared at her as if she was insane. "Talos is going to fucking kill you, Alisa."

She was about to argue her point when they came to a rolling stop at an intersection where some Worker Poppets were standing around, waiting for the trolley to take them back to their hovels in the inner city. Their heads were craned heavenward, reminding Eliza of poultry birds waiting to drown at the first instance of rain.

"Maybe that's why Talos paid Grott a visit," Derek persisted, dropping his voice to a conspiratorial whisper as the Poppets boarded even though none of them looked bright enough to understand any part of their conversation. "Maybe he refused to hold up his end of the bargain. Maybe Talos was sent to gather the schematics and any prototypes, but when he got there, he discovered that Grott had destroyed all of the evidence. Goodbye, Dr. Grott."

"That does make sense," Eliza agreed. She dug out the bullet in her pocket and turned it idly in her gloved hand. "What I don't understand is why Dr. Grott would let someone bully him into building arms when he was so against warfare. He was a pacifist, Derek. He didn't believe in the end justifying the means."

Derek sighed as they rumbled into midtown. "People make mistakes, Alisa. People get desperate. Good people do bad things all the time. Nothing is black and white."

She closed her eyes. Derek was right. She couldn't help but be reminded of Mr. McGillicuddy. Foxley implied he was an evil man, a monster who'd done terrible, inhuman things, but maybe he was just a man, neither evil nor good, a decent man who had made some bad mistakes. She couldn't figure him out. She couldn't figure out where the monster ended and the man she might have fallen in love with began. Maybe they were even one and the same.

Thankfully, by the time they'd reached the heart of midtown, her thoughts were starting to clear out like someone pulling cobwebs away. She suggested returning to the Starlight Casino instead of going back to Derek's apartment. Derek gave her one of his looks like he didn't get her, so she added, "I don't want to be seen at your place twice. The guards might notice and think it's odd you're bringing the same guy home."

Derek's jaw ticked. "I don't bring guys home. I don't bring anyone home."

She looked at him with surprise. "What about the clothes in your closet?"

Derek blinked and smoothed out his face professionally. "What about them?"

"You have clothes of all kinds in there, for men and women." It only took Eliza a moment to figure it out. "You're part of the Red

Doors, aren't you?" She whispered it barely loud enough for him to hear. "You help Poppets like Maria. You put them up in your place until they can find their feet, don't you?"

Derek looked mildly embarrassed, and she knew then that she was right.

Maria leaned against her and Eliza wrapped her arms protectively around the girl's shivering shoulders. "Can you arrange a room for us down at the casino for a day or two?"

The casinos were among the few generators of hard cash in Poppettown, and most nights, they teemed with tourists. A person could lose themselves in a crowded room. It would make for a good cover.

"I'll pay for it," Eliza insisted. "I'll do whatever is necessary."

Derek looked like he might argue, then shook his head and folded his hands. "No. A gift."

He didn't sound particularly thrilled with all of her plotting. It would be so easy to go with Derek, to let him take care of her. Leave all of this behind. Run away with him. But she couldn't do that to Derek or the Red Doors. To Maria. To anyone.

Maybe one day they would have their time. Just not now. There were simply too many bad guys out there looking for her right now.

* * *

Derek set her up in the high-rollers suite at the Starlight Casino Hotel. Eliza was pleased with the accommodations; the suite was popular with visiting celebrities, and she needed her lodgings to be a little flashy to pull off her plans.

After she'd gotten Maria cleaned up and under the covers of the king-sized bed in one of the suite's two enormously posh, interconnected rooms, she went to explore the rest of the suite.

She soon found the things she needed. The first she found inside the big double-door wardrobe. As she had hoped, the suite came with complimentary evening clothes, three black-tie suits and six evening gowns of various sizes and designs. She pulled the smallest of the suits out, rummaged around until she found the complimentary sewing supplies in the drawer of the desk, and settled down by the big picture window that had a panoramic view of the swarming streets below to hand sew her alterations by false moonlight.

Two hours later, three knocks fell on the door, their signal. "Alisa?"

She let Derek in. He was pushing a room service cart ahead of him. "What are you up to?" he asked, sounding concerned.

"Oh, this and that."

He looked over the room, then at the chair by the window, noting the clothes hanging across the back of it. "Do you ever stop working?" He sat down on the edge of the bed and glanced at it longingly.

Eliza uncovered a dish and sniffed appreciatively at the contents. "If I stop doing things, I'll wind up dead." She covered the dish up. Her body was hungry enough, but her stomach was too nervous and fluttery to handle food. She kept thinking about all of the things that could go wrong tonight.

She looked at Derek, still staring expectantly at her. "Can you pass a message along for me to any interested parties in the casino circuit?"

He blanched. "Like?"

"Like a certain vampire named Lord Westmacott is visiting the casino on important business but is receiving threatening letters from an unknown party. The Lord wishes to hire an experienced security detail. He is willing to pay handsomely, of course." She hesitated. "Do you know who you can inform to get the word out?"

Derek stood and moved to the window to examine her sewing. He lifted the slacks she had cuffed and sewn, then the jacket she had altered. "There are channels," he admitted. He turned and glanced at her, holding up the clothes to eyeball her fit. "But I've never heard of a Lord Westmacott."

"Of course not." Eliza went to take the clothes from him. "I've just made him up."

* * *

The suit fit her exactly, snug and glossy, though she'd needed some very tight bandages to bind her rather generous cleavage. She combed her short black hair straight back away from her ears, using liberal amounts of hair oil, then applied a sheen of pale foundation primer to emphasize her cheekbones and forehead. With her dark coloring, she knew she would look just like an undead creature wearing foundation to make him appear more human.

She started tying a formal black bowtie around her neck, then switched it out for a bold red silk cravat with a gold pin. It was what a vampire would wear.

When she stepped out of the bathroom, pulling on a pair of embroidered white evening gloves, she found Derek staring at her in blatant shock as if he didn't recognize her, which was exactly the reaction she was looking for. She strutted across the room, then pivoted like she was on a catwalk, the tails of her tuxedo flying. "Convincing or no?"

"Convincing. But why a vampire? And why a man?"

"If Talos is as desperate for money as you say he is, he'll want to score big tonight." She smoothed the cravat knotted just high enough to hide her lack of an Adam's apple. "Only a Vampire Lord would have the kind of funds he's looking for. He wouldn't want to miss an opportunity like this."

"A lot of big Hollywood stars try to look like vampires, you know. Mostly, they fail horribly at it."

She was ready for that volley. "Most Hollywood stars haven't grown up among vampires." She returned to the vanity mirror in the bathroom and searched her reflection for flaws. Her vampireness was extremely understated, just the way she wanted it, and just as a real vampire's would be. After all, she was a human pretending to be a vampire pretending to be a human.

Derek watched her carefully. "You could go in as a vampiress, you know. There's always a chance you might blow your own cover."

Eliza bit her lip and touched her hair. "But Talos raped Maria." She stared long and hard at the mirror, trying to fight down the almost rib-cracking anger that was trying to rise up inside of her again. She closed her eyes and relished the feeling—embraced it. If she was angry, then she wouldn't feel scared half out of her skin about the idea of facing the clockwork man tonight.

"She told me that while I was helping her bathe. There was just too much blood. He ripped her up something awful, Derek." She swallowed and waited for her heart to stop ticking so fiercely. "That means Talos hates women. I have a better chance of earning his respect as a man."

"If he shows up."

"He will. I hope he will. Red Collars often do bodyguard service between jobs, if it pays well enough."

According to Derek, word had been circulating through the casino for a good few hours, and she knew too many people were far too interested in the business of a visiting Vampire Lord not to talk. If Talos was close by, he'd probably already heard about the job. Chances were good he kept his ear to the ground around the casinos in order to collect jobs. Work was easy to get that way.

Swallowing hard, she lifted her eyes in the mirror one last time, straightened the cravat, and stepped back into the room, trying to perfect the effortless glide that vampires were so capable of.

"Alisa." Derek took her by the wrist as she was heading for the door.

"Yes, Derek."

He gathered her into his arms, being careful not to disrupt her clothing. He gave her a poignant look. "You know how I feel about you."

She swallowed nervously. "Yes, Derek. I know."

"You belong with me. With the Red Doors. We do so much good." He hesitated. "There's a place for you here, Alisa. A place among us. With me."

She nodded. "I know that." She stared deep into his simmering blue eyes. She touched his face. "But I have to do this first, Derek."

"Is it really so important?"

"It is to me."

"After, then?"

"Perhaps."

He let her go and she moved to the door.

He watched her, the moment solemn, his thumbs in the loopholes of his trousers like an Old West gunslinger made to carry a heavy burden. Finally, he smiled, breaking the mood. "Good luck. And don't get yourself killed, you crazy girl."

She smiled more bravely than she felt as her hand fell on the doorknob.

| xii |

"Come on, you dogs. Come and get me!"

As the first of the Poppets reached Edwin and started snatching at his clothes with the intention of pulling him down into their irate numbers, he spread his wings and leaped up and out of their reach. He then raised his wrist to his mouth and bit deeply into his own flesh. A long viscous stream of black vampire blood flowed.

He was a weak bloodkinetic, having inherited the trick from Lord Foxley. Though, unlike Foxley, he could manipulate only his own blood and not the blood of others. But the things he could do with that were...interesting, to say the least. Before his blood reached the ground, he willed it to reform into a long, chain-like manriki, then added some barbs just for the hell of it.

Long ago, as a young vamp, he'd studied bujutsu, the art of war, at the Temple at Shingon in the shadow of Mount Koya. His less than brilliant expertise with swords and knives had made his sensei despair, but he unexpectedly excelled with whips and chain weapons. He did not tell his sensei, a woman, that he had learned the art of the whip from a disciple of the Marquis de Sade; she would have likely kicked him in the balls.

As he floated back to earth, he gripped the end of the blood manriki in one hand and flicked it out in sentient loops.

The weapon could not actually harm vampires of his own bloodline, and it couldn't really hurt humans, but it was strong and, more importantly, scary as hell. He wrapped it about the ankles of the man grabbing at him and yanked his feet out from under him. With a grunt, the man went down hard.

A woman immediately replaced him, crawling nimbly to the top of the milk crate he stood upon and flinging herself at him, her hands hooked into claws. He cracked the manriki and it encircled her shoulders and lifted her up and off her feet, knocking her back into the wall of angry Poppet protesters. Others rushed forward and met with similar fates.

After a few minutes, Edwin found himself losing patience with this lot. He cracked the blood whip like a lion tamer, and the fierceness of it drove the crowd back in fright. When someone approached, he lashed out at them. The attacks were more psychological than physical. The manriki was loud and left behind a sizzling psychic hum where it touched human skin, giving the victims the impression of pain without actually inflicting any damage. They deserved a lot worse than some pseudo-pain for what they had done to the vampiress tied to the stake, but if he wanted to kill everyone who had ever offended him, there wouldn't be many people left on planet Earth.

The crowd was composed mostly of Worker Poppets and ex-Pleasure Poppets. Despite their genetics, none had the reflexes he had. As soon as they learned that they couldn't ambush him, they started backing off or running away while making all kinds of empty threats.

When the lot had mostly cleared out, Edwin snaked the manriki up around his shoulder and glared at the few who lingered, daring them to approach him. They decided that discretion was indeed the better part of valor and took off running, leaving him standing in the dirt lot with only Cesar and the burning vampiress, still tied to the stake like some medieval witch put to flame.

There was nothing he could do for her; the vampiress was dying. But he couldn't let this travesty continue. He climbed down off the milk crate and used his coat to beat out the remaining flames of the funeral pyre. The coat quickly went from white to a singed black color, not that he cared.

The vampiress' flesh had melted and burned right to the stake, forcing him to rip the whole thing out of the ground and lay it down gently amidst the debris. There were iron chains about her wrists, but those had long since burned her flesh down to the bone. Her body was little more than a flaking black husk, though her eyes were alive. Aware. He knew it was silly, but he couldn't help but pull the iron shackles away, despite there being very little of her hands left. No one deserved to die in chains.

She tried to form words, to say his name, but she had no mouth to speak. He put his hand on her shoulder and said, "I'll discover who is doing this. I'll end it. I swear." He waited until the spark of her life went out of her eyes—it didn't take very long—and then he picked up his charred coat and laid it over her lifeless body. He crossed himself and said Last Rites, then sent up a short prayer to God that He would see fit to forgive the vampiress any transgressions and welcome her home. After that, he climbed slowly to his feet.

Cesar stood beside Edwin, looking pale and surprised by the care he had taken with the vampiress. "Look, I'm sorry..." he began, searching for the right words. "I'm sorry about your friend."

"She wasn't my friend," Edwin explained. "I didn't know her."

"Then...why?"

He glared at the young man. "If you'd found a human dying in similar conditions, what would you have done?"

Cesar looked uncomfortable.

Edwin ignored him. He couldn't understand it, looking at the dead vampire. Poppets and vampires had always had their differences. That was true enough. But it had never been like this, the violence so overt and...crude. When had the Poppets grown so bloodthirsty?

A dark figure was crossing the lot toward them, its footsteps so light its feet hardly seemed to touch the earth. Cesar flinched and darted behind Edwin, fearful it was another insane Poppet closing in on them, but Edwin immediately recognized the tall, sexless figure wrapped in a coat and a scarf. He felt the pull of her blood. His blood.

The manriki melted off his shoulder as he stood up and turned to her. "Mouse," he said.

"Lord Edwin." Mouse's voice rasped in a way that was course, ambiguous, and familiar.

Edwin lurched forward to meet the figure. His heart was ticking very loudly in his throat. At first, he thought it was surprise or relief, then he felt the mechanics of his clockwork heart stuttering like a piece of bad machinery. A sudden, terrible lethargy overwhelmed him. He realized—belatedly, and with some concern—that his overwound heart was locking up.

Too soon, he thought. He tasted blood on his mouth. He couldn't die without seeing Miss Book one last time. He couldn't die without saving her. He dropped to his knees, and Mouse lunged forward, embracing him before he could fall to the ground. Her face, creased with worry, was the last thing he saw before darkness overwhelmed him.

* * *

He woke in the dark in a storeroom lined with boxes and bottles, lying on an unfamiliar cot. Shadows shifted dustily around him, halos of light. A woman stood over him. For a moment, he thought it was Miss Book here to wake him for some engagement, and he hoped that everything that had happened to him had been a bad dream. He even rejoiced. Then he realized who it was: Mouse. But that was still better than nothing. That meant he wasn't dead. Not yet, anyway.

"Lord Edwin, tell me what to do." Mouse crouched over him, sounding frantic. "Do you need blood?"

No, he mouthed. Blood could not help him with this. He forced his voice up. It sounded sandpapery to him. "...mustn't tell... anyone." He reached for the key around his neck, under his shirt. He had trouble holding it in his fingers, which felt fat and numb.

Mouse helped him guide the little scarab key out.

"Tell me what to do, my lord."

He lowered her hand until the key was flush to his chest and pushed against her hand until he felt the spike pierce his flesh and heart. The sensation made him jump. It hurt this time, quite a lot, actually. He grunted, sweating through the pain as he showed her how to wind his heart six times.

A frightening darkness clouded his vision. His heart jumped in an unpleasant way, and he sucked in a dry breath that felt like hot concrete in his lungs. He coughed until he tasted blood, and then his clockwork heart turned over and started ticking along again in a more regular way. He pulled the key loose and let it fall against his chest. He felt nauseated and headachy. Exhausted.

Mouse sat down on the bed beside him and tenderly touched his hair. "Lord Edwin is unwell."

"I'll live," he told her. He squinted through the dark that was full of moving shadows. "Where are we?"

"Your club, my Lord."

He sat up slowly. There was a large picture window with one-way glass on the far side of the room. Once he'd gained his balance, he limped over to it and peered down. In the early 1960s, a former speakeasy had come up for sale in Poppettown. Edwin, being a good businessman and having learned a few tricks from Foxley, snatched it up and renovated it into a discothèque in preparation for the new wave of "sound" that the youth of America had seemed to have taken to. But he hadn't wanted Foxley taking a percentage of his profits, so he'd staffed it with his own people, hired Mouse as his manager, and never mentioned a word of it to Foxley.

Xanadu, once his steamy Grecian disco, was now called Tokyo Hoes. It looked something like Hooters, except it seemed to cater to a much more...eclectic clientele, he noticed. More than twenty tables were set up around the darkened room, many clustered around a stage where several exotic dancers were pole dancing and shucking off incredibly complex Cosplay costumes. There was even a Furry doing a moonwalk. He'd been to his share of stripper clubs, but this one took the prize. Hentai animation writhed along the walls on gigantic screens, and the motion-sensitive lights were enough to induce epilepsy in even the most stalwart soul. A techno remix of a popular J-pop song drowned out all sound unless you were on top of the person you were speaking to.

"What happened to Xanadu?" he asked. "Where's my club?"

Mouse bit her lip. "I decided it needed an upgrade. It seemed the right thing to do after the fire."

Edwin raised his eyebrows. "My club was on fire?"

Mouse shrugged. "The Poppets have been acting erratically these past few months, my Lord. They burned us out."

"You should have come to me, told me," Edwin chastised her. "I would have found you protection, Mouse."

Mouse's stubborn jaw quivered. She moved her coat aside to reveal the pancake holsters she had crisscrossed across her broad, flat chest like a gunslinger. He ogled the massive twin Desert Eagle semi-automatics she was packing. "I can handle it," she insisted.

And she was right. Mouse was not an ex-Poppet like so many Heirs these days. Poppets did not exist back in the days when she'd first been made a vampire. A hundred years ago, she'd been an Irish immigrant who came to London to escape the Great Potato Famine. Fresh off the boat, she'd been selling herself in Whitechapel, barely scraping by alongside the other Ladies of the Night, when Edwin found her.

She'd been less than pretty, and, as a result, starving, but there was something about her, a primal Gaelic savagery, that spoke volumes to him. It was a snap decision on his part. During a bout of extremely vigorous lovemaking on both their parts, Edwin found the straight razor under her pillow. She'd been using it to give her clients Glasgow smiles when they refused to pay her. She said that way, everyone left with a grin.

When he teased her about it, she smiled innocently and said she was "Nae but a wee mouse running in the streets, no threat at all."

"A mouse?" he asked dubiously. He was already in love with her beautiful brogue. "You've sharp He knew then that she'd make a lovely vampire. He leaned down and buried his teeth in the soft throat flesh under her chin. She hadn't formally accepted his offer (at least, not within the strictest sense of Court Law), but he hadn't cared about that at the time. If she had refused him, he would have taken her anyway, she was that delicious. He watched her choke on her own blood and shudder in her death throes beneath him. She looked beautiful and glacial with her throat half torn away and blood bubbling over the wound and soaking into the mattress beneath them. In that moment, he offered her his wrist, warning her that she would need to make the initial bite.

She bit. She drank him. And she lived again.

With the exception of Foxley, Mouse was the most amoral person he had ever met. Within a fortnight, she was feeding herself regularly from the British upper class. In fact, regents were her favorite delicacy. She enjoyed dressing up as various visiting viscounts, affecting accents, and dallying with married upper-class ladies in private drawing rooms all over the Empire. Sometimes, she ate her intended prey. Other times, she only lured the poor woman into a compromising position and blackmailed her, adding to their ever-expanding coffers.

Foxley never learned about her existence. Mouse was his Heir, his Enforcer, his little secret. Her love for him was unconditional, absolute, as it was among all Heirs. But Mouse also possessed enormous will and determination. She was quickly becoming her own Lord. He kept expecting her to leave him and establish her own Court, but Mouse never wandered very far from him. She liked guns and bloodshed. She liked being his Enforcer.

He glanced around his club. It was obvious that Mouse ran a tight ship and knew how to change with the times. She was a survivor. But it hurt his pride to know he hadn't been there for her when she needed him, that she might have been killed.

Sensing his distress, Mouse moved closer to him. He hugged her, winding her lovely, bony body around his. He had been gone three years. He'd missed his little darling. He turned to her and kissed her hair and her eyelashes in a way both pious and familiar.

She turned her head, offering her throat to him. "My blood is yours, my Lord. Now and forever. Drink me."

* * *

"I keep thinking about the young one who died," Edwin said. "Did you know her?"

The two of them sat at the back of the club, nursing sake bombs in an effort to look innocuous. Two tables down, Cesar occupied a booth while two girls in teeny-tiny waitress kimonos mooned over him and played with his hair. Edwin wondered how long it would take before the girls discovered that Cesar was batting for the opposite team, or if they even cared about that.

He glanced around. He had to admit the club was an excellent cover. Mouse had done well to transform it into a fantasy world where the employees and regulars dressed in costume. There was no way to tell who the real vampires were.

"No," Mouse answered his question. She ran her finger affectionately down the side of Edwin's face, tracing the worry lines that were visible only when he was thinking. "She's an orphan."

"What happened to her Court?"

"Vampires have been dying, my Lord. The Courts below are almost gone."

"Vampires dying above, vampires dying below," Edwin mused. He sipped his sake—it was mixed with Mouse's blood—and took a hit on his clove cigarette, relishing the warm burn of blood, alcohol, and tobacco moving like liquid gold through his system. It felt almost like the good old days when speakeasies were all the rage and everyone smoked Cubans and danced the foxtrot in flapper dresses. "Soon, we'll be on the endangered species list, my little mouse."

Mouse frowned with concern. "What's been happening in the overworld, my Lord?"

"Do you remember Rathbone?"

"Rathbone disappeared years ago."

"Apparently not." He went on to explain about the Court killings, and about his suspicions that the Poppets' actions were being controlled by a powerful bloodkinetic. As he spoke, he kept his voice voce sotto and just below the level of human hearing.

"The Poppets here are quite capable of killing vampires without the Lords interfering—as you have seen," Mouse said when he had finished his story.

She sat very close to him, dressed in her favorite dark business suit and tie, a white opera scarf swirled around her neck. To anyone looking on, she looked like an Ivy League youth, nothing like the hundred-year-old vampiress she was. She inclined her head and buried her face in the side of his neck, pulling his scent deep into her lungs. He knew his familiar presence filled her, strengthened her. To anyone looking on, she looked like a young man making out with his lover.

"Are you telling me that we have come so low, become so human, that we have begun killing our own kind?"

"It would seem that way. Nobody knows where Rathbone is—or what he's up to." Mouse suddenly sat up straighter. "Is Rathbone the one pursuing your Courtesan?"

"What do you mean?"

"The woman who smells like you, my Lord. I've met her."

"Miss Book?" He sat up, almost toppling his chair. "Eliza? You've seen her?"

Mouse nodded. In the dimness of the club, her big, deceptively innocent eyes glinted like raw jewels. "Near the rail yards. That's where I first encountered her. My spies have been watching her ever since. She has been all over the city, hunting for something, accompanied by a man."

Edwin felt a slow rage building inside of him. It made sense Eliza would have gone to ground with vampires after her. But still...

"That foolish wench is looking for Rathbone!" he said, knowing it was true. Eliza Book couldn't leave well enough alone, and it would likely get her killed one of these days. "And you said she's with some man?"

He didn't know what irked him more, the idea that she thought she could take on a Vampire Lord all by herself, or that she was keeping time with some bloke. He took Mouse by the chin and pinned her with a hard look. "What does he look like, this man?"

Mouse flinched as if struck. "He is a Poppet. Handsome and well made. Like Clark Gable." Then she saw his anger boiling over and hastily added. "But not as handsome as my sweet Lord."

Edwin jumped to his feet and started pacing along the perimeter of the club's dance floor, trying to decide on a plan of action.

"My Lord," Mouse said, catching up to him.

He watched the flickering predatory light in Mouse's eyes. She was almost as dangerous to Miss Book as Foxley or Rathbone...or farking Clark Gable, whoever that was! "You didn't touch her, did you?" he said, giving her a dangerous side-eye. "Didn't nibble on her or anything?"

She gave him her innocent eyes. "The pretty one is yours, my Lord. I would never touch what is rightfully yours." She sounded almost cartoonishly indignant by his accusation.

"You said that about the Duchess Duchovny, as I recall. But then I walked in on the two of you in that drawing room with that honey stick. You'll have to forgive me if I don't exactly believe you, my little mouse."

Mouse straightened her soldiery shoulders as if insulted. Standing straight, she was nearly as tall as Edwin and as imposing as a Navy Seal in fatigues. She radiated strength and desire. It made lesser men, and women, crawl. "I do not take what will be freely given to me with time and patience, my Edwin gave her a concerned look. "What do you mean?"

Mouse smiled, showing heartlessly perfect teeth. "There is time to enjoy the pretty one when you have remade her." Her smile grew. "Time for her to come and know her sister in the dark."

Edwin narrowed his eyes in warning. "She's different, Mouse. She does not want to be your sister. And she will not be remade."

"As you say, my Lord." But her eyes remained dead.

He ignored her look—or tried to. "You said you have your spies keeping an eye on her. Take me to her, Mouse. Now."

| xiii |

Eliza glided down the long, curving staircase to the casino below, trying to appear both mysterious and vampiric. It was more difficult than she'd thought.

The casino swarmed with people. She saw men in tacky evening suits of metallic moiré and women in big, daft dresses and giant feathered hats like something out of Revolutionary France. The crush of bodies made the place feel like a furnace, and she found herself sweating uncomfortably under her smart, conservative tuxedo.

"Sir?"

Before she even reached the bottom of the steps, a waiter had rushed a martini glass of some neon blue liqueur to her. She took the glass but said nothing, as was customary among Vampire Lords. They took great pains not to appear to mix unnecessarily with the humans.

She carried the glass cradled in her white-gloved hand, her chin held high and proud as she wandered through the cavernous, bustling casino halls. Like haute couture and teeth filing, carrying a drink or cigarette at all times was all the rage among the always fashion-conscious Vampire Lords. Anything to look human, as vampires loved irony almost as much as they loved blood.

She wandered into the main gambling hall and chose what looked like the largest, busiest poker table. She took a seat, nodding appropriately but maintaining her silence. The players around the felt instantly fluffed up. They were special now; their table had a genuine Vampire Lord attending.

A popular pop singer sat down on the armrest of her chair and started introducing herself. As she spoke, she carefully wagged her buxom, silicone-infused breasts in Eliza's face. Massive amounts of plastic surgery had given the woman the almost perfectly symmetrical look of a Poppet that was so popular among entertainers. Eliza took pains to ignore her while she was dealt some cards. Meanwhile, a busboy rushed up to offer her a tray of chips.

She started to play. She wasn't very good at poker, but the others at the table kept folding no matter how bad her hand was. They were just thrilled to have a Vampire Lord in their midst, and they had no intention of driving him away.

The night wore on. The women came and went, one more beautiful and buxom than the last. Then the men gave it a shot. She encountered aging rockers, popular socialites, politicians, and burned-out celebrities. One determined woman, a popular reality-star, wiggled into her lap and boldly hung her long, evening-glove-clad arms about Eliza's neck. She started kissing Eliza's neck and giggling drunkenly. Eliza endured it until one of her gloved hands began to wander down Eliza's body, edging toward her nether regions that were a dead giveaway.

Eliza turned the woman's head and gave her a good sharp bite. The woman screamed in sudden horror and jumped onto the poker table, where she crouched like a scalded cat and started whining about being a vampire while clutching her wound. Sure, celebs loved hanging around the undead, but becoming one of them was something else.

The woman was working her way into hysterics when Eliza spotted the monster wending his way across the floor. The woman spotted him as well and started scrambling off the table, kicking cards and chips away in her haste to escape.

The thing cutting a path through the crowd stuck out like a rabid bull among a flock of fleeing swans. He was at least eight feet tall and built like a locomotive that had been in a deadly, metal-mangling derailment. The analogy was apropos, she decided, because at least half of his body seemed to be made of escapement prosthetics, a mountain of moving clockwork parts that chugged slowly along in the vague shape of a man but was nothing of the sort. A small, ugly pinhead sat atop all the moving parts, tiny, piggish eyes swiveling back and forth over the heads of the crowd before settling on her.

The clockwork man, Eliza thought. She felt her heart lurch inside her, and suddenly, she was sweating profusely.

Talos was here.

* * *

They retired to one of the casino's private gambling lounges to conduct their business. It was full of plush, fall-into-the-cushions brocade furniture and vases full of peacock feathers. It looked more like a boudoir out of an Old West cathouse than anything else, complete with private entertainers in skintight corsets, hot pants, and ostrich fans. But the girls quickly cleared out when Talos rumbled into the room, following Eliza's lead. They weren't paid enough to take his kind of abuse.

Eliza indicated a wing chair that looked much too small for Talos to occupy, then went to stand against the showy but non-functional fireplace mantel. Until their business here was concluded, there was no way she was going to be able to sit down.

Talos stayed on his feet, making the large, vaulted room feel positively tiny. "I don't work cheaply. A thousand an hour, plus expenses," he informed her. His voice sounded like an engine being turned over constantly. He let out his breath in a long, hot hiss of steam. "And I expect full payment upfront. No games, little Lord."

"I don't play games. And I don't pay cheaply," she returned, trying to look braver than she felt. She held her martini glass in one poised hand, trying hard to prevent it from trembling and sloshing liquid over the front of her tuxedo. Part of it was fear. Part was rage. Each time she looked at Talos, she thought about Maria and Dr. Grott. She thought about the things he had done to them...and then she shut off her imagination before it completely overwhelmed her.

A part of her wanted to jump on Talos and hit him repeatedly with her bare fists, not that it would likely do him any real damage. "Naturally, I'm curious to know if you're worth the money I'm willing to pay. Do you have much bodyguard experience?"

Talos glared down at her. His gyros ground together, a sound like nails on a blackboard. "No."

"Then why should I pay you so well?"

"Because you pay me, I do what you want. I do good work."

"What kind of work have you done in the past?" It was a fair question.

He smiled, showing sharp little bullet teeth. "I protect and I harm. Your choice, little Lord."

"I hear you're a mercenary. A Red Collar. Is it true you've worked for Lord Rathbone in the past?"

He drew back just a little. "Why do you ask me that?"

Had she blown her cover? She didn't know. She cleared her throat. "I might be looking for a reference. Is that so unusual?"

Derek was right, of course. She was completely out of her league. Something passed behind Talos's eyes. It looked like rage. "Nobody asks for references from Talos!" he bellowed.

Then he hit her and her world went black.

※ ※ ※

Edwin ducked out of the cab that had ushered him uptown to the steps of the Starlight Casino, the last place Mouse's agents had spotted his employee. Almost immediately, he detected Miss Book's unique scent—like morning mist and vanilla fields. It was heavy on the air, emphasized rather than diminished by the copious amounts of sweat and alcohol pouring off the patronage. She smelled...afraid.

Trying to stay calm, Edwin paid the cabbie, then turned to glare at Cesar standing practically on his heels in the gutter. The girls at Tokyo Hoes had stolen away his supervisor's uniform and dressed him foppishly in a suit of rich royal dark blue with black piping. Beneath it, he wore a white buccaneer's shirt sporting froths of lace at wrists and throat like some kind of modern-day air pirate. They'd even given him a French manicure. He looked ridiculous. (And more than a little tasty when he turned his head the right way to reveal his slender brown throat.)

Edwin looked him over. "What do I have to do to get rid of you?"

Cesar scowled. "Pay me money. Two million dollars. Now." He extended his hand. "Don't have it? Tough shit. You're stuck with me, then."

"You're really pushing it, mate," he said and started up the steps of the casino.

The moment he was inside, people noticed him, waiters surrounded him, and women—and not a few men—gravitated toward him. He brushed them aside, barely noticing them. He had caught Miss Book's scent stronger than ever. She'd been here less than an hour ago.

He pulled a credit card from his wallet and shoved it at Cesar. "Go entertain yourself. Buy a hooker or something."

Cesar glared at him but eventually stalked off toward the poker tables.

Finally alone, he could do what he was good at. The scent trail led him across the casino hall, down a long corridor, and right to the door of a private gambling lounge. Security was tight here, and before he knew it, an armed guard started toward him.

Edwin shot the man a menacing look that immediately killed the spring in his step. There were some advantages to looking like a B-movie Dracula, he supposed. "Turn around and go back before I lay you out and fill your mouth with your own intestines, lad," he said.

The guard stopped and started backing down the hallway, his eyes fixed on Edwin.

Edwin took the doorknob in hand, finding it locked. Eliza Book was right there, just behind the door, and from the way she smelled, frightened half to death and probably in trouble.

It didn't matter that she didn't want to see him, that she hated him. He'd realized something during the past two days of their separation, something important. None of this was about him, his pride, or his personal needs. It was about her, about keeping her safe. He no longer felt he was unredeemable. He would redeem himself through her. For her. He would rescue Eliza, rescue the damsel in distress from the dragon, and then he would set her free. It was the only way he could properly call himself a man.

And, anyway, he loved her. Loved her even if he could not have her. There was nothing else for it.

Edwin twisted the mechanism, breaking the whole knob and plate off the door, then just decided to rip the door off its hinges.

Inside, he discovered a giant pile of walking junk pinning a young Vampire Lord to the floor. For one moment, he was confused by the dissonance of Eliza's scent and her lack of presence. Then he looked more closely at the vampire on the floor—the black youth he did not immediately recognize—and then the junk pile monster gripping him by the lapels of his tuxedo jacket as he slammed his head repeatedly against the floor, and realized it was Eliza. Eliza was the young Vampire Lord!

The tiny pinhead swiveled on the huge, misshapen body, and pitiless dark eyes centered on him. The monster spoke. "Little man, go away."

Edwin bared his teeth and charged forward. "I'm not going away. And I'm not a man!" Gripping the monster by a servo sticking out of his spine, he turned and heaved him against the far wall. It surprised even him; he hadn't known he was that strong.

The monster hit the wall like a bomb going off, pulling down drapes, crushing furniture, and even ripping a huge raw hole in the wall itself.

The monster scrambled up, not hurt, but mildly pissed off. "Good job, little man."

Edwin let out his breath, hissing between his teeth. He fully extended his wings, which easily tore through the back of his suit jacket. "I told you! I'm not a man!"

Finally, the monster seemed to realize this. It unfolded itself to its full eight-foot height, its head missing the vaulted ceiling by inches. It stared at him as vapidly as a machine.

Edwin hesitated. In his time, he'd fought a great many enemies, but a monster cyborg was novel even by his standards. He edged around so he was stationed in front of his secretary, shielding her. He glanced behind and saw she was mostly conscious but stunned. "Miss Book? Eliza? Can you hear me, love?"

She groaned as she forced herself to her hands and knees. There was blood in her close-cropped hair from a wound somewhere on the back of her head. Head wounds bled a lot, he reminded himself, so the blood wasn't so unusual, but he didn't want to take any chances. She needed medical attention immediately.

The mechanical man charged him.

It was like a train hitting him, literally. The impact knocked the breath right out of his body. He felt the wall close in behind him fast. But a body in motion tends to stay in motion, and the speed and force of the monster's body was irresistible. His back hit the wall, then the wall gave, studs buckling as the monster kept up its forward momentum. Drywall, studs, and, finally, bricks, exploded outward, and then the two of them hurdled right through the wall of the casino and into the alley beyond.

The monster stopped. Edwin kept going, flying backward until he hit the chain-link fence surrounding the employee parking lot. He bounced off it as if it was a net before falling face-first onto the wet, hard asphalt. His teeth, nose, and at least three ribs cracked on impact. Funny, but despite already being dead, things continued to hurt an awful lot.

He groaned as he spat out blood and broken bits of himself. He choked and scrambled on the asphalt, trying to find purchase. But before he managed it, something grabbed him by the back of the neck and hauled him up as if he was a ragdoll.

The monster. It eyed him critically, not injured at all, dammit. "Little vampire, who are you?" it asked.

Edwin choked on the blood in his nose and mouth. It took him two tries to summon his voice. "Your...pain in the arse!" He kicked at the monster's steel jaw, but it just hurt his foot and the monster only grunted in response. It wasn't fair. The witty comebacks and defensive assaults always worked in the action movies he watched. Why couldn't life be like a movie?

"Not such a big pain," the creature commented. "Your name, little vampire?"

Edwin stuck his chest out, which wasn't very impressive, he supposed, seeing how he was dangling off the ground. "Lord Edwin McGillicuddy."

"The Prince!" the creature rejoiced.

"That's right."

"I get to kill the Prince today. Good day!"

This wasn't going well!

"Put me down and fight like a man...or whatever," Edwin demanded.

"I think no. I think I'll just crush you, little vampire, make your brains run like soup." He turned around and threw Edwin like a piece of weightless flotsam against the wall of the casino.

It was like being fired out of a cannon, whatever that felt like. The wall slammed into his body and he felt more ribs crack like kindling. The broken ones that were in the process of mending crunched alarmingly, and Edwin slid down the wall, his body so full of pain that he felt darkness hovering like a black angel over his head. He snorted blood through his twice-broken nose. Blimey, he thought, he was getting too bloody old for this shit.

The monster lunged at him again. Edwin moved at the last second and the creature plowed right through the wall. Edwin rolled out of the way of the falling bricks, crushing his poor bruised ribs under his weight in the process. The creature swiveled around, bellowing like a behemoth, and let out a belch of white steam.

Edwin, sensing imminent doom, tried to crawl away over the debris. He had suddenly decided that discretion, valor, etc., etc...but the creature grabbed him by the wings and yanked him up. Edwin hung limp in the monster's giant metallic hands, feeling about as significant as a fly.

He moaned in pain. It felt like his skin was two sizes too small for him, and all his bones felt loose and rattling. "You win...you're bigger and stronger. Happy?"

The monster smiled humorlessly. "I'll be happy when you're dead!" He threw Edwin back at the fence. Edwin hit it, bounced, and fell like a sack of concrete to the ground. His kung fu wasn't all that, he decided, and this was a very good wake-up call to his lack of invulnerability, he decided. If that walking pile of junk threw him around anymore, he was going to end up looking like someone's day-old laundry.

"Now, I tear your wings off like a bug and beat your face in!" the monster roared. It was a very effective threat because Edwin was sure he could probably back it up. The monster took a step toward him, readying himself for a new assault.

Behind him, through the hole in the wall, Edwin saw Eliza climbing to her feet, weaving slightly as she stumbled through the ragged aperture in the bricks. She put a hand to her head, then stared in wonder at all of the blood on her hand. Looking angry, she clenched her fist defiantly and something like a spark danced along her knuckles.

Her formerly cloudy eyes focused on him, and he spotted a spark burning in them. She had taken a licking that would have killed a normal person and was walking it off better than most of the men he'd known in the East End. It was the only advantage to being a Poppet.

"Mr. McGillicuddy?" she said in surprise and wonder. "What are you doing here?"

Edwin climbed unsteadily to his feet. "S-saving you?"

She stared at him long and hard for a moment. "You came here to save me?"

He nodded, the gesture nearly toppling him. "I said I would come back for you."

She looked the situation over. "Well, you're not doing a very good job of it."

Edwin raised his eyes to the pile of moving parts chugging toward him. "You may be right."

"Is he being a bother?"

"A wee bit, aye. Nothing I can't handle." Then he fell back against the fence like a dead man.

* * *

"Talos!" Eliza shouted, and the mountain of mechanical refuse stopped dead in his tracks and turned to glare at her. She felt an instant of panic...followed by an even stronger spike of rage. Her head still hurt, and she was unsteady on her feet, but what Mr. McGillicuddy said was motivating her.

I said I would come back for you.

Her heart ticked faster and faster at the realization that he was slowly killing himself to try and save her. Well, if Mr. McGillicuddy couldn't save her, she would just have to save him.

"You leave my employer alone!"

Talos snorted in disgust and started toward her. "Little Vampire Lord isn't a Vampire Lord at all." He stopped and reached for her. When he was less than a foot away, he swiped his big hand at her.

Eliza felt like Fay Wray being cornered by King Kong. She swatted his hand away, a sudden electrical spark blooming between them.

Talos jerked and pulled his hand back, looking at it and wriggling his fingers in surprise. "What did you do?"

"That was a warning. Do you want more?"

Talos roared and reached for her again, wrapping both huge hands around her body and lifting her right off the ground. It was like being stuck in a vice; she couldn't move at all. So, instead, she focused all her energy on him. She had to make physical contact with mechanical devices to affect them, it seemed.

And so, she did. She opened herself up like a live electrical current and pushed her power into Talos's body.

Talos roared again, this time the sound escalating into a scream of agony as sparks danced along his hands, up his arms, and into his misshapen body. His whole mountainous form began to tremble as he sucked up her power like a machine siphoning off energy from a live circuit.

She pushed harder, feeding more and more electrical energy into him, feeding power into his body until she could feel his gears grinding, trying to negate the overload. When it was too much and they finally reached their limit, they locked up and his entire body went stiff, his fingers flexing open.

Eliza fell...and Mr. McGillicuddy, standing below, caught her.

It knocked him down so she found herself in a sitting position in his lap. He sat there with his back to the wall of the casino—what was left of the wall, anyway—staring at her in wonder, shattered debris surrounding them.

Far above them loomed the frozen figure of Talos, his circuits burned out by whatever it was Eliza had done to him. He looked strangely like a piece of modern art...if the artist was utterly insane. Slowly, he teetered, then tumbled over with a smash of gears that left the ground trembling beneath them and cogs and screws spinning off into the dark.

Eliza flinched and stared at the pile of steaming rubbish a long moment before turning her full attention on Mr. McGillicuddy. He looked disheveled, frightened, and battered, and his face was a horrible mask of bruises and blood. She felt the need to reach out and touch him, but she was afraid that would hurt him.

"You came here to save me?" she said again.

"Did you think I would not?"

"You don't even know me. You don't know who I am. What I am."

"Tell me." His voice was sincere, his attention unflinching.

She held his even gaze and told the truth. "My name is Alisa. I was created as a Poppet in my Lord's Court, but when I was fifteen, I escaped and came to this place. I changed my name to Eliza Book. Then I came to work for you."

Mr. McGillicuddy nodded. "It's nice to meet you, Eliza. My name is Edwin Oliver McGillicuddy. I was born in the East End of London in 1806. I used to be a vampire Enforcer and a gangster. I...erm..." He looked away. "...I guess I still am."

He looked sad about that. But then, as he looked back at her, his expression changed. He reached out and touched her face with his big cool hands as if to prove that she was real. "You cut your hair." He ran those hands over it.

Eliza, suddenly overwhelmed by everything, covered her face with both hands and burst into tears.

Edwin waited, letting Eliza cry herself out before saying in a soft, careful voice, "What is it, love? Tell me."

She hiccupped, shaking so badly in his arms that she was afraid her bones might rattle apart. She wiped at the unladylike snot running out of her nose in rivers. My god, the two of them made such a romantic pair, she reflected. They were such a damned mess.

Finally, she wailed at the false sky, "I'm cold and tired and so sick of running all over this goddamned city! And I don't want you to fire me!"

He looked distraught. "I'm not firing you!"

She lowered her hands. "I said such terrible things to you—and thought much worst. You must hate me!"

He gathered her close and wiped the tears from her eyes. And then, unexpectedly, he kissed her, long and hard. She had never been kissed like that by anyone before, and she immediately gave into it, into what she was feeling. What she wanted. Him.

He was still kissing her when security showed up to see what in hell had happened.

| xiv |

Understandably, the establishment was upset about their esteemed guests being attacked on business premises by a well-known mercenary. The manager himself apologized profusely to Edwin and Eliza and expressed his concerns for their health and well-being. Mostly, though, the man was just terrified of a lawsuit—or of pissing off the High Vampire Courts, which he assumed Edwin was a part of. As such, he gave the two their choice of a free room for the night.

They looked at each other. It was cute. The manager thought they were a couple. A Vampire Lord and his Bride.

Eliza was about to request a double when Mr. McGillicuddy interrupted. "The honeymoon suite, my good man. The best you have."

She raised her eyebrows at that, but he gave her a sly look that made her quiver a little inside. Oh god, those eyes...

Around three in the morning, the police finished questioning them and the paramedics finished patching Eliza's head wound. Mr. McGillicuddy gave her that look again and then suddenly swept Eliza off her feet and into his arms, effortlessly carrying her up the long, curving staircase to their room. Eliza squealed. The gesture was grand and romantic even though her employer looked like hehe had been in a bar fight. But the moment they were inside the large, posh suite, Mr. McGillicuddy sagged and nearly dropped her to the floor.

"You'd best put me down," she said, her arms around his neck.

"Nah. I'm good." He straightened up. He wouldn't stop looking at her even though she too was quite a mess in her tattered, bloodied tuxedo.

They hardly looked like a romantic couple, yet he carried her to the king-sized bed with the mirrors in the ceiling above it, kicked away the tacky red coverlet, and set her down. Then he sank down beside her and just looked at her. He ran his fingers over the curve of her cheek, but his eyes looked unfocused.

"Mr. McGillicuddy, are you all right?"

He blinked and refocused. "Y-yeah. And I think we are far, far beyond the formal 'Mr. McGillicuddy' stage, don't you agree...Eliza?"

"Lord McGillicuddy," she tried.

He shook his head.

"Edwin."

"Perfect."

"Edwin," she said again, tasting his name and rolling it around her mouth.

He looked awful, as if he'd gone ten rounds with a heavyweight champion—and lost.

His eyes started to drift again as if he was on the edge of passing out.

"Edwin...are you okay?"

"It only hurts when I...do anything," he coughed. His voice sounded worse than ever, nasally, because his broken nose hadn't straightened itself out yet. He touched it and winced.

This wasn't exactly the romantic setting she had fantasized about. Eliza scrambled off the bed and hurried to the bathroom. She found a first aid kit in the linen closet and brought it back to the bed with her. She had no idea if it would help Edwin or not, vampire physiology being a great deal different than human or Poppet, but she had to do something. She couldn't leave Edwin looking like the victim of a gang hit.

She applied an antiseptic to a sterile pad and started on the scrapes and bruises that decorated one whole side of his face. He flinched at the deeper wounds but bore it all like a lifelong soldier.

"Handsome devil, eh?" he said and coughed again. Loose stuff rattled around his chest disconcertingly.

"Yes." She smiled. "Not so sure about the accent, though."

He laughed at that, which brought on a new fit of coughing.

He let her work, watching her but saying nothing at first. Finally, reaching up, he reset his broken nose, which brought fresh tears to his eyes and made Eliza flinch at the sight—and sound of crunching bones. Then he said in a more normal tone of voice, "You saved me from that monster."

"Yes," she agreed shyly as she attended to the bruises and abrasions that decorated his chest beneath his shredded shirt. "I seem to be a walking CPU of some kind."

"Techkinetic," he said, still sounding odd with his slowly healing nose. "You're the first I've ever seen to be able to do things like that."

"The first of my kind, huh?"

"It would seem so."

Eliza thought about that. Her powers were very odd, and she was still learning how they worked. She didn't even know where they came from, but she knew that anytime she concentrated on Dr. Grott's computer, new data automatically filtered into her mind —not all at once, thankfully, but in pieces. There were files about many things, including Poppet physiology, and she knew from reading some of them in her head that the scientists who created her kind had experimented in all kinds of different ways.

Even Talos had stored an astonishing amount of data on his hard drive—or whatever it was that passed for his brain—and she'd been privy to that information, too. "You know, when I...shocked Talos...or whatever it is I did to him...I got a good look inside of him. Everything he was made of, including most of what was in his head."

"Was there anything in his head?" Edwin joked. "That bloke struck me as all brawn, no brains."

She widened her eyes. "You'd be surprised."

"What did you see?"

It took her a moment to formulate her thoughts. It was like having the key to the entire Internet. The information was overwhelming. She had to index it all or she'd go insane. She took a deep breath and decided to fill him in on her "investigation," such as it was.

She told him about escaping Foxley's ship and her experience with the Hummingbird, then her encounter with the shooter down here in Poppettown—he looked momentarily horrified until she showed him the now nonexistent wound in her shoulder—and then, finally, about Dr. Grott's lab and what she'd found on his computer.

"I saw primitive schematics for a new type of firearm, a kind of high-frequency handgun that can disrupt the orbit of molecules. A tiny nuclear weapon, if you will. It has me worried, Edwin. A lot."

She took a deep breath as she continued. "Talos had similar schematics embedded in his hard drive. In fact, Dr. Grott erased them from his computer because he was so appalled by what he had done. I only found them because I was able to access their pathway—there's no way to totally delete a file on a computer, you see."

She stopped when she realized she was babbling about things he probably only had a passing understanding of. Then she frowned at her own realization. "And yet, Talos had those exact same files. It doesn't make sense. Why would Rathbone hire Talos to torture Dr. Grott and extract files that Talos already had access to?"

Edwin thought about that. "Maybe he got them from the doctor's computer the same as you did?"

She shook her head. "I don't think so. I had to find special deleted pathways. I don't think Talos was sophisticated enough to un-erase files. Anyway, why would he torture Dr. Grott if he could have access to the files anytime he wanted? It makes no sense."

Edwin stared gravely at Eliza for a long moment before finally plucking at her sleeve. "Smoke and mirrors."

"What do you mean?"

"Think about it. No one sees Rathbone, yet his influence is felt everywhere. With Foxley, it's understandable. He's so bloody vain and insecure that he won't let anyone see him. And yet, there are still those among us who know what he looks like. It makes me wonder if Rathbone might not exist anymore."

"You mean someone is using his name," Eliza suggested. "Like a big bogeyman in the dark?"

Edwin shrugged, then eased himself up off the bed and hobbled to the window. He leaned in the window well and peered down at the streets below for a long, poignant moment. She could see him thinking, and could almost hear the gears turning. For the first time, she realized he was much cleverer than he let on. Finally, he dropped the curtain and turned to face her, his wolfish eyes keen. "Have you noticed the unrest in the streets? The violence?"

Eliza sat up on the bed. "Yes. Even the vampires down here are afraid of the Poppets."

She thought about the soap boxers and all of that propaganda stuff on the street about the Great Mother, whatever that was. Vampires were certainly not on the Most Popular List down here.

"It's always been bad, granted, but it seems to be getting worse. It's almost like the Poppets have been galvanized to take action. All that Great Mother business," Edwin said as if to read her thoughts.

She stared at him steadily. "You think Rathbone is dead and a Poppet is using his identity to stir up trouble." It wasn't a question.

"I think all of this smells a mite peculiar."

"Perhaps we could—" she began, then started when Edwin suddenly lurched against the window.

She stood up. "Why aren't you healing?"

He pushed himself upright. "I seem to be having a spot of bother with the old ticker, as it were."

"Edwin! Why didn't you say something?" She immediately went to him and unbuttoned the remnants of his shirt under his suit jacket. She laid her ear to the wall of his chest, frowning. "You're completely overwound. You'll need to rest for at least a few hours before I can rewind you. Otherwise, you'll lock up."

"Already did that."

She gave him a stern look. "Hasn't Foxley been properly winding your heart up in the morning?"

Edwin made a face. "As if I would let him do that."

She gave him a cross look.

"No." His face turned hard, his eyes as piercing and sharp as amber stones. "I'd rather die than give Foxley any more power over me." He glanced morosely out the window. "I have my nightmares. I don't need anymore."

Eliza stared at him in mute surprise. She'd judged him harshly, she knew, in absolutes. Edwin wasn't an evil person—wicked, perhaps, but wicked wasn't the same thing as evil. Her clockwork vampire was impetuous, overzealous, oversexed, and overwound, but none of those things made him evil.

She felt like crying all over again. She wasn't sure what she would have done in his place, with Foxley holding her leash that way. For all she knew, she might have done worst. She wanted to hold him and cry all over his suit, but she thought that would probably only hurt him.

He swayed slightly as he got to his feet, his eyes looking frighteningly dilated.

"You need blood, Edwin. Blood and rest."

He steadied himself against the wall. "Perhaps you're right. Would you be good enough to ring room service, love?"

"No," she said. "I won't."

He raised his eyebrows at that.

She reached up and touched his cheek. He touched her hand touching him and closed his eyes. She figured all the blood on the two of them wasn't helping with the urges much. He struggled to keep his face passive and his expression neutral, not wanting and hungry, but she saw. She knew.

She looked up at him, her face set. She wasn't afraid. "I want you to take from me tonight, Edwin."

Her offer seemed to take him by surprise. "They have blood substitute in the bar downstairs," he reminded her.

"I'm a Poppet." She took his hand and, with a gentle tug, led him back to the bed. He followed like a little puppy on a string. Once they were sitting side by side once more, she touched his face again, lovingly, with just her fingertips. "You'll heal faster with my blood."

He shook his head, took her hand, and kissed it. "No."

She raised her chin defiantly. "I can help you. And this is my decision."

He looked at her long and hard. Then he ran his hand along her cheek. She turned her face instinctively into his touch. She could all but feel the yearning inside of him. Slowly, tenderly, he cupped the back of her head. His mouth came down on hers. He kissed her, and it was slow and soft and lingering and sad.

She liked it. She wanted it to continue, but he started to draw back.

It was so infuriating!

Eliza grabbed a hank of hair on the back of his head and kissed him back, hard, harder, licking the inside of his mouth. Their tongues touched.

She smiled against his mouth. "You haven't thought about it? About...us?"

He groaned and his eyes fluttered closed. "I always think about us."

"Really?"

He sighed tiresomely. "All the bloody time, woman."

She laughed at that. She'd suspected, of course, but to hear him confirm it was very empowering. Resolute in her decision, she climbed back onto the bed and he followed, crawling after her over the coverlet.

She smiled impishly. "What do you think about? I mean, what do you think about when you think about us? What kinds of things do we do?"

He swallowed nervously, his throat so dry it clicked. "You mean...what don't I think about us doing."

His words were thrilling and frightening. She'd had no idea he thought about her that way...so intensely. She finally stopped when they were kneeling together in the center of the bed. She ducked her head under his chin, kissed and nibbled the side of his throat. He needed a shave, but she liked it. It gave a touch of ruggedness to his otherwise smooth, prince-perfect face.

"I want you to be my Lord tonight. I want to be your Poppet." The admission made her blush despite her absolute confidence in him that he would never hurt her.

Edwin groaned, eyes closed. "Oh, lovey."

Maybe she was being too forward? Too pushy? She didn't know. She had never taken the initiative like this. But it was so much fun to be in control for a change. Especially with a man she truly liked—maybe even loved.

He opened his eyes, took both of her hands, and drew them to his mouth to kiss. "I don't want to hurt you."

"Would you? Hurt me, I mean? If you did it?"

He looked horrified. "Of course not. I would never hurt you."

Her heart fluttered at his words. "I trust you, Edwin."

"I know."

She licked her lips nervously and told him the truth. "I don't want to be afraid of this anymore. I don't want to be afraid of vampires." She let him go, but when he didn't immediately leap upon her, she lay back on the pillows, even undid the first two buttons on her shirt. She knew he wouldn't be able to resist that, and she was right.

After a few hesitant seconds, Edwin leaned down and kissed her softly, sweetly, on the corners of her mouth, like the prince trying to awaken Snow White from her glass coffin. She groaned in response, his kiss setting her whole body alive with an electrical jolt.

They made out for several minutes, all of their kisses so fluttery and soft that they barely touched. Meanwhile, their hands moved gently and unhurriedly over each other. But it wasn't enough.

"Please, Edwin." She unbuttoned her shirt completely and lay back on the bed, the shirt rumpled around her, and just watched him watch her so intently.

He looked worried.

"I want this," she confessed. "I want to do this, and I want it to be my choice." She was near tears. "I've never…" She turned her head away so he wouldn't see the tears spilling from her eyes. How could she explain? "I've never had a choice, Edwin. I want this. I need this!"

He swallowed. "I know."

She stared up at him, a hand roaming up to touch herself, to trace her breasts with her fingertips, even though it was completely unnecessary. She was already so aroused she could barely lie still, and her nipples hurt. Her entire body ached to feel him atop her, having her and protecting her. "I'll be your Poppet if it's what my Lord commands."

"You need to stop talking like that, lovey. You're not my Poppet."

"Your Courtesan, then."

He seemed to come to a decision. "My girlfriend. My love." He leaned down and kissed her fully, tasting the inside of her mouth. He drew his hungry mouth down the column of her throat and then down farther, replacing the fingers she was drawing about her nipples with his tongue. He ran his sharp teeth across her sensitive flesh.

The sensation made her suck in a sharp breath. He wasn't exactly gentle. But just then, she didn't want gentle. He spread his wings, covering them both. She reached up and grappled his shoulders as he ravished her, her grip perhaps too harsh because he grunted with pain as all his sore spots were aggravated by the sudden, jarring motion.

"Sorry," she said.

"No bother," he answered, moving upward to kiss her, first gently, then not so gently. His hands roved over her, ripping at her costume clothes. She tried to move to accommodate him, but he held her still against the mattress.

She swallowed nervously. She had a feeling that Edwin wasn't big on slow, gentle lovemaking. He was a violent man with a violent past. It would have frightened her to death if she didn't trust him so completely. To distract herself, she started unbuttoning his shirt, but yanking on the fabric only made him grunt in a completely unromantic way, so she stopped doing that. The shirt, and pretty much everything else he was wearing, would have to stay on. He was going far too fast for her to keep up, anyway.

She dropped her hands, running them down his sides as he pressed his bruising kisses to her throat under her ear. The sensation sent chills coursing through her body. He worked on loosening his trousers and hers just enough for them to come together with very little guidance from her. He growled deep in his throat and gripped her by the hips. Eliza grunted and watched in the mirrors above.

His lovemaking was fast at first, but soon he slowed down. "Are you all right?"

"Move a little...yes, like that. Yes, that's...that's just lovely," she sighed, enjoying the sensations washing through her. She liked that he was listening, that he was taking his time.

She jumped inside each time he hit her sweet spot. She'd had no idea it could be this nice...this sweet...this amazing. Each time he moved, it made the pleasure swell within her. Meanwhile, he ran his teeth over the sensitive skin under her ear, somehow never disrupting his rhythm.

Edwin was an amazing multitasker. She giggled at the thought.

He stopped for a moment. "I hope that's a 'he's bloody amazing' giggle and not a 'blimey, what in fark is this wanker doing?' giggle."

That made her giggle, too. "The first," she agreed.

That seemed to satisfy him. She turned her head and put her hand to the nape of his neck, inviting him to take. He kissed her throat deeply and she felt the first serious pricks of his teeth, then his lips withdrawing as he had second thoughts.

"I trust you, Edwin," she said softly, hoarsely. "I love you. Take me."

Her words galvanized him. This time, he kissed until he had sucked in a bite of her flesh. He bit down and she felt a sharp, brief flash of pain...and then the shock of his bite ripped like knives right through her body, from top to bottom.

Eliza sucked in a deep, sudden breath and arched her back as she climaxed hard with a partner for the first time in her life. It hadn't been like this with her Lord, nor even with Derek. The pleasure bordered on pain, and then, for one sweet second, it went beyond pain, into ecstasy, and she screamed.

It triggered his own release. With a grunt, Edwin came inside her, his teeth still embedded in her throat. She realized with a heart-racing intensity that her own orgasm was feeding into him and he was now feeding from her like an electrical current with no end.

Eliza fell back on the mattress, shuddering so violently that Edwin had difficulty staying atop her as he drank from the tiny wound he had made. The sensation was beautiful and amazing, like nothing like she had ever experienced in the past.

"Edwin..." she croaked, all the sound she could articulate. And then, just when she thought the wave of her orgasm was beginning to ebb, it built again, this time stronger than before. She wrapped her legs around Edwin's waist and sank her nails deep into his side to hang on as sparks of electricity danced quite literally over her body and his and the light on the nightstand exploded in a burst of ozone, plunging the whole room into darkness.

Edwin didn't notice, or else did he care. He rode her pleasure over and over again, drinking and loving on her until she screamed once more. He yanked his head back, pulling his teeth out of her flesh, his mouth covered in her blood. He growled like a wild animal, and this time, the electrical discharge between them was so powerful that a long row of lights on the avenue outside gave a series of angry, wasp-like hums before exploding and blanketing the entire block in darkness.

Then they were up, with Eliza's back to the headboard as Edwin took her yet again, his eyes all black with neither whites nor irises. Eliza clutched the back of his neck, trying to entice him to return to her wound, to feed again. But Edwin was old and experienced, and he knew what could harm her. Thank goodness at least one of them had enough presence of mind to act responsibly.

He loved her one last time to climax, panting with the effort. And then, finally, he was done, though it took some time for his eyes to clear and return to their normal, golden-yellowy appearance. Eventually, they slid down and lay exhausted side by side on the pillow. He looked like Edwin again, only a little tired.

"Bloody hell, are you all right?" he asked, hoarse with concern.

Eliza touched the side of her throat. Edwin's bite—his mark—ached almost as much as the rest of her did, but it was a good ache, an ache she treasured. In the dimness, she could still see faint bruises on his face, but they seemed to be fading to yellow as her blood healed him with nearly preternatural speed.

"No," she told him, panting to catch her breath, "Absolutely not." Her heart was running like a machine in her chest, her body humming with electricity, and she couldn't seem to stop pressing herself against him. "Edwin, that...that was the most amazing thing I've ever experienced...ever."

He watched her, looking dazed. "Me, too."

"Really?"

"Aye, really," he answered, far too high on her blood to be lying. "You don't feel...sick or drunk?" he asked with concern.

She shook her head.

He smiled and laughed. "I've never met anyone who could resist El Mal de Amor. Are you sure you're all right?"

She pulled him to her and kissed him, sparks skipping between them and biting like little wasps. "I'm fine, Edwin. I'm perfect."

He ran his hand protectively over her boyishly short hair. "No wild desire to fulfill my every desire?"

She thought about that. "No." Other than the good achiness and the exciting, heart-pounding afterglow of their lovemaking, she felt no different at all. "I don't have to do that whole 'my Lord' nonsense all the time, do I?"

He smirked. "Only if you want to. I mean, I don't mind or anything. We could make it our thing." He wagged his eyebrows.

She laughed. "We have a thing?"

"Aye," he grinned. "We have a thing. You and I."

She ran her hand over his ribs where the bruises had been almost black. "So, how do you feel?"

"I'm fine. I'm good." He hesitated only a moment. "Do you want to do it again?"

"What? Our thing?"

He nodded rather eagerly.

"Edwin." She tugged on his shirt. "You need to rest and reset." The motion pulled him atop her. He was already ready for round two. How could he be ready so soon after everything they had experienced? It wasn't human, like him.

"Do you ever think about anything except sex?"

He thought about that, long and hard.

"Never mind." She wrapped her arms around his neck and pulled him down for a kiss. The electricity between them began to build again. "Yes, my Lord, I want to do it again."

***

"Why must you resist me, woman?"

Eliza seemed amused by his question the following morning. She sat on the edge of the bed, pulling up her stockings. "I am not resisting. I simply refuse to sit around in a club somewhere with your lazy vampire wench while you go hunting that lunatic." Eliza spread her hands, which were capable of amazing things, and he wasn't talking about her techkinetic powers. "Do you have any idea how sexist that is, putting baby in the corner?"

Edwin stood in the bathroom before the large oval vanity mirror, running the edge of a straight razor over his chin and throat while he watched his girlfriend in the glass. "Bloody hell, it's not sexist, Eliza, just good sense! And Mouse is not a lazy vampire wench. I don't create lazy vampire wenches."

"Just oversexed ones, I'm sure."

He turned to look at her.

She was grinning to show she was teasing him. She was a fetching sight, half-dressed in her chemise.

"She won't touch you on penalty from me, if that's what you're worried about. She may be oversexed, but she's also obedient." He toweled off and started buttoning up his freshly laundered linen shirt. The hotel owner, wanting to impress the Vampire Lord staying at his establishment, had sent up practically a whole wardrobe for them both, which was convenient, considering the sad state of their clothes.

Rank has its privileges, he thought, not for the first time.

Eliza finished dressing and stood up. She put her hands on her hips, swaying slightly in the bustled green day dress that was about half a size too small for her—in all the right places—and gave him a direct look. "So you have her cowed as well?"

Before he could answer, she tugged on the snug-fitting bodice. "What size is this? I look very fat in it, don't I?"

"You're not fat." He snapped up his braces and turned to feast his eyes a bit more on her deliciously curvy shape. No, not fat at all—more like a plump partridge he wouldn't mind sinking his teeth into a second time...

Eliza stood in the doorway, jaw clenched in righteous indignation, while her generous cleavage strained the buttons of her dress. It made him want to go up to her, rip the dress open, and have his way with her again—against the wall, or maybe on the edge of the desk by the window, except that she seemed to have something to say.

"Edwin! Focus!"

So much for the obedient little Poppet.

Blimey, he thought. Here it comes...

"While we're on the subject of Mouse, do you two...you know...have a thing?"

He slid into his brand new suit coat in a natty shade of dark hunter green as he searched for the proper response. He had perhaps gone a bit overboard on the honesty bit when he'd told her about Mouse—though he had to admit he rather liked his woman jealous, though he would never admit to it.

"We did," he finally admitted. "But we're not together anymore. Mouse is my little darling—my daughter, if you will."

"Your daughter." She gave him a dubious look.

It made him uncomfortable, all this revealing of souls, so he lit a cigarette and pointed it at her. "Why don't you tell me about Clark Gable?"

She looked confused. "Who?"

"The bloke you've been running about the city with." He started picking through the collection of ties hanging over the vanity mirror, finally settling on a bright red one. He held it up in the mirror, the cigarette clenched in his teeth. "While we're on the subject of deep, dark secrets, why don't I know about him?"

"Derek?" She sounded surprised. Stepping forward, she picked out a more appropriate color to go with his suit. "Since when do you have any interest in Derek?"

"I take it you two go back a ways?"

She hung the more conservative black tie around his neck, giving it a snug little tug. "Are you jealous?"

"Pot, meet kettle."

"Now wait just one minute...!"

But he'd had it with all his mincing around. He threw the cigarette in the sink and started stalking her, backing her into a corner of the suite. He saw an almost dangerous excitement in her eye. It whet his appetite in a way nothing else could.

When they reached the desk, he lifted her up and sat her down upon it, then shifted her legs apart and slid her skirt up her legs with a sensual slide of his hand. Holding her hungry, demanding gaze, he moved forward to take her again until she gripped his shoulders and cried out his name. He lowered his head, cupped the side of her neck, and drank from the mark under her ear, which opened automatically for him, allowing him to take without needing to harm her a second time.

After a few moments, the strong, gentle suckling of his lips on her wound made her climax so hard that they would have blown every light in the room, had any remained intact.

Take that, Clark Gable, he thought.

He withdrew, touched her cheek tenderly, and kissed her.

He was proud to say it took her a moment to compose herself.

"What...what was that for?" She looked flustered and disheveled, just the way he liked his women. The way he liked her.

"You said you loved me last night. Is that true?" His heart ticked nervously inside his chest at the question.

Again, she blushed. "Y-yes."

"Good. Because I love you, too."

She looked stunned by his admission.

He indicated this...them. "And this was because you're mine. You're my woman. And I want you to remember that. Though I have no issues reminding you." He ran his hand along the line of her thigh.

"Only yours?" she teased, sounding unimpressed by his display of machismo.

"Mine and mine alone. And you should know I don't appreciate other men dallying with my woman."

"There are no other men! There was no dallying!" Getting serious, she blew out her breath. "And don't go changing the subject, Mr. McGillicuddy. Just because I'm yours doesn't mean I'm about to let you put me away like some silly female while you go traipsing all over the city, hunting this Chimera character. I'm more than capable of taking care of myself in a fight, as I have more than adequately proven to you."

He glared at her, let out an exasperated breath, and returned to the bathroom to fix his rumpled clothing. He thought about influencing her through his mark to stay, but honestly, she seemed inured to his glamour, as she had already proven. Besides, it would probably only make her cross with him, and he didn't want that. He didn't want to admit it, but he was sort of/kind of afraid of her.

"Why must you resist me?" he repeated, throwing up his hands.

She followed him into the bathroom and reached up to fix his tie. "Because I can. Because it's fun. Because you're being an ass." She snagged the tie tight around his neck, almost painfully so, impressing him. "Take your choice, my Lord."

He pressed his lips together in frustration, but Eliza only smiled up at him, her hands flat on his chest. He liked the confidence in her eyes. This was a fierce and powerful Eliza, different from the quiet, bookish one who took his notes and dictation, though he didn't know which one he liked better, if he was being honest.

"I saved you from Talos," she reminded him. "You said so yourself. Doesn't that make me valuable to you as a partner?"

He bit back a smile. "Chimera isn't Talos, Miss Book. There are no circuits to bypass, and you won't be able to electrocute him, trust me. You'll be dead before you even see the whites of his eyes. Plus, I need time to discover who's behind the gunman who shot you outside the casino." He put his hand on her wounded shoulder, but she never so much as flinched. Tough as nails, his woman was.

"I thought that was Chimera."

"If it was Chimera, you'd be dead, love, not standing here." He leaned forward. "Chimera doesn't miss, trust me. I know firsthand what he can do." He tapped his chest over his clockwork heart. "Somebody unrelated to Foxley wants to see you dead. I mean to find out who that person is. Chimera is bad enough on his own, but an unknown quantity is even worse. Understand?"

He watched her, expecting her to protest further. He didn't expect her to tear up suddenly. "Bloody hell!" He closed his eyes. The old Eliza was back, and he couldn't stand to watch either one cry.

"I just don't want you to die," she sniffed. "And something bad is going to happen. I just know it."

"I'm not going to die," he said, taking her hands and pulling her against him. He wrapped his arms protectively around her. "I did that a couple of times. It's never worked out."

"You know what I mean. He nearly killed you last time." She snorted at her tears. "I can protect you, Edwin. I can help you!"

He sighed, searching for a way to approach this logically. "It would help me tremendously to know you're safe. It would be one less thing for me to fret over. Try to understand, Eliza."

She wiped her eyes with her sleeve. "But why do you have to hunt Chimera? Can't you tell Foxley there's no Rathbone? That it's all a hoax? Maybe the High Vampire Courts can use that to investigate this whole business."

"But that won't stop Chimera from hunting you."

"I don't understand."

Edwin thought about telling her how personal this was to Foxley. He meant to kill Eliza and, frankly, it had nothing to do with this Rathbone business, but Edwin didn't want to talk about the wanker. Foxley continued to be a black cloud hanging over them both.

Instead, he took her hand and put it against his chest so she could feel the minute, complex mechanics of his clockwork heart clicking along. "The reason Chimera was able to get close enough to nearly kill me the last time was because he made himself look like someone I trusted. He very nearly killed me, Eliza. In two hundred years, he's the only one who has ever come so close."

She waited, watching him with frightened eyes brimming with tears.

Edwin pressed his lips together with determination. He needed her to take this seriously, even if it meant he had to frighten her. "He means to find you, to hunt you, and he will try to kill you, Eliza. He likes it, the hunt. It's the air he breathes. I have to kill him so that never happens." He took her hand in both of his and kissed her knuckles. "Now, will you do as I ask? Please?"

"What about Derek and Maria?"

"What about them?"

"I can't just leave them here!"

Edwin closed his eyes and bowed his head in defeat. "Bloody hell."

"Edwin, please. We've been seen together. Chimera might hunt them, too. I can't just leave them on their own if he's as dangerous as you say."

Edwin sighed, eyes still closed. "What makes you think Derek will listen? Do you think he'll just go off with you and stay at the club and everything will be hunky-dory?"

"Don't use American anachronisms. You sound weird."

"Eliza..."

"He'll listen. He loves me and he'll listen."

Not the words he wanted to hear. He looked at her seriously. "Do you love him?"

Her lips parted and she looked surprised. "Oh, Edwin. I did love Derek, but that was years ago. When he was only a boy, the vampires abused him. They did horrible things to him. He needs my help."

He squeezed her hands. "But will he be willing to stay with Mouse? She is a vampire, you know."

"I'll talk to Derek. I'll make him understand how important this is."

"Shall I come with you? Help convince him?"

She shook her head. "It's better if you didn't. I'll talk to him and then I'll be right back."

She started rushing off, but Edwin grabbed her by the hand and drew her back into the circle of his arms almost as if they were ballroom dancing. He kissed the back of her left hand. "Hurry back, woman," he said. "I'm not done with you yet."

| XV |

D erek was playing solitaire in the casino downstairs, a bottle of rotgut on the table beside him and a big, middle-aged matron sitting in his lap, when Eliza spotted him. She tightened the white silk scarf around her neck and started toward him. She had to wind her way through a cotillion of half-drunk patrons teetering on their feet—and it wasn't even mid-morning yet!

Derek noticed her at once and shooed the matron out of his lap. She tumbled to the floor and scrambled around a bit before crawling drunkenly away on hands and knees.

Eliza reached Derek and sat down at the table. "Good morning," she said, probably too cheerily.

But Derek continued to play in silence.

"I've arranged a safe house for you and Maria."

"Whatever for?"

Eliza frowned at his tone of voice. "To keep us safe while Mr. McGillicuddy hunts Chimera—Foxley's agent. He's put a mark on me, you see. And, presumably, you, too, because you've been seen with me."

Derek stared blindly down at his cards. "Your employer...Prince Edwin McGillicuddy, the Angel of Hell."

She blinked at him. She'd forgotten that when Edwin swept her into his arms, and then up the stairs Margaret Mitchell-style (minus the big frou-frou ball gown, of course), that everyone in the casino had gotten an excellent view of them together, including Derek, who was working the floor. But she hadn't been thinking about that at the time. All she could think about was Edwin and being alone with him.

She felt a stab of remorse. Derek hadn't even entered her mind until he came up in her conversation with Edwin this morning. "You don't understand, Derek. All of this is so much more complicated than it seems."

"It's complicated? When you were delirious in my bed, you said McGillicuddy was a mistake. Now you're telling me it's complicated?" He flipped through his cards again even though he'd already lost the hand of solitaire. "I find it interesting this revelation comes on the heels of a very good shagging on the part of the Prince."

"I don't understand."

Derek glared, his once young and handsome face cut with hard lines she'd never noticed before. She almost didn't recognize him. "He's hypnotized you, Alisa. You think you're in love with him, but it's just vampire magic. He's using you. He's turning a trick."

She shook her head. "You don't know Edwin the way I do."

"I know he spent years bullying people and filling the streets with his own toxic mixture of drugs and prostitution. Do you think any altruistic intentions now can ever change that? Do you think he's changed…that something like him can change? He's a vampire, for Chrissakes, a goddamn monster!" Derek threw his cards down, mouth a savage slash in his quivering face.

She felt her cheeks burn. She had hurt Derek. She had never, ever, wanted to do that to him…

Derek suddenly leaned across the table separating them and pulled away the scarf around her neck. Eliza sat back, putting a hand over Edwin's mark, but he'd already seen. He knew.

Derek's eyes clouded up. "You let him feed on you?"

She hastily pulled the scarf back into place to hide the sore little mark under her ear. "That," she said pointedly, "is none of your business."

"So, you're giving him your body and your blood?"

Eliza felt a jolt of anger. "I don't ask for the details of what you do with your clients."

"My clients are human," he grumbled. "I don't service vampires like some poor, lovesick Poppet!"

He'd finally crossed a line.

"I'll say this only once, Derek. For three years, I've been on my own. I've made my own decisions, my own mistakes, and I'm not ashamed of what I've done." She took a deep breath before continuing. "I've also been alone. But now, for the first time in my life, I don't feel that way with Edwin."

"You chose to go above. You chose to be alone!"

She felt the tears start. "You know my reasons!"

Derek suddenly banged his fist on the table, making glasses and cups jump. "You left me!"

She sat there in stunned silence, watching him. Horrified by him.

Derek started to speak, but she held up her hand for silence.

"I begged Mr. McGillicuddy to let me help you, and he agreed to it, despite him being a vampire and a devil and no particular fan of yours. But if you don't want my help, then it's obvious I'm wasting my time here. I'll just take Maria and be on my way."

Derek's jaw ticked. He said nothing.

Eliza stood up, staring down at him sadly. "I'm sorry, Derek. I'm not Alisa anymore. I have to live my life. I hope you realize that someday."

Leaving him sitting there, Eliza went solemnly up the stairs to collect Maria.

Derek had meant so much to her once. Maybe he still did. But nothing had changed. Nothing ever changed with Derek. But, just like with her vampire master, she refused to belong to him. At least Edwin gave her options and didn't try to control her.

Maria was sitting up in bed, swinging her legs and slurping hot porridge from a bowl on the room service tray when Eliza let herself into the room. There seemed to be more color in her cheeks, and much of the swelling in her face had gone down with the ice packs she had applied last night. It revealed a very pretty girl with a heart-shaped face, violet eyes, and long blonde hair shampooed to the sheen of yellow silk.

The sight of the girl put a catch in Eliza's throat. She remembered what it felt like to be frightened, alone, her life in everyone's hands but her own. She wondered if, when this was all over, it wouldn't be such a terrible idea to invite Maria home with her and Edwin. They could find her work. Maria could really be someone someday.

Eliza knew Edwin wouldn't mind, even if he did grumble about it a little at first. Her heart fluttering with the possibilities, Eliza went to draw the drapes, letting the colorless, artificial lights of Poppettown in. "Good morning, Maria. I hope you feel up to a trip today."

The girl blinked in the brightness and rubbed her eyes. "Where are we going?"

Eliza turned and approached the girl. She touched her airy blonde hair. The girl flinched and Eliza felt her heart break just a little bit more. But she had hope. With time, patience, and plenty of love, Maria would emerge from her shell, and she would heal as Eliza had healed. In time, she would see that not everyone meant her harm, that there were still good people in the world—people who loved her.

"Are you afraid of me, Maria?" She hoped it wasn't so.

Maria shook her head bravely.

"Good." Eliza sat down beside the girl and started telling Maria about herself and Edwin, emphasizing the fact that Edwin was not at all like the vampires she had encountered in the past.

Maria looked wary but not frightened.

Then she told Maria that the clockwork man was gone, that he could never hurt her again. That seemed to drive some of the tension out of her young shoulders.

"Mr. McGillicuddy is going to keep us safe for a few days while he hunts down the rest of the bad guys. And then, when that's done, we'll all go home together. Would you like to come home with me?"

The girl nodded emphatically. "I work really hard."

Eliza smirked. "You won't have to work, Maria. But you will have to go to school. Would you like to go to school?"

Maria shrugged. "Don't know. Never been."

After she got Maria dressed and in a coat, Eliza gathered up their luggage and guided Maria out into the hall.

She was surprised to find Derek waiting for them. His face was still stoic, but there was something new in his eyes. A kind of light. Even before she closed the door, he said, "I saw Edwin down in the casino. I talked to him."

Eliza stiffened, and her voice was guarded. "Did you give him a hard time?"

He shook his head. "No. But he's an overbearing jerk, just so you know. And he sounds funny, like a Monty Python sketch. What the hell is that accent?"

Eliza glared at him.

"He said he got a lead on Chimera and didn't want to waste any more time waiting around here. He said you were in charge and I was to protect you and Maria. He said I was to take you downtown to see his friend Mouse." He touched his suit coat where his gun was tucked away in his armpit holster. "He emphasized the 'Eliza is in charge' part. I don't think he trusts me."

Eliza sighed. It was typical of Edwin to go haring off, guns a-blazing, like some kind of cowboy. And people wondered how he came up with feckless characters like Doctor Blood. But she supposed this was his way of keeping her out of the line of fire. It didn't make her feel any better about being dumped, but she knew why he was doing it.

"Should I have stopped him?" Derek asked.

"No," she said, letting out her breath in a puff of exasperation. "Let Edwin do his thing. Let's go."

Downstairs, Eliza stood with Maria on the curb and waited for the slipstream trolley to arrive. She kept a hand near her pocket where she still had Derek's gun. After all, Edwin warned her that Chimera could look and act like anybody, and she intended to protect herself and Maria. She might have suspected even Derek, except that Chimera didn't know Edwin was putting her and Maria under Mouse's protection.

A few moments later, Derek pulled up in his roadster.

"I'd rather we didn't take your car," Eliza said when Derek came around to open the door for her.

"Did Edwin give you the address of the club?"

"Yes, but—"

"Then why wait for the trolley?"

"That shooter, whoever he is, knows your car, Derek. He could have spies on the street. We could be leading him right to Mouse."

Derek smiled long-sufferingly. "Mouse is a vampire, Alisa. I'm sure she can take care of herself."

Something wasn't right. Edwin emphasized that she was to take a trolley to Mouse's club. Eliza took a step back, but someone stuck the muzzle of a gun in her back, halting her in mid-gesture.

"Get in, Miss Book," Maria said, her voice much older than Eliza was used to hearing. "And, Derek, you drive."

Stunned and numbed by the sudden turn of events, Eliza climbed silently into the car. Maria slid in beside her. She was holding a short, fat pistol of some translucent plastic with big round tumblers. The gun had a strange, non-standard design, but it matched the schematic in Eliza's head. She suspected it might be a boomer gun. In fact, she was pretty certain about that. It was smaller and more compact than she expected, scarcely larger than the palm of Maria's hand. Maria would have had no trouble concealing it on her person, in a pocket, or in her garter.

"I don't understand," Eliza said, starting to edge toward the opposite door.

Maria turned and pointed the gun at the casino through the open window of the roadster. "Behave yourself, Miss Book, or I'll bring the whole building down with your vampire inside of it. You know what this is, don't you?" She stroked the gun.

"I know." Eliza stared at it.

Derek, his eyes as fixed as a zombie, got in the driver's seat and turned the engine over, saying nothing.

Eliza sat on the fine white vinyl seat in stoic silence, her heart hammering, her mind wheeling…the gun still in her pocket. She looked at Maria. "I don't understand," she repeated. "Are you Chimera?"

Maria smiled sweetly, pulling the bleeding edges of her broken lips apart. "Wrong bad guy, I'm afraid. I'm Rathbone. Or what's left of him. I hear you've been looking for me?"

The car pulled out into the street.

* * *

Edwin's favorite gun was a pretty, nickel-plated Rainmaker that fit exactly in his long, slender hand. He'd won it in a poker game with Old West gambling outlaw Belle Starr. It had been still warm from her garter when she handed it over to him. It was an early design, a five-shot Colt with a bad habit of jamming after the first shot. Gunfighters loathed it. Edwin kept it more for sentimental reasons than anything else. It made him remember Belle and her attempt to snooker the gun out of him after the game. She hadn't succeeded, though he'd allowed her to ply her trade on him repeatedly against the wall of the cathouse. Negotiations could be fun.

Over the years, "Belle" had been modified many times over to accommodate ever newer and more modern types of munitions. More recently, he had upgraded it with a new stock and barrel that allowed him to fire magazines full of blooding bullets—bullets that contained a single drop of his own blood, deadly on contact to any vampire not of his bloodline. It was cute, sexy as hell, and deadly to both humans and vampires.

He was sitting at the hotel room's desk, cleaning Belle, loading her for bear, and thinking about what fun he and Eliza had had on this very spot only an hour earlier when the love of his unlife returned.

She stepped quietly into the room and closed the door soundly behind her.

Edwin glanced up. "Did you talk to Derek?"

Eliza nodded as she started across the room toward him, affecting a soundless glide.

"And what did he say? Any trouble?"

She shook her head. In the dimness of the artificial early morning light pouring through the windows, her face was painfully bare and her eyes a deep, ocean blue in her frank, open face. Eliza always managed to look so guileless, so innocent, and that surprised him, considering what she had been through. It made Edwin's heart melt a little bit more. She was absolutely perfect for him, perhaps even his Anam Cara.

"Cat got your tongue?" Edwin asked as he finished inserting a fresh magazine. He cocked the gun and aimed it straight at her chest.

Eliza stopped and watched him carefully. Hungrily.

"What do you have to say for yourself, then?"

Eliza frowned with concern, saying nothing.

So, Edwin shot her in the chest. In the heart.

The bullet knocked her to the floor.

He stood up.

The creature on the floor began to scream. It screamed like a machine, a sound that went on and on as noxious black fluid poured out of the massive, poisoned hole in its heart. He hoped the creature appreciated the irony of the shot.

It flailed against the floor, then seemed to melt and reform, to become other things, other people from other times, some random, some calculated. He saw dead friends and past lovers. For one moment, it looked like Mouse, then like Foxley. Finally, as the blooding bullet ate through its queer anatomy, it began losing form altogether and become instead a kind of viscous black sludge that slowly melted right through the cracks in the floorboards.

Chimera was very good at what he did. He'd even managed to smell like Eliza, like vanilla candles and morning rain. But his silence was a dead giveaway.

"Tit for tat, ya bloody git." Edwin kicked at the remnants as they melted away. "Back to hell wit' ya."

He swung back toward the door, the gun still warm where it was clenched in his hand, intent on finding Eliza. If Chimera had been able to infiltrate the premises, God knew what else was here.

Edwin was halfway down the hallway when his mark on Eliza opened up and he was struck with a massive psychic blowback that staggered him into a nearby wall.

Eliza was in mortal danger.

* * *

As they glided seamlessly downtown, Eliza asked the inevitable question. "Where are we going?"

"You'll see." Maria stared out of the window. Her voice was toneless, revealing nothing.

Eliza studied the girl's reflection in the glass, suddenly overcome with dread and regret. Maria didn't even have the self-respect to look maniacal like a good villain should. Instead, her expression was empty, like a bored girl riding to her first day at school.

"You're not going to say anything?" she said to Derek in the front seat.

She received no answer, so she kicked his seat, hard. "You bastard! You lie to me, kidnap me, and you don't even feel the need to explain yourself?"

"Don't bother him," Maria snapped. "None of this is his fault. He's only doing as I say."

"Why would he do that?"

Maria turned her head, rotating it in a funny way that made Eliza think of a doll in a creepy horror movie, and pinned her with huge, pale, unblinking eyes. They were the eyes of a child. Yet, like Foxley, there was something there not childlike at all. Something dark and soiled.

"Because I am the Great Mother. The Hive does as I bid, and Derek is part of the Hive." Maria smiled—not unkindly. "So, if you feel the need to rage, Miss Book, then rage at me."

"Of course you don't. There is something wrong with you, Poppet. Your brain is not wired properly." Maria shifted the gun into her lap but kept her finger firmly on the trigger.

Eliza felt a surge of rage; she was getting tired of people telling her she wasn't right in the head.

"I still don't understand. How do you know that? Who are you?"

Maria ignored her question. "You're a Deaf, Alisa. Your brain is damaged...different. That's why you were able to walk away so easily from your Vampire Lord. In case you ever wondered. You cannot hear me."

Eliza scowled. "Who are you that I should listen?"

"I told you. I am the Hive." Maria smiled then. It was an empty smile, the smile of a brilliantly constructed robot. "The Great Mother." When she saw that Eliza still did not understand, she sighed wearily as if burdened with a particularly stupid pupil.

Her eyes moved mechanically as she searched for the right words. "When we are taken by our Vampire Lords, we are marked. This causes certain psychic changes to occur within us. We become linked...a smaller part of them. We can only do their will. But you don't know this because you have never been affected that way."

Eliza swallowed drily and heard a sharp click.

"I am the Hive Mother, Alisa. The Queen Poppet, if you will. I am in your head. I am in everyone's head. Everyone who is a Poppet. I was with you last night when you made love to Edwin. I was with you when Derek helped to get the bullet out of you. I was with you in Lord Foxley's cage. But you cannot hear me because you are a Deaf."

"I'm not—"

"I don't mean in some physical way. I mean here." She pointed at her temple. "One in every ten thousand Poppets is like that. Even those Poppets meant to live as Courtiers and Courtesans are developed without a prefrontal lobe to prevent anxiety and introspection

—essentially, a genetic lobotomy. But nature abhors a vacuum, so sometimes the fetus develops a secondary lobe to compensate. This can change the whole topography of the brain. It can also trigger powerful psychic vibrations, especially when the Poppet is under duress."

Maria looked at her knowingly. "You and I are both different, Eliza. We do not function like other Poppets. There are a few others, as well. Mr. Stephen, for instance. We're all almost like siblings."

"We're nothing alike," Eliza insisted.

Maria shrugged as if Eliza's words were of no consequence. "It was the same with me. After Lord Rathbone took me...used me...I changed for the better. I found I could communicate wordlessly with the other Poppets at Court. In fact, I could communicate with other Poppets anywhere in the world."

She stopped and blinked thoughtfully as if relishing the memory. "I was no longer alone. With time, I learned to control and then to increase my power. Eventually, I discovered that I could not only talk to other Poppets but influence their thoughts and actions."

"Control them, you mean."

"I prefer to think of it as groupthink, a communal experience. We all have the same goal in mind—that is to say, freedom." She glanced askance at Eliza. "Before I came along, the Poppets were scattered and weak. I brought them together. I gave thoughts to the ones who were thoughtless, and purpose to the ones who were without a path. I made them strong. I did that."

"Congratulations." Eliza stared at the weak little bruised figure sitting beside her. It hardly seemed possible that such a small, wounded body could possess so much power. She licked her dry lips, suddenly afraid of that seemingly innocent creature. "What happened to your Lord?"

"Rathbone? I killed him. Or, rather, I influenced his Poppets to kill him. They disemboweled him very slowly. Removed all of his internal organs. It took many days."

Eliza felt the blood drain from her face.

"Don't mourn, sister. Rathbone was an evil piece of shit."

Something was happening to Maria's voice. It was deepening, roughening, reverberating in the open air as if other voices lurked beneath it, all talking softly at once.

Eliza shuddered, wondering if she was going insane—or maybe she was just hearing the Hive speak.

"He'd been raping me regularly since the age of five. I'm not unlike your Derek in that regard. We have both suffered at our masters' hands. You, on the other hand, have been mostly spared this indignation and do not understand pain. You kept your innocence much longer than most of us. You have been protected, sheltered from much of the pain."

Maria smiled bitterly at her, tears in her eyes. "I assure you, sister, the world is a much brighter place without Lord Rathbone's presence."

"But you killed his Poppets. Your own people!"

"No, I only let the Poppets kill each other." Maria's eyes went blank, empty, soulless.

The eyes of a perfect sociopath, Eliza decided.

"It didn't please me to do so, of course, but it was a necessary evil. I wasn't as strong as I am now, and if any of the Poppets had survived, they might have talked, then investigators from the High Vampire Courts would have found me, broken me, and that I cannot permit. Not until I finish the will of the Hive."

"I thought you were the Hive."

"We are all the Hive," Maria said, her voice echoing with dozens of angry, buzzing voices.

Eliza felt the little hairs on her arms lift and brush against her sleeves as the collective Hive voices washed over her like flitting moths. "And the other Courts?" she asked, dreading the answer. "Did you kill them too?"

"What do you think?"

"I think you're disturbed. I think your power has unhinged your mind."

Maria shrugged. "It's simply a matter of perspective. When one is fighting a war, there are bound to be casualties. I assure you the end will justify the means, sister."

"What ends? What means?"

"That," Maria responded, "is a surprise."

Eliza thought about snatching up the gun in Maria's lap, turning it on her, and demanding that Maria let her go, but she doubted she could get to it in time before Maria squeezed the trigger.

She needed more information. "The shooter. That was you?"

"He was a Poppet acting under my command. One of the Hive. They are many down here now, and many more coming all the time. The Red Doors are quite useful in that way. In their extreme ignorance and zealotry, they bring us new soldiers every day."

Eliza felt sick. "Why try to kill me? I have no real power. I'm not part of your Hive."

Maria smiled. "Your presence disrupts the Hive, Alisa. As a Deaf, you are an opposing force."

"A force you mean to kill," she said miserably.

"Well, now, you are developing interesting tricks, such as your ability to communicate with machines, so I may forgive you. We shall see."

Eliza squeezed her eyes shut. "You're too kind." Her fingers inched toward her pocket where she had the gun. "Do you kill all opposing forces? Did you kill Dr. Grott?"

"Dr. Grott was human. Therefore, not part of the Hive. He could not be controlled."

"Why did you pretend to be his assistant? Because your Hive couldn't control him?"

Maria looked poignantly at her. "It is not my Hive, Alisa. It is our Hive. And I really was his assistant. I needed someone with the skills necessary to engineer this." She held up the gun in her hand, stroking it like a beloved pet.

Eliza stared at the little, innocuous-looking weapon. "When you learned you couldn't bend Dr. Grott to your will, you programmed the schematics into Talos, then erased Dr. Grott's computer databases, didn't you?"

She wondered if that was the reason Maria needed her, to make weapons. The idea made her sick. Would she force Eliza to make arms meant to kill vampires—and other Poppets?

"You know about Talos." Maria sounded impressed. "And, no, I do not need your talents for that purpose, sister. I only need one of these for the task ahead." She held up the gun.

"But Talos," Eliza insisted. "He killed Dr. Grott. He hurt you. Raped you."

"On my orders," Maria said. She looked out the window as they slid by through the muzzy patches of darkness and light that were the slums. The streets looked bleak and graphic. Worker Poppets trudged by, their eyes set steadfastly ahead of them. How many of them were now part of the Hive?

"I told you there must be casualties. I subject even myself to the rigors of the Hive."

"Why?" Eliza indicated the car. "Why this game?"

Maria's face grew placid, almost young. "To get close to you, of course. I needed to see if your power could serve the purposes of the Hive." Maria smiled to indicate that Eliza had passed approval, then turned her attention back on the street as they pulled alongside an alley wedged between a tenement building and a nightclub.

"And, last night, when you darkened so much of the city with your wild talent as a 'techkinetic'—as your clockwork vampire calls you—I finally realized you would make a powerful ally of the Hive."

"I'm not your ally, Maria."

Maria ignored her as they turned down the alley. "We're here," she announced, indicating a door at the end of the alley. "From here we go to the overworld."

Eliza slid her hand inside her pocket and gripped the gun.

"Do not draw your weapon, Alisa. You know what this gun can do. Behave, or the blood of the thousands of people who will die in the rubble of these buildings will be on your head."

Eliza loosened her grip on the little gun.

Derek opened her side, reached in, and took the gun from her. He kept his eyes fixed on Maria as if she were some holy messiah who had descended to Earth to save his soul. He did not seem to notice Eliza at all.

"Come, sister," said Maria, linking her arm through Eliza's and dragging her from the car as if she really was a sister. In Maria's other hand she gripped the boomer gun, hidden in her skirts. "We really shouldn't keep the esteemed Lord Foxley waiting, now, should we?"

***

Eliza was gone.

Edwin knew, even without checking, that she was not in the casino downstairs, nor on the sidewalk outside or anywhere in the general vicinity of the building. He could not smell her at all, though he could feel the dull, insistent vibration of her fear. The unique bloodlink they had forged between them the night before sang like a wire being thrummed. He knew even without thinking about it that the Hive had taken his woman.

Frustrated, he stood on the casino's ground floor, wings fully extended, trying to get his rage under control before something untoward happened and the police had to do a return trip. People sitting around craps tables and the roulette wheel stared warily at him, frightened by what moved in their midst.

When he got his hands on those two wankers, they were dead. Or, they would beg to be when the Prince finished with them. He turned and punched a sizeable hole in the wall, startling some old biddies sitting around the blackjack table.

He needed a plan.

Edwin returned to the main lobby and approached the night concierge. At first, the man was reluctant to tell him what room Cesar was staying in, but a few less-than-gentle mental pushes later, Edwin was on the second floor, standing in front of room 205.

He broke the door and lock soundly, thinking what a bad habit he was making of this, and stepped into the room. He half-expected to find Cesar in bed with some fine young stud, going at it like the red-blooded, All-American male he was.

Instead, he found the boy sitting up in bed, clutching his pillow, eating a quart of Edy's Double Fudge Brownie ice cream, and watching an old rerun of Buffy on cable television.

Edwin looked and looked again. Talk about safe sex. He decided his first fantasy about Cesar was more fun.

Cesar, sensing danger, climbed slowly off the mattress and stood there, backlit by the image of Sarah Michelle Geller ramming sharpened stakes into multiple black vampire hearts. When his eyes met Edwin's, he dropped his carton of ice cream to the floor. "Um…"

"Oh, please, don't even bother explaining what you've been up to. It'll be a very dull story, I'm sure." Edwin marched up to the young man, grabbed him by the front of his pajamas, and threw him down on the mussed coverlet of the bed.

A look of surprise on his face, Cesar tried to scramble backward, but Edwin moved too quickly, springing onto the bed like a cat and pinning Cesar under his weight.

Various magazines lay scattered across the bed. Edwin held out hope that a few were *Playgirl* or even *GQ*, but everything was either aviation- or anime-related. He resisted the urge to roll his eyes and instead ripped Cesar's pajama shirt wide open, buttons flying.

Cesar gaped, his eyes going wide.

Edwin studied the lovely, tanned, military-inspired muscles of Cesar's waxed chest and the sweet little pulse ticking in the hollow of his throat. Now, this was what he called chocolate. "Want to be a vampire, mate?"

"Uhhh..." Cesar shuddered.

"Good. I need you."

He needed a vampire who could fire a gun and fly a ship. A vampire who knew his way around security on board the *Gypsy Queen* was a definite plus if what he had seen briefly in Eliza's mind was true—and, by extension, this so-called Hive.

Cesar swallowed nervously and gripped Edwin by the lapels.

Edwin reached down and stroked Cesar's cheek with his thumb. Cesar looked very pretty lying there on the rumpled bedclothes. Delicate. Delicious. Edwin leaned down and inhaled his chocolaty breath and the vanilla heaven of his skin. He was practically a virgin. His blood would be incredibly sweet.

"You said you wanted to be part of my Court," Edwin breathed softly in Cesar's ear.

Cesar quivered in response and his fingers bunched up in Edwin's clothes. He whimpered, and Edwin took that as a yes.

"Welcome to the family."

Taking Cesar by the chin, Edwin turned his head and buried his teeth in the boy's delicate throat flesh.

| xvi |

A car was waiting for them in the overworld. The ride was short, silent, and uneventful. Eliza sat in the backseat next to Maria. Maria kept the gun discreetly in her lap but made no pretense of hiding it. Derek drove without acknowledging either of them.

When they finally arrived at JFK Airport, they transferred to a shuttle a little larger than a Hummingbird, the type used to bus groups of wealthy tourists and their piles of luggage up to the gyro. Derek piloted the craft.

Eliza, regaled to the back once more, was forced to sit on the floor with her back to the wall of the shuttle with Maria on the backward-facing seat before her, the gun resting in her lap.

"I still don't understand one thing," Eliza said at last. She glanced at the boomer gun. It was probably a bad idea to go for it. It wouldn't take more than a millisecond for Maria to jerk the trigger, and that would be that. It would likely vaporize them all in mid-air…not to mention what the sonic wake would probably do to the city below. But she couldn't stop thinking about it.

Maria would do it, too, she knew. If she was willing to submit to rape at the hands of Talos just to get close to Eliza, she had no doubt the girl was more than willing to vaporize all of them and become a martyr to her cause.

Maria smiled as if she knew exactly what Eliza was thinking. "What's that, sister?"

Eliza narrowed her eyes. "If it's true that you can control all Poppets everywhere—well, almost all Poppets—why not simply command all the Poppets all over the world to destroy their Vampire Lords? Wouldn't that be easier than carrying on with all this complicated cloak and dagger business?"

Maria pursed her lips. "The answer to that is simple. We have no desire to make martyrs of vampires."

"We as in the Hive, or we as in you?"

"There is no longer any difference between me and we, sister." Maria glanced out the window at the passing clouds in the gunmetal grey, overcast sky. "We are almost there."

She knew where there was. "There...where you plan to kill Foxley like all of the other Vampire Lords," she guessed. "What a coup for you."

Maria shook her head. "I will not kill him. His own Poppets will kill him for me."

"Then why do we need to be on board the *Gypsy Queen?*"

Maria narrowed her eyes. "Lord Foxley is a special case."

"Because he's old and powerful."

"Because he owns the *Gypsy Queen.*"

"I don't understand."

"You tire me with your questions, sister."

Eliza smirked. "I'll probably be dead before this night is over. Humor me."

Maria thought about that. She looked out the window again, very solemn. "More than one and a half million people are living on the Island of Manhattan. There are another fifty thousand people on board the *Gypsy Queen.* If close to one and a half million people were suddenly erased because of a vampire attack, do you really think anyone, even the most liberal progressive, would dare pass the Vampire Bill?"

Eliza sat stunned for a long time. She could hear the nearly silent hum of the artificial air circulating through the shuttle. She could hear her own pulse thudding in her ears. It took her a while to find her voice. "You really are a psychotic little bitch, aren't you?"

"Again, that's a matter of perspective."

"You can't kill that many people because you've suffered. That's insane!" She started getting up, to reach for the gun in Maria's lap, but Maria was right; she was inside Eliza's head. She knew Eliza better than she knew herself.

Maria grabbed Eliza by the front of the dress, effortlessly tossing her against the far wall of the shuttle. Her strength was enormous. Eliza felt her skull crack against the wall. She grunted and slumped down, pain and unconsciousness painting the corners of her vision.

Maria stood up. She took a step toward Eliza. For the first time since all this insanity had begun, her face showed real life as it twisted into a mask of vapid, mindless, animal rage—a rage that made Eliza's hair stand on end.

"What do you know about suffering, Alisa?" she screamed, covering Eliza in spittle. She swung the boomer gun at Eliza's head like a billy club.

Eliza had seconds to react if she wanted to survive. Armed with her peculiar power, she gripped the metal floor and instantly connected to the shuttle's internal circuitry. She didn't try to do anything in particular, but the pulse of wild, rampant energy still made the craft shudder, which caused Maria to stagger. Eliza jerked away from the wall and ducked under Maria's swing.

She kicked out at the level of Maria's knees, knocking the girl over. The gun went flying into a corner as Maria toppled to the floor. She had one chance. The gun was too far away to reach, so Eliza lunged at Maria, jamming her arm against Maria's throat, pinning her to the floor.

Maria choked. Eliza gritted her teeth and pressed down. If she had to kill Maria to stop this madness, so be it. It wasn't like this was the first time she had ever killed anyone. It was unfortunate but necessary. Maybe that made her a bad person, as bad as the monsters that had enslaved them, but she didn't care. All she knew was that a city full of people, both innocent and guilty alike, could not be allowed to die because of one girl's pain. It wasn't fair.

Maria, her face strangely placid, reached up and wrapped her hand around Eliza's throat, her iron grip causing her fingers to dimple her skin. Eliza held on. Already, Maria was losing strength. A few more centimeters and her windpipe would be crushed and all of this would be over. Maria was strong; Maria was a Poppet. But so was Eliza. She kept applying pressure until she heard a sharp click near her ear.

Derek had heard the panicked cry of the Hive Queen from his place up front in the cockpit. Every Poppet in the world had heard the cry of the Queen, she figured.

"Stop, Alisa."

"No, Derek! You don't under—"

"Let the Great Mother go, Alisa."

"She's not—"

"She is our strength. She is the All..." He pressed the cold barrel of the Colt to Alisa's head. "You must not harm the Hive, Alisa."

Eliza glared up. "Derek, she isn't the Hive! She's a disturbed girl who is going to kill this whole fucking city if we don't stop her!"

Derek seethed. She saw that clearly. Most of it was Maria and the Hive. But there was a part of his pain that was purely her doing, she knew. He'd loved her once. As children, they had been everything to each other. But, now, his love was tempered with disappointment and jealousy.

With a roar of frustrated rage, Derek clipped the side of her head with the butt of the gun.

Eliza's world went black.

* * *

Mouse and Cesar stood in Tokyo Hoes' storeroom, wearing dusters like Old West riflemen. Edwin wore an old coat of his made of soft, black, broken-in leather. Mouse had kept it as a memento. It fell to his heels and covered the bulky Remington Blooding Rifle under it well enough if he didn't move too quickly. But then, he reflected, if he had to move quickly, hiding the rifle was a moot point.

Mouse had done well. Edwin had phoned ahead and told her to expect them, and to gather supplies for a little expedition. Since this was Poppettown, finding contraband like the Remingtons they were currently armed with had taken Mouse exactly two phone calls and twenty-six minutes. They were huge, sexy as hell, and could kill an army of Nazi werewolves on the march. The police used them to put down rogue vampires since they took special blooding bullets laced with iron particles, making them poison on contact with any of the undead. Not to mention, they left a hole you could put your entire arm through. Edwin loved them to pieces.

He looked his two Enforcers over. Mouse was ready. She wore her scarf and hat so that most of her face was covered, her body strong, agile, and sexless under the coat. She had her gun slung across her shoulder and the bloodlust glinting in her eyes.

Cesar looked less sure. His skin was still very grey despite the copious amounts of blood that Edwin had poured down his throat, and his eyes looked feverish and slightly unfocused, like a young, untried gunfighter. Under normal circumstances, Edwin would have spent several days teaching a new Heir and getting to know him, but that was a luxury they could ill-afford at present.

"Cesar," he said, his voice cracking like a whip.

Cesar snapped to attention and looked at Edwin. In life, he had been a soldier. In undeath, it was the same thing. "I feel weird," he said, slurring his words as if he were dead drunk.

Edwin pointed at himself. "You watch me. You listen to me. You do nothing that I don't tell you to do."

Cesar nodded dumbly. His hand went to his throat where Edwin's mark was still sore and half-healed, then to his mouth where he was the beneficiary of a new pair of shocking, wolf-like incisors. Gradually, his eyes began to drift again. He'd lost his mortality and gotten a whopping dose of El Mal de Amor. It was a miracle he could stand up straight.

Mouse grabbed him by the back of the neck and jerked his head around so he was looking directly at Edwin. "You do not look away from our Lord when he speaks. Our Lord keeps us alive. You watch him every moment you are not watching for enemies. Understand?"

Cesar nodded again, looking more frightened than ever.

As Edwin loaded up on ammo boxes, sticking them in all the available pockets of his coat, he said to Mouse, "Keep an eye on the pup, will you?"

"Of course."

A tenement building three blocks down led to the overworld. The three of them headed that way, marching down the strangely derelict streets. Poppettown was never like this, not even in the middle of the night. An occasional car passed, but there were hardly any people on the street.

So, when the crowd rounded a bend and started marching toward them in military formation, all three vampires stopped dead in their tracks in the middle of the street, Edwin in the center with Mouse on his right and Cesar on his left. He was half expecting this.

Poppets of different ages, races, and divisions poured into the streets and formed ranks so deep they forced traffic to a full stop.

Edwin watched them. They looked empty-faced, like giant walking dolls. Many carried weapons—shovels, pipes, or whatever debris they could scrounge from the city corners. All of them had eyes set fast on the three vampires standing in the middle of the street, their dusters blowing around them like gunslingers in a spaghetti western. All were ready to block their path and keep them from returning to the overworld.

Mouse and Cesar looked to him. Edwin shifted on his feet. He glanced at his Enforcers; both looked nervous, and for good reason —this was peculiar behavior, even for Poppets.

He opened his bloodlink to both of his Heirs, and it was like throwing open a door in his mind. Suddenly, he could feel what they felt. Mouse—eternal hunger, resolution, indomitable spirit, a creature of impulse and careless violence. Cesar—a naïve creature, innocent, randy as a sixteen-year-old lad, frightened to death of his own desires. Of the two, Cesar was still so close to his humanity that it hurt. And, under that, both vampires' raging, heart-pounding desire to rend and consume every vessel of blood standing before them, even knowing it would never fill them, never sate the low-grade madness hissing through their blood.

"Skirmish line," Edwin ordered, drawing out the Remington from under his coat. The others followed suit. Mouse licked her lips in anticipation. Cesar worried his bottom lip but tried to look tough.

Edwin moved the Remington to his shoulder, where it rested in clear sight, a warning to the oncoming crowd of Poppets. With less than a thousand yards separating them, the crowd finally stopped.

"Who are you?" Lord Edwin demanded of the crowd. "What do you want with us?"

The crowd of Poppets mulled about restlessly for a few moments before one of their numbers stepped to the fore, a big, bulky Worker

Poppet with barely the IQ of a young child. He nevertheless pinned Edwin with a cynical look far beyond his intellect or experience.

"McGillicuddy," spat the Poppet. "The Angel of Hell. Get thee back."

"And you are?" Edwin said, cocking an eyebrow at the Poppet's bravado. He pushed subtlety against the Poppet's thoughts, rooting out answers. There was more going on here than it seemed. The Poppets barring their way were much more unified than they ought to be.

The head Poppet swayed lightly, blinked, and said, "We are the Hive. You will not pass tonight."

Lord Edwin's mouth quirked up on one side. "What is the Hive? And why will I not pass?"

Again, the head Poppet swayed as Edwin pushed for more answers. This time, though, Edwin sensed that the Poppet really didn't know very much. He could feel a unified consciousness at work, yet no one part of the whole seemed completely aware that invisible hands were pulling its strings. It simply bounced along on those strings as any good poppet would.

Irritated, the head Poppet took another step toward them and raised his fist, shouting angrily, "The Hive is all! You will not pass, devil. She will not allow it!"

Mouse leveled her rifle on the Poppet as it drew nearer. For one heartbeat, Edwin was fully prepared to give her the signal. Then he looked at the head Poppet and realized that Eliza would never forgive him if he killed a Poppet caught up in some kind of giant, malevolent groupthink, no will of his own.

"Stop," he said, and Mouse obediently lowered her gun, though not by much. "We're not going to kill the Poppets."

"We're not?" Mouse sounded disappointed.

Edwin tossed his gun to Mouse, who caught it one-handedly. He put his wrist to his mouth and bit. A few seconds later, the shining black manriki flew, enwrapped the head Poppet, and with a simple, practiced motion, he had deftly jerked the man into his arms. The other Poppets jostled undecidedly at this new development.

Edwin turned the Poppet around so his back was to him, jerked his head to one side, and bit deep into his shoulder.

The Hive entered Edwin through the Poppet's bitter blood. Edwin swallowed, taking into himself all the knowledge of the Hive, all the history of the Hive Queen's suffering. It was like sitting down in a vast library and reading every book in it in fast forward. A library of dark, violent knowledge that he absorbed in seconds. It was also like sitting down at a vast banquet and eating rotten food. It made his head spin. It made him ill.

He saw all. He knew all. And he despaired.

***

Lord Foxley, who had been slumbering in his library at New Versailles, one of Edwin's novels resting in his lap, suddenly jerked awake as an ancient bloodlink was suddenly ripped wide open like an old wound inside his head.

Pleasure Poppets stirred around him, disturbed by his sudden intake of breath.

"My boy?" For one moment, he was certain that Edwin was in the room with him. The invisible presence felt distinctively like Edwin—warm and honey-sweet, rough, cynical, and it left a bitter aftertaste in his mouth.

Edwin was certainly not the oldest vampire in the world, but he was still a very powerful one. It took a powerful vampire to open such old bloodlinks so quickly and efficiently. But then, Foxley knew that about Edwin, had always known that. A weak vampire would not have become his own Lord in only two hundred years. A weak vampire wouldn't have developed the tricks Edwin had so quickly—one of which was the ability to not only induce unbelievable, orgasmic pleasure through his bite but also control those he bit, dead or alive. He could have effectively raised an army of zombies if he so desired.

It was a trick that Foxley had utilized in the past when Edwin worked as his Enforcer.

Foxley stiffened and slumped back in his wing chair as Edwin began filtering information down the invisible umbilicus of their bloodlink and into his head. It came in a tumbling rush, like books falling off shelves, their pages fluttering open, their words imprinted on Foxley's retinas and brain.

And then books did start falling off shelves, a few at first. And then hundreds tumbled to the floor as Edwin's power ripped through the room like a sharp October wind. The Poppets at Foxley's feet began scrambling away, heading for the door as books began mounting up around Foxley's chair.

Foxley remained seated, undisturbed by Edwin's show of power. If anything, it comforted him. Edwin always comforted him, saddened him, and piqued his hunger. Foxley had made many Heirs over the long centuries of his existence, but it was Edwin he regretted. Edwin he missed. Edwin he ached for. It was an endless, ongoing agony that he had come to relish.

He watched the last of the books tumble down at his feet.

"But why tell me this?" he asked. "You ran away...again." His voice sounded hurt even to his own cynical ears.

Well, it ain't 'cause I bloody like you, Edwin's voice came distinctively into his head. He let his breath out in frustration—at least mentally.

Our enemies are en route to the *Gypsy Queen*. I'm willing to cut a deal. Place Eliza under the seal of your protection and I'll do a bit of rat-catching for you.

Edwin was a very good negotiator. Foxley had taught him that.

It took Foxley but two seconds to make up his mind. The sad little Poppet made his Prince happy, and that interested Foxley. He wanted Edwin happy—for now. He could rip her away from him at any time and make Edwin's pain the sweetest thing either of them had ever experienced.

"Very well." He wetted his lips with the tip of his tongue. "But she is destined to hurt you in ways you have yet to experience in even two hundred years of life."

I know.

"On my life and blood, your Poppet is under my protection," he vowed, then leaned forward. As if you would release me, Edwin answered.

Foxley laughed. "You know me so well." He paused. "Why not bring her into the fold? That way, we can both enjoy her charms."

Because she's mine, Edwin warned. She is part of my Court.

"Your Court. I like the sound of that. You really are coming into your own, my boy." He hesitated. "Do you really love her that much?"

More.

"Then make her like you."

You wouldn't understand. Edwin sounded sad. If you lived another twelve thousand years, you would not understand. Now, clear out your Poppets. All of them—except for Mr. Stephen. The Hive Queen can control Poppets anywhere in the world. If the Poppets catch you, they will kill you and take control of the ship. Trust only vampires and Deaf Poppets. She has no control over them.

"Are you certain about all of this?"

Bloody hell! Would I bloodlink to you if all of this wasn't true?

Edwin had a point. He'd had no contact with Foxley in over fifty years, hadn't even sent a Christmas card! And yet, now, he was wide open, vulnerable.

When he had opened the bloodlink to Foxley, he had also left himself wide open to Foxley's inspection. Foxley could see everything inside of Edwin, every shame, every pain, and everything he cherished. Centermost to his desire was Eliza, tying him to the remnants of his humanity, but she was not alone. There were others: his little Heir Mouse, the friends he had made on Earth, even the new one, Cesar. Edwin was a fool and a Gael—obsessive, impetuous, stalwart. When Gaels loved, they loved for life. It was the same when they hated.

Where is the main Command Center for the *Gypsy Queen?* Edwin asked. He had been rummaging around Foxley's mind as well, but he had been unable to discover that information. Foxley had hidden it too well.

Foxley was reluctant to share such sensitive information, but he realized he no longer had any choice. The hour was growing late. "That's here, with me."

You keep the Command Center at New Versailles?

"Despite what you think of me, I do not spend my days merely cowering away with my Poppets here, indulging in pleasure and fantasies. One of my duties is to maintain the gyro's course, secure its orbit, and see to it that everything is maintained properly." Foxley bared his teeth. "I built this ship. I was a master shipbuilder and captain twelve thousand years ago, Edwin. I engineered the *Gypsy Queen* and everything aboard it."

Foxley stood up amidst the cataclysmic piles of books, tall and angry that someone—a Poppet, no less!—would believe herself his equal, that she would try to overthrow him, a Vampire Lord twelve thousand years steeped in his craft. It was contemptible. It was arrogant. It was something he would have done.

"I shall attempt to secure the premises around the Command Center. I'll meet you here. Do you have reinforcements?"

I have two Enforcers with me. But I formerly request Lady Claire. I require her blades.

"You have her." Foxley paused. "Why does the Hive have your woman, Edwin?"

Maria means to use Eliza to bypass your security system.

"That's impossible. She cannot do that."

Eliza can tear through your security system as if it was made of tissue paper.

Foxley maintained his stance but, inwardly, he cringed. He believed Edwin. Edwin had no reason to lie to him about that.

He sent out a silent command for Lady Claire to join him at the Command Center, then moved to one of the bookshelves and put his hand on the wall where a sensor read his DNA. The shelf slid back to reveal a dark, round passageway beyond. He had many such passages honeycombing the palace so he might better reach the Command Center in a hurry.

"You realize my first duty is to protect the *Gypsy Queen*," Foxley stated as he started down the passage, his eyes easily piercing the almost impenetrable darkness. "And if that requires me destroying your woman in the process, then it must be so."

That would upset me greatly.

And that, frustratingly, upset Foxley greatly.

The passageway was smoothly metallic and smelled faintly of electricity. It twisted off in dozens of different branches that led to various command ports around the palace, but Foxley had been down these corridors so often that he could have found the main corridor that led to the Command Center in his sleep.

"Really, Edwin, you are a fool. You could have destroyed me easily by saying nothing at all. And then you would be free."

He sensed that Edwin agreed.

"Why help me?"

Edwin shrugged mentally. *I want to be a superhero?*

"You are a romantic. You read too many books." Foxley smiled as he passed through the final door and stepped into the somber blue light of the main Command Center, the very beating heart of the *Gypsy Queen*, and gazed upon the helix that kept the whole ship suspended in orbit. It throbbed with pale azure light that was almost too painful to look upon. "If I see your woman, I shall do what I can to...preserve her."

I'm sure you will. Edwin shut down their bloodlink like slamming a heavy metal door.

Despite the imminent danger, Foxley laughed.

* * *

Edwin pulled his teeth out of the Poppet, blood gushing over his chin as he let the man go. First, the Poppet staggered, then toppled into the street, not dead but out cold.

The other Poppets were mulling about again with agitation. Some turned to glare at him—not a friendly look. Some began to speak, not more than a sentence each—and sometimes just a fragment of a sentence—but it all came together like a chorus. Edwin knew he was hearing the voice of the Hive speaking.

It started talking about killing him in various creative ways.

Edwin weaved slightly on his feet as he tried to absorb all the sudden knowledge carved into his brain...stories about Maria, about the cruelty she had experienced at Lord Rathbone's hands...then her sudden explosion of power and control...the ability to speak to other Poppets, first in dreams, then literally mind to mind...an innocent game, really, a way to stave off the long, lonely hours...her pain, their pain...the Poppets coming together...not entirely Maria's doing. She thought she was the Queen because she was the apex, the glue that held them together, but she was more like a lightning rod, a focal point for this great, worldwide outpouring of misery.

Out of the few and scattered grew a massive group intelligence. The Hive had been born not of the misery of one lost soul, but thousands. Edwin had to shut it all down before it completely swamped his mind and broke him.

Several Poppets pointed at him. "You'll die, McGillicuddy! Die like Rathbone!" they said as one. Slowly, they started forward again, marching toward the three vampires.

Edwin danced back a step, their collective anger chilling him to the bone. "If I had a shilling for every time someone said that to me, I'd be able to retire," he said, trying to sound tough in the face of their outrage. He only sort of succeeded.

He turned to glance behind him. More Poppets were bringing up the rear. They were going to hem the three of them in, then take them apart at their leisure.

Edwin turned to Mouse. He saw the panic in her eyes. When he'd absorbed the knowledge of the Hive and fed it into Foxley, his bloodlink had naturally filtered the information down into his own Heirs as well—the two vampires who were, by blood, closer to him than anyone. For a moment, all four of them had been linked together in a massive mental orgy.

Now, his Enforcers stood white-faced with shock and understanding.

"What's the play, my Lord?" Mouse's voice quavered, though her hands were rock steady around the stock of the Remington resting on her shoulder.

Edwin pointed down an alley. "You and Cesar get to the overworld. Get above by any means necessary and secure transportation. We need to hurry and find Maria if we're going to stop all of this."

Mouse nodded determinedly and snagged Cesar by the collar, which was a good thing since the baby vampire was staggering in the street from information overload. "And you, my Lord?" She sounded deeply concerned.

Edwin pulled the whip off his shoulder. He snapped it, and it responded appropriately with a long, insinuating hiss. "I'm buying you time, little mouse. Now run along. And watch Cesar!"

Mouse knew better than to argue or protest the will of her Lord. She slung her arms about Cesar's waist, spread her wings, and was airborne in seconds while Cesar let out a scream of sudden surprise.

Edwin turned back to the crowd that was quickly closing in on him on all sides. He snapped the manriki again and smiled. Wickedly. "Okay, you dogs, let's play."

***

"You shouldn't have hit her so hard. You could have damaged her brain!"

Eliza came around to those words, which were being spoken in a scalding female voice. She was lying on the floor of the shuttle on her back. As she lifted her head, she was struck with an almost debilitating wave of nausea. She pushed herself upright, then gained a small sense of satisfaction when she tossed her cookies all over Maria's shoes, making the girl dance back a step. But since there wasn't much in her stomach, it was almost anticlimactic.

A pair of strong male arms encircled her waist and pulled her upright. For one moment she thought—hoped—that it was Edwin, her dark knight, come to rescue her, to hold her, to soothe her hurt and take her home. Fuck this strong-willed heroine shit, she thought. She wanted to run away. All this bravery shit was for the birds.

But it wasn't Edwin holding her. It was Derek. His placid, handsome, empty face shone down on her, more horrible than anything that Edwin could ever show her. Edwin was a monster, yes, but at least he had the self-respect to recognize it. At least he was in charge of his own will and not some mindless puppet without strings.

"Get away from me!" she shouted, struggling.

"Alisa, please."

"Don't call me that! I'm not Alisa!" she cried. "My name is Eliza Book. I'm the Courtesan of Lord Edwin McGillicuddy!"

Derek's eyes flared with rage. She realized after a moment (and a jolt of understanding) that he was acting under his own will again. Maria had let him go. She could see the difference in him, in every line of his body, in his suddenly animate face. Yet it made no difference.

Maria had gotten to him, really got in his head the only way a zealot can, through sheer, twisted logic. Eliza shouldn't have been surprised by that, she supposed. In her heart of hearts, she'd always known that the "pre-conditioning" that Derek had endured as a child had been horrible beyond measure. Unforgivable. She couldn't pretend that it was anything less than what Maria had endured at Lord Rathbone's hands.

Rape. The vampires had been raping him since he was a small boy. How do you ever get over something like that?

The shuttle had landed on the airstrip of the visitor's center just outside New Versailles. The windows framed the cool grey darkness of artificial night aboard Foxley's gyro.

Maria went to the door and unlocked the latch.

Derek grabbed Eliza's chin and turned her head to face him. He held her with his large, square hands, his strength enormous.

She stopped struggling when his pain-filled eyes pinned her. She was terrified he would break her neck in his rage.

"Alisa...Eliza, listen to me. Maria's right. It's important we do this."

Her first instinct was to shout obscenities into his face, kick him, punch him. But that was less than useless. He'd just knock her out again and carry her off to Foxley's palace. There was no stopping him now.

"You can't let this happen, Derek," she said, looking for reason in his eyes. "You can't be a party to this madness!"

"It's not madness," Derek insisted. His eyes, though not wholly crazed like Maria's, were sad and thoughtful and somewhere far off in the past where he dreamed of revenge. "Think of all of the wars that have been fought for independence. The Civil War, the Revolutionary. This is exactly the same thing. What we're doing is waging a war for independence for our people. We're fighting for freedom!"

He looked deep into her eyes and brushed his thumbs along her jaw. Finally, he leaned down and kissed her. Eliza closed her eyes and concentrated on not gagging. It was a sweet kiss, it was Derek's kiss, but behind it was all of the pain and loathing he'd stored up for years. Loathing not just for vampires but also for himself, for the entire human race that had made him and subjected him to such pain and humiliation.

He let her go.

She staggered back a step. And then she slapped him smartly across the face.

Derek stared at her, stunned.

"I'd sooner throw my lot in with Edwin and the vampires. They aren't nearly the monsters you two are." She lifted her chin defiantly. "I'm glad you never came to the overworld with me, Derek. You're weak and no man at all. Edwin is ten times the man you'll ever be."

Darkness clouded Derek's eyes, a killing rage that turned his face monstrous. He put his big, strong Poppet hands around her throat, his fingers pressing into her windpipe. Eliza glared at him, challenging him to do it. To end her. She was glad she had gone above and escaped this hell of an existence.

"Derek, no."

He stared past her at Maria, standing by the door.

"We need her," said Maria.

Derek let her go but gave her a deadly look as she rubbed at her sore throat. He looked a hundred years old. "When I see your vampire, he's dead." He drew his Colt and turned it on her, wagging it from side to side, indicating that she was to follow Maria down the steps of the shuttle to the runway.

Maria led the way with Eliza walking obediently behind. They climbed down to a loading bay in the visitor's center just outside New Versailles. Ahead loomed an enormous white gravel pavilion lined on both sides with rippling, long-armed willow trees. They led up to the imposing, one hundred-foot-tall iron gates of Foxley's estate, Foxley's crest engraved in the arch of the gate. Beyond it stretched an expanse of well-manicured green lawn sporting Grecian fountains, exotic flowers of every imaginable type, and even a flock of all-white peacocks strutting proudly across the grass.

And, beyond that, rose the glowing, white-stone palace of New Versailles, looking like something from a fairy tale.

Derek pushed her roughly toward the gates.

"Why are we here?" Eliza asked. "This is Foxley's estate."

Maria smiled grimly. "It's also the place where the Micro-Electro-Mechanical System gyroscope is located—the device that vibrates and emits its own false gravity and keeps the whole gyro in orbit. Even Foxley's staff isn't aware the device is here, but Foxley's Poppets know. And, now...so do I."

Maria never broke her stride as she walked purposely down the path toward the gate.

Eliza gave her a cold look. "So, why not just bomb it? You've been bombing other establishments."

"Don't be fooled by its appearance. New Versailles is lead-cased and impervious to all but the most powerful explosives—only a nuclear detonation could rupture it. Foxley built it that way to protect himself and the gyroscope from being damaged. He's very clever, you see. But that's the secret to his long existence. Foxley lets others believe he's immature, lazy, and reckless. He's really none of those things. "

"You sound like you admire him."

Maria lost her wry smile. "I admire his engineering genius. He created the *Gypsy Queen*. He invented the concept of the gyro in the first place, and the use of MEM gyroscopes to power airships. But, at the end of the day, he's still only a vampire. A monster."

They'd reached the imposing black iron gates. This being the tourists' off-season, they were closed and electronically locked. Beyond it stretched the estate where guards swarmed the grounds, moving in regulated patterns. None did more than glance their way. The gate was impervious; one would need a special access pass to bypass Foxley's passkey system.

Maria moved aside and indicated the gates. "Open them," she told Eliza.

Eliza glanced at the gates' elaborate security system. She had no idea how to bypass it, but that hardly mattered. The computer would tell her how it worked—if she touched the gates. She shook her head. "No."

Maria reached across the space between them and took the Colt from Derek's hand. She grabbed Eliza by the short hairs at her scalp, and, as she yelped, dragged her forward on her knees, shoving the gun into her mouth, cracking her teeth.

Eliza choked, tasting blood and bitter gunmetal. Maria's eyes were blank and empty, her grip so strong that Eliza had no doubts she could crush her skull in if she chose to. In a soft, concentrated voice, Maria said, "Open it or I'll shoot your brains out the back of your fucking head, bitch."

Eliza gritted her teeth around the barrel as she considered her options. She shook her head. She might be a Poppet like Derek and Maria, but she was nothing like them. She wouldn't be a party to this madness and so much blood on her hands. Living wouldn't be worth it.

Maria could go to hell—along with her Hive.

Maria narrowed her good eye as she read Eliza's thoughts. She, too, considered her options. She took the barrel of the Colt out of Eliza's mouth, turned, and fired it point-blank into Derek's chest.

xvii

Edwin was very good with the manriki. But even with all his training and experience, he was unable to halt the huge collection of Poppets closing in on him. He raised the manriki high overhead like a lion tamer's whip and cracked it in the open air, momentarily startling the oncoming crowd, but it didn't stop them from pressing him back until he reached the sidewalk in front of a club.

"Kill the Prince!" the Poppets screamed, faces twisted into masks of rage. They shambled forward like a pack of flesh-hungry zombies.

Edwin swore, letting the manriki melt away. This wasn't working. He extended his wings in a truly demonic manner, but the Poppets didn't seem overly impressed by his show of bravado. He glanced up at the fire escape on the second floor of the club. It seemed so far up. He wondered if he could do it...

He was terrible at flying, and heights horrified him. But then he looked at the demon-eyed crowd getting closer, wanting his blood...

And then he knew. For Eliza...aye, he could do it. He would fly or die, he thought bravely as he lifted his great scarlet wings and cupped the dense air beneath them, terrifying himself. He rocketed upward at such a speed he nearly missed the safety rail, only snatching it at the last moment, which halted his lift. He struggled a moment like a kite caught in a windstorm as he pulled himself down and onto the fire escape.

Meanwhile, the crowd filled the space beneath him, arms reaching, hands grasping. The Poppets milled, calling him the worst kind of coward in a rather lame attempt to lure him back down.

Fuck that noise, he thought. And then the realization that he'd just flown caught up with him, and he experienced the rare pleasure of throwing up all over his enemies. After wiping his mouth, he turned, ripped the security bars off a window, and shoved his leather-clad elbow through the glass. Moments later, he found himself inside a crumbling tenement building and heading for the staircase that led to the upper part of the structure that rose up through Poppettown and into the New York City streets above.

The basement aboveground was dank and dusty, but moonlight —real moonlight, not manufactured subterranean light—poured through some broken boards up ahead. It was a relief to see real sky again as he scrambled through a break in the boards. Within minutes, he found himself in a dead-end alley, standing in a foggy, poorly lighted corner of Market Street in lower Brooklyn, not very far from home.

He'd barely gotten his wind when an old Duesenberg swept around the corner and barreled toward him, its lights momentarily blinding him. He leaped at the last moment, landing shakily atop the hood of the car as it screeched to a halt inches away from a dead end wall, its headlights illuminating some creative gang graffiti.

Now, he was pissed! His fists crackled as he balled them up, ready to bust in the face of the idiot driver who'd nearly run him down.

The driver's side door flew open and Mouse popped out. She looked breathless, her scarf coming unwound. "Cesar says there's an airstrip with Hummingbirds not far from here." She pointed west, then paused as she looked at him standing atop the dented hood of the car, glaring down at her. "My Lord, what's the matter?"

"You stupid chit, you nearly ran me down!"

"But I didn't."

"Do you even know how to drive?" It occurred to him that he'd never actually seen Mouse behind the wheel of a car before.

Mouse looked stricken. "No. But I watch a lot of television. Cops and robbers shows." She pantomimed twisting the wheel of a car this way and that.

With a growl, Edwin leaped off the hood of the car and went around to the passenger side. "Let Cesar drive," he said, getting in.

Mouse bared her formidable teeth but obediently got in the backseat while Cesar assumed her place behind the wheel. She slammed her door very hard to indicate her displeasure. She leaned between the seats. "Lord Edwin..."

"Stay! That's an order."

"But, my Lord..."

"Mouse, do not make me turn this car around!"

Cesar sighed and put the car in gear. "Are we there yet?"

* * *

Eliza caught Derek before he slumped to the ground. He was heavy, but she was strong. As a child, she had held him like this when he would do nothing but curl up in terror and stare blankly at the walls of the Scholomance for hours at a time.

Now, he lay shuddering in her lap, blood darkening the front of his suit and painting his lips. "Alisa..." he said, his voice hoarse and distant. Then he corrected himself. "Eliza..."

His eyes flickered over her, so young and pain-filled she felt her heart breaking all over again.

She kissed his forehead, moving aside a long black curl of his hair to do so. He felt hot, feverish. She looked over at Maria, who stood motionless beside the gate, the Colt lying on the ground at her feet. Her eyes were flat, like painted pools, with no life, no soul, in them.

"You fucking devil," Eliza whispered, though it solicited no reaction whatsoever from the girl. Everyone was expendable to Maria, Eliza reminded herself, even Maria herself.

Ignoring her, Maria withdrew the boomer gun and indicated the gate with it. Her voice was calm and unaffected. "Foxley has an excellent medical bay. When we get inside, we'll get help for Derek. Or, alternately, you can sit here and let him bleed all over you. It's your choice, sister."

Eliza bit her lip. She had no choice. She couldn't let Derek die, not after everything he had been through.

She started easing Derek to the ground. He instinctively clutched at her in a blind panic, eyes rolling like a frightened prey animal that knows it's been trapped in some canned hunt.

"I'll get you help, Derek, I promise." She eased his grip off her one finger at a time. "Just lie still."

He stared at her, wanting to believe. He had always believed in her. Slowly, he let go.

Eliza stood up and turned her attention to the security gate. She had to work fast. She wrapped her hands around the smooth cold metal bars and summoned her bizarre talent.

The shock was instantaneous and nauseating. For one moment, she felt she was part of Foxley's security system, that she was, in fact, the system. Every part of her was fused to the gate and the electronic system connected to it, and now that she had made first contact, she realized the computers all over the estate would do anything she wanted, and she didn't even have to reconnect physically with them anymore!

The lock disengaged and Maria pushed the heavy gate open. The Security Poppets paroling the parameters of Foxley's estate took immediate notice, turning as a unit and starting toward them.

Spotting Maria and her gun, they reached for the weapons they wore on their hips.

But Maria was faster. She raised the boomer, toyed with something under the trigger that Eliza figured probably controlled the output, and aimed the gun.

Eliza shouted a warning, but it was already too late.

Maria squeezed the trigger. There was no kick, but the gun emitted a high-pitched, headachy noise like sonar at full volume. The gun tore through the wall of guards like a laser, rendering them so much bloody flotsam.

Seeing her chance, Eliza lunged forward and grabbed Maria's hand, trying to twist her wrist to make her release her hold on the gun, but Maria's hand felt like rubber, as if she wasn't real anymore.

Her eyes looked like boiled white eggs as she turned to Eliza. "You bitch," she said and backhanded Eliza.

Her blow packed incredible power. Eliza fell hard against the bars of the gate, her poor abused skull clanking against the metal. She groaned as she slid down to the ground, her hair matted with new blood, her body trembling with weakness.

She hurt all over, and her mind felt like it was full of angry hornets. She blinked to clear her vision. "Is this how you do it?" she croaked. "Slaughter whole Courts?"

"You'll see, sister." Maria wagged the gun at Eliza. "Get up."

Eliza climbed slowly and unsteadily to her feet, glaring at Maria as blood dripped from her wounds and into her eyes. They started down the path that led to Foxley's pristine, white-brick, quasi-medieval palace. As they neared the remnants of the mangled guards lying in a heap on the cultivated green, Eliza experienced a dizzying wave of nausea.

They were no longer men or women; just red and gold uniforms full of broken bones, torn flesh, and bloody, raw-meat faces. The boomer had flayed the skin from their bodies and crushed their bones—and yet, despite the awful sight, they seemed to twitch like invisible wires were attached to the bloody remains.

Eliza flinched, wondering if she'd gone insane. Slowly, those invisible wires jerked each of the tattered security guards upward into semi-upright positions as if a cruel puppet master was hard at work. The dead—undead—soldiers with their naked meat faces swayed in place, their eyes, lidless and empty-white, swiveling to Maria as if waiting for orders.

Eliza covered her mouth and stumbled back, slipping on the blood-soaked grass. She fell hard on her ass, her hands clamped firmly over her mouth to keep from vomiting at the sight.

More Security Poppets began pouring out of the palace, guns at the ready. Maria turned her gun on the new guards and squeezed off another wake of razor-sharp sonic frequency. Like some form of invisible automatic machine-gun fire, the impact lifted the guards off the ground and ripped them to tatters before tossing them in random directions like raggedy dolls.

"Dear god." Despite the insistent pounding of her skull and the nausea boiling up her throat, Eliza managed to scramble up onto her knees, intent on escape. But there was nowhere to run. The guards that Maria had chopped down earlier were tottering toward her like a collection of big, broken toys, their bloody claw hands reaching for her.

Eliza tried to crawl away, but the legion of the undead broke apart, systematically hemming her in on all sides before closing the circle around her. Zombie Security Poppets eyed her, their flayed faces showing little emotion past an eager desire to please the All-Mother. They grabbed her, their greedy hands ripping at her hair and clothes.

Whimpering, Eliza tried to jerk away, but their fingers were like iron vices, and the shards of their fingerbones razored through the thin skin of her arms, drawing blood.

"Bring her," commanded the Hive Mother. Maria started marching down the path toward the palace, stepping over the newly slaughtered bodies that were even now beginning to shiver with new and unnatural life.

The army of undead Poppets brought her.

* * *

Cesar checked their aircraft's altitude. Everything on board the Hummingbird looked good. He adjusted his headphones, turning the white noise down to a mere whisper, as the sound of it was giving him a massive, migraine-intense headache. He toggled the landing gear as he slowed the Hummingbird in preparation for their descent, then rechecked all the instruments one last time.

He did all the required landing tasks with a speed and aptitude that was...well, supernatural. It would have blown his squad leader's mind back in the service. That was one good thing about being a vampire, he supposed—he had super strength, super reflexes, probably a super brain. Super everything.

Something to compensate for the fact that the world had suddenly become too loud, too bright, too pungent, too everything. Not to mention, his teeth hurt in his mouth and he was horny as hell—and he wasn't even thinking about sex. Thanks to McGillicuddy, he was on a carnival ride that would likely never end. He wondered how vampires endured it all without having a nervous breakdown.

In the chair beside him, his Lord and maker looked paler than normal—rather greenish, in fact. "Sir, we're coming in," Cesar said. "Where should I land the bird?"

"On the ground," Edwin answered simply, scrunched back in his seat, his fingers digging holes in the upholstery.

"That's...not exactly what I mean. I need a destination."

Edwin narrowed his eyes as if he was in pain. "On the roof of the palace, if you can manage it."

Cesar jerked the joystick as they entered the air space around New Versailles. Edwin looked like he was going to hork all over the lighted dashboard. Cesar gave him a grim, determined look. "Sir?"

"Yeah?"

"Can you fly?"

Edwin looked annoyed. "No, I can't fly. If I could bloody fly, do you think this would be an issue?"

"But...vampires fly, right?"

It had to be true, Cesar thought. Else, why would they have wings?

"Why do you ask?" Edwin peered through the windshield with narrow eyes.

Cesar bit his lip. "I can fly."

"You are flying."

"I mean...you know." Cesar made whirlybird gestures in the air. "That's how I got to the second-floor window of this building. Mouse and I were standing in the alley when it happened. Just like that."

"What happened...just like that?"

Cesar undid the buttons of his coat and tilted his shoulders. Under the coat, his clothes were in tatters because a nicely shaped pair of brand new bronze wings were rustling restlessly beneath them.

"Huh," said Edwin. "So you're a bottle blond."

"What? No. I mean...yeah, but...that's not it." The timbre of Cesar's voice rose. "I grew them. I grew wings."

"That happens, flyboy."

Cesar looked stricken. "But I can fly!"

"You can fly. Congratulations. But can you land this bird without killing us?"

Cesar swore softly. He angled the craft sharply downward as they approached the roof of the palace's airstrip, making Edwin swallow against the vomit creeping up his throat. That pleased Cesar immensely.

"You really are a bastard," he said, glancing over at his heartless creator. "You keep using me! You don't care about me at all!"

"You'll get used to it."

"How long before I become my own Lord?"

Edwin frowned. "Why do you ask?"

"I want to know how long it'll be before I can really start hating you."

"Land the craft, Cesar."

Cesar landed the craft.

* * *

Cesar and Mouse fairly leaped from the cockpit of the Hummingbird, but Edwin was a little slower in deplaning. He felt like the ground was lurching slightly under his feet even after he was down and on the palace's paved rooftop landing pad. He crouched low to steady himself.

Mouse grabbed his arm with concern. "Are you all right, my Lord?"

"He gets airsick," Cesar said with a devious smile that showed off his bright new vampire teeth. "And he can't fly because he's afraid of heights."

Edwin glared. "Shut up, Cesar."

"Blarney, you two argue like old washwomen," Mouse complained, looking from one to the other. She stopped and glanced out over the estate where the grass was stamped flat and churned over to produce a muddy bog. "What in hell...?"

Blood coated the grounds, the fountains, the trees, and even the formerly white peacocks prancing about and picking at the bloody remnants of what might have once been human beings. Everything was spattered crimson as if a war had been fought here not very long ago...fought and lost.

Edwin straightened up as the wavering nausea finally left him. He would have to deal with Cesar and his insecurities some other time. He examined the grounds, then reached into the boot of the Hummingbird and pulled out the three long Remingtons. He tossed two to his Enforcers, balancing the third one on his shoulder.

He smiled. "Let's join the party, ladies."

* * *

It was like stumbling through hell.

Once the two of them were inside the palace, Maria began making more zombies. They would go a few hundred feet down a corridor, and a new set of Security Poppets would pop up to stop them, armed, dangerous, and very well trained. And, each time it happened, Maria aimed the boomer in the general vicinity of the guards, blowing their bodies into bloody rags.

Soldiers went down in broken heaps. Then Maria would wait as the piles of bloody rag-people lying on the floor began to stir and slowly climbed to their feet, their uniforms in smoldering tatters, their flesh shorn away to show the insides of men and women that no one should ever see. Then those new zombies would form a rank behind Maria, and the march would continue until she encountered another group of Foxley's soldiers.

Rinse. Repeat. Scream.

More and more soldiers joined the ranks of Maria's undead army. And, directly behind Maria, and being pushed relentlessly forward by the growing ranks of the undead, Eliza stumbled along. If she didn't walk, or if she lost her footing and fell, they would drag her along, their bony, bloody claw hands digging deep into her scalp and dragging her by her hair or her skin until she screamed in agony. She learned to walk very quickly despite her various injuries.

She was exhausted, and she could feel herself teetering on the knife-edge of hysterics. She was sick of running, sick of crying, sick of being afraid. Her head ached fiercely and she limped down the long corridors like an old woman, sometimes leaning on the horrid zombies for support.

She wondered where Edwin was and if he was all right. If he would come and save her.

Every time Maria reached a security door, she couldn't breach, she directed a zombie to drag Eliza to the forefront of the ranks, and, there, the zombies threw her upon the security panel. The system automatically recognized her, flashed a few green lights, and the door clicked dutifully open. Then the zombies let Eliza go and she crumpled to the floor and had to scramble to get to her feet before the walking packages of raw meat yanked her up and started dragging her along the floor again.

They moved ever inward toward the heart of New Versailles—through Security Poppets, through locked doors, through corridors, through blood. Foxley's whole palace resembled a maze, one corridor looking the same as another, but Maria seemed to know exactly where they were going. She seemed to have a set of directions in her twisted head.

They turned a bend and came upon a collection of Pleasure Poppets clustered together, cowering at the end of a dead-end corridor like children afraid of the dark. They looked strangely pink and defenseless in their nearly diaphanous little strips of clothing, their eyes lemur-large as they took in the sight of Maria's blood-drenched visage and the zombies filling the corridor beyond.

They lived like caged exotic birds, Eliza knew. They had no way to deal with something like this, no coping mechanism whatsoever. They existed for simple pleasures.

Maria looked at them with big, deep, pity-filled eyes. She seemed to consider them very carefully. Then she began lifting the boomer in her right hand.

Eliza felt the panic leap up into her throat like vomit. She pushed past the grappling hands of the zombies and shouted, "Maria, don't!" She snatched Maria's arm at the elbow, trying to yank the gun down. But Maria was cold and unmovable; it was like wrestling with a stone statue of Maria instead of a real, flesh-and-blood person.

The Poppets whimpered and mewled, childlike faces turned up in uncertainty. The girls crouched low to the floor, clinging to each other. The young men stood over them, galvanized by a primordial instinct to protect their women. She recognized one of the young men as the Poppet Jeremy, the boy who had helped her escape. They looked so human, so vulnerable.

"You can't kill them!" Eliza screamed, hanging onto Maria's arm. She realized she was hysterical at last, but she didn't care. "They're like us! Maria...!"

Something passed over Maria's face and behind her eyes, something almost like life. Maria trembled, shining tear tracks pouring from the corners of her eyes as she watched the cowering Poppets standing in her way.

"You're right about that, sister," she admitted. She tossed off Eliza's hold, then lowered her gun hand. She turned and nodded to the ranks of zombies waiting behind her.

Slowly, they shuffled forward as one, reaching and grasping, making delirious groaning noises of anticipation as they closed in on the Poppets trapped at the end of the corridor.

The Poppets screamed like tortured kittens as the zombies fell upon them. Eliza sank to her knees on the floor, covered her ears, and screamed.

***

In another part of Foxley's facility, Edwin stumbled almost drunkenly against a wall, groaning. His head was abuzz with the cries of dozens of dying Poppets.

Mouse caught him by the arm. "My Lord," she said with concern.

"Eliza's in trouble," he said, trying to drown out the cacophony of voices in his head. His teeth were suddenly achingly sharp in his mouth, and he knew his eyes had bled to a stark, glistening black.

Eliza's horror pulled on him like a magnet. He picked up his Remington and started down the corridor again, hurrying now, letting their bloodlink lead him on.

"We need to hurry, Mouse...now!"

***

Eliza cowered against the wall, trying not to hyperventilate, scarcely able to bear the sight of the massacre that painted the walls around her. There was blood on her hands and in her hair. The corridors seemed awash with it as if someone had taken a can of bright red paint and kicked it around.

Maria stepped past her and directed her new zombies to break down the door of a room that seemed to be very important to her. One of the reanimated Pleasure Poppets, a male who'd had his legs and torso torn away at the waist, and who was trailing a long line of intestines, crawled forward on his elbows to obey. Others shambled forward to help break down the door.

Eliza didn't care anymore; she was finished. She tried to crawl back down the corridor, but she kept sliding on the blood on the floor, and she couldn't find any traction. A zombie grabbed her by the shorthairs and tossed her into the room ahead of them. Eliza landed hard and stunned on her hands and knees, then had to scrabble to sit up.

It looked like a library, though the books were scattered all over the place as if a windstorm had passed through here. She shirked as partially eaten Pleasure Poppets moved to surround her.

Maria scanned the room, then went to one of the vast, empty bookcases that rose up toward the vaulted ceiling. Zombies pressed in behind Eliza, forcing her to hobble after Maria. She nearly fell over the piles of books and warm, steaming offal. Her head was full of a stark white static as if her brain could register no more death or bloodshed. They pushed and she went. She felt nothing, and yet she couldn't stop shaking.

"Sister, come," Maria ordered. She had found what she was looking for, a security keypad lurking behind a secret panel in the bookshelves.

"No," Eliza answered, backing up. She stared around at the ruined things in the room with her, the zombies watching her, some of whom had once been simple, pretty Pleasure Poppets. Hands like cold wax grabbed her by the shoulders and started propelling her forward. She dug in her heels. The zombie pushed and Eliza finally began to scream in protest.

She couldn't do this anymore, couldn't go on—

There came a blast from out in the corridor as if someone had set a bomb off. The zombie who had her in its grasp let her go, startled by the sudden percussion.

Eliza tumbled to the furry, white, blood-soaked carpeting of the library floor. She was so exhausted that it took her a moment to realize that what she was hearing was a high-caliber rifle crack echoing around the corridor. She sat up as a second percussion made the whole palace shudder, and then a zombie exploded into a mound of bloody debris in the hallway beyond. Another followed, blown not just to bits but atomized particles.

"The Prince," Maria said, enraged.

Eliza sobbed in relief. The cavalry was finally here!

***

Edwin sighted down a zombie through the scope of the Remington and shot it neatly in the back of the head. The skull exploded like a porcelain teapot, scattering blood and grey matter everywhere, then the entire body, infected with the toxic blood of the bullet, trembled and erupted into bits like a geyser. He felt very much like an action movie hero at that moment.

Edwin was a very good shot, with more than a hundred years of target experience, plus some hands-on training he'd received from Sheriff Virgil Earp during the Gold Rush. He ejected the spent cartridge, took the next casting from between his teeth, reloaded, aimed, and fired again as the zombies turned as one to face him. Utilizing a rapid-fire and reloading system, he took out zombie after zombie, the blooding bullets making the creatures explode not once but twice in what he felt was a very impressive display of blood and guts.

"Ladies!" he called and his two Enforcers rounded the bend and took aim beside him, Cesar to the left of him and Mouse to the right. "Lock and load. Let's clean house."

Three more rifle shots took down three more zombies. All three reloaded.

Edwin was impressed. He knew that Mouse could shoot—she loved online shooting games—but Cesar was proving to be a surprisingly good investment of his blood. They'd come armed for bear, which was good, seeing how the whole palace was swarming with the undead.

He'd seen zombies, even made them on occasion. Some vampires like himself could raise the dead for a short time and propel them along by sheer willpower. But he'd never seen anything on this scale before. At the onset, he'd been afraid young Cesar might freak out. But Cesar seemed to enjoy killing almost as much as Mouse. Unfortunately, the Remingtons were bolt action and could only get off one shot at a time, which made for slow killing.

They needed to find Maria, the Queen Poppet. Now.

"Orders?" Mouse asked, reloading her rifle.

"Aim for the head," Edwin said, taking out another zombie as the horde began moving toward them. "Keep going until we see Maria. Eliza is near; I can feel her fear clearly."

Cesar made a disgruntled noise, snapped a new cartridge home, and took aim once more. "I think I saw this in one of the Romero films. What do we do when we run out of ammo?"

"I'll think of something." Edwin blew another zombie to fragments, the sound explosively loud in the close corridor.

"What happens if they catch us?"

"We get eaten."

"Zombies will eat a vampire?"

"Zombies will eat anything."

"The undead eating the undead. Lovely."

"Shut up and fire."

Cesar fired.

As one, the three of them cut down more than a third of the zombies crowding the hallways before the creatures through sheer number began pressing the three vampires back down the corridor. This was taking too long, and Cesar was right—they didn't have enough ammo. It was also painfully obvious the zombies were there to prevent them from entering Foxley's library, the place where the vibration of Eliza's fear was the greatest.

Edwin swore and tossed his rifle to Mouse. "Cover me," he said. "Keep firing until you see the blood in their eyes."

The two Enforcers continued their rapid-fire system of loading and firing while Edwin started down the corridor, headed right for the heart of the zombie horde shambling toward them.

"What in hell is he doing?" Cesar asked.

"You'll see," Mouse answered.

Edwin reached the first zombie and grabbed it, swinging it around so its back was to him. He stumbled away from the advancing crowd, dragging the zombie with him. He snapped its head to the side and bit.

The zombie struggled, then went limp in his arms. Zombies might eat a vampire if it was injured or trapped, but they certainly weren't stronger than one. As the others clustered about him, their claws raking over his leather coat, Edwin released the newly infected zombie and pushed it into the crowd. It immediately lunged at the nearest zombie and bit down on a skinny, ragged arm. The second zombie gave a dry cry.

A zombie crept up and bit down on the crook of Edwin's arm, but the leather coat protected him. He grabbed it and swung it around, giving it his bite before letting it go. The second zombie followed suit, attacking its compatriots. The first zombie he'd bitten had turned at least three others, and those were biting others, turning even more, a lovely geometric effect.

Edwin darted away from the crowd of infighting zombies and rejoined his two Enforcers. He "What now?" Mouse asked, her face piqued with war lust. There was no getting through the waves of chaos in the corridor as zombies began tearing into each other like a feral pack of hungry dogs. But at least they were no longer worried about the vampires standing right in front of them.

"The direct approach." With a wild grin, Edwin took up his gun, turned, and fired straight into the wall. It left a tremendous hole in Foxley's imported English wainscoting. He pointed at Cesar. "Know martial arts?"

"No." Cesar looked sad.

"Seen martial arts movies?"

"Well...sure."

"Kick that wall down."

Shrugging, Cesar did as his master bade, round-housing the wall as if he was Bruce Lee. Most of the remaining wall crumbled inward, leaving them more than enough room to duck inside. Cesar gasped in amazement, then jumped straight up and punched the air, his wings fully extended.

"That is so fucking cool! I love being a vampire!"

Edwin ejected his spent cartridge. "I'm happy for you. Now get in there and kick some more monster ass."

"Yes, sir!"

* * *

The panel behind the bookcase slid soundlessly back on an unseen mechanism to reveal a long, dark corridor. Eliza grunted in defiance, kicking and punching at the zombie that had her, but it was like trying to fight something made of rubber, something unreal and unfeeling. No matter what she did, she couldn't get a reaction from the dead thing dragging her along by one arm.

"You bitch, let me go!" she shouted at Maria as they moved into the corridor. "My vampire is here and he's going to kick your ass!"

"Prince Edwin has his hands full at the moment, I'm afraid." Maria smiled nicely. "Don't worry, sister. Your usefulness is almost over. Then you can join the others."

Maria, Eliza, and a small retinue of ten or so zombies moved steadily down the tunnel, which twisted and turned into a seemingly endless number of different passageways. But Maria seemed to know exactly where she was going even though it was almost pitch black and every tunnel looked the same.

After a few hundred feet of being dragged literally kicking and screaming down the passageway, Eliza spotted a dim, bluish glow up ahead. At the same time, she became aware of a kind of subliminal vibration that she more felt than heard. It immediately gave her already splitting head an almost crushing migraine.

A few moments later, they emerged through a door and into an enormous, white, egg-shaped chamber unlike anything that Eliza had seen up to this point. The walls were honeycombed and faintly glowing. It looked like something that belonged on a spacecraft in an old science fiction movie. In the center of the room was a giant glowing blue helix containment unit that loomed a hundred feet above them. It was coiled protectively around a high central dais upon which rested the gyroscope—the final, beating, all-important heart of the *Gypsy Queen*.

Eliza stopped fighting, momentarily stunned by the sight of the device. She couldn't help but gape in wonderment. The gyroscope was made of some shining brass alloy and had a circumference of at least twenty feet. It spun like a lazy satellite on its spin axis, rotor, and gimbal, taking any direction it wanted, which was its primary function as it emitted the gravity necessary to keep the billions of pounds of weight that was the *Gypsy Queen* self-sustained in its own orbit above New York City.

It was...gorgeous, an engineering marvel, and it took her some moments to remember to breathe. The gyro hadn't seemed real until now, and now that she'd seen it, she couldn't look away from Foxley's amazing invention. She was utterly in love with it.

Six high-ranking Security Poppets in red and gold uniforms noticed them immediately. They appeared to be attending the computer station, which encircled the gyroscope's containment unit, a final defense against anyone tampering with the device that ensured all aboard the airship lived and not died, burned to cinders in a massive crash with a wake equal to a hundred nuclear explosions.

"You, halt!" one whispered savagely, grabbing at a slim, wand-like weapon on his utility belt that looked about as imposing as a high-tech cattle prod. He aimed it at Maria and her zombies.

Eliza wondered where their guns were and why they weren't armed to the hilt, considering the importance of their function.

Maria turned and looked at her, reading her thoughts. "Percussion weapons are not permitted in the Command Center. They are too likely to interfere with the gyroscope's sonic signal." She pointed to various warnings posted in English and Upyrese along the walls. "In fact, sister, it would be wise of you to keep your voice soft and at a whisper."

Maria put her finger to her lips in a shhh motion. She smiled, full of empty, childlike glee.

"Bitch." Eliza spotted a decibel counter affixed to the wall that moved gently up and down. For the moment, it was registering a safe green zone.

Maria looked at the guardsmen with her ghostly white eyes. She smiled, and the first guard approaching them lost all expression, his face blanking out as if someone had sucked out all of his emotions. The others stationed around the room did the same as the Hive mind took them over.

"Shhh," she told them as well. Then she commanded her horde of ravenous zombies forward.

* * *

By the time Edwin, Mouse, and Cesar reached the Command Center, the whole place had erupted into a state of chaos. With a single mental command, Edwin halted his two Enforcers mid-step, quickly evaluated the situation in the room, and then decided they were extremely and profoundly fucked.

Maria had the Security Poppets who protected the gyroscope in thrall as her small army of zombies converged on them. At Maria's feet huddled Eliza, looking bedraggled and frightened, her hands clamped over her face as the zombies tore gaping red holes in the flesh of the soldiers just standing there, impassively staring into space like big dolls.

The guardsmen were being devoured alive, piece by bloody piece. He could scarcely bear watching it himself, and he'd seen his lion's share of bloodshed over the past two hundred years of his life.

He had to do something now, but what? Zombies were clustered around Eliza and Maria like a protective wall, hindering direct fire. He swore violently; this was going to be far more difficult than he'd thought.

Cesar started lifting his Remington rifle as he prepared to take a bead, but Edwin automatically reached out and caught the barrel of the gun, lowering it. "You'll hit my woman...or you'll disrupt the gyroscope." He pointed to the warnings posted all over the chamber. "Both are very, very bad things for you to do."

He wasn't at all mechanical, but through the power of his blood-link with Foxley, he'd gotten a crash course in gyroscopic mechanics. He didn't understand most of it, but what it all came down to was this: Firing a gun in the Command Center was bad. From what he'd learned, shouting here was a bad idea and could disrupt the whole ship.

He glanced aside at the decibel reader on the wall. In the ensuing chaos, it had crept up from green to yellow, and a digital warning flashed below it, a cute, low-res bat with Foxley's face that put its finger to its lips, indicating that they should lower the noise factor in the room immediately.

"What now?" asked Mouse.

"We do things the old-fashioned way." Edwin bit his wrist and let the blood flow into the manriki, using it as if it was a lasso to rope three more zombies in, allowing Mouse and Cesar to snap their necks quickly and efficiently.

Not more than a few seconds passed before Maria realized what was going on behind her. Finally, she'd come to realize her little zombie army was under siege. She swung around, eyes narrowed, zombies parting automatically for her passage. She took a few steps, arm extended, at the end of which was a gun, its make something Edwin didn't recognize, which was a shame because he liked guns very much. Maria's face was as blank and expressionless as a doll as she fired directly at them.

Edwin detected an actual visual disruption in the air as the percussion rocketed toward him. It reminded him of a wave of heat off a desert deadpan, and he suddenly decided he didn't like this gun at all. Mouse moved faster than all of them, shoving him out of the way and taking the blast full on. It shattered her body as if she was made of bright red glass, and for one long moment, Edwin found himself kneeling on the floor, aghast, as he watched little pieces of burning Mouse floating down all around him.

The severance was sudden, absolute, and painful, like a limb being sliced off. Edwin keeled over on his knees until the crown of his head touched the floor. All he could do was make gasping noises as if he was choking on his own blood. All he could think is, *Mouse is gone. My darling is gone.* Then his mind instantly switched gears, tucking the sorrow and the loss away for later contemplation. Already, he was thinking about his one remaining Heir.

Cesar, only a baby vampire—so young, so inexperienced—stood frozen in place, his boyish face aghast as he watched the burning flotsam of his sister drifting down around him. Maria had her queer gun trained on him next, determined to destroy all of his Heirs and peel away every last layer of his sanity until he crumbled.

With a cry, Edwin leaped, driving the boy to the floor and covering him as Maria's gun emitted an ear-splitting sonic screech that felt like an ax slamming into his brain. That gun, whatever it was, was the devil.

He was proven correct in his assumption when it punched a gigantic hole in the opposite wall and sent shrapnel and a rain of dust and debris skittering down, blinding them—but also cloaking them from Maria's view for the moment.

Edwin sat up, shaking, dreading the worse, but the gyroscope was still turning in lazy centrifugal arcs far above them. The decibel reader, which had hit the orange level for one breathless second, was slowly descending to yellow again.

Edwin sat back, pulling his coat off Cesar's head. "Still alive?"

Cesar, trembling violently, sat up and wrapped both arms around Edwin's neck, burying his face in his master's throat. "I'm sorry!" he sobbed. "I don't really hate you! Oh, Christ, I don't want to die tonight!"

"Easy, lad, easy." Edwin held him, rubbed his shoulders, then gently unlaced Cesar's arms from around his neck.

Cesar looked like a ghost amidst all the clouds of dust, only his painfully innocent, tear-struck eyes shining through the mask of grime on his face. Edwin snapped the manriki up around his shoulder. "I want you to stay down. I don't want you to move at all."

"But..."

"I'll take care of this lot."

"But what are you going to do?" Cesar asked, sounding hysterical.

Edwin smiled, showing teeth. "I'm going to send that bitch back to hell." He rubbed at Cesar's tears, tracing a path through all of the grime.

Without waiting for a response, he stood up and leaped from the clouds of dust, landing catlike beside a zombie, his manriki already snaking around its shorn neck. One hard twist and the zombie's head popped off like a bottle cap and rolled across the floor, knocking another zombie off his feet.

Zombies converged on him from every side, but Edwin was beyond fear, beyond caring. He snapped the manriki, straightening it into a fifty-inch blade with the keen edge of a razor. Swinging it, he started tearing through the ranks, beheading two or three zombies at a time, all of which exploded messily on contact with the poisonous blood blade.

Zombie blood splashed him like warpaint, and limbs and chunks of dead grey flesh hit him from every angle. Foxley used to say he was a bloody impetuous Gael and that it would get him killed one of these days. He was prepared to prove Foxley right this night, if necessary.

He smiled like a shark, lips drawn back over jagged teeth as he bisected a zombie falling upon him. Only one thin wall of zombies remained between him and Eliza, and he meant to break that wall down!

***

Edwin was here.

Eliza sensed him long before she saw him breaking through the clouds of dust, debris, and bloody zombies, swinging the biggest blade she had ever seen at the undead surrounding him. Only Edwin could induce this kind of frenzied chaos, she reflected.

Maria, too, spotted him and raised her arm, aiming her gun at him and squeezing off a shot.

"Edwin!" Eliza shouted a warning.

He blocked it at the last second by extending his sword into a wide shield. Unfortunately, the sonic wave blew his huge black shield to shards in his hands.

"Bloody crazy bitch!" he roared, balling both fists up in fury. For the first time, he looked—and moved—more like an animal than a man. He whipped around as zombies jumped at him, then drew an old-fashioned Colt that didn't look like it could do anything to this lot. Cocking the Colt, he raised the hem of his long leather coat, draped it over the long muzzle of the gun, and fired the whole magazine through the coat and into the lot of undead while simultaneously muffling the percussions.

Zombies imploded on contact with the bullets.

Eliza was so glad Mr. McGillicuddy was a former gangster! His aim was spot on, and the zombies went down in heaps, their insides on the outside.

Maria raised her gun again, trying to take Edwin down. Eliza jumped on her back, driving her to her knees. Maria went down hard, firing the boomer. It blasted a second, even larger hole in the wall above Edwin's head, driving the decibel meter up to the red line for one perilous second.

Furious, Eliza jerked Maria around, trying to wrest the girl's arms to the floor and the gun out of her grip before she got them all killed.

In response, a zombie fell upon Eliza, yanking her back into their ranks.

Eliza screamed.

***

Edwin, on hearing Eliza's cry, swung around, his eyes all black, his saber teeth bared in a grimace of war lust, and aimed his gun at the zombie threatening his woman.

He hit on an empty cartridge.

Hell! He smacked his pockets, finding them distressingly empty. The zombies had ripped his coat to shreds, scattering his magazines all over the floor.

He swore violently, cursing the fact that heroes in action films never seemed to run out of ammo. Then zombies jumped him from all sides, at least ten of them, their numbers driving him to the floor on his face under the ferocity of their weight. Claws ripped long, bloody furrows into his back as they tried to drag him back into their ranks.

Edwin roared and twisted around. A zombie leaped at him—once a pretty Pleasure Poppet, now a horrible, sexless, blood-slathered nightmare—and opened its broken, badly hinged jaws like a snake, bloody saliva dripping onto Edwin's face. Edwin snarled in response and drove the heel of his hand into her nose, breaking it further.

The zombie girl spat teeth at him but otherwise seemed unharmed. But before she could clamp her jaws down over his throat and rip his pulse out at the root, her head was cleaved cleanly off her shoulders.

Edwin sat up, throwing off the body as something that resembled a ghost on skates glided past him. It took him a moment to realize it was Lady Claire, two iron fans fully extended in both hands as she did a graceful ballet de action on her inline skates across the blood-slathered floor. She skated past the wall of zombies, harvesting more of their heads with several sharp swipes of her fans, the blades working so efficiently there was barely any blood and the bodies simply folded like pieces of laundry.

Edwin let out a sigh of relief and offered her a salute. "I owe you one, chit."

Claire saluted back with one bloodied iron fan. "You better believe it, McGillicuddy," she said. Then she skated off to kill more zombies.

A magazine lay on the floor a few feet away. Edwin started to reach for it but a pair of shuffling feet kicked it away as more zombies pushed through the wall of their fallen comrades. Oh, hell and double hell!

Edwin lunged after it, and a zombie jumped on his back, its claws snagging in his coat. He twisted around, trying to shake it loose, when suddenly it jerked back as a thin, black cord cut through its ragged larynx. Mr. Stephen, standing behind it, ripped his garrote through it. He was smiling savagely, enjoying his work. He stopped for a moment to give Edwin a Jeevesque tip of the hat as if to say Good day to you, sir! Then he was off to help Lady Claire cut down more zombies. Now, there was a valet!

Edwin scrambled for the magazine, snatched it up, snapped it home, and leaped to his feet with the newly reloaded Belle in his hand. The scene, thought Edwin, looked like something Dante Alighieri would have dreamed up—were he shagging Hieronymus Bosch at the time. He rushed into the fray, determined to find Eliza in the heart of all of this bloody madness.

* * *

A zombie grabbed Eliza by the front of her dress as she was trying to crawl away and flung her down, knocking the breath from her body, along with half of her senses. It took her a moment to realize it was Mr. Laurel who had her—a newly resurrected Mr. Laurel!

He looked rather the worst for wear. His suit hung on him in bloody tatters, his once-broken nose was bitten off, and part of his face had been shaved away on the left side. He grinned at her and licked his broken teeth like a lascivious animal. His eyes rolled in his head, blind and white as the power of the Hive rolled through him.

"How uncouth!" Eliza exclaimed. She was getting just a little sick of Mr. Laurel threatening her, first alive, now undead! Sitting up on the floor, she spotted a piece of debris from the shot-out wall, a long, thin metal rod of some kind. She glanced at it, then back at Mr. Laurel, imagined where she wanted it, and it leaped forward at her behest, plunging deep into Mr. Laurel's belly.

Mr. Laurel looked surprised by what she had done. Then he began to scream. Fueled by fear, exhaustion, and raw, enhanced Poppet strength, Eliza grabbed the end of the rod sticking out of his body and dragged it up to widen the hole.

Mr. Laurel dropped to his knees.

Eliza withdrew the rod and deftly swung it, knocking his head from his shoulders. Mr. Laurel's head continued to scream as it flew the length of the room, bounced across the floor, and finally exploded like a bottle rocket against the far wall. The rest of the zombie folded at her feet.

"Blimey!" someone exclaimed close beside her.

Eliza jumped at the sound and turned, the bloody rod shaking in her hand, only to find the owner of the voice at her elbow, cutting down zombies as if he was pulling weeds. Edwin! She nearly sobbed with relief.

"Remind me to never piss you off, woman," he said, eyebrows raised in appreciation at the way she had taken out Mr. Laurel.

She threw herself into his arms. "Oh, god, Edwin! Edwin!" She clenched him tight, all the blood between them squicking in an extremely disgusting way.

"I'm glad to see you too, lovey," he answered, gathering her close and kissing her hair.

Their reunion was short-lived, however. The guardsmen that Maria's zombies had attacked—what was left of them, anyway—had begun climbing to their feet and shambling toward them—or crawling, if there wasn't much left. Eliza and Edwin instinctively put themselves back and back, Eliza armed with her sad little piece of shrapnel, Edwin gripping his little gun, and prepared for the second wave.

| xviii |

Her mind is a sea—dark, fathomless, all-consuming, like waves drifting and taking her actions here and there. And, like the sea, she is really in command of none of it. She is the Hive Mother. She is the Hive. She is the All. But she lives at the mercy and behest of a massive collective intelligence. She stands with zombies hemming her in on all sides in a protective platoon and watches her enemies cut down her Poppets—her children.

She feels a great swelling scream rise up within her as the Vampire Lord Edwin McGillicuddy massacres her legion, skillfully and without remorse. The scream pours out of her, as well as out of her countless followers all over the world.

The gyroscope hasn't yet sustained enough damage, despite the intense racket of war in the room around her: the gun blasts, the snarls of the vampires, and the screams of her fallen children. The decibel reader bounces up and stretches toward the red warning line, then, maddeningly, falls back down to orange.

The Hive tells Maria to turn, lift the gun in her hand, and train it on the gyroscope itself. That will end it, it tells her. That will end everything—including her intense pain, the claws of agony scratching at the insides of her skull like beasts begging to be released from an iron cage.

She obeys their voices and raises her hand, the gun in it. She is about to squeeze the trigger when one of her own zombie guardsmen suddenly grabs her and spins her around. She doesn't immediately recognize him. He is dressed in the tattered gold and red uniform of a guard. He is covered in blood. He is young and beautiful like a Poppet, but he is not one of them.

Maria is confused. She doesn't understand why he does not obey. Then she reaches into the collective intelligence of the Hive and realizes that this creature is still alive, after a fashion.

She is looking at a vampire. She is looking at Lord Foxley in disguise. Lord Foxley—the creator of the machines and the ship she is trying to destroy. He is so painfully young, so boyish and innocent looking that she would never have recognized him were it not for the collective intelligence.

For the first time in a very long time, Maria panics. She struggles, trying to break his hold on her. Then Foxley says in a rumbling basso completely at odds with his lovely face, so untouched by age or sorrow, "Look at me, my Poppet."

His voice is sweet, gentle, and compelling. It warms her throughout like fine wine.

And Maria looks. He is beautiful, a fey angel made of snow and dreams. He smiles on her so benevolently and with such forgiveness that Maria finds herself smiling in return. She immediately loves him—loves him the way one loves the quick sighting of an arctic wolf in deep woods or the primal majesty of a mountain that has stood for millions of years, insolent in its sheer existence. A love that is so deeply ingrained in the human psyche that it borders on religious agony.

His smile warms her cold, vampire-touched flesh, and his eyes touch her inside like a prophet. She loves his white perfection, his gentle, wise eyes. She has never been in love until him. But he also makes her sad because she knows that she will never love another.

He is everything, the All. The All-Father to her Great Mother. He touches her, his white fingers moving as feathery as angel wings through her long hair.

"Come, my girl," he says, and his voice is like a drug—like music or wine. She could never have enough of it. "Come. Let me hold you, my little lost angel. Let me heal you."

Her body no longer hurts. Her heart no longer hurts. Nothing hurts.

Maria lowers the gun and is about to step into his welcoming embrace when the Hive suddenly roars to life within her, bowing her back with agony and making her clench her teeth until she tastes her own blood. It distorts Foxley's image, turning him back into what he truly is: a dead thing with a grey face, feral black eyes, and demonic wings fully extended, ready to clutch her.

He is leering at her like all vampires everywhere, hating her and hungering for her all at once. In that moment, he becomes Rathbone. He becomes the Prince. He becomes all vampires everywhere, because all vampires, like all Poppets, are ultimately connected. They are all one. They are all part of the All.

Maria screams. She tries to withdraw from his poisonous embrace, but he closes his thin, cold iron fingers around her wrist, his fingers easily breaking her bones like kindling. The harsh pain rips the remaining veils away from Maria's eyes. She screams in pain and outrage and swings her gun hand around, the Hive roaring through her mind like a virus.

She fires blindly at Foxley, missing him, but tears a gaping, smoldering hole right through the protective helix surrounding the gyroscope.

Foxley roars at her destruction, his saber teeth fully extended like a shark about to bite, and grabs the boomer, ripping her whole hand off at the wrist so that it, and the gun, fall at her feet.

His coldness sears her. And yet, she feels no pain suddenly. Still, she continues to scream as the fantastic, electrical current of his power rips through her flesh like blades.

"You bitch," he snarls, spittling her with his rage. His power is irresistible, absolute, his anger cataclysmic. There is a reason why they call him the King of the World. His twelve thousand years of rage and power enmesh her so completely that she feels helpless, a small fly stuck at the center of a spider's massive web.

He jerks her around, spreads his wings, and rockets upward, stopping just short of the vaulted ceiling. His wings encase her. He bends her neck sharply at an angle, breaking it, but not killing her. Oh, no. She can see his thoughts, his intentions. His mind is wide open now. He wants her to see.

He means to keep her alive for a while, to make her suffer every moment of her defeat. She will suffer all through the last few seconds of her life. She will taste her own death on his lips.

"Poppet," he says, "your revolution is at an end."

Maria, her body as limp as a ragdoll, continues to scream while Foxley bites deep into her throat and rips the red, wet life from her body.

***

It wasn't enough.

There were simply too many zombies, and even between the three of them—Edwin, Eliza, and Claire, and their various weapons—they were still being quickly overwhelmed. Mouse was gone, and Cesar was too young and inexperienced to continue. Claire had managed to dodge most of the attacks, but Mr. Stephen, not being a vampire—and certainly not invulnerable—had had to retreat into the relative safety of the corridors of New Versailles.

Edwin and Eliza stood back to back in the middle of the Command Center. Edwin wielded Belle in one hand and the manriki in the other. Eliza had several bits of debris from the walls hovering over her like a lethal halo. Each time a zombie lunged forward, one of them lashed out, sending it tottering back a step, sans a piece of itself or with a metal fragment embedded in it.

Edwin decided that he really, truly, hated fast zombies.

"I never imagined I'd die like this," Eliza admitted. Her voice sounded shaky and tired.

"At least, if we die tonight, love, you can never say that our life was boring and uneventful."

A zombie reached for Eliza. She pantomimed a gesture and a shard of sharp metal whizzed by, cutting off its hand at the wrist so it flopped around on the floor like a fish out of water. She stomped it under her heel and kicked it back into the melee. The zombie withdrew but watched her hungrily as it searched for an opening. "Knowing you has never been boring, Edwin. I only wished it had lasted longer."

"Do you mean that?" he asked, sounding emotional.

"Yes," Eliza admitted sadly. "I think we could have had many fine adventures together."

Edwin lashed out, winding the manriki around the throat of a zombie lurching at him. The moment the manriki enwrapped the creature, it began screaming and clawing at it as his blood began poisoning it. He reeled in the screaming zombie, lifted his gun, and emptied a bullet right into its head. It imploded, coating them both in a fresh new layer of Je Suis Un Zombie.

The other undead shuffled back uncertainly at the sight.

"Do you regret it?" he asked, swiping at the gore on his face with his sleeve, his tone serious. "Meeting me? You wouldn't be here now were it not for me."

The one-handed zombie began edging toward her again. Eliza slashed at its head with another shard to warn it back. "I don't regret meeting you, Edwin, no."

"I love you, Eliza. I loved you the first time I saw you." He lassoed another zombie and pulled it in for quick disposal. "But I was too afraid to say so. Too afraid of what you would think of me."

She knew that, of course. Edwin was very conservative about his feelings. He didn't bandy about words like love without meaning them. And, for that reason alone, they were even more precious—even if he was telling her on a battlefield full of zombies.

"I regret lying to you, Eliza. Not telling you about my past."

"You didn't lie to me, Edwin."

"I didn't tell you the truth, either."

"I didn't ask."

He sighed wearily. "Can you forgive me?"

"For being a vampire?"

"For being a gangster."

"I already have." Eliza smiled and felt the familiar burn of tears. Despite their ridiculous situation and the fact that they would most likely die tonight at the hands of a dozen blood-hungry zombies, ripped limb from limb, she felt a rush of relief. It felt so good to be honest with Edwin, pressed against his back and breathing in his familiar scents of leather, blood, and tobacco. She felt...safe, as insane as that sounded. She knew she was safe with him.

"And I lied, too." She swallowed the bittersweetness in her throat. "I lied to you from the beginning about being a Poppet. I was a Courtesan at the Court of my Lord in the years before we met. I was fifteen when I ran away."

She bit back on the awful tears clotting her throat. "I'm not a woman, Edwin. I'm an it, a toy. I never told you because I was so ashamed."

There was a long silence during which they both lashed out at the encroaching zombies. Then Edwin said, softly, "I knew what you were, Eliza. I knew from the moment I saw you."

"And you never said anything?"

"Does it matter, Eliza?"

"I was a vampire's property," she sobbed. "A thing. A possession. Not a real woman. I've never been real."

Edwin slid Belle into his armpit holster—he was out of bullets, finally—reached behind, and took her hand. He entwined his fingers in hers. "Mo Anam Cara," he said, rolling the words along on the sweet sound of his Gaelic accent. "You are a woman."

"Oh, Edwin," she sobbed.

The zombies began closing in, this time in force, like a wall collapsing around them. The stench they gave off, like freshly butchered meat, made her want to heave. Hive zombies glared sightlessly at the two of them, their jaws slackly open, drooling in anticipation.

This is it, she thought as she clung to Edwin's hand. And yet, she wasn't afraid. At least they were dying together. They weren't going to die with lies between them. That meant something. And Edwin, after all, had given her the most wonderful six months of her life. Six months of being alive, of being a woman, not a Poppet. When presented with such a fantastic and unexpected gift, could she really complain when it ended unexpectedly?

Edwin turned and pulled her against him, wrapped her in his coat, and rested his chin atop her head. She squeezed her eyes shut. She was awash in his cologne, the damp smell of leather and blood, and the smell that was uniquely him, the smell that was just Edwin.

The first zombie finally pounced and sank its broken teeth and clawed hands into the back of Edwin's coat. He grunted at the pain and pressure, closed his eyes…and, suddenly, one by one, the zombies seized up, tottered, and dropped to the floor around them.

She watched them crumple up into odd positions as only truly dead things can.

Eliza raised her head, gasping in surprise, and watched at the bodies piled up around their feet. "What's going on?"

"Foxley." Edwin nodded at the opposite side of the room.

Eliza looked past the sea of falling zombies and saw that Foxley was hovering near the ceiling, but not flying, no. His wings were folded about himself while his power of bloodkinetics sustained his altitude through sheer will so he resembled a giant, mutant chrysalis.

She had just started wondering what was going on when he fully extended his wings and she saw he held the limp but still shuddering body of Maria in his arms. His face was awash in her blood as he continued to gnaw at her throat and collarbone, worrying it like a dog might worry a bone. Maria looked like a big, tattered, bloodstained doll.

Then he let her go, and she dropped heavy and lifeless to the floor far beneath him.

The last zombie fell with Maria as her hold on the horde of undead was finally broken.

The silence in the room that followed was thunderous. The once sterile landscape of the Command Center, now decorated with so much blood and so many bodies, felt starkly surreal.

Foxley turned and glared at them both, his face masked in Maria's blood. He didn't look like a child anymore. He didn't even look like a vampire. He looked like what he was: a monster from the deepest, blackest pit of hell. And Eliza knew she would never get that demonic and unnatural image of him out of her mind. It was imprinted on her brain forever like a childhood trauma.

He grinned through the blood, showing off his blood-yellowed teeth. His eyes were cold and mechanical as he fixed them on the two of them. She didn't need a bloodlink to feel his insult and his childish jealousy, both amplified by the blood he had just gorged on. Foxley hated her, hated her with every fiber of his being, hated her with a vengeance born of pain and loneliness and freakish isolation. Because of her, Edwin would never be his...

She opened her mouth, prepared to shout a warning to Edwin that Foxley was about to fly at them both, but suddenly the whole room shuddered, tossing Foxley back against the wall, where he slid down to the floor. He lost his interest in them at that moment of impact and glanced aside at the gyroscope instead.

It looked undamaged, but the sonic waves it was generating on an almost subliminal level like a dull toothache were disjointed and making palatable and erratic wakes that rocked the room from side to side.

"What in hell is going on?" Edwin asked. He swayed on his feet as if he was drunk.

"It's the gyro." Setting her fear of Foxley aside for the moment, but keeping one eye on him at all times, Eliza moved to the computer station at the foot of the giant glowing helix and studied the reports rapidly scrolling up the screens.

Foxley moved up behind her, and Eliza felt the little hairs on the back of her neck stiffen. She gripped the edge of the console, swallowed against her fear, and glanced aside at the blood-splattered vampire.

"There's something wrong with your gyro," she stated simply.

Foxley looked at her starkly. His face, lost in half shadows, looked as ancient as a primordial mask under all of the blood. He narrowed his feral, black, unblinking eyes and licked at the thick grue on his lips. "It would appear so," he answered, his voice surprisingly calm —and at complete odds with his appearance.

She half expected him to jump on her, to rip her throat out with his great jagged teeth. It made her want to cringe and crawl away.

But Foxley closed his eyes and blinked his black eyes back to grey. He then moved around her, considered her deeply, then turned his attention to the computer console. His hand slipped past her and his fingers flew nimbly over the keyboard as he imputed a long series of command lines. Eliza watched, trying to follow what Foxley was doing, but he was going much too fast, and many of the commands coming up were in Upyrese, the language of the High Vampire Courts.

Foxley swore, hooked his long ashen hair behind one ear, and tried a few more command lines. When nothing changed, he finally slammed his fist into the monitor in front of him, cracking it like an egg, though his hand sustained no obvious injuries.

"When Maria fired the gun so close to the gyroscope, she disrupted its sonic impulses," he said at last.

"That's why the oscillation feels off."

"That's correct, Miss Book."

Edwin came up behind Eliza and put his hand on her shoulder, keeping one eye on Foxley. "Is there something happening to the gravity?" he asked.

The room lurched as the *Gypsy Queen* struggled to maintain altitude, and Eliza clutched the edge of the workstation with both hands and leaned forward. The instantaneous jolt she received from the computer made her head swim and her teeth ache like small electrical impulses were dancing across her molars. She stiffened as the gyro's many schematics fluttered through her mind. It took her but a few moments to run a full systematic diagnostic.

Suddenly, she knew what was going on. Foxley was right. "The sonic impulse from Maria's gun has disrupted the central axis. The gyroscope has moved off its center of gravity. Its axis of rotation is tilted sideways."

"But what does that mean in English?" Edwin asked, his grip on her shoulder tightening.

Before she could explain fully, emergency signals started going off all over the Command Center, turning everyone's face a lurid shade of red. Warnings and damage reports began scrolling up on all of the undamaged computer monitors. Unfortunately, there was no staff left alive to attend to them. Everyone was dead.

Foxley turned to glance grudgingly at Eliza, the only one in the room who understood anything about his gyro. "The *Gypsy Queen* is moving out of orbit."

"I'm aware of that, Foxley."

"If it continues to move out of orbit—"

"Yes!" she insisted. "I know what will happen."

She nudged Foxley aside, her hands dancing across the computer keyboard, her fingers giving off little blue sparks of electricity. "We're entering a one-hundred and eighty-five-degree axis spin, and, so far, we've lost two hundred feet."

"Two-fifty," Foxley corrected her, reading the screens.

"No course resetting?"

"The computers can't readjust with the angle so severe."

"I don't understand any of this," Edwin complained bitterly.

"My boy," Foxley explained, glancing up, "the *Gypsy Queen* is falling out of the sky."

* * *

There were only five of them left—Edwin, Eliza, Foxley, Cesar, and Claire, and Claire had been terribly injured in the battle, one of her wings nearly bisected. Still, everyone still alive or undead gathered around the workstation to see what they could do to keep the *Gypsy Queen* from crashing into the Island of Manhattan.

Unfortunately, only Foxley and Eliza understood anything about the ship, and Foxley was at a loss as to what to do without a full work team to fix the helix. He kept pacing around uselessly with Claire close on his heels.

Eliza worked frantically over the station, with Edwin and Cesar close beside her. Neither of them understood anything about engineering, so they were no help at all, but just having them near was a comfort to her. She kept summoning up programs and diagnostics, dragging screens with her fingertips and then dismissing them. None of it did any good. It would take a moderately sized crew days to fix this kind of damage. And they didn't have days. They had maybe thirty minutes before they crashed into the island of Manhattan—if they were lucky.

Finally, she stopped and simply glared at Foxley while the gravity continued to weaken in the room around them, making the blood on the floors float in unnatural ways like a series of giant Rorschach tests. His nervous and unconstructive pacing was getting on her last nerve. "The whole system needs a complete overhaul."

Sensing her burning dark eyes on his back, Foxley stopped and turned to glare at her. For the first time since she had met him—maybe the first time in his whole long life—he looked helpless and confused. Like all of them, he was a prisoner of forces much larger than himself. I took him a moment to consider and then to speak.

"All of you should evacuate the premises immediately." He folded his wings about himself protectively. "You can take a shuttle. I shall alert the nearest gate..."

"Abandon ship?" Edwin said. "What about you?"

Foxley looked directly into his Heir's eyes when he said, "The captain does not abandon his ship."

Edwin looked beyond surprised by his creator's statement. "You're going down with it?"

"I created the *Gypsy Queen*. She's mine. I'll not abandon her." A small smile ticked one corner of his blood-slathered mouth. "My boy, perhaps I'm not the monster you think I am."

"No one is going down." Eliza took a deep breath and started digging through the computer diagnostics again, touching screens and absorbing the knowledge of Foxley's flying marvel at nearly preternatural speeds. It was a terrific learning experience, but it told her very little about the problem the ship was having. "Anyway, I doubt any of us would get off this ship in time. Besides, Foxley, we can't leave millions of people to die below us."

He made a disparaging sound in his throat.

Eliza bit back a scathing remark. She knew fighting with him about human worth would be like trying to teach the proverbial pig to sing. It wasn't like she'd suddenly be able to convince him to care about a few million measly humans.

"What exactly is wrong with the gyroscope? Mechanically, I mean." Despite the mighty well of knowledge she had absorbed, she couldn't find the schematics for the gyroscope anywhere. Of course, Foxley probably didn't keep such files on the workstation computers due to Patent and his own flagrant paranoia.

Foxley shook his head slowly. "The tuning fork resonator is cracked." He stared up at the gyroscope far above them, spinning in too many random directions at once, and then glanced down at the diagnostic reports scrolling wildly across the screen before him. "It needs to be replaced."

Eliza followed his look. "Well, do you have a replacement?"

"Little Poppet, it would take a specialized group of engineers days to repair this kind of damage, and we have less than twenty minutes before impact." He gave her a nasty, vulpine look. "You need to take Edwin off this ship now."

"We're not letting this ship fall! It'll be like dropping a hundred atomic bombs on the City of New York."

But Foxley wasn't listening. He perched on a nearby workstation and just sulked. Useless wanker, as Edwin would say.

She'd just about figured out the engineering mechanics of the gyroscope. "Can someone get me up there?" She pointed.

"The gyroscope requires specialized tools," Foxley explained, looking up. "There is no way you can fix it, Poppet. Not in the next few minutes."

"Give me the benefit of the doubt," she said. "Take me up, Foxley. And stop calling me 'Poppet!'"

Edwin reached for Cesar and pushed the boy toward her. "Take her up," he commanded.

Cesar obediently moved to one side and took Eliza's arm. Eliza looked over at Foxley. "Come on, Foxley. Stop sulking and do something constructive."

Foxley's eyes burned with hopeless rage. "It will not work."

Eliza shrugged. "So, let's do it anyway. It will give us something to do while we wait to die."

Edwin, obviously exasperated, picked Maria's boomer up off the floor where it had fallen and sighted down the barrel at Foxley. "You have no idea how satisfying this is, old boy. It's like a dream come true for me. Now, do what Miss Book asks."

Foxley gave Edwin a dirty look but obediently moved to Eliza's other side and took her arm. Eliza had to work not to shirk at the vampire's ice-cold touch. Together, the two vampires flicked their wings and started drifting upward, Eliza wedged between them.

She swallowed nervously with a throat so dry it clicked and resolved not to look down. If she looked down, she would be sick. Instead, she concentrated on the gyroscope looming before her, giving off sonic waves so powerful that they felt like soft physical punches hitting her.

"Can you get me close enough to touch it?" she said.

The two vampires grimaced under the intense sonic pressure. But, together, they drifted a few inches closer to the vibrating satellite. The pounding, electrical waves slammed into Eliza like a legion of dull sledgehammers, giving her a kind of all-over-the-body headache. But it wasn't electrical waves she was experiencing, she knew. The gyro acted on a self-sustaining torque, not electric power. The machine, sensing her presence, had begun speaking to her in shocks of almost blinding data and ambient power.

Around them, the room began to tilt dangerously, forcing the vampires to compensate for it. The *Gypsy Queen* was moving so far out of orbit that they'd likely break up long before they ever crashed, which might actually be worse than crashing. Instead of one gigantic airship slamming into the middle of Midtown, the city would be assaulted by a massive meteor storm of apocalyptic proportions not seen since the dinosaurs' era.

She knew she was running out of time. She also knew this might not work.

Biting her lip to keep from crying out, Eliza reached out and made first contact, touching the cool, metal helix of the gyroscope. For one second, she experienced almost heart-stopping agony. Then a spark seemed to leap off her skin and ignite her power so she felt only the mind-numbing rhythmic spinning of the gyroscope in her head.

Foxley was right. To do a proper job of it and change out the resonator, she would need specialized tools, raw materials, and a crew of at least a dozen men—none of which she had at present, seeing how almost everyone at New Versailles was dead.

She had to do this herself. All by herself.

Closing her eyes—because everything she was seeing now was in her own head anyway—she used the computer to map out what materials she needed and where she could find them in various parts of the Command Center. The whole room became transparent in her head. She saw what she needed, and she saw where it could be found.

Metal squealed around them in an alarming way as she ripped the walls wide open like a series of wounds. She sensed both vampires flinching at the sight. She summoned electrical fuses, wires, and whatever raw materials the ship could spare, tearing everything right out of the walls in long eviscerated electrical ropes and gathering them close in a drifting halo around her just as she had the debris earlier.

She then began sewing it all together into a new package, metal twisting, fuses melting together. She didn't have time to do neat work. Her hands moved quickly, orchestrating the operation.

Turning her attention back on the gyroscope, she ripped it wide open like a giant metallic egg, tore the wounded electronic guts from the device in a shower of sparks, and then, with a series of gestures, sent the new materials snaking inside the aperture she had created. She tied up all of the fuses and loose ends and resealed the reinforced titanium casting as best she could. It was shabby work, a quick fix, at best. The whole Command Center would need a complete overhaul, but she hoped it was enough for now.

She slowly opened her eyes and waited. The gyroscope hummed even louder as it acquired a steadier resonance. She thought everything would be all right, but the *Gypsy Queen* suddenly lurched again, this time the other way. Violently.

The two vampires jerked backward, and before she knew it, Eliza was in freefall. She didn't even have time to scream. She just fell.

A pair of strong arms caught her and she grunted as she landed atop Edwin, her weight and the sudden gravity in the room driving them both to the floor a bit too hard. She sat up, stunned. She was straddling Edwin's hips in a most unladylike position!

She mashed both hands over her mouth at the sight. "Edwin, are you all right?"

He blinked his bright wolfish eyes, then gave her a goofy smile as he glanced down at their position. "Um...bloody great."

"You're incorrigible."

"I love you too, lovey." He leaned up to cup her cheek and kiss her.

Across the room, the body of Maria, which looked more like a smashed insect than anything that had ever been human, began to stir. Edwin swore under his breath at the sight, scrambled out from under Eliza, and found his feet as the other flayed soldiers in the room began lurching and swaying once more to their feet, the hideous determination of the Hive mind flashing across the remains of their faces, turning them bestial.

He yanked his old-fashioned gun from his holster even though Eliza was pretty certain he was out of bullets and took aim.

It was beginning all over again.

* * *

Maria, enlivened by the Hive, tottered on her feet, battling with her broken bones and lifeless flesh. Her face was blank, her empty white eyes seething out of the almost black veil of blood obscuring her face. Her head lay brokenly on her shoulders, a huge chunk of flesh gone from the side of her face and neck where Foxley's primordial teeth had torn into her.

She stared sightlessly across the room, a dead thing, yet she seemed to see her enemies, to sense them in some instinctual way. She started limping determinedly toward them, stopping only to retrieve the fallen boomer where Edwin had dropped it with her one remaining hand.

Eliza gasped at the sight, her heart plummeting.

Maria lifted it and sighted down the lot of them...then suddenly jerked spastically as someone fired repeatedly into her body from behind. She danced like a poppet at last until one of the shots finally collapsed her skull. Maria and her undead army slumped down, shuddering and finally lying still in a big broken heap of doll-like parts as the final death claimed them all.

Derek moved stiffly into the Command Center, one hand pressed to the seeping gunshot wound in his upper chest, the other hand clutching his Colt. He kept it trained on Maria as he staggered across the room with pain-narrowed eyes, his bloodied lips peeled away from his teeth, which were locked tight in a grimace. He studied Maria's lifeless body for a long moment before emptying every last bullet into her head. Finally, satisfied, he lurched against the wall and slumped down.

Eliza rushed forward to catch him. "Derek!" she said, taking his head into her lap and carefully pushing aside his jacket. The bullet had tagged him high up—not his heart, exactly, but close. Being a Poppet that was harder to hurt than any human had helped. He had lost a lot of blood, but with a little medical care, she thought he should recover.

She wiped some blood from his lips. "Derek," she said again, but he didn't respond. His eyes were fixed on a spot above her head.

Glancing up, she saw that Edwin stood over them, staring down at Derek's prone form. Derek's eyes roved all over his tall, blood-coated figure, so hate-filled that Eliza could feel a kind of kinetic energy pouring off him. Slowly, he raised his gun hand and cocked his empty Colt at her boyfriend. He pulled the trigger compulsively even though he kept hitting on empties.

A look passed across Edwin's face. Eliza felt her own heart leap up and lodge somewhere in her throat where it ought not to be. "Edwin, don't!"

Edwin checked his own gun's munitions and grunted in surprise. "Huh, I thought I was done, but there's one bullet left. What do you know?" He cocked the modified Rainmaker and aimed it at Derek's prone figure. His voice was steady and as cold as a black winter's night. "Someone put a bullet in my heart once, lad, and I killed the creature that did it."

The two men stayed that way for a remarkably long time while Eliza and the small group of survivors held their collective breath, waiting to see what Edwin would do.

Derek's hand trembled with weakness but didn't move an inch from its intended target. His eyes burned feverishly. If he could have taken down the whole vampire race, he would have. Eliza knew that. If Maria had succeeded in killing everyone in New York and pinning it on the Vampire Courts, he would have rejoiced. She knew that, too.

Edwin smiled grimly. He licked at all of the blood rouged over his lips. "Lower your gun, lad, or I'll empty this last bullet into your fucking head," he said.

Eliza finally found her voice. "Don't do this to him, Edwin, please. You have no idea what he's been through."

* * *

No, Edwin thought. He knew exactly what Derek had been through.

He'd been through much worse in two hundred years. He knew what this kind of suffering did to a man. He knew how it broke you down, how it made a monster of you. He considered ending Derek's existence then and there. It would be a kindness, really, better than what waited for him down in Poppettown—an insipid and useless life full of useless pain and impotent rage.

But then he saw Eliza's eyes. Her pain. In that moment, he made his decision. He lowered his gun—the first time for him, as far as he could remember. But he didn't do it for Derek. He did it for her.

Eliza sighed with relief. She reached up and prized the Colt from Derek's hand. Derek let it go. Eliza put it down on the floor and cradled him close, though her eyes never strayed very far from Edwin.

Edwin slid Belle back into her holster. "I'm still the Prince, lad," he said, offering Derek a deadly smile full of sharp, bloodstained teeth. "And if you ever point a gun at me again or endanger my Eliza, you're a dead man. Remember that." He lit the last cigarette in his pack and walked away, thinking Doctor Blood would have been bloody proud of him.

| xix |

Two days later, accompanied by a media blitzkrieg not seen since 911 or the Kennedy Assassination, vampires were formally recognized as America's newest minority group, with all rights and privileges attendant thereof. Edwin and Eliza attended none of the nationwide parties going on. Foxley, though not a good man, was at least sporting enough to afford them a private suite at New Versailles to say their goodbyes.

Edwin had agreed to return to Foxley's Court for two thousand years, which would at least satisfy the little tyrant. And Eliza, now under Foxley's protection, would be free to live her life in the city as a free Poppet. A free gentlewoman. Naturally, Eliza did not like the deal he had brokered, but she understood its necessity. She had made the decision not to undermine his sacrifice by fighting against it, and for that, Edwin was grateful.

Edwin laid his woman down on the vast, soft, four-poster bed in their room and joined her there. Their lovemaking was uncharacteristically soft and prolonged. Wordless. Eliza turned her head and placed her hand on the back of his neck, inviting him to take her. Edwin found his mark and drank, being careful to cause her no pain.

Eliza closed her eyes and luxuriated in the feeling of his mouth taking nourishment from her and his body giving back pleasure, a full circuit of sensation that caused all the lights in the room to flicker and dim.

When he had taken her to the edge and over it several times, he settled down to just kissing and touching her, doing everything he could to memorize her taste and scent and everything that made her Eliza. He knew he would need it in the long, lonely years and decades and centuries to come.

The light in the window softened to the color of a blush and the shadows lengthened as synthetic day gave way to manufacture night aboard the gyro. He was surprised; they'd spent hours together without saying a single word, without needing to.

"I like that this was our last time," he finally said.

They lay quietly resting, holding each other, fingers clasped.

* * *

Eliza felt sad but content. Overwhelmed. "Yes," she answered him.

Soon, Foxley's soldiers would come for her, to take her back to Earth. Soon, it would all be over. She would return home to a free life. She would find new work, or perhaps she would work for herself or travel to others lands, places she had never had the opportunity to visit. She would live as a free human being.

She should be happy about that, she told herself. But she wasn't.

She studied Edwin for a long time, trying to burn everything about him into her memory. For perhaps the millionth time, she ran through all their options in her mind. They could run away together and hide in Poppettown like fugitives. They could fight, dying together like a strange Romeo and Juliet in a hail of bullets. But even as she thought these things, she knew how ridiculous and impossible they were. Edwin would never do something like that to her, not now that she was free, a truly free gentlewoman.

She thought about staying here aboard Foxley's gyro. She thought about being Edwin's Courtesan in full...then his Favorite...and, finally, his Heir, his vampire bride.

He sensed her thoughts. He said, stroking the side of her face, "You have a chance to live free down on Earth, Eliza. How many Poppets get that chance in a lifetime?"

Her eyes burned with unspent tears. "I don't want to live down there alone. I don't want to be free without you."

"Lovey," he told her with a tender smile, pushing himself up on one elbow, "please don't be sad. You'll live free like the woman you are, and you'll go places and do things. You'll experience life in a way few people like you ever do. And you will not be alone, because someday you'll find someone just right for you, someone who is your Anam Cara."

She felt a great wellspring of sorrow open up inside of her, the kind that no amount of crying can fix. She couldn't see those things the way he could. And, as a result, she couldn't seem to stop clutching him. "And you? What will become of you, Edwin?"

He thought about that. "I'll continue to work for Foxley."

"How long? Two thousand years? Ten thousand?"

He didn't answer her.

***

Foxley held all the cards. He always had.

There was no escaping the Mad King of New Versailles. Edwin learned that long ago. He was a fool to think otherwise. But at least Eliza had a chance to live free where he could not. The idea appealed to him even as it ripped his clockwork heart to pieces. He'd been a pickpocket, a gangster, a monster. A villain. But in his heart of hearts, he'd always liked the idea of being a superhero, the lone cowboy, the knight in shining armor.

Besides, there was no point in continuing along these ideas, nurturing unrealistic dreams. He could be as pragmatic as Eliza when he needed to. He smiled. "Miss Book, do you want to do it again—for old time's sake?" He wagged his eyebrows up and down, hoping to lift her spirits.

"Our thing?"

"Aye, our thing."

They did it again until Eliza cried.

The guards appeared soon after, knocking insistently on the door. Edwin and Eliza redressed and followed them down the long garish corridor until they reached a door to Foxley's self-styled arboretum. Outside, the synthetic sky was a stark azure, and the gardens were full to brimming with deliriously blooming roses. They walked hand-in-hand down the garden path, saying nothing. They had said everything to each other hours ago.

Foxley stood at the end of the path, clipping off rose blooms, busily choosing which ones would live and which would die. The guards moved to either side, allowing Edwin to approach the little Lord of New Versailles, but Eliza stayed behind. Edwin knew she did not want to talk to Foxley. She had nothing to say to him.

Edwin approached his master, doing his best to stem his anger. Honey, not vinegar, he reminded himself. "I'd like to know for certain that my woman will be returned to Earth unharmed. I'd like to see to it myself, if you wouldn't mind."

Foxley turned to look upon his Heir, a red rose in his hand. He was again the young, unsullied boy, his face impassive and full of light. It reminded him of that fateful night in London when they first met at the prison. How Foxley had shone like some young god. Edwin wondered how something as starkly evil as Foxley could look so angelic. So pure.

Foxley gestured to Edwin with the rose. "Walk with me. We have something to discuss."

They started down the garden path together, wending around the big vulgar roses. Edwin thought about ranting and raving, stomping Foxley's rose garden into the dirt in front of him, but what good would it do? Foxley would just plant another garden.

Foxley was old and powerful. Iron. Untouchable. Pleas and insults meant nothing to him, as did love.

"Your clockwork heart," he asked suddenly. "How is it?"

The words caught Edwin off guard. "All right, I reckon. I didn't know you cared." He responded drolly, sliding his hands into his jacket pockets.

Foxley looked hurt. "I should never have sent Chimera after you. I should have punished him for what he did to you."

"Are you actually apologizing?"

He stopped to prune another rose and offered it to Edwin, though Edwin did not take it. "I'm very proud of what you have become, my Heir. Did you know the media is hailing me as a hero for killing 'Mad Maria,' as they're calling her, and for stopping the Hive from destroying New York?"

Edwin smiled wryly. "I'm thrilled for you. I know how much you love good PR."

Foxley looked toward the synthetic sky, the rose clenched in his fingers. It almost made him look like a real little boy instead of the bloodthirsty, sociopathic freak he was. "I find the concept of being a hero strange and...interesting, to say the least. The President of the United States wishes to visit New Versailles. He has asked that I act as an ambassador to my people."

He paused to smell the sweet scent of his rose. It was a shade of azure, genetically modified, no doubt. "I am to be the 'Strong, Kind Face of Vampirekind,' as he has put it. I have not yet formally accepted his offer, of course. It means a public life, you see."

Somehow, Edwin just couldn't find his enthusiasm. Tomorrow, he would be Foxley's Enforcer. His right-hand man. His living weapon. Tomorrow, Foxley would live like a hero among both humans and vampires, a man who had stopped a terrorist organization from obliterating New York City and crushing nonhuman rights for vampires everywhere. Tomorrow, they would be two of the most powerful and respected vampires in the entire world, dining with kings and presidents.

Tomorrow, he would be without Eliza.

Foxley stopped in the center of the garden and sat down on the edge of a huge Grecian fountain full of stone gods and water nymphs pouring out a sparkling fury of water overhead. He crossed his legs and let his hand drift in the cool water. "I rather like the attention," he said with a boyish shrug. "Though, of course, many things in my life will need to change. I shall have to project a fair and positive image to the world. After all, I will be the face of vampires everywhere."

"I wonder how we'll ever survive."

Foxley laughed at that, a lighthearted sound that hinted at nothing dark beneath the surface. "As my first act as Ambassador of Vampirekind, I shall officially release you from all obligations to my Court." He flicked his fingers as if performing a magic trick. "You are free to leave with your Courtesan and your Heir anytime you please. However, I do recommend my five-star golfing resort. It is tres magnifique—enough to get even your pathetic game up."

The words stunned Edwin and put him in a surreal place. "Are you bloody serious?"

Foxley narrowed his eyes. "I understand your pup Cesar, being a fine pilot, knows the way back to Earth?"

"You want me to take Cesar, too?"

"He is your Heir. Your Enforcer...my Lord."

Edwin didn't know how to respond. He wanted to hug Foxley. But he also wanted to punch him in the damned face. "What's the catch?"

"No catch." Foxley grinned up at him.

Edwin waited, but when nothing changed, when Foxley did nothing to stop him, he turned back on the path. In only a few long strides, Edwin had returned to Eliza's side and swept her like a bride into his arms, where he proceeded to spin her round and round. She was so startled that she could do nothing but gasp in surprise until he stopped to lean down and kiss her.

Sparks flew.

Eliza put her hand on his chest, feeling the faint vibration of his clockwork heart ticking along just for her. "Edwin...I don't understand."

He smiled at her, devilishly. "Eliza, we're going home."

***

From a distance, Lord Henry Foxley smiled and narrowed his eyes cattily at the sight of the two lovers frolicking in his garden. They made a lovely couple, hugging and kissing, although he knew nothing the sad little Poppet felt for her clockwork vampire could compare to what Foxley felt for Edwin.

Edwin didn't understand him. He never had.

He loved Edwin with a love greater than his ship or his Court. Edwin was his magnum opus. Edwin was his world. But Foxley was a patient creature by nature and could wait. Wait for the rather extraordinary Poppet that Edwin loved to expire. And if it did not happen naturally and soon, there were other ways and means.

There were always ways.

Then Edwin, in his grief and his despair, would be all his. Forever.

Ilya smiled insouciantly up at the beautiful, manufactured sunlight warming his vampire cold skin. He laid the blue rose to his cheek thoughtfully. He had forever on his side, after all.

ABOUT THE AUTHOR

K.H. Koehler is the bestselling author of various novels and novellas in the genres of horror, SF, dark fantasy, steampunk, and young and new adult. She is the owner of KH Koehler Books and KH Koehler Design, which specializes in graphic design and professional copyediting. Her books are widely available at all major online distributors and her covers have appeared on numerous books in many different genres. Her short work has appeared in various anthologies, and her novel series include *The Kaiju Hunter, A Clockwork Vampire, Planet of Dinosaurs, The Nick Englebrecht Mysteries,* and *The Archaeologists.* She is the author of multiple Amazon bestsellers and was one of the founders and chief editors of KHP Publishers, which published genre fiction from 2001 to 2015. She has over fifteen years of experience in the publishing industry as a writer, ghostwriter, copyeditor, commercial book cover designer, formatter, and marketer. Visit her website at https://khkoehler.net.

www.ingramcontent.com/pod-product-compliance
Lightning Source LLC
LaVergne TN
LVHW030317070526
838199LV00069B/6483